PRAISE FOR DAV

'All too plausible, with complex cha
—Antony Joh.

'*A Long Shadow* is a terrific, high-octane crime thriller with a frighteningly plausible plot. Antonia Conti is a superb creation – fierce, dogged and loyal – and I can't wait to see what she gets up to next.'

—M. W. Craven, author of the Washington Poe series

'A gripping thriller that presents an all too plausible vision of a dystopian future. *A Long Shadow* by David Beckler is a propulsive and thought-provoking read.'

—Adam Hamdy, author of *Black 13*

'Fans of not-quite-superhuman heroes will eagerly embrace this series kickoff. Pow!'

—*Kirkus Reviews*

A NUCLEAR REACTION

ALSO BY DAVID BECKLER

Antonia Conti Thriller series

A Long Shadow
A Stolen Memory

Mason & Sterling series

Brotherhood
The Profit Motive
Forged in Flames
The Money Trap

Anthology

The Road More Travelled: Tales of those seeking refuge

A NUCLEAR REACTION

DAVID BECKLER

THOMAS & MERCER

Text copyright © 2023 by David Beckler
All rights reserved.

Published by Thomas & Mercer, Seattle

www.apub.com

Amazon, the Amazon logo, and Thomas & Mercer are trademarks of Amazon.com, Inc., or its affiliates.

ISBN-13: 9781542034722
eISBN: 9781542034739

Cover design by Dominic Forbes
Cover image: © Mihai Simonia / Shutterstock; © dynasoar / Getty Images

Printed in the United States of America

This book is dedicated to B. E. Andre.
Boz took me under her wing when I joined her
writing group and has played a big part in my
development as an author. Despite not reading in
my genre, she has read and given me feedback on
everything I've published. Her sometimes harsh —
but always fair — comments keep me honest.

CHAPTER 1

Bright light woke Rick Grainger, and his befuddled brain attempted to make sense of his surroundings. People were in his bedroom. Before he could react, hands grabbed him and wound tape round his mouth. He threw a punch, catching air as he struggled to make out the shadows behind the light. Hard steel pressed into his temple.

'Give me an excuse to use this,' a sibilant voice whispered in his ear.

Grainger stopped struggling. Hands appeared from behind the light and grabbed his wrists, twisting his right arm. He resisted until the pistol barrel pressed harder. He let them roll him over. As they turned him, he glimpsed Erika, rigid on the bed next to him, flat on her back with her hands clasped in front of her. Her expression puzzled him, but as they wrenched his arms behind his back and shoved his face into the mattress, the pain took over. Rough hands squeezed his wrists together and cable ties secured them, pulling tight.

Two people pulled him upright. Was one the gunman, or were there three of them? Torch beams criss-crossed the bedroom, fleetingly illuminating Erika, still lying on the bed.

'Please don't hurt her,' came out in a jumbled mumble through the tape.

Then the light beam blinded him again until the rough fabric of a hood brought blackness. A stale smell of damp cereal filled his nostrils. Two men half-dragged, half-carried him across the bedroom floor.

Erika cried out. He struggled, freeing one shoulder. As he spun round, a blow to his kidney brought him to his knees, then another to the back of his head slammed him face first into the wall. Bone and cartilage crunched. Pain coursed across his back and head, and he struggled to breathe as tears, snot and blood filled his nostrils.

'Now get up.' A different voice.

Unable to breathe, the fear he'd die here gave him strength. He thrashed around like a beached marlin, yelling through the tape until someone removed his hood and ripped the gag from his mouth. He spat out the bloody mixture before gulping mouthfuls of air.

'Right, get up. Now.' The lights returned to his eyes.

Blood dripped from his ruined nose, but at least he could breathe.

'We can't have you dying on us yet, but you make a sound, and you *will* regret it. Understand?'

He nodded, and the man behind him pulled the hood back over his head. Powerful hands gripped his upper arms and pulled him to his feet. Panting in pain, he staggered upright. In between the sound of his breathing, he heard low sobs. If they hurt her, he'd make sure they paid. As they pulled him, stumbling, towards the door, he kept that thought in his head. Low voices came from behind, but he couldn't make out the words.

They stopped him at the head of the narrow stairs and one of them released his arm before brushing past him and guiding his foot down to the top step.

The man's head must be around knee height. If he attacked now, he'd catch them unawares. The sharp tap with the pistol told

2

him he wouldn't. He concentrated on keeping his balance. Who were these people? What did they want? They'd not asked for jewellery or money. . . Of course they hadn't. *Shit!* He knew why they were here.

He listened as they negotiated the stairs. He'd not seen much, but thought he'd detected three of them. At least two accompanied him. He tried to sense them but had enough on his plate staying upright. As the thought of why they'd seized him sunk in, terror paralysed him. Please God, stop them harming Erika.

A sharp prod in his back. 'Come on, get a move on.'

They'd reached the ground floor, and he had to trot to keep up. They were taking him out the back. A door opened and icy air enveloped his legs. Despite it being summer, a T-shirt and boxers weren't suitable attire for two fifty-seven in the morning. How did he know the time? He recalled the flash of illuminated numerals as they'd spun him round.

Wetness infused his feet, then something slimy and crunchy underfoot as they dragged him through the back garden. Damp grass brushed his left foot as his right stayed on the rough brick-work of the path. A sharp pain made him gasp as his ankle smashed against concrete. He staggered, but they held him upright. He wasn't small, a hundred kilos, but these two had no problems with him.

The ground changed to cobbles. They'd slipped out of the back gate. He always locked it. Had Erika forgotten last night? *Don't start blaming her.* With any luck, she'd contact the police before they got him to the car. But why would they leave her? They didn't have time to tie her up. Had another team already dragged her out? Terror seized him, stopping him breathing.

A car door opened, then they lifted him off his feet. The sensation of helplessness filled him with panic. He fell, landing after a sudden heart-stopping drop. He lashed out with his legs, catching

3

someone with his bare heel. A man swore, pushing his leg away, then the lid of the car boot slammed into his shins. He cried out. Panting to catch his breath, he flinched when the boot lifted, certain they'd broken his legs, or if not, they would this next time. Instead of hitting him again, they shoved his feet in and slammed the lid.

By the time he'd unscrambled his brain, the car surged forward, the electric motor silent. He sniffed, and above the musty smell of the sack, he detected the familiar odour of his dog blanket. They'd stolen his car, Erika's really, the cheeky bleeders! Why hadn't Buster barked? Had they killed him? Maybe he'd run off. He looked fierce, but he wasn't the bravest.

He checked his injuries. Some of his teeth felt loose and his lip three times the normal size. They'd broken his nose, but no worse than the last time. He wanted to throw up. It must be due to shock and the blood he'd swallowed.

A blast of music made him jump, then it stopped.

'What's this shit!'

Despite his predicament, he wanted to object. Then the speakers blasted a series of radio channels until it settled on a repetitive techno-beat.

A sharp object dug into his back. He'd not put the jack away when he'd changed the wheel and, wishing he'd kept the boot tidier, he rolled off it. The car braked. They must have reached the junction with the main road. Something rolled into his back. What the hell was it? It wasn't like anything that should be in there. Still disorientated, he reached for it, but it rolled away as the car moved off.

Next time they braked, he attempted to grip it, but couldn't reach it. Ignoring the discomfort, he manoeuvred round. Next time it rolled into his forearms, but his swollen hands didn't respond. Twice more he tried with the same result. Frustration and a determination to succeed took over. On the next bend, it bumped into

4

him, and he trapped it against the bulkhead. A bottle of wine. He rolled it round until the neck pressed into his right palm.

Grainger remembered now. He'd thought the beggar hanging round the car had nicked it. It must have fallen out of his bag. He'd give the guy a fiver next time he went in. Could he use the bottle? He remembered a story he'd worked on where a rival gang took the head of a drug cartel hostage. The man had freed himself by using a broken bottle and killed two of his assailants.

He concentrated on closing his right hand until his fingers gripped the bottle. Making sure he didn't drop it, he moved back towards the jack. Could he smash the bottle against it? When the metal pressed into his buttocks, he visualised where the jack lay. He swung the bottle, which hit with a solid clunk. It slipped but stayed intact. He tightened his grip and hit it again. The glass against the metal sounded loud, but he hoped the seats would muffle the noise. He took four more attempts to break the bottle. The heady odour of wine filled his nostrils and cold liquid soaked into his boxers, but he didn't care.

The car stopped and seemed to stay a long time. He froze. Had they heard him above the music? But if they had, someone would have checked straight away. Don't say they'd arrived before he'd freed himself. He couldn't tell if the engine had stopped by listening, but he no longer detected the faint vibration. The music stopped, voices carried, doors slammed, then laughter. He lay still, staring at the lid, waiting for it to open. After a long pause, the car moved off.

He didn't know how long he had and searched for somewhere to wedge the broken neck of the bottle. His swollen hands barely obeyed him now. He hadn't closed the jack, the reason he'd left it out. Would the V between the two sides hold the neck of the bottle? Grainger manoeuvred round until his hands touched the cold metal. He could barely feel them now and needed to get the bottle wedged before they stopped working. He adjusted his grip until he held the broken end. The razor-sharp edges lacerated his hand, but he pushed past the pain and worked the neck of the bottle into the V. When he thought it secure enough, he paused for a moment.

The pain and fear exhausted him, but he couldn't rest. He moved round until the jagged edge pressed against his wrist near the cable ties. Working with the motion of the car, he moved his wrists and sawed at the ties. He grunted in pain as the glass cut into his flesh. Sure that they'd come for him at any moment, he hurried. Then, when he'd almost given up, his wrists separated as the plastic securing them parted. He flexed his hands and pulled the hood off, using it to wipe his blood-slicked palms. Once his hands regained a semblance of feeling, he reached for the neck of the bottle and retrieved it. Despite the pain and discomfort, having his hands free and a weapon of sorts gave him a boost. Whoever opened the lid was in for a surprise.

The journey seemed to take forever, and his cramped limbs stiffened. His thoughts returned to Erika. He imagined their home crawling with police. Having reported on crime for many years, he knew what would happen, but Erika was strong enough to get through it. He flexed his hands and feet, keeping the circulation going. Despite the pain from his many cuts, the fear of who his kidnappers worked for dominated his thoughts. He'd heard enough rumours to believe at least some of them were true.

He wiped the blood from his hands again. How much had he lost? Not enough to weaken him.

Despite his waiting for it, the end of the journey took him by surprise. The road noise ended, and the car stopped vibrating. Voices nearby warned him of someone's approach. Where was his bottle? He realised he still had hold of it. He flexed his shoulders and gripped the neck of the bottle tighter. Then, all too soon, the boot opened. Bright light haloed two heads looking in.

Half-blind, he yelled and lunged at the nearest. The man lurched back, but Grainger caught him with his makeshift blade. The impact almost ripped the weapon from his hand, and the man screamed.

Someone else shouted a warning. Then, before Grainger got the second one, something hit him across the forearm. He lost all sensation in his hand and dropped his weapon. Another blow caught him on the temple and knocked him back. Hands grabbed his shoulders, and a headbutt smashed into his already ruined nose.

Almost unconscious, he couldn't resist as they dragged him out and dumped him on to a concrete floor like a sack of wet washing. Feet, fists and weapons rained blows on him, and he covered up, hoping they hit nothing vital.

After what felt an eternity, the beating ended. Grainger sucked in air, then a boot slammed into his lower back. The pain took his breath away, and he gasped, tensing as he waited for another kick.

The man with the sibilant voice shouted, 'Stop!'

'Look what the bastard did!'

'You should have been more careful.'

'You what?'

Even curled up on the floor, semi-conscious and with a hood on his head, he sensed the tension. After a few seconds, the atmosphere eased.

The team leader gave terse instructions, and they dragged him across a concrete floor. Waves of pain made his head swim, and he must have lost consciousness because he found himself in a chair with his arms secured behind his back and his ankles fastened to the legs. The hood, or another like it, covered his head. A scene from a story he'd covered in Iraq flooded back. That hadn't ended well for the man in the chair. He dismissed the thought. This was England, not a lawless country.

He no longer felt cold. In fact, sweat trickled down his neck. Where the hell was he? The hot, dry air reminded him of a boiler room. God, he needed a drink. He listened. Was it someone breathing? It sounded too loud, like an enormous creature. His imagination created monsters, but he snuffed them out.

Despite the pain from his injuries, he dozed, waking with a start when steps came closer. Several people drew near, but none spoke. He swallowed, wishing he had some water. They stopped, and he imagined them stood round him in a circle. Steps came closer, and he couldn't help cringing. Someone ripped the hood off his head, flooding his eyes with light. He squinted, trying to see where he was. As he blinked to clear his vision, he saw the rails on the floor in front of him. The heat came off a metal door in the wall in front of him, at least ten paces away.

The roof of the space he sat in loomed far above and the walls on each side were even further away than the one facing him. What the hell was this place? He focused on the surrounding figures. They stood on each side of him, not wanting to stand too close to the heat. Three of the figures he guessed had brought him here, including one with a bloody bandage on his cheek, but the fourth seemed out of place. Smaller than the others, he had the air of an accountant or banker. Brown hair worn short with a side parting. The suit looked like one of those made by that Norwegian designer who claimed not to sell anything for under ten grand. Grainger recognised him with a sinking sensation as his worst fears were confirmed. Gustav Reed-Mayhew, one of the most powerful businessmen in the country. And someone he was investigating. But how had Reed-Mayhew found out? Grainger hadn't told anyone.

Reed-Mayhew's cold hazel eyes appraised him. 'I see you recognise me, so no need for introductions.'

'What do you want?' Grainger couldn't keep the panic out of his voice.

'The story you're working on—'

'That's nothing to do with you.'

'I decide what concerns me. Who have you told?'

'Nobody.'

Reed-Mayhew smiled. 'A bit too quick, Mr Grainger—'

'I've told no one.'

'Interrupt me again and you'll regret it. Now, who have you told?'

Grainger waited a few seconds to make sure Reed-Mayhew had finished. 'I've told no one. I wasn't sure there was a story.' *Until now.*

'Hmmm. In that case, this' – Reed-Mayhew made an expansive gesture – 'will have been unnecessary.'

'It is.' Sweat dripped off Grainger's nose. What the hell was this place, and why so hot?

'Excuse me if I don't take your word. You must have discussed it with your boss, that insufferable meddler who imagines herself some sort of knight in shining armour.' Real hatred distorted Reed-Mayhew's features. 'And the old cripple in the wheelchair.'

'I planned to tell Antonia today.' What day was it? How long had he been here? 'I've said, I've told nobody.'

'Not even your wife?'

Grainger swallowed. 'No. Nobody.'

Reed-Mayhew laughed, a loud sound that echoed. 'That's definitely a lie. How can I believe anything you tell me, Mr Grainger?'

Grainger's sluggish brain caught up with his situation. The fact that neither Reed-Mayhew nor his thugs had bothered to hide their identities meant only one thing. 'It's up to you. Believe what you want.'

Reed-Mayhew addressed the men flanking him. 'I believe Mr Grainger has worked out his fate. They always think they've got nothing to lose at this point. I think we need to disabuse Mr

Grainger of that notion.' He gave a nod, and the men moved forward.

Grainger's bladder loosened. He'd always believed he had a high pain threshold, but he was in no hurry to find out. 'Look, I've told nobody, not even my wife. I've been a journalist for twenty years. I keep my mouth shut until the story's ready.'

The men approached, and their leader produced a knife. Grainger couldn't take his gaze off it as it came closer. Then, all three men walked out of sight behind him. Still tense, he waited. Then his hands parted. The men grabbed his wrists and pulled his arms round before him. Cuts caused by the bottle had stopped bleeding, and the beginnings of ugly scabs crawled across his pale skin, making it look like he'd attempted to kill himself.

The man holding his right wrist pressed it against the chair arm and the team leader secured it there with a metal band, then went back behind him. Metal clanged against metal. *What the hell?* Did they have some sort of torture machine?

The team leader returned holding a bracket and Grainger realised there were slots at the front of each arm of the chair. He examined the chair itself for the first time – all metal, and it sat on wheels. This second bracket fitted into a slot in the front of the chair's left arm and stuck out before it. After securing the bracket with a wing nut, the man holding his left wrist slammed his forearm on to the bracket, securing it with another metal band at the front end. Grainger's left arm stuck out, like he intended stopping traffic.

'I can see you're wondering what's going to happen,' Reed-Mayhew said. 'It's something I designed myself. You'll be impressed.' He nodded at the men and two disappeared behind him.

A motor came on and the chair slid forward. Slow, but straight towards the door, which shimmered with heat haze. The heat increased. He slid past Reed-Mayhew, and, with a clank, the door opened. Behind it, a mass of flame. The blast of heat stretched Grainger's skin over his cheeks. Within seconds, the hairs on his knees shrivelled. Grainger tugged at his wrists but could free neither. Blood dripped from the wounds he'd reopened. The chair moved inexorably closer.

'Look, I told nobody.'

'You said.'

His left hand felt on fire. 'How can I convince you?'

'Tell the truth.'

'I am.'

The chair stopped.

He turned his head away and opened his eyes. Flames roiled and crackled less than two paces away. 'Please, I'm telling the truth.'

He had to shut his eyes and tucked his chin in. The stench of burning hair filled his nostrils. Did Reed-Mayhew believe him? The motor started again. *Thank God!*

Then he realised he was still going forward. His scream echoed.

CHAPTER 2

3 MONTHS EARLIER

The demonstrators moved along The Mall in a noisy but peaceful procession. Antonia snapped a photo of a group carrying a five-metre-long model of a Polaris submarine with two young women dressed as Trident missiles perched on the top. After carrying it for two hours, they looked like they regretted their decision.

A young man circulating with a courier bag full of anti-nuclear weapons leaflets approached and offered her one. Despite the warm spring weather, he wore a jacket buttoned up to his throat. He looked familiar, and she remembered seeing him at a similar protest in Bristol the previous week.

Something about him made her uneasy, and she refused his leaflet. She wove through the good-natured protestors, taking pictures and talking to people who looked interesting. The phalanx of police and private security guards lining the route looked on with grim expressions.

A young woman with blonde dreadlocks produced a megaphone from her backpack and started a chant. 'NO NUKES IN MY NAME!'

Within thirty seconds, a snatch squad emerged from the watching security guards and surged into the protestors. Antonia filmed it, forcing herself to stay detached. The people nearest the chanter moved to protect her, but using brute force, shields and batons, the guards got to her. One snatched the megaphone, while two more grabbed her. She fought back. Another guard joined in, pulling her hair and forcing her head back.

This part of the march paused, and an angry crowd surrounded the snatch squad. More officers streamed into the crowd, using chemical sprays and batons indiscriminately until they reached their target and absorbed her and their colleagues into their dark uniformed lines, then washing back to the side like a dirty tide receding. All around Antonia, people coughed and retreated from the chemical cloud, which caught in her throat and made her eyes stream.

A violent shove from behind pitched her forward and as she stumbled, someone grabbed at her arm. She kept her balance but almost dropped her camera. The man holding her arm jerked her, pulling her towards him, and instead of resisting, she went with it. Her left fist whipped out and crunched into his nose.

Surprise and pain made him release her arm. Another hand grabbed at her, but she twisted away.

A shout of, 'Leave her alone!' and a dozen protesters surrounded her. Her assailants slunk off, one holding his bloodied nose. She trained her camera on them until the crowd swallowed them.

'You okay?' one of her rescuers asked – a stocky guy of about forty, with cropped greying hair and an amused smile on his thin lips. Like her, he'd used ghost powder to break up his profile and make it harder for the face-recognition cameras to track him.

'Yeah, thanks for your help.'

'It didn't look like you needed it. The guy you punched didn't look too clever.'

'Did you see who pushed me?'

'Yeah, a guy with a courier bag, handing out leaflets. Very subtle. I wouldn't have noticed, except I'd seen him in Brighton a couple of weeks ago and was watching him.'

'I saw him in Bristol. You think he's undercover?'

'I'd bet on it. Along with those two.' He gestured in the direction her attackers had run. 'You're Antonia Conti, aren't you?'

'Yeah, and I've seen *you* before.'

He held out a hand. 'Rick Grainger.'

The name took her back to a press awards night. She'd gone with Eleanor after *The Electric Investigator* had been nominated for their story into the manipulation of prisoners' memories. Grainger won the award for a story he'd covered on corruption in the awarding of council contracts.

'Congratulations on your award.'

'Nah.' He waved her comment away. 'You should have won, but I work for the sponsor, so . . .'

Protesters swarmed round them, and they were now less than a hundred metres from the line of police vehicles shepherding the back of the protest. 'We should move up to the front,' she said. 'The speeches will start soon.'

'Yeah, and I don't like the look of that lot.' Grainger pointed at a knot of officers who'd gathered at the edge of the protest, in line with them and keeping pace.

Antonia led the way, weaving through the crowd, heading to the front. After a hundred paces, Grainger said, 'I'll see you around.'

'Yeah, sure. Thanks again, Rick.'

He waved and melted into the protest.

Antonia, still buzzing from the confrontation and buoyed by his comment, looked for people to interview. As she spoke to protesters, she kept a lookout for the guy with the courier bag and his two companions. She suspected they worked for the undercover private security company who'd infiltrated protest groups and caused hundreds to be convicted of the 'crime' of plotting to cause distress. If she saw them again, she'd put them on her front page.

As she neared Trafalgar Square, angry shouting greeted the marchers. A counter protest had arrived from Whitehall and those at the front of it were attempting to break through the lines of security people. The protesters in the main march reacted with angry gestures and insults. Antonia moved across the rows of protesters towards them. She knew what the narrative would be tomorrow, and news outlets would assign blame for any trouble based on their political leanings.

She came closer to the counter protesters. Although supposedly made up of shipyard workers and defence contractors whose jobs depended on the new Trident, they looked like the usual rent-a-mob she often encountered at these protests. Young men with short hair and tattoos, looking for trouble.

She filmed them, using the short extendable pole an inventor engineer Eleanor knew had made for her. It extended from thirty centimetres to two metres and weighed a kilo, making it heavy, but a useful weapon. Some of the mob noticed her and started making monkey noises. How witty. A couple of cans flew over, and Antonia decided she'd filmed enough. With jeers and catcalls following her, she returned to the body of the march, arriving in Trafalgar Square as the speeches started.

She scanned the audience as she listened to the speakers. The usual earnest activists, who didn't appear to have rehearsed, or even spoken in public before, provided the warm-up acts. After ten minutes, she spotted a familiar figure. The leafleteer. She zoomed in on him and took a picture, but she needed to get closer. As she closed on him, he turned and strode away.

Blast! He must have seen her. Then she saw Grainger in close pursuit. She followed. The leafleteer slipped through the security lines, but they stopped Grainger. As he argued with them, Antonia moved along the security line to where it thinned. She got through and looked for her quarry.

Behind her, the distinctive voice of the principal speaker thundered. The protesters cheered, and the counter march reacted, surging forward. The security guards focused on this new threat and Grainger slipped through their lines. He jogged towards someone Antonia couldn't see and she followed. Up ahead, the leafleteer strolled away from the protest, mobile to his ear and seemingly unaware of Grainger.

Before Grainger reached him, shouts came from their right. A group of the counter marchers appeared out of an alley. Both Grainger and the leafleteer paused and watched. The leafleteer ended his call and strolled away. The men advanced towards Grainger. He ran, and the men followed.

Antonia hesitated. Could she get help in time? She knew the people guarding the protest wouldn't help, and although Charing Cross police station wasn't far, she suspected it would be deserted. She followed, soon catching up with the men, her long stride eating up the distance.

Eight men chased Grainger. They stretched into a column as the slower men fell behind. Antonia would soon pass the last man, but she didn't want them to see her. She slowed, shadowing the backmarker. A hundred metres ahead, the front man had almost caught Grainger.

The reporter swerved into a gateway and stopped, facing his pursuers. Two ran past him, intending to circle him. He ran forward, catching them by surprise. He hit the nearest one, a slashing blow to his collarbone. The man collapsed with a scream. The others hesitated, and Grainger leapt back, taking up a defensive position.

Antonia retrieved her camera pole, and, making sure she'd locked it so it wouldn't extend, shadowed the backmarker. The two men nearest Grainger surged forward. Antonia hit the backmarker. He collapsed with a grunt. She'd felled the next man before any of the others realised she'd arrived. Two ran at her. Big men, but not skilled.

She avoided the punch the nearest one sent her way. As she straightened, his other fist caught her a glancing blow high on the forehead. She ignored it and swung her makeshift baton at the side of his knee. It hit him with a sickening crunch, and he fell, his shriek of pain stopping his companion two paces away. Antonia feinted with the camera pole at his head and, as the man swayed out of range, launched a sidekick into his thigh.

He staggered and grunted. She followed up, and he went to step away, but his leg didn't work. Antonia swung the pole at him. He lifted an arm to block her. She adjusted the aim, and it shattered his elbow. His arm fell, and he stared at the unnatural bend in it. She caught him on the chin with the backswing and he collapsed.

Grainger had felled another of his assailants and when the two remaining men realised the fate of their companions, they fled.

Antonia ran up to Grainger. 'Are you okay?'

'Yeah.' Blood leaked from cuts on his face. He bent over, hands on knees and breathing hard. 'Fuck!'

Antonia scanned the battleground. The first man Grainger had hit staggered to his feet, arm hanging down, gripping his elbow. The other one writhed on the floor, hands cupping his groin. Behind her, three she'd hit lay still, and the fourth used a street lamp to support himself on one leg. A few people stood fifty paces away, keen to watch but not wanting to get involved. Some held phones up, filming, and one held his to his ear.

'Shall we go?' Antonia said.

'Yeah, okay.' Grainger took a step. 'Fuck!' He grabbed his knee. 'What have you done?'

'When I kneed matey there in the balls, I twisted it.'

'Can you walk using this?' Antonia extended the camera pole, locked it, and handed it to him.

'I think so.'

'Good, let's go.'

A shout from behind them spun them around. It came from the two who'd run off, and with them at least ten more.

'Fuck!'

'Come on.' Antonia offered him a shoulder.

'No, you go on.'

'I'm not leaving you.'

They'd gone ten paces, Grainger leaning against her on one side and using the pole on the other, when one of her victims shouted, 'Get the black bitch!'

Her pulse spiked, and she almost dragged Grainger.

'Leave me,' he told her. 'It's you they want.'

She ignored him. Behind them, their pursuers closed in. Up ahead, a door swung open. A brown face appeared in the opening, its owner waving them over. Antonia put on a spurt and, thanking him, they threw themselves into the opening. The man slammed the fire-exit door behind them.

They paused for a moment, Grainger panting. Had they got away? They waited, not daring to talk. A loud banging on the doors made their rescuer jump. The doors trembled but looked solid.

'This way.' He led them down a corridor lined with bins and trolleys.

Grainger refused her help. 'I'm okay now. I've run it off.' He hobbled a few steps using the pole, then his gait improved.

She followed, checking on him limping along. They reached a door, shut tight. Their rescuer stopped with a look of panic. He ran his hands along the edge of the frame, then kicked it. 'Shit!'

Behind them, the banging on the doors changed to loud thuds. 'Is there another way out of here?' Antonia said.

18

The young man's eyes darted, then he said, 'Yeah, follow me.' They turned a corner, and he led them to a ladder fixed to the wall. He jerked a thumb upwards to a trapdoor. 'Up through there. There's a corridor takes you to the back of the building.'

Grainger stared at the trapdoor, at least five metres above them. 'No way with my knee.'

'I'll carry you,' Antonia said.

Behind them, the thuds grew more vigorous.

'Is there another way?' Grainger said.

'Down there.' Their rescuer pointed down a gloomy corridor at ninety degrees to theirs. 'There's a staircase. You go up three floors, it brings you to a fire escape and you can get outside.'

'I'll go that way and you and Antonia go up there.'

Behind them, wood splintered. 'Thanks, mate,' Antonia said. 'You'd better get up there.'

He swarmed up the ladder, and before Grainger could argue, Antonia set off ahead of him towards the stairs. His shoes slapped the floor behind her. Unable to see far, she slowed her pace. After a few steps, she no longer heard her pursuers, but doubted they'd given up. She almost tripped over the stairs and skidded to a halt.

Grainger stopped himself with a hand in her back. 'Sorry.'

'Will you be okay climbing this?'

'Yeah, if there's a handrail. You go first.'

She didn't argue. If she got up there first, she could at least suss out the fire escape. Faint illumination from a light-well leaked in through grimy windows. She'd reached the first floor when sounds from below told her their pursuers had broken in. Excited shouts and banging as they overturned the metal bins in an orgy of destruction. A burst of adrenaline propelled her up the stairs. She reached the top and looked around her.

A green fire exit sign hung over a doorway a few paces away. Grainger scrambled up the stairs, at least one floor behind her. She reached the door in four strides. A bolt with a glass tube secured it. A short chain hung down, missing its hammer. She looked for something to break the tube.

Apart from an extinguisher, the short corridor contained nothing. Five doors led off it. She tried the first, locked. Grainger arrived and halted on the top step, panting.

Voices came from below, then a shout. 'They're up here.'

She snatched up the extinguisher and, using the edge of the base, swung it at the glass. She cleared the glass splinters before pulling at the bolt. Unused for an age, it resisted.

Grainger stood beside her. 'Let me have a go.'

She drew the bolt as he reached for it and pushed the door. It moved a few millimetres. The sounds of pursuit grew closer, and she threw her shoulder against the door. It opened wide enough for one person.

'Go.' She gestured to Grainger.

'No, you—'

She pushed him through the gap. 'I'll catch you up, now go!'

She picked the extinguisher up by the neck as his shoes clattered on the metal treads of the fire escape. A head appeared at the top of the stairs and with a war cry she lifted the extinguisher and charged. The man froze and another figure came up behind him, blocking his retreat. The extinguisher connected with a clang and the first man fell back. His companion jumped clear of him, but without hesitating, came straight at Antonia. Still off-balance, she didn't have time to swing her makeshift weapon and she thrust it at his head. He threw his hands up and not only blocked the blow but caught the cylinder.

Antonia tugged, but he held tight. He wore a vest top, and chemically assisted muscles gave him a cartoonish appearance. At least twice her weight, he jerked the extinguisher. Antonia held on, but she slid along the floor. She braced her left leg against the foot of the bannister and arrested her movement. The handle slipped through her fingers. Her assailant showed a gap in his front upper teeth. Behind him, his companions bunched on the next flight, enjoying the show and shouting encouragement.

Grainger must have reached the ground by now. She stopped pulling and released the handle. The bodybuilder reared back, and she followed up with a roundhouse kick straight at his head. Unable to lift his laden hands, her foot caught him on the side of his head, which snapped back. He fell senseless, and lurched into the gathered spectators, taking at least three with him.

The cries of alarm and pain followed Antonia, and she threw herself through the gap in the doorway, kicking it shut before bounding down the staircase.

CHAPTER 3

Antonia walked into the bar like she owned it, reminding Chapman of the Antonia he'd first met; before she lost her confidence. It wasn't surprising after what happened to her last December. Chapman half-rose from his seat and waved. With a smile, she acknowledged him and strode to the table he occupied. People she passed noticed her. She wore her uniform of jeans and black leather jacket and her armoured backpack swung on her left shoulder. She looked well, although as she got closer, he thought he detected a faint mark above her left eye. They exchanged greetings and settled down with their drinks.

'What's wrong with your office?' He gestured at the surrounding room.

'I needed to get out. I've been holed up in my bunker since first thing and fancied some fresh air.'

'Why don't you move offices? I appreciate it's Eleanor's place, but you're falling over each other.'

She held up a finger. 'That's about to change. Eleanor's bought the house next door and wants to convert most of it into our new headquarters.'

'Bloody hell. Where did she get the money?' How many million would it have cost?

'Investments and a pension she cashed in.'

'Is she okay?'

'Yeah, fine. She's just decided she won't retire, so no point in having a pension.'

He intended to make the most of his pension, his ambition being to emulate a retired inspector he'd met who'd racked up forty-three years on his. 'You staying in the basement?'

'No way. Eleanor has promised me a large office overlooking the garden at the back.'

'There will be no talking to you then. When's it happening?'

'Soon, I hope.'

He checked the time. 'Are you done for the day?'

'I hope so. This is my last meeting.'

'Oh, so this is a "meeting".'

'And a catch-up with an old friend.'

'Do you fancy a bite afterwards?'

'Sorry, I can't.'

'Gym night.'

'Erm, no.' She sounded uncharacteristically evasive.

'A date then?' A man in her life would explain her newfound aura of confidence.

She looked embarrassed and sipped her water. 'I'm seeing my mental resilience counsellor at six thirty.'

He hid his relief. 'What's one of those?'

'She's helping me strengthen my mind. You remember what happened to me when those women messed with my memory? I'm determined I won't end up in the same position again.'

He still had nightmares of the night he'd stayed up waiting to find out if they could retrieve her memories or if she would end up a shell of a person. 'Maybe we should offer it to our lot. We've got loads off with stress and mental health problems.'

'I can give you a card, but she's not cheap.'

Chapman believed a team bonding session in the pub with your mates did wonders. He gestured at the mark on her forehead. 'So, you get that in the gym last night?'

She brushed her hand over the blemish self-consciously. 'I covered the protests in Trafalgar Square and encountered some thugs in the counter demo.'

'What happened?'

She told him about flattening the thugs in a matter-of-fact tone. She'd done something similar to him the second time they met, leaving him sprawled on the floor, unable to breathe.

She paused her account. 'What are you smiling about?'

'Just remembering the time you flattened me.'

She returned his smile, then continued describing their flight into the building and her assault on the bodybuilder.

'I'd like to have seen that.' He'd have hated it. The worry of what might have happened to her made him nauseous. 'What happened when you got out of the fire exit?'

'Rick had already got out and bumped into some of the security guys and a few of your lot from Charing Cross. Someone had called them. The idiots wandered off. The security guys were useless.'

'If they'd been off duty, most would have joined the thugs chasing you. I don't know where they recruit them. Low-level criminals who've avoided getting a record.'

'I got that vibe off them.' She checked the time. 'We could have a bite here. I've got time.'

'What about after your session?'

She frowned and took another sip of her drink. 'Okay, you can pay.'

'Great.' He'd take her to the new Italian. Not cheap, but a nice, relaxed atmosphere. The sort of place you'd go with an old friend.

Antonia got down to business. 'I'd better tell you why I asked to meet you. You know I've been looking for Alan's killers since he . . . Since that day.' Alan Turner, Eleanor Curtis's nephew and Antonia's friend, had run *The Investigator* until his murder by the men hired to guard him.

Chapman would never forget. The young man who'd looked too timid to confront his own shadow, taking on killers with automatics armed with just a chair. The inevitable outcome had enabled Antonia and Chapman to escape, and the thought that he'd spent too little time looking for Alan Turner's killers filled him with guilt.

'You found someone?'

'Not yet.' She produced a laptop from her backpack. 'We investigated a self-storage unit business. A young guy with a load of containers on waste land undercut the big boys. Somebody didn't like it and sent the heavies round.'

'Are you serious?'

'Do you realise how much money people spend on those things?'

He did realise. He'd spent a fortune on them his since his divorce. Although he should just empty it. If he hadn't needed the stuff in there for seven years, he'd never need it. 'Yeah, okay, it's big business.'

'And they're used to hide stolen goods and proceeds of crime.'

'So, some dodgy people are involved in the business.' He suspected the guys he paid were dodgy, but they also made sure nobody touched their clients' stuff.

'Yes, very dodgy. Anyway, the guy in charge of the heavies they sent sounds like "The Smoker".'

A hot, clammy hand clutched at Chapman. The man had subjected him to a beating he'd never forget. 'What happened to the lad?'

'Nothing serious. But the guys who sent the boys round now own the container park.'

'Is the lad making a complaint?'

'No, he won't even talk to me. His girlfriend contacted me. She recognised another of the heavies. They'd gone to her school.'

'Do you want me to track them down?'

She shook her head. 'No need. I found him, and spoke to him, but he's now inside and I need someone to talk to him.'

'And you want me . . .'

'He's on remand, so they won't let me interview him, and too many of the guards there would recognise me if I posed as a visitor.'

'What about one of your other reporters?'

'If it was a story, I'd send one of them. But this is personal. We owe Alan our lives. One of us must do it.'

Feeling he'd been railroaded, he swallowed some of his beer. 'Okay, when?'

'Oh, Russell, thank you.' She leant across and hugged him, enveloping him in a faint floral scent. She sat back and tapped at the laptop keys. 'I'll email you the details, including why he's there. I've listed the crimes he and his cronies are involved in and I'm sure you could investigate him for one of yours.'

He laughed. 'You knew I'd say yes, didn't you?'

'You're a decent man, Russell. We owe Alan.' She finished typing and closed her laptop before sliding it away.

'Yeah, we do.'

She drained her drink. 'I'd better go. Text me where we're eating. I promise to put my phone on.'

With another hug, she left. Chapman finished his drink. The reason he'd avoided looking for 'The Smoker' was that finding him would open a Pandora's box he'd rather keep shut. His last encounter with the man had not only led to Chapman being tortured, but Antonia killing Chapman's torturer in order to free him, leaving behind plenty of DNA evidence. An uneasy sensation tugged at his insides.

◆ ◆ ◆

'Ms Conti, your visitor's arrived.' Jean Sawyer stood in the doorway to Antonia's cramped office.

Antonia glanced around the room. She'd tidied up, but it looked tired. 'Thanks, Jean, please show him in.'

The call from Rick Grainger had come as a surprise. He'd been mysterious, not telling her what he wanted, but she'd find out his reasons soon enough.

She rose to greet him. 'Welcome, Rick. Take a seat.'

A slight limp, as well as bruising round his eyes, remained from his ordeal four days earlier. 'I wanted to say thank you again. I doubt I'd have got away from those thugs without your help.'

'You could have sent a card – or phoned.'

He laughed. 'Yes, I could.' He sat opposite her and cleared his throat. 'You don't seem happy to see me.'

'I'm surprised you're here. I read your account, blaming the anti-nuclear protestors for the trouble.'

'Ah. Right.' He looked embarrassed. 'That's one reason I'm here. I read yours and wished I'd written it.'

Although pleased at the compliment from a fellow profes-sional, especially one with such a stellar reputation, she remained wary. 'What do you want?'

'You're very direct.' He seemed amused.

'I find it the best way to be and am always suspicious when someone comes here, buttering me up.'

'I meant I wish they'd allowed me to. My original version left no doubt the trouble came from the counter protest, which we both know – and which you could say, in your piece – was organ-ised to discredit the original protest.'

'Had someone done that to my piece, I wouldn't have let them put my name to it.' *Was that true?* She'd never been in that position.

'Someone warned me you were uncompromising. I thought it only applied to the way you fought.' He paused, clearly waiting for her laugh. 'I told them to take my name off, but they claim a mistake by a sub-editor.'

'You've not come here because you want my good opinion.'

'No. I've got a story for you.'

'How does that work? You're a star reporter for one of my rivals—'

'Not really rivals. They're much bigger.'

Don't underestimate me. 'And we were much smaller once.'

'Good point.'

Despite her misgivings, she wanted to discover what he'd come to say. 'Do you want to tell me?'

'As you point out, my current employers won't appreciate me taking this to a rival.'

'You want a job?' She laughed. The idea of having a reporter with his profile working for them sounded absurd.

'I'm quite good.'

'You're more than quite good, but half a dozen other publications would snap you up, so why us?'

'None of them will touch this story.'

'You've tried them?' *And we're also-rans, then?*

'Not all directly, but I've got the contacts to make discreet enquiries. Most have heard rumours, but they're either steering clear out of deference, or someone warned them off.'

'Royals?' She wasn't interested in gossip, however 'big' a story.

'No, I wouldn't bring a royal story to you. Give me some credit. I know you wouldn't touch something like that. I might work as part of a big team, but I can do my own research.'

'I don't doubt it. Do you have evidence to back up your story?'

'Not enough yet. But I can get it if I'm allowed to.'

'And how much did you have to reveal to the ones you approached before you got turned down?'

He laughed. 'You're a lot brighter than *my* editor. Enough to get their attention, but not enough to enable them to run a spoiler.'

'Do you want to tell me?'

'Are you offering me a job?'

They'd discussed taking on a new reporter. Jean was already working on some stories, mainly on technology, and they'd talked about offering her more, but they needed an experienced investigative reporter. It would probably put Jean's nose out of joint if they brought someone in ahead of her. But she couldn't object to someone like Rick Grainger. He would have been way above their expectations *and* salary. 'What's your salary?'

He told her.

'That's twice what I get.'

'You're undervalued. I'd look for another job.' He winked at her.

What would Eleanor do? Although they'd done well since the big story at Christmas, the work converting the new place next door and integrating it with the existing offices would eat into their reserves. But having someone like Grainger on board would boost their subscribers. 'How much would you accept?'

He quoted a figure still above what she got, but more manageable. 'Plus, I'd want to do some freelance TV presentation, which I can't do now, mainly in France and Germany.'

She considered this. They'd deliberated expanding into Europe. She should discuss this offer with Eleanor, but Antonia was in charge. 'I'd want a veto on what stories you work on. Nothing to harm our brand.'

'No problem. You know the type of stories I want to work on. The type of stuff I got the award for. You wouldn't believe how many stories I've shelved because my editor spiked them.'

She could well believe it. Many of his reports she'd have happily published. 'Okay.' *You should at least see the story he's offering you.* Too late: she stuck out her hand.

29

'Thank you.' He took it, exuding relief and excitement.

'We haven't got a lot of room, but we're expanding into next door.'

'I saw the sold sign. But I don't need a lot of room. A desk and chair, plus access to unlimited coffee.'

'We can manage that.' They could offer him a desk, just, but would a reporter of his stature accept hot-desking?

'I can also do a lot from home – if you're happy for me to do so?'

'No problem. Do you want to tell me the story nobody will touch?'

'Okay. The reason for the trouble at the protests last week is because they're going to ban protests. The trouble gave them the excuse.'

'I'd worked that out myself.' Would his offering disappoint her? 'Helped by stories like the one your paper produced.'

'Sorry.' His ears grew pink. 'But that's not the story. The reason is, they're going to approve the Trident replacement.'

'That isn't a surprise either.' She'd heard rumours.

'No, but do you know which cabinet ministers own shares in the companies who get the contracts?'

'Have you got evidence?'

'Oh yes, and I can get more. It just needs digging out.'

Antonia tried to suppress her excitement. 'How high does it go?'

'All the way.'

This would bring the government down. A wariness mixed with her excitement. She knew they'd also do anything to defend their position.

CHAPTER 4

Sabirah arrived at work full of enthusiasm. She and the children had enjoyed a wonderful weekend away with her friend Jean, and she loved not having to work as a cleaner for the first time since she'd arrived in the UK. Losing her part-time cleaning job four weeks ago had come as a blow, but when the shop extended her hours, she'd believed she'd finally made progress. Although easier, the work paid better.

A strained atmosphere greeted her when she arrived. Her boss hadn't been his usual cheerful self for at least a week, and she wondered about the rumour that his wife had cancer. She hoped it wasn't true. She was a kind woman. As she changed into her uniform, a call over the speaker summoned her to his office. She finished changing and made her way up the stairs.

'Come in, Sabirah.' He gestured to the seat in front of his desk and waited for her to sit. 'There's no easy way to say this, but I'm going to have to let you go.'

It took her a few seconds to grasp his meaning, and then it hit her like a punch in the gut. She took a deep breath and gathered her wits. 'Why? You just give me more hours.'

'It's unfortunate timing, but business is tough, and I've got to cut my overheads.'

'Is my work not good?' She knew this wasn't true, having received several excellent appraisals.

'Nothing wrong with your work, and I'll give you an excellent reference. It's just a business decision.'

'So, are we all out of work?' As she'd got to know her colleagues, she'd learned their stories, and it would hit all of them hard.

'It's not that bad.'

That was something, but why her? 'Who else is going?'

He looked uncomfortable. 'It's not any of your business, but it's just you.'

She'd learned how these things worked. 'But I'm not the newest.'

'You are. You signed a new contract three weeks ago.'

'But I work here for more than one year before.'

'Sorry, but that's the way it goes.' He wouldn't meet her gaze.

'This is wrong. You—'

'I'm not getting into it. Take it up with your union if you don't like it.'

He'd discouraged Sabirah from joining the union, and, insecure about her refugee status, she'd not joined one. Determined not to let him see her upset, she left the room. She returned to the locker room, numb inside and wanting to leave before she spoke to anyone else. She pulled the overalls off, not bothering to hang them up, put her outer clothes on, grabbed her handbag and left.

As she emerged from the locker room, two of the others saw her.

'Are you okay, Sabirah?'

She wanted to ignore them and run out, but these were good colleagues, friends even. 'I have—' Had he sacked her, or made her redundant? 'I have finished.'

'Aww. That's a shame. Was it because of the graffiti on the shutters?'

The shutters were always up by the time she arrived. 'What graffiti?'

'You shouldn't let it get to you. They're just sad racists.'

'What did it say?' Sabirah could imagine.

Her friend looked embarrassed. 'Something about illegals and them being . . . No, it's not worth repeating.'

Weariness weighed Sabirah down. She'd hoped to leave those comments behind when she received Indefinite Leave to Remain for her and her children.

'Ignore them, Sabirah. Tell him you want your job back.'

'He sacked me.' She left before they could recover and offer more sympathy. She'd break down if they did.

On her journey home, she churned over what she'd discovered. He must have decided to get rid of her after the graffiti appeared. What he did must be illegal. Even though she wasn't in a union, she could find out. Antonia would know. But did she want to come back and work for a man who would do this to her? She needed a job, and if she stayed out of work too long, not only would she run out of money, but the Internal Security Agency would come knocking.

Antonia heard the whirr of Eleanor's electric wheelchair as she arrived in Antonia's office for their Monday morning management meeting. They had a huge amount to discuss, even before Antonia's rash decision to hire Rick Grainger. She worried about how to break the news, *and* how much it would cost them. As usual, Eleanor produced an agenda and Antonia intended to bring it up in 'any other business' at the end, hoping to have come up with something in the meantime.

Eleanor studied her across her desk. 'You've got something on your mind, Antonia.'

Antonia took a sip of her coffee. 'There's a lot to go through. Shall we start with the first item?'

'Okay. The proposed refurbishment of our new office. I'd like us to appoint Sabirah as lead architect to oversee the conversion and integration of next door into our offices down here.'

'Wow, I thought you'd asked your friend Brody to do it.' Antonia was unsure how she felt about this. Although more than happy to give her friend this opportunity, she also wanted their new offices to be fabulous.

'It will give Sabirah the chance to turn her life around.'

'Yes, but I thought she'd assist. She's not worked as an architect since she left Syria.'

'She's brushed up her skills and I think she's ready. I'm surprised at you, Antonia. I expected you to support my decision.'

'Of course, I want to support Sabirah, but it makes sense for her to assist first, then once she's back in the swing she can take on more responsibility. This will pile a lot of pressure on her.'

'I'm sure she can handle it. She managed much bigger projects in Idlib. Anyway, I've asked Brody if he's happy to supervise her and he is.'

'You've already discussed it with him?'

'Of course. If he didn't want to do it, there's no point even thinking about it.'

'If Sabirah feels she can handle it, I suppose we can try it.' Considering she'd not discussed taking on Grainger with Eleanor, her protests seemed hypocritical.

'I'll tell her – unless you want to.'

'No, it's your idea. We need to decide what we want so we can brief her.'

They spent an hour deciding what they needed to create a state-of-the-art news-gathering facility. After topping up their refreshments, they moved on to the next item.

'"Increasing the amount of reporting Jean does",' Eleanor read out. 'How much of her time do you propose taking up with reporting? We will need to get cover for the days she's not doing her normal job. She's your PA, so you decide.'

Antonia had already decided. 'I've got two investigations I want her to work on, plus I think we should give her a role in designing our computer system for the new offices.'

'That sounds almost full-time. I presume you're not proposing managing without a PA.'

'What about Tomasz Zabo?'

'What about him? Has he recovered?'

'He's ready to start work.'

'But the poor lad lost a leg in the attack on you.'

'Yes, but he's got a prosthetic leg and can get around well enough to work as my PA.'

'Will he manage all the stairs when we move next door?'

'We're putting in a lift so *you* can get around. He can use it if he needs to.'

'I presume he's available, but do you think he's still up to the job? Loss of mobility can play havoc with your confidence.'

'It hasn't harmed yours, Eleanor.'

She laughed. 'But you mustn't offer him a job out of a misplaced sense of duty.'

'Misplaced? A van aimed at me smashed into him on his first day working for us. If he hadn't been with me, he'd still be walking about on two complete legs.'

Eleanor gave her a sympathetic smile. 'If you put it like that. Have you spoken to him?'

'We had a long chat last week. He appeared the same as before.'

'When have you told him he can start?'

Antonia's cheeks grew warm. 'I've confirmed nothing. Once we've agreed to it, I need to speak to Jean.'

'I've said it before. You're in charge.' Eleanor glanced at the agenda. 'Any other business?'

Antonia decided to just come out with it. 'I've taken on a new reporter.'

'We've only just agreed to appoint Jean as a reporter. Taking on someone new seems . . .' Eleanor searched for a word. 'Ambitious.'

'Taking over the house next door is ambitious.'

'Especially by someone of my senior years?'

'You'll outlive us.' The fact Eleanor was nearer eighty than seventy still amazed Antonia. Sharing the house with Sabirah and the children had given her a new lease of life.

'Will you tell me who it is?'

'Sorry. It's Rick Grainger.'

'*The* Rick Grainger?'

'Uh-huh. The one who beat us to the award last year.'

'You should have won it.'

'Rick agreed.'

'Did he? How very fair of him. How did you persuade him to leave his current employer? I understand he has a lovely office with views of the Thames.' Eleanor looked round Antonia's less than salubrious office.

'I didn't need to. He came to see me because he's got a story nobody else will touch.'

'And that is?'

Antonia lowered her voice. 'Ministers owning shares in the companies winning the Trident replacement contracts.'

Eleanor raised her eyebrows. 'Has he evidence?'

'He says so.'

'What if it isn't strong enough to run? His current outfit must have seen the evidence and decided not to go with it.'

Antonia hesitated. She'd worried she hadn't insisted on making his employment conditional on seeing the evidence. 'Do you think he's the sort of person to do that?'

'Based on his record, I'd say no.'

'You haven't asked me how much.'

'I assume enough to attract him, but not too much. The audience he brings should more than pay whatever you've agreed.'

Antonia told her the sum, holding her breath for the reaction.

'I'm sure he'll be worth it. We should raise your salary. The boss should always get the most.'

'I need no more.' She barely spent half her current salary.

'Let's revisit it once we've finished the building work. Well done, Antonia. Getting someone of his calibre is testament to what you've achieved.' She held her arms out and Antonia walked round the desk to give her a hug.

She untangled herself. 'I've had two excellent mentors and I've only built on what you and Alan established.'

'Yes, it's a pity Alan isn't here to see this.' An uncharacteristic wistfulness entered Eleanor's voice.

'We should call the new place Alan Turner House.'

Eleanor's eyes glistened. 'Thank you.' After a few seconds, she gathered herself. 'I'll leave you to it. We must celebrate.'

She wheeled herself out, leaving Antonia to her thoughts. She remembered Alan patiently befriending her when she first arrived to live with Eleanor as a damaged teenager. He'd spent months breaking through the hard shell she'd built around herself and had helped her reconnect with people. When she started at *The Investigator*, he'd mentored her, teaching her all he knew about her new career. She missed his wise counsel and wished she could consult him about her decisions, especially this one.

What if Grainger's story didn't stand up? She'd been so excited by the idea of having a reporter of his calibre, she hadn't considered potential downsides. She hoped this was just buyer's remorse, and that she hadn't made a serious mistake.

◆ ◆ ◆

By the time she arrived home, Sabirah wanted nothing more than to curl up in bed with a hot water bottle. A note on the bottom step from Mrs Curtis asked her to see her in her office. She contemplated ignoring it, but she couldn't wallow in self-pity and needed to put on a positive facade before the children came home.

She took the lift down and put on a false smile before the doors opened. As usual, the basement offices contained too many people. Sabirah greeted those not too busy to notice her. Mrs Curtis's voice came from Jean's open door, and she halted in the doorway.

'You're home early, Sabirah. Thank you for coming down. We'll use Antonia's office. Do you want to wait in there?'

Sabirah exchanged a look with Jean. Apart from a misunderstanding early in their friendship, when Sabirah thought Jean had kidnapped her children, they'd become good friends. Mrs Curtis knew this and would discuss things with Jean present. For a horrible moment, she thought Mrs Curtis intended to give her more bad news. Was she going to ask them to move out of her beautiful flat on the upper floors of her house?

Sabirah went into Antonia's office. She wasn't comfortable taking her friend's chair, but it would be strange if Mrs Curtis sat alongside her. Antonia needed a bigger office. She sat, and Mrs Curtis wheeled herself into the room.

'Suits you, Sabirah. I can see you behind a desk, or maybe a drawing board.'

'Even in Syria we used computers.' Her life as an architect in Idlib felt a lifetime ago. She'd had a husband then, before they killed him. Busy closing the door behind her, Mrs Curtis didn't seem to notice the tears gathering in Sabirah's eyes.

'How are the children? I've not seen them for a week. We normally see you over the weekend.'

'We went with Jean to the New Forest.'

'She's a good woman, if odd at times.' They exchanged a conspiratorial smile. 'We've just promoted her to full-time reporter.'

'That's good.' Her friend's good fortune mocked her.

'We'll have to get a replacement PA for Antonia.'

Was she going to offer her the job? Sabirah's English still wasn't good enough. 'I don't think—'

'No, I'm not offering it to you. Sorry, Sabirah.' Mrs Curtis's pale cheeks flushed.

'Of course, no, I don't think you do.' *No, I'm just a shop assistant or a cleaner.*

'I *do* want to offer you a job. More of a short-term commission.'

'Commission?'

'We anticipate it taking three months, but you may not want to give up your new job for something temporary.'

Sabirah gave a wry smile. 'I'm home early because I . . . He sacked me.'

'What for?'

'He said he make me redundant, but the others mention racist graffiti.'

'And the solution is for you to leave?' Mrs Curtis shook her head. 'Oh, Sabirah, I'm so sorry.'

Her eyes prickled. *Don't show me sympathy, please.*

Appearing to read her mind, Mrs Curtis became brisk. 'It's serendipity.'

Sabirah frowned. 'Sorry?'

Mrs Curtis laughed. 'It means fortuitous. I want to offer you the job of architect, to oversee the conversion of our new offices.'

Sabirah said the first thing on her mind. 'I'm not ready.'

'Nonsense. I've seen your work. You're perfect for the project. And Brody Innis thinks so too.'

'Mr Innis is very kind, but he helped me a lot when I intern for him, and I only did three weeks.'

'He'll oversee your work. You're not able to practise yet, so he'll put his name on any plans, but you'll do the work.'

Sabirah couldn't speak. This was more than she could have dreamed.

'You're not going to turn me down?'

'No, of course not. Thank you. Thank you.' She rose and rounded the desk, hugging the old lady. 'Thank you.'

Everything that had happened hit her, and the floodgates broke open.

Rick Grainger waited for his wife to come down to breakfast. He'd heard her moving about. Erika got back late last night and had the next two days off to make up for working over the weekend. He was contemplating making another coffee when she swept into the kitchen, looking like she'd just returned from a restful weekend break rather than a gruelling business trip to Zungharistan, a ten-hour flight away.

He got up and took her in his arms. 'What time did you get home?'

'Three-ish. You were on another planet.'

He checked the time. Just past ten. 'Why didn't you sleep in?'

'I have. It's well past my normal getting-up time. Anyway, why are you still home? Won't the Ogre bite your head off?'

He pointed to his open laptop. 'I told him I'm working from home first thing and would go in later. You ready for a coffee?'

'Hmm, yes please.' Erika busied herself getting her superhealthy breakfast together as he made them both coffees.

He passed her a cup and sat, still undecided how to break his news.

His wife pre-empted him. 'Okay, what's on your mind?'

She could always read him. 'I've got a new job.'

'Oh, no wonder you're prepared to risk upsetting the Ogre. More money or promotion? Or both?' Her eyes widened.

He focused on his mug and sipped the strong brew. 'Neither. In fact, it's a pay cut and I'm working for a much smaller outfit.'

Erika raised her perfect eyebrows. 'I assume you've got your reasons.'

'You're not angry? I've not told Elfyn yet. I wanted to make sure you're happy with the decision.'

'It's your career, and we don't need the money, especially with the news I've got—'

'What? Jacinda's sharing more of her obscene profits with you workers?' The hedge fund Erika worked for as finance director had recently made a lot of money, shorting a car maker who'd fiddled their emission results. Grainger suspected Jacinda had used insider information, but he'd avoided looking any closer.

'You first – you're not getting out of it so easily. You must have thought it through. Who's your new employer?'

'*The Electric Investigator*.'

Erika drank from her cup. 'That *is* a surprise.'

'I told you. Antonia Conti, their editor, saved my life at the riot—'

'But I'm sure she didn't expect you to sacrifice your career to repay her.'

'I'm not sacrificing anything. They're going places. She's not like Elfyn or the others. She doesn't give a shit who she upsets if she's got a story.'

His wife studied him with her shrewd brown eyes. 'You've taken the Trident story to her, haven't you?'

He shifted in his seat. 'Yes. You're going to find out when we publish it, so . . .'

'Haven't you been warned off it?'

'By Elfyn, yeah. But you know what he's like. Anything to preserve his "access" to Number 10.'

Her eyes clouded. 'But he's right, it could end your career, or worse.'

'Rubbish.' He spoke with a confidence he didn't feel. 'They just keep you cowed by using hints of dark acts committed by clandestine groups protecting their cabal.'

'What about those two reporters who ended up dead in a car smash—'

'That was an accident. The driver was a known alkie, three times over the limit.' He'd not expected his wife to object to the story he'd chosen to pursue. 'Anyway, you brought me the story.'

'I wish I hadn't now.'

'Do you want me to tell Antonia I've changed my mind? I've not signed anything and I'm sure she'd understand.' He suspected Antonia would either rip his head off or take the story on herself, *after* ripping his head off.

'Have I ever stopped you?'

He stood and walked round the table to give her a hug. 'Thank you.'

'Well, you'd have been unliveable with. Is that a word? But you promise me you'll be careful.'

'Scout's honour.' He gave the three-fingered salute. 'I'd better tell the Ogre. But what's your news?'

'It's good.' She hesitated and smiled. 'Great. But you'll have to wait to find out. Now off you go.'

He left for work, energised at overcoming the first obstacle. Erika already out-earned him and now it sounded like she'd be even better off. At least he wouldn't feel so guilty about the pay cut.

He spent the train journey into work preparing his approach to Elfyn. He'd be furious, but it was all bluster. The sun shone off the windows of the tower block housing the paper. The architect who'd designed it for them described it as representing a sword of truth. But in reality, it resembled a cudgel of propaganda.

When did you become so cynical? As he made his way up in the lift, he realised he'd felt like this for a while. Would he rediscover his youthful idealism by working with Antonia? She still refused to make the compromises so many news people ended up making. *Rick Grainger, social justice warrior.* He smiled at this vision.

'Glad you think it's funny.' Elfyn waited in front of the lift doors. 'Where the hell have you been?'

'I told you I'd work from home—'

'But you didn't say what on. I told you—'

'Can we do this in your office?' Although pretending to be occupied with anything else, the people in reception were all listening in on the exchange.

Elfyn looked around, almost in a daze, then strode towards his office, leaving Grainger in his wake. Once they'd both entered the room and closed the door, the editor turned and stepped into Grainger's face, forefinger jabbing at him.

'I fucking told you to leave that story alone. If you want to carry on working here—'

'I don't.'

'What do you mean?'

'I'm giving you notice.'

'You can't.'

'Of course I can. I only need to give you four weeks.'

'Stuff that. You can clear your desk and fuck off now. I'm not having anyone I can't trust in my team.'

'Fine, you can pay me in lieu, and for the leave you owe me, which I intended to take instead of notice.'

'Fine, like I care. It's not my money and we've got plenty of it.'

'I'll wait here for security. You wouldn't want someone untrustworthy wandering around, would you?'

Like it did so often, Elfyn's rage evaporated as quickly as it had arrived. 'No need.' He slumped into his chair. 'So where are you going, Rick?'

'*The Electric Investigator.*' He waited for the snort of derision.

'Well, they *are* punching above their weight. But the girl down there's pretty feisty. With her and the old bat in the wheelchair, you'll have your work cut out.'

'I'm looking forward to it.'

'I bet you are. Your woke campaigning side will have plenty of opportunity to assert itself.' He stood again and held out a hand. 'Good luck, Rick, I've enjoyed working with you.'

Grainger gripped the large hand in his. 'Thanks, Elfyn, it's been a pleasure.'

Elfyn held on. 'I'm assuming you'll take the Trident story to them. That's why you're working on it again.'

'How did you find out what I've been doing in my own time?'

'I got a call at home last night. You activated a trip wire.'

Grainger considered the people he'd spoken to about the story. He'd been discreet, but obviously not enough.

'They were fucking furious,' Elfyn continued, 'and I mean incandescent, threatening me with all sorts.'

'You can tell them you've sacked me if it makes it easier for you.'

'It's good of you, but no need. A word of warning.' He leant in, still gripping Grainger's hand. 'You and your new boss need to watch your backs.'

'Why are you bothered? You didn't want to run it.'

'I'm not. In fact, I hope you expose the whole fucking lot of greedy scumbags. But the people who rang me won't give you a free run at the story.'

'Thanks for the warning.' Grainger extricated his hand and moved to the door.

'And, Rick. You won't get a phone call, like I did. They *like* me. You and the girl you now work for, not so much.'

CHAPTER 5

Jean Sawyer stared at Antonia through her bottle-bottom glasses. 'Full-time reporter?'

'Yes, we discussed the possibility when you started working on stories. You've got an aptitude for this work, Jean. You're organised, meticulous and tenacious. I've used Miles to cover any technology stories, but it's not his forte.'

Jean rolled her eyes. 'He usually asks me if there's anything technical.'

'Exactly, and if you're doing the job, he can focus on the stuff he's good at.'

'I'm good at being your PA and covering reception.'

Once they'd got Jean out of the habit of interrogating people who contacted them with confidential information, she'd become a good PA receptionist. 'Of course, but we can find someone who can do that job. What we haven't got is a reporter who can cover the technical desk. And you've showed us you're good at that.'

'Not everyone can do my job.'

'The new job means more money, and more variety.' She still wasn't sure if money motivated Jean, and variety might be the wrong thing to emphasise.

It was. Jean looked panicky.

'I'm sure once you get used to doing it, you'll be fine. You've done well so far.' Antonia had expected a bit of pushback, but not this level of resistance. Eleanor had warned her Jean wouldn't like change.

'But who's going to do my job?'

'A young man, Tomasz Zabo. He did it for a very short while before you did.' One day counted as very short in anyone's language.

'Oh, the cripple.'

'I suggest you don't use that term, Jean. Thomas lost part of his leg, but he's recovered now and is raring to go.'

Jean studied her. 'What if I refuse the reporter's job?'

'Are you going to?'

'Oh, no. Mummy said we need to up our income. The house needs some repairs, and she can't earn much.'

Antonia hadn't met Jean's mother, but from Sabirah's reports, her personality explained Jean's eccentric views and less-than-PC language. 'Good, we've got some investigations I want you to take over.'

'When do you want me to start?'

Jean's expression of alarm made Antonia uneasy. Had she made a mistake? 'Tomasz can't start until a week next Monday. He's temping.'

'Okay, it will give me time to get used to the idea.'

'You won't change your mind, will you?' Antonia dismissed visions of having two PAs fighting over one desk.

'Oh, no. I just like to get used to things.'

'Great. Welcome to the world of reporting.' Antonia didn't offer her hand, knowing Jean's aversion to physical contact. 'You'll be typing up your own contract, so make sure you don't inflate your salary or give yourself extra holiday.'

Jean reacted like Antonia had propositioned her. 'I would never do such a thing.'

'I'm joking, Jean.' Antonia checked the time. She had half an hour. 'Are you busy?'

'Not too bad. Do you want me to get my pad?'

'Get your pad and ask Miles to join us. And I'd love a coffee.'

She made the final changes to an article from one of the other reporters while she waited. She'd call Zabo at lunchtime. Despite her reassurances to Eleanor, she still felt guilty about what had happened to him. Who wouldn't? She hoped he'd take the job. She'd sounded him out a week ago but hadn't offered him the post until she was certain Jean would take the other one. Serve her right if he'd taken one in the last few days.

Jean returned with two coffees and set one down in front of Antonia. 'Who's the other one for, Jean?'

'If I'm going to be a reporter, I'll drink coffee like the rest of you.'

Antonia studied the pale, milky liquid in Jean's mug with distaste.

'Not all of us,' said Miles as he sat down next to her, a mug with a tea bag string hanging from it in a large hand. 'Jean told me. Great decision. She'll be an asset.'

'That's what I told her.' She'd have to thank Miles. Jean seemed to grow as she heard his praise. 'I want her to take over the story you've just started on. How's it going?'

'The insider dealing? I've only scratched the surface. I'm focused on the housing scam in Newham – I thought it more urgent.'

'It is, which is why I want you to hand the insider dealing to Jean. Go through what you've found with her and set her up on any databases you think she'll need, not just for this story, but for any others she might work on.'

'Okey-dokey.'

'Come and see me when you've finished.'

Miles and Jean left. Not much more than a year ago, Miles had been her predecessor's PA, and he'd become one of her most trusted reporters. Would Jean show her value as soon? And how would Miles take the news she'd taken on Rick Grainger? She'd tell him when he gave her an update on Jean's progress.

At lunchtime, Antonia rang Tomasz Zabo, and he agreed to start a week on Monday. She was writing Rick's contract when Miles returned with Jean.

'I know you only wanted to see me, but I thought Jean should tell you what she's discovered.' His excitement communicated itself.

They both waited while Jean settled herself and opened her tablet. 'Miles showed me the information he'd uncovered on JN Partners. It looks like they had insider information on the sunglasses manufacturers who fiddled their test results.'

'Manufacturers? I thought we were only looking at one?'

'I was,' Miles said, 'but Jean spotted another three small funds shorting shares in other manufacturers in the same pattern. It's too similar to be a coincidence.'

'You think it involved several hedge funds?' Antonia got the tingle she'd learned to trust.

'Or a network of funds controlled by one person,' Jean said.

'Have you any evidence?'

'Not yet, but I'm sure I'll find it if there is.'

Antonia believed she would, but would her methods cause them problems? 'And this inside person must work for a testing company?'

'I'd looked for someone at the manufacturer, but it makes sense to look at who's doing the testing as well, and Jean's discovery makes it almost certain that it's someone there. The chances of four employees at different companies all deciding to leak information seems unlikely.'

'Well done, Jean.'

A pink flush suffused her assistant's cheeks.

'There's more.' Miles displayed pride, suggesting he saw Jean as his protégé. 'I'll let Jean tell you.'

'I checked the fund's history. Jacinda Nieto started the fund in 2006 and they've made huge profits every year. I think they've been at it for a few years. I've got indications they knew about Bear Stearns.'

'You're joking?' 2006. Antonia had been a happy child in an obscure small town in South Sudan then. She doubted anyone in the town had even heard of a merchant bank.

Miles's heavy brow furrowed. 'Six weeks after forming, JN Partners shorted fifty million dollars' worth of Bear Stearns shares, in January '07. By the time the shares plunged to near zero, they'd made forty-eight million.'

'How come nobody noticed?'

'They were small fry, and with so much shit flying around then, nobody looked. We only noticed because we looked at their latest deal and worked back. I say we, but again, Jean picked it up.'

'Good work, both of you, and especially you, Jean.'

'Can I start work on this now?'

'I'll need you to do some jobs for me until Tomasz starts.'

'The same Tomasz who worked here before?' Miles said.

'Yes, he starts Monday.'

'Excellent, he's a likeable lad.'

'He is. Can I have a word, Miles?' She waited until Jean left and hesitated, unsure how Miles would greet her news. 'We've got another new reporter starting soon.'

'Oh, right, where will they fit in?'

'It's tight, but we will have more room once we've converted next door.'

'Wouldn't it make sense to recruit them once we've moved?'

'Yes, but the man in question approached us, and he's got a big story.'

'It must be big for you to offer him a job. Who is it?'

Antonia wasn't sure how much she should share with Miles. She trusted him, but it was Grainger's story. 'It's Rick Grainger.'

'*The* Rick Grainger?'

'Yes.'

'Wow, no wonder you took him on. Wow.'

'You're okay with it?'

'God! Of course. I could learn so much from someone like him. When's he starting?'

'He's negotiating his severance with his existing employer, but I hope soon.'

Miles's eyes shone. 'When will you tell the others? I'm sure this will give everyone a lift, having someone like him in the office.'

'We've got a staff meeting tomorrow morning.'

'Great, and thanks for letting me know first.'

That was easier than she'd feared. Things were going well, so why did she feel so uneasy?

◆ ◆ ◆

The email alert pinged, telling Chapman he'd received a message from someone he shouldn't ignore. His sergeant, Alice Sanchez, had set up the alert, which disregarded the myriad emails he received from colleagues covering their backs by including everyone they could think of. He checked the sender: DCI Gunnerson. What did she want?

Russell, please come and see me re your request to visit Bradwell.

What the hell? Why would she get involved in this? Still grumbling, and certain someone had it in for him, he locked his screen and left his office.

'What's up, boss?' Sanchez studied him from her desk.

'The request I put in to see Hughes at Bradwell. The DCI wants to see me about it. She shouldn't even be at work.'

'That's her choice, but she probably wants to know why you're seeing him.'

'I told you.' He'd told Sanchez about a fake bodyguard shooting Alan Turner, Antonia's editor, but hadn't mentioned that both he and Antonia had witnessed it. Despite Sanchez's involvement in a more recent incident, during which both he and Antonia had killed some people holding Antonia prisoner, he didn't want to tell Sanchez too much.

'But that shooting isn't our case.'

'That's why I didn't put it on the request.' He'd found a tenuous link between Hughes and an open case from six months ago. One Gunnerson wanted him to close.

'I told you it was thin,' she said. 'She's going to want more before she okays a day out to the seaside.'

'*Day out*. Have you been there? Someone described it as the "arse end of nowhere", and she was being generous.'

He made his way to the DCI's office, his mind whirring as he rehearsed arguments as to why he needed to visit Hughes. Gunnerson looked less stressed than he'd seen her in months. Her husband of thirty years had recently died of motor neurone disease.

'Russell, I wanted to thank you for coming to the funeral. I appreciated the support.'

'I liked Rex. You sure you're okay to come into work? The funeral was only Monday.'

'Best place for me.' She glanced at her screen. 'Your request to see this prisoner at Bradwell. They've come back and asked if we can send someone else.'

'What?'

'I'm sure you've not forgotten what happened the last time you visited.'

How could he? 'I thought they'd changed the entire management team to keep their contract.'

'They have, but GRM still runs it, and they have long memories. Can't Alice go?'

'She's tied up with something else. Anyway, you're not letting them dictate who you have investigating your cases?'

'No, I'm not, Russell. They asked me to look into it, and now I have.'

'Okay. Is there anything else?'

'Have you seen the vacancy for an inspector in the Child Protection team?'

'You trying to get rid of me?' He wanted promotion back up to DCI, not a sideways move, and definitely not into Child Protection.

'I meant for Alice. It could be a great opportunity for her. Unless you think she's not ready.'

She was more than ready, but losing an experienced sergeant would have a detrimental effect on his chances of moving on back up the ladder. 'I'll mention it to her.'

He returned to his office, wondering who in the GRM hierarchy had objected to his visit to one of their prisons. It couldn't be their owner, Reed-Mayhew? He doubted he even knew Chapman existed.

Sanchez sat at her desk.

'Alice, Yasmin mentioned a vacancy in Child Protection. You're not interested?'

'I was. I've got the application here.'

Bugger! 'Are you sure? I thought you said they couldn't pay you enough to do that job.'

'Well, now we're having one of our own, it changes your perspective.'

He'd forgotten she and her partner were adopting. 'Oh, right. Of course, I'll give you a good write-up.'

As he walked away, she laughed.

'What?'

'Your face. No, I'm not interested, thanks. Stevie Gillich mentioned it to me a few weeks ago when she put in for her transfer out of the unit.'

'Ha, ha. Funny. You can do the paperwork for last month's overtime figures for that.' He checked the time. He'd better go. 'I'm going to Bradwell. I'll see you in the morning.'

'Have fun.'

He gave her the finger and, collecting his coat, went to his car. As he'd suspected, the traffic out of town was a nightmare, but he listened to his latest audiobook. His daughter had introduced him to them, although he wasn't impressed by Abby's YA listening material and preferred the latest Jack Reacher. The dual carriageway ended, and his progress slowed. He'd got a lift from an ex-colleague last time he came, but after he'd trashed her force's investigation into a suspicious death, he doubted she'd even speak to him now. Another bridge he'd burnt.

As he got closer to the prison, the landscape changed as the hedges lining the road gave way to low fences and ditches framing prairie-like fields of uniform crops. What happened to the 'green and pleasant land'? The weather also took a turn for the worse as the spring sunshine disappeared behind threatening clouds. The bulk of the prison appeared on the horizon, an ugly squat block.

He parked in the half-empty car park and walked towards the main entrance with a sense of foreboding. He couldn't imagine how he'd feel if he arrived here for a stay.

The new corporate branding on the exterior extended to the interior. But GRM still ran it, despite carrying out illegal memory experiments that had led to the death of at least one inmate in here.

GRM's Reed-Mayhew had a habit of getting his own way with the great and the good, often using a combination of threats and bribes. Chapman's experience suggested he preferred using threats and doubtless gathered plenty of dirt on those in power.

'Inspector Chapman?' The prison officer inspecting his ID scrutinised him. 'You need to leave your phone.'

'It's in the car. Everything else from my pockets is here.' He pointed to the keys in the plastic tray.

With a scowl, the officer placed his ID and email confirming his visit in the tray and waved him to the body scanner. The management might have changed, but the prison guards were probably the same ones from the last time he'd come, and they'd almost lost their jobs because of him.

After making him wait ten minutes, another guard wearing a scowl came to collect him. They walked past a series of interview rooms and approached the main prison building.

'What's wrong with those?' Chapman pointed at the unoccupied rooms.

'They're all booked up. We've put you in one on the East Wing.' He paused at a barred gate and unlocked it before waving Chapman through.

The unmistakable sounds of a prison assaulted Chapman's ears. He hated these places and suppressed a shiver. A few figures milled about, prisoners by the look of them, beyond another barred gate ten paces away. The door clanged behind him. Chapman waited for the guard, but he'd remained the other side of the gate.

'What's going on?'

'One of my colleagues will take you through.' He waved Chapman on towards the second gate, enjoying his discomfort.

As Chapman got closer to it, he realised they'd left this gate unlocked. He rushed back to the first one, but the guard had gone. The sounds of the prisoners grew louder.

'Oi, what the hell are you doing?' A note of panic entered Chapman's voice.

He grabbed the gate and called again, conscious of the prisoners behind him.

'You all right, mate?' Two guards stood at the second gate and watched him through the bars. The one who spoke made a show of unlocking it. 'You gonna join us?' They sniggered.

Chapman, hot-faced, walked towards them as they swung the door open. He kept a tight rein on his temper as they escorted him through a labyrinth full of prisoners. Pig sounds accompanied him, letting him know the residents recognised what he was. They passed through another 'airlock' arrangement before they led him to an interview room. He entered and waited, letting his pulse slow, certain he hadn't needed to come here via the route they'd led him.

Following another wait, the door opened and two guards came in with a manacled prisoner. Several inches taller than Chapman, he had a shaved head and a nose bearing signs of much violence. He wore a vest and tracksuit bottoms, and although slim, corded muscles covered his tattooed arms.

'Give us a shout when you're done.'

The two guards left, and Chapman stared at Hughes. 'Take a seat.'

Hughes gave him a long stare before he sat. 'You're trying to fit me up. I had nothing to do with—'

'I'm here on behalf of Antonia Conti.'

Hughes studied him anew as Chapman sat opposite him. 'Why couldn't she come?'

'She's not welcome here. Nor am I, come to think of it, but they don't have a choice about letting me come.'

Hughes relaxed a bit at this but said nothing.

'You told her you could give her information on someone we're looking for.'

'You can fuck off. I'm not a snitch. She told me he'd killed one of her mates—'

'Alan was my friend as well.' This wasn't true, but he needed Hughes back onside. 'I'm not here officially, which is why I had to say I wanted to interview you about the other case.'

Hughes glared at him for a long time. 'Okay. But I'm only talking to her.'

'I told you, she's not welcome.'

'You'll have to get me out, then.'

'How will I do that? You're here on another case, nothing to do with me.'

'Not my problem.'

'How do I know the man you know about is the one we're looking for?'

'Tall, about my height, but much wider. Short black hair. Stupid beard and a scar here.' He pointed to his right cheek. 'He speaks like he's got a bad throat and his left knee's fucked.'

The knee was the result of his encounter with Antonia. 'I'll see about getting you out, but don't even think of messing me about.' He ignored Hughes's glare and summoned the guards.

As they led Hughes away, unshackled, they told Chapman to wait. Another unnecessary delay and two more guards came to collect him.

'Are we going the direct way this time?' he said.

'Don't know what you're talking about, mate.'

Chapman followed them. Once he got out of here, he'd never come back, no matter what.

At the nearest 'airlock,' the two guards repeated the disappearing trick. Chapman, expecting something like this, waited for their colleagues to show themselves. Five minutes later, footsteps approached.

Figures appeared, but they wore the wrong uniforms. Five or six evil-looking convicts gathered round the far gate. Chapman swallowed. One of them pushed at the gate, which swung open. Chapman looked behind him, but the guards had gone.

CHAPTER 6

'They've put me on gardening leave pending the end of my contract.' Rick Grainger's voice issued from the speakerphone on Antonia's desk as she studied Jean's email.

'You happy about that?'

Jean has been busy.

'I suspected they'd do something like that. Elfyn's a bit of a hothead and didn't like me telling him I'm leaving.'

'I'm sure. Will you take a holiday before starting here?' She'd have to sort out a desk for him. Even if he did most of his work off-site, he'd need somewhere to call his own here.

'Can I start straight away?'

'How soon?'

'Lunchtime?'

'What, today?' Eleanor appeared at the door, and Antonia beckoned her in.

'Yeah, I'm keen to get going.'

'We haven't sorted you out a desk yet.'

'No worries. I told you, I can work off-site. I just need to bring you up to speed.'

'Okay, what time?'

'Twelve?'

'Great, see you then.' She ended the call. 'Morning, Eleanor.'

'You might have shown a bit more enthusiasm, Antonia.'

'He caught me by surprise, that's all, *and* we haven't got room for him.'

'You're not having second thoughts?' Eleanor scrutinised her, making Antonia feel defenceless.

'Of course not.' They didn't have space for him, *and* she didn't feel ready to manage him. Would he compare her management style unfavourably to other editors he'd worked under? She'd had little experience as a reporter, let alone an editor. She told herself not to be silly; she managed the other staff without problems. Although none of them had Rick's depth of experience.

'Good. I'm looking forward to having him work for us. It's a real coup. How will you announce it?'

'I'm going to tell everyone at the staff meeting at ten. I've already told Miles.'

'I meant to our readers. We can leverage having someone like Rick on board to get more subscribers.'

'Of course.' Too focused on the stories in the pipeline, she'd done nothing about it.

'We also need to publish it before our competitors get wind of it.'

She'd better check to see if Grainger's old paper mentioned it in this morning's edition. She didn't have time to write the article, but she had an idea. 'I'll get Miles to write something. He's very enthusiastic about the prospect.'

'Good.' Eleanor hesitated, a note of concern in her demeanour. 'Jean's a bit subdued. Do you think she's worried about the change in status?'

'I've not noticed, but I haven't seen her much today. She's keen to start, and she's done a lot of research in her own time.' Antonia tapped her screen.

'You need to reassure her she can always return to her old job—'

'Tomasz Zabo has already accepted it.'

'I'm hoping it won't come to that. Just the knowledge she could go back to her old job should reassure her. But if she wants to, we'll have to deal with it.'

'Okay.' Antonia reminded herself Eleanor had lived three times as long as she had, and had a lot of experience to pass on, especially about managing *The Investigator*, having done it for longer than Antonia had been alive. 'I'm worried about managing Rick Grainger.' She explained her misgivings.

Eleanor laughed. 'I would imagine some absolute arses have managed him. Egotistical idiots with the ear of the paper's owner. Someone like you will be a breath of fresh air. I'm sure you'll be fine. Just make sure he knows you're the boss. I'll leave you to it and see you at the meeting.'

After briefing Miles, Antonia got ready for the staff meeting. Conscious they often became time-consuming habits, she rarely called them. Today she had news of two new staff and a change in status for a third. She zipped through the agenda, buoyed up by the positive response to her announcements, especially getting someone of Grainger's profile on board.

Once back in her office, Antonia focused on the insider dealing story she'd given to Jean. The details Jean had already uncovered excited her. As she went over them, her excitement grew. This could be a big story, maybe too big for Jean.

'Snap out of it. When did you become this worrier?'

'Sorry, Ms Conti?'

'Jean, I didn't hear you. Come in and sit.' She'd have to mention her growing propensity for worry at her next meeting with the mental resilience counsellor.

'I thought you were talking to me.' Concern leaked out of Jean as she settled into the chair.

Eleanor was right. Had she changed her mind? 'Are you okay, Jean?'

'Is the new man doing my job definitely starting Monday, Ms Conti?' She yawned.

'He is, but if you'd rather stay in your current job, we'll deal with it.'

'Oh no. I wanted to say I'm really enjoying being a reporter.' She yawned again. 'Sorry, I didn't get much sleep last night.'

'You've uncovered a lot of hidden tracks. I'm impressed.' Six months earlier, Jean had uncovered an attempt on Antonia's life by hacking a gangster's emails. 'How have you uncovered them?'

'I've not done anything illegal, Ms Conti.' Jean shook her head, making her jowls wobble. 'You explained we mustn't break the law.'

'Okay, that's great, Jean. So, how did you identify who was passing the information to JN?'

Jean gave a smile. 'Only one laboratory worked with all four manufacturers. So I investigated the finances of each of the employees and ex-employees.'

'How did you manage that without hacking their bank accounts?'

'I assumed they'd not put the money in their bank accounts, and they'd have to launder it. I checked if any has an overly extravagant lifestyle, but none seem to. The candidate I identified has two daughters. One runs an antique shop and the other a cake shop. Both made huge profits and because they're limited companies, they publish their accounts.'

'He's laundering his money through his daughters' businesses?'

'There's a correlation between when the hedge funds paid their informer via a series of offshore accounts and his daughters' businesses getting a cash injection.'

Antonia leant forward. 'And how did you get that information?'

Jean blinked. 'I've got access to a forum where whistle-blowers share data on suspicious financial transactions in tax havens.'

Antonia had a few questions but decided to keep them to herself, as she didn't intend to publish these details. 'Okay, can you produce a timeline with the relevant dates and amounts?'

'Are you planning to expose him?'

'We're not interested in him. Our targets are the hedge funds, but we can use the information to put pressure on him to give them up. We'll speak to him and tell him we plan to publish what we've got. I'm sure he'll decide to talk. Well done, Jean.'

The praise made her preen, but she still looked unhappy.

'Anything wrong?'

'Do you want *me* to speak to him?'

'I'll do it.' She doubted Jean would ever be ready, or happy, to interview strangers.

With the air of someone reprieved from an onerous chore, Jean returned to her desk. Antonia was still deciding where to put Grainger when the front doorbell rang. Miles beat her to the door, and, recognising the caller, introduced himself. Antonia greeted Grainger and gave him a quick tour, introducing him to his new colleagues, and led him to her office.

'I had an enthusiastic response when I announced your arrival. Everyone's looking forward to working with you.'

To her surprise, Grainger looked embarrassed and mumbled a response.

'You wanted to bring me up to speed?' she said.

'Yeah, here's what I'm working on.' He pulled out a laptop from his courier bag and opened it, angling the screen so Antonia could see it. 'As you know, there's a network of companies involved in producing the hardware for our nuclear deterrent. Most are multinationals, but the government is under pressure to put the business with British companies. The problem is, there aren't many UK companies which can do the work.'

'What's preventing them from gouging the government on price?'

'The audit commission spotted it and have got the government to agree they've got to meet a "competitiveness threshold", so if a foreign competitor is over ten per cent cheaper, they have to go with them.'

'What's the betting every company puts in a bid only nine per cent more expensive?'

'How very cynical.' He smiled. 'The policy means that because so few companies can take part, the people who knew of the decision bought shares in these companies.'

She wondered if Jean's story would intersect with this one. 'You mentioned ministers.'

'Yep. I'm reliably informed that at least seven cabinet members have bought shares in the companies expected to get the contracts.'

'And you've got evidence?'

'They've used proxies and networks of contacts, companies hidden in tax havens and secretive partnerships. But I've untangled some of them and can link three cabinet members to the shares. Including the Home Secretary.'

A surge of excitement energised Antonia. 'You mentioned the PM?'

'I'm still working on him, but I'm confident we'll get him. I'm hoping we'll turn one of the others.'

'What can you offer them? Once we expose the network, they'll all go down.'

'But if I keep their names out of it, until they go to the authorities, confess their sins, they'll get more lenient treatment.'

'You got someone in mind?'

'I'm confronting the Home Sec at lunch tomorrow. You fancy coming?'

'Try keeping me away.'

He hesitated. 'There's one downside.'

Antonia had thought of at least two.

'At the moment, they think they've got away with it. Once we approach them, they'll realise they haven't.'

'Or she could refuse to cooperate.'

'She could, but I doubt any of this lot has the moral fibre. I'm more concerned they may get nasty. Cornered rats and all that.'

'If you're happy to take them on, I am.' She knew all about cornered rats.

◆　◆　◆

'Are you going to report the arseholes?' DC Louisa Walker asked Chapman when he told her about his experiences with the guards at Bradwell.

'What for? Nothing happened, they were just playing games.' As he'd suspected, and hoped, the guards arrived to 'rescue' him before the prisoners did anything, but it had been a frightening moment.

'How did you get on with Hughes?'

'I've got to get him released. He wouldn't tell me anything until he's out of there.'

'If I had my way, he'd rot there.'

'You know him?'

Walker scowled. 'He and two of his oppos cornered me when I was in uniform. I don't know what would have happened if Darren hadn't turned up.' She jerked a thumb towards DC Darren Baxter on the other side of the room, perched on a chair that looked two sizes too small.

'Did you arrest him?'

'Sergeant refused to process him. Said nothing had actually happened. But it would have, evil bastard. Darren offered to break his legs, but I didn't want to get him into trouble. Wish I'd taken up his offer.'

Chapman would have helped Darren if he'd known about it, but they needed Hughes to talk. He'd speak to the officer who'd put him on remand. He returned to his office, closed the door, and made the call.

The detective inspector answered straight away. 'Hughes? No chance. He's threatened witnesses in a major fraud case. We're keeping him in custody until we've finished the case.'

'How long do you expect it to take?'

'Six weeks minimum, but you know what these fraud cases are like.'

Chapman did. It could take twice as long before he got Hughes out. The chances were he would then refuse to talk to Antonia. Chapman should ring her and tell her the bad news, but it could wait. He'd better finish the paperwork about his visit.

Sanchez arrived back and came to his door.

'You don't look happy, Alice. What's up?'

'The boss wants to see you in—'

'I spoke to Yasmin ten minutes ago. She didn't say.'

'The big boss. The *new* big boss.'

'I'd forgotten we were getting a new chief super. What's he or she like?'

'Um . . . You'll find out.'

'What?'

'I wouldn't keep him waiting.'

'Right, thanks.' He locked his computer and stood, stretching.

It wasn't like Sanchez to be mysterious. What did the chief superintendent want? He'd not done anything to justify a serious bollocking. He probably wanted to give him the usual bullshit pep talk. Funny, he'd heard no rumours, and Gunnerson had said nothing about the new guy.

After a brief wait, the secretary led him to the office, opened the door and left him on the threshold. Chapman halted in the opening, dumbfounded. Chapman's nemesis, Ian Harding, sat behind the desk wearing a chief superintendent's uniform and a smug smile.

'Russell, come in and close the door.'

Chapman, remembering all the times Harding had thwarted his investigations into powerful business figures, couldn't speak, but did as asked.

Harding gestured at the chair in front of his desk.

Chapman found his voice. 'What are you doing here?'

'Did nobody tell you? I just spoke to your sergeant. She seems very capable.'

'She is.'

'Don't look so worried, Russell. I don't expect to stay here too long.' Harding made his arrogant claim in a matter-of-fact tone.

Chapman sat, before his legs gave way. Yasmin had always warned him Harding would one day be able to do him *real* harm. What better than being his boss?

'I've asked you here on a confidential matter.'

'Why me?'

'We've had our differences, Russell, but you've always been a good officer, and this is a job for someone with your skill set.'

The last time their paths crossed, Harding had done his best to derail Chapman's investigation into Reed-Mayhew. 'Do you want to tell me what you want me to do?'

'Direct as ever, Russell.' He gave a smile that didn't touch his cold blue eyes. 'What I tell you must go no further, and you report to me, nobody else.'

'I understand.' *Fuck!* That was all he needed. Regular contact with this arsehole.

'I knew you would, Russell.'

This Mr Nice Guy act gave him the creeps. He waited for Harding to continue.

'You're aware DCI Gunnerson's husband died recently.'

'I went to the funeral.'

'Of course you did.' Harding seemed unsure how to continue. 'Well, this is very embarrassing.' He produced a large envelope from under his desk diary. 'Read this.'

Chapman reached for the envelope. Inside, a single sheet of pale blue paper. He pulled it out and studied the three lines of text. Laser printer, so no chance of tracing it. Faint smudges of fingerprint powder peppered the edges and the folds.

'Anything from the envelope?'

'No fingerprints, but they're checking it for saliva.'

Chapman doubted it would yield any results. Most stamps and envelopes now were self-adhesive. Not that he could remember the last time he'd sent a letter.

One of your officers has murdered her husband. I overheard him telling her he wanted her to do it and she agreed. Two days later, he was dead.

A well-wisher

Chapman hoped this person never wished him well. 'No signature, no date. Are we taking this seriously?'

'There's a date on the stamp. But we don't have a choice.'

'Are you planning to suspend her?' Chapman would be favourite to step up and do her job, but much as he wanted promotion, he didn't want it this way. He didn't envy whoever got the job of investigating Gunnerson. She was very popular.

'I'm not suspending her.'

'Sorry?'

'I want you to investigate and see if there's anything to this claim.'

'I don't think that's a good idea.'

'You're not here to critique my decisions.' The old testy and insecure Harding surfaced.

Chapman swallowed. He'd seen the bastard's vindictive streak. 'Sorry, sir, but she should have someone from outside investigate her. If not Professional Standards—'

'I'm quite aware of that, Inspector. But I don't want one of my officers' reputations besmirched unnecessarily. Especially in my first few days here.'

No, you don't want any banana skins to arrest your inexorable rise to the top. Chapman knew how these things played out. Even if she hadn't done it, the 'no-smoke-without-fire' mob would love it. And what about Yasmin? Being accused of killing Rex. 'But if I clear her, and it turns out she did it – they'll accuse us of covering it up.'

'Yes, they'll accuse *you*, Inspector. So, make sure you get it right. Report back to me in person when you've got something.'

'I'm assuming you don't want the DCI to know about this?'

The chief super looked at him like he was an idiot. 'Clearly, Inspector.'

'How do I explain my absences from my other investigations? She *is* my line manager.'

Harding opened a drawer and produced a file. 'I've already spoken to her and told her I want you to do a confidential efficiency study of the station. These are your findings. Reword them in your own language before you submit them. I've told her to give you plenty of leeway. There's a Battersea postmark on the envelope, which is close to the hospice where her husband ended his days. I want you to start there.'

Chapman raced through possible objections, but couldn't think of any more and took the folder. He left, his thoughts churning. How could he do this without Yasmin finding out? And if she had done it and it got out *he'd* done the dirty, his life wouldn't be worth living. *Bugger! Bugger!* Harding had really stitched him up.

CHAPTER 7

Although already mid-morning, Sabirah sat at her kitchen table and finished her drink. The three days she'd spent in the architect's office preparing the drawings of Mrs Curtis's house had left her exhausted. She'd forgotten how tiring having to use your brain could be, and the three weeks she'd previously spent in Mr Innis's office hadn't prepared her for the intensity. The fact she'd not done it for so many years made it even harder, but she hoped familiarity would make it easier.

She studied the digital models one of her new colleagues had prepared for her. The practice she'd worked for in Idlib had discussed getting this software before Rashid died and she and the children escaped. The memory of Rashid's arrest and murder visited her anew, but she pushed it away and focused on the screen. She closed the laptop and left the apartment to make her way down to the offices of *The Electric Investigator*. She found Antonia in her office and, unusually for her, wearing a smart dress.

Sabirah sat in the visitor's chair and placed her laptop on the desk. 'Do you want to go through the proposed changes for next door? We can decide what facilities you need.'

'Sure, I've got a couple of hours before I've got to go out. Why don't we go through the building? It will give me a better idea.'

After collecting the key to the house next door, they left the basement offices. After the gloom of the basement, the sunshine surprised Sabirah. The neighbouring house looked tired and almost dilapidated, although Mrs Curtis's original house also needed freshening up. She'd suggest doing the outsides together. Antonia led the way up the front steps and opened the faded black door.

A pile of junk mail and free newspapers behind the door made it stick. A musty smell combined with ancient cooking smells. A stained, cheap carpet covered the floor and another with a different garish pattern covered the stairs.

Sabirah, who'd only been in there once before but knew it from working on the plans, led the way. A door on her left led into the main room. She pushed it open on stiff hinges and stepped inside.

The contrast to the same room in Mrs Curtis's house couldn't have been starker. Someone had smashed the cast-iron fire basket, and pale-yellow paint covered the marble fireplace surround. A pile of broken furniture and rubbish lay in one corner.

'They've wrecked the place.' Antonia pointed at a stained and damaged ceiling rose.

'We can repair or replace it, no problem.' She hoped she was right.

Antonia didn't look convinced. 'How will we integrate the existing offices?'

'I'll show you.' Sabirah led the way to the basement stairs.

A damp, rotting odour greeted them when they opened the door. The light switch clicked with a dead sound. Sabirah retrieved her phone and clicked on the flashlight. Stone steps led down into the darkness. Cobwebs criss-crossed the ceiling and as she shone the light on the floor below, creatures scurried away. She looked at Antonia's smart dress and shoes.

'I can show you on the model.' Sabirah backed out and closed the door. 'Shall we check out your office upstairs?'

'Sure. I'm on the first floor?'

'Mrs Curtis said you should have the best room.'

'Oh, did she?' Antonia looked like a girl whose parents had praised her, and Sabirah reminded herself how young her friend was.

She led the way up the stairs and pushed open the first door, which led to the rear living space, preceded by a poky room with dilapidated kitchen units along the side wall.

A partition split the tall sash window. 'Once we remove this, you'll have a beautiful big room.' Sabirah pushed the sliding door in the partition open.

It led to a larger room with a broken-down sofa in it. An open doorway in the far partition led to a smaller area split into a bedroom and mouldy shower room.

'All of this will become one room, your office. I'm creating a meeting area here.' Sabirah indicated the bedroom. 'You can have your desk here and see outside.' She peered out of the window. 'We'll have two seating areas in the garden so you can work out there – or have lunch.'

Antonia joined her. Broken furniture, including at least two fridges and a cooker, lay on the remains of a lawn. 'My imagination isn't up to seeing it, but I'm sure you'll make it beautiful.'

A surge of affection made Sabirah blink. Before she could respond, her phone rang. Nadimah's school. With a tinge of panic, she excused herself and answered.

'Are you able to come to the school, Mrs Fadil?'

'Is Nadimah okay?' Her panic grew.

'She's not hurt, but she's been involved in a serious incident. You need to come in.'

What did they mean? She'd get a cab, but walking might be quicker. 'Give me fifteen minutes.' She ended the call. 'Antonia, can you—'

'Give me the keys and don't worry, I'll lock up. Let me know what's happened and if I can do anything.'

Sabirah thanked her and raced down the stairs. She half-ran to the school, arriving hot and out of breath ten minutes later. The look the receptionist gave her before taking her to the Head's office didn't ease her disquiet. Nadimah sat in the office, wearing a defiant expression Sabirah had become too familiar with. Sabirah gave her a tight smile before taking the offered seat.

The Head studied them over steepled fingers. Her long blonde hair pulled back into a severe ponytail stretched the pale skin on her forehead but left the lines around her eyes untouched. 'Ah, Mrs Fadil, so glad you recognised the urgency of the situation.'

'What's happened?' She ignored her daughter, wanting to know what had happened before responding to her.

'We caught your daughter fighting—'

'I was defending myself,' Nadimah said.

The Head gave her a withering look. 'If you can't control yourself, this discussion will continue without you.' Nadimah subsided, and the Head continued. 'We take a dim view of pupils fighting.'

'I understand. I haven't brought my children up to fight.' She could hear her servility and hated herself for it.

'I believe you send her for boxing lessons, which I can't condone, especially for girls.'

'It's not just boxing, she does advanced self-defence. Why shouldn't girls learn to defend themselves?'

The Head sidestepped Sabirah's question. 'She broke a boy's nose, and fortunately for her, he's declined to press charges, but if he decided to, we would back him a hundred per cent.'

Nadimah wanted to speak, but Sabirah signalled for her to wait. 'Have you investigated?'

'Of course. We spoke to the witnesses, and they confirm the boy's version of—'

'Of course, they're his friends—'

'Nadimah, please, let the Head finish.'

'Thank you, Mrs Fadil. As you can see, she has issues with authority.'

'My daughter is defending herself. What happened, Nadimah?'

'I told her.' She gestured at the Head. 'The boy and his friends cornered me in the corridor, laughing and giggling. Then when everyone except his friends had gone, he grabbed me.' She blushed and gestured at her breast. 'Then he put his hand up my skirt.'

The Head leant forward. 'That's not true, Nadimah.'

'Are you calling my daughter a liar?'

The Head backpedalled. 'The other witnesses disagree.'

'They weren't *witnesses*,' Nadimah said. 'They. Were. His. Friends.' She was almost in tears.

'Is that true?' Sabirah demanded.

Nadimah nodded.

'Well, of course, they all know each other. This isn't a big school.'

'Do you want me to call the police, Nadimah?'

'There's no need, Mrs Fadil.'

'My daughter will decide. Nadimah, do you want to go to the police?'

'I'm sure this is all a misunderstanding. When we have cultural differences, these things happen.'

'Are you saying an English girl would let the boy do those things without complaining?'

'No. What I meant . . .' The Head took a deep breath. 'Cultural differences make it easy to misread the situation.'

'Misread? You think my daughter misread the boys assault her?'

'No, I meant misunderstandings can exist on both sides.'

'What is there to misunderstand? These boys sexually assaulted my daughter. We might be from a foreign country, but even we have heard of the "Me Too" movement.'

'No, Mamma.'

'Sorry?' Sabirah studied her daughter.

'No, I don't want to go to the police.'

Sabirah didn't let her relief show. She knew how these things played out. 'Okay, we'll go home now.'

'Before you go, I have to decide what sanction to apply to your daughter.'

'You want to punish her?'

'She punched the boy, which she admits.'

Sabirah fought to keep her temper. 'What will you do to the boys?'

The Head looked surprised. 'What do you mean?'

'You heard my daughter. They assault her.'

'But it's her word against theirs.'

'So, this is what you teach your children? The girls have to put up with assault, and the boys don't get punished.'

'That's not fair.'

'What's not fair is you punishing my daughter but letting the boys off.'

'I haven't decided what to do to the boys. But I think your daughter should stay away until next Tuesday.'

'If you do nothing to the boys, she will stay off far longer. And I will explain to the press why I'm taking my daughter out of this school.' Sabirah stood. 'Come on, Nadimah.' She swept out of the room, overcome with a mixture of anger and fear. What if she couldn't get Nadimah into another school and how would it affect their refugee status?

◆ ◆ ◆

The call from Nadimah's school still on her mind, Antonia studied the paperwork Grainger placed in front of her.

'You can see the beneficial owners of those shares are the Home Secretary's children. One of them's still at uni and the other works as an intern at his uncle's brokerage business.' Grainger's eyes shone with excitement as he spoke. 'There's no way they could afford to buy so many shares.'

'What was the share price?'

'It opened at twenty-two quid this morning, up from seventeen last week. Once the government confirms they're going ahead with the Trident replacement, it will only go one way.'

Antonia did a quick calculation. Each of the children owned nine million pounds' worth of shares and had made two million in a week. She whistled. 'Not bad money for an intern and a student.'

'Not bad for a corrupt politician.'

'And you showed this to your last editor.'

'I didn't have all the documentation, but he knew I'd get the evidence.'

'And he told you to stop investigating?'

'You know how it works. The big boys get privileged access to ministers in return for not rocking the boat too much.'

Antonia always suspected this happened, but having it confirmed made her disappointed *and* furious. 'But you did the exposé of the Agricultural Secretary, which got him sacked.'

'Someone higher up wanted him out. Win-win for my old paper. They get to act like fearless crusaders and someone with a lot of power owes them a favour.'

'But this could be huge. Why would any news outlet pass it up?'

'Too risky. If the government falls, who's going to get in? Probably someone else from the party and they'll never trust you. If the current lot somehow survive, you end up in the wilderness. If it leads to a general election and the other lot get in, the opposition don't trust you anyway, so equally bad.'

'It's not something *we* have to worry about.' Antonia lifted the documents. 'And where did you get this from?'

He laughed. 'You know I can't tell you.'

'I need to know it's credible.'

He hesitated, then seemed to decide. 'The shares are owned through a series of offshore companies and held in the Cayman Islands. I've got contacts over there. Whoever set up the transactions didn't take as much care in covering their tracks as they should have. It looks like the son at the broker's office was involved.'

'I wouldn't like to be in his shoes when his mum finds out.'

'Spoilt, arrogant shit, from what I hear. I wouldn't cry for him.'

'I won't be. When did they get these shares? Even at seventeen pounds, they would have needed fourteen million to buy them. Has the Home Secretary got that sort of money?'

'The short answer is yes. Jilly Bucklin and her husband are worth a lot more than fourteen mill, but they got the shares at under twelve quid, so they'd have cost about ten mill. And they didn't buy them. Someone who owns a lot more shares has "lent" them. They get their ten mill back when they sell.'

'I wish someone would lend me ten million pounds' worth of shares.'

'If you can make them millions more, I'm sure plenty would do it. The person who lent her the shares is sitting on paper profits of two hundred mill, with much more to come.' Grainger checked the time. 'Should we get going?'

A dull, overcast afternoon provided a contrast to the morning's sunshine, and Antonia wished she'd worn something warmer as they made their way to the waiting cab. Jilly Bucklin went for lunch at a restaurant in South Kensington, fifteen minutes from her office in Westminster. Apart from the area having fewer cameras and security patrols, few political hacks frequented it. Any journalists seeing her and Grainger together would certainly show a special interest in them. The article Miles wrote yesterday had created a splash, and bigger outlets picked it up, speculating Grainger had taken a big story with him.

The taxi neared the restaurant, and a mixture of excitement and apprehension made Antonia tingle. They'd agreed on their approach and Grainger looked super-relaxed, but she sensed a tension. He rubbed his neck as the cab pulled into a parking bay.

They headed for the entrance, the hollow sensation in the pit of her stomach growing with each step. If Bucklin took the fall, they'd have a good story, but not the great story she hoped for. The restaurant looked busy and, despite the weather, they'd even filled the tables out on the pavement. They skirted the roped-off area and approached the main door. A young, black-jacketed waiter opened the door.

Before he could speak, Grainger flashed an ID card and said, 'We're with Ms Bucklin's party.'

Seeming impressed, the young man led them to the back of the restaurant and through an archway. Antonia would have to ask Grainger what his ID said. The aroma of rosemary and garlic reminded her she'd not eaten yet.

Bucklin and her entourage stood out. She sat at an isolated table in the far corner of the large room, opposite a junior minister Antonia recognised. Between her and the entrance sat four men who picked at their food whilst they scanned the room. The men spotted them as the waiter pointed out the Home Secretary. Two rose and intercepted them.

One stepped in front of them. Big and bulky, he had a florid drinker's face but sharp eyes. 'You and your floozy can turn around and go straight back out.'

'This "floozy" is my editor, and your boss will want to talk to us.'

The man studied Antonia, and she glared at him. 'Make an appointment.'

'Get stuffed.' Antonia went to step round him.

He grabbed at her arm. Expecting the move, she twisted away, leaving him grasping at thin air. Moving faster than she expected, his left hand shot out. She swayed away, cursing her shoes as she almost lost her balance. His strike missed, and he stumbled into an unoccupied table. Glasses fell and crockery clattered.

Someone cried out in alarm and a man swore. Antonia readied herself for another attack. His companion reached into his pocket and the other two security men stood.

'Ms Bucklin, do you have a comment to make about your children's ownership of millions of pounds of defence shares?' Grainger's voice grabbed everyone's attention.

'For God's sake, let them through.' Bucklin's plummy voice cut the tension. The glare she gave the florid drinker suggested he wouldn't enjoy their debrief.

Antonia brushed past him, and Grainger followed. The excited hubbub from the other diners died down. Antonia had attended press conferences where Bucklin spoke, but she'd never seen her close up. She looked about fifty and, like most women in public life, took care of her appearance, a jolly hockey-sticks type, Antonia guessed. She studied them with a glowering expression.

'I'll see you back at the office before the PM's briefing, Jilly.' Her companion got up, leaving a half-eaten steak.

'Yes, thank you.'

Antonia took his vacated seat and Grainger pulled one across from a nearby table.

'Don't make yourselves too comfortable—' She paused as a waiter arrived.

'Will your guests be ordering?'

'Don't be ridiculous. And you can take these.' She waved a hand at the two plates of half-eaten food.

Red-faced, he scurried away with the plates.

Once he'd left, she focused her attention on the two reporters. 'You have two minutes.'

Grainger checked nobody could overhear them. 'As I said, what do you have to say about your children's ownership of shares in Ajax Engineering PLC?'

'What my children spend their money on is none of my business, nor of yours.'

'When the children of a powerful public servant like you receive multi-million-pound share portfolios, it's all of our business.'

'Who told you this preposterous pack of lies?' Her throaty voice rose.

'I've got evidence.'

'Rubbish.' The uncertainty in her expression undermined the vehement denial, and Antonia picked up her sense of panic.

Grainger made sure the politician's bodyguards could see his hands and retrieved papers from his inside pocket before sliding them across to her.

She read it, a small tic below her left eye the only betrayal of her unease. 'Someone's had you for a mug, I think the phrase is. I hope you didn't pay for this forgery—'

'I intend to publish this.' Antonia indicated the papers.

'Whoever you work for won't publish. They wouldn't be stupid enough.' The corner of her eyelid fluttered.

'Feel free to sue me.' Antonia gathered herself to go.

A variety of emotions crossed Bucklin's face until resignation dawned in her eyes. 'What do you want?'

As they'd agreed, Grainger took over. 'Once we publish my article, you and your fellow conspirators—'

'We're not conspirators.'

'Call yourself what you like. That's what you are. And you'll all be swept from power in disgrace. You can salvage a modicum of respectability if you help us.'

'How? I don't know anything. I was—' She looked around. 'Can we discuss this somewhere private?'

'Sure, where?'

'Why don't you come to my home tonight—'

'Won't it look suspicious if we're seen rocking up to your place?'

'I meant my constituency home. There's a rear entrance. Nobody will see you.'

Antonia shook her head. 'That's what worries me. We need to choose somewhere else—'

'I'm not meeting you anywhere public. Do you think I'm stupid?'

'Do you think I am?'

Bucklin sighed. 'Look, I'm not some sort of gangster. I'm a respected MP and government minister.'

Antonia held her gaze.

'You're going to publish what you have anyway.' She appealed to Grainger. 'As you said, by speaking to you I can salvage something. I need you on my side.'

'Antonia?'

She could see Grainger really wanted the interview, as she did. 'Okay. I'll tell my staff where we've gone, so if anything does happen . . .'

Grainger gave her a smile and addressed Bucklin. 'Shall we say seven?' The minister lived in Kent, just over an hour away.

'Impossible. I've a cabinet meeting. Nine.'

Grainger checked with Antonia, and she nodded, happy to let Bucklin have this minor victory.

'Great, nine it is, then. Make sure the goons know to expect us.'

Antonia stood, and Grainger followed. The three remaining guards glowered at the two reporters.

As they passed, the one embarrassed by Antonia muttered, 'It's not over, you black bitch.'

She gave him a cold smile. The skin in the centre of her back itched as she imagined his and Bucklin's gaze following her. Part one over. She'd find out at nine if it had worked.

CHAPTER 8

'I'm going out, Alice, don't contact me unless it's urgent,' Chapman said.

'Oh, okay. What do I say if anyone wants you?'

'I'm doing a job for the chief super.'

'Sorry about not warning you yesterday. He told me not to.' She looked embarrassed.

'He enjoyed my reaction, but as the prick says, he shouldn't be here long.'

He intended to spend every moment off-site while Harding remained here. Why the hell had the bastard chosen to come to his station? Chapman realised he was being paranoid, but the guy was haunting him. The Friday afternoon traffic didn't improve his mood, but he'd call it a day once he'd finished at the hospice. He'd had a long week and looked forward to his days off with Abby. She'd so far reserved the worst of her teenage tantrums for her mother, so both parents looked forward to her coming to him.

A thin drizzle accompanied him when he arrived at the hospice. He'd expected something nineteenth century, like a converted stately home, but this looked like a modern care home – red brick, and tiles with lots of angled roofs and dormer windows. He acknowledged the similarities between the two institutions, although in a care home, the time between arrival and departure lasted longer.

After parking in a visitor's spot, he made his way to the reception. The institutional smell he associated with these sorts of places, a mixture of piss, disinfectant and boiled cabbage, was less noticeable than he expected. He'd considered his approach since Harding handed him the investigation twenty-four hours earlier. He needed to find the writer of the letter.

A smiling receptionist in a smart uniform greeted him. He introduced himself and asked to speak to the manager. The receptionist made a call and a woman in a grey suit came to meet him. About his own age, mid-forties, she wore her thick auburn hair long, and her blue eyes stood out against her pale freckled skin. Her name badge read Jean Adair. She held a glossy brochure in her hand.

'Inspector Chapman, how may I help you?'

'Can we speak in private?'

After arranging for refreshments, she led him to an office furnished in pale wood and pastel fabrics.

'I'm here to investigate an anonymous complaint about one of your—' What should he call them, clients? Patients? 'Residents.'

'We call them patients, Inspector.' She frowned. 'I hope the complaint wasn't about the care we provide.'

'I'm afraid I must keep that to myself for the moment, but if I discover anything critical of your hospice, I'll tell you.'

She seemed mollified. 'How can I help you?'

'Can you tell me which staff took care of Rex Gunnerson?'

'Oh, his wife's a policewoman, isn't she? Did she make the complaint?'

'I can assure you; it wasn't her. She'd have come to you with any complaints.'

'Yes. She struck me as a very straightforward person.' Adair's slight Scottish burr came out. She clicked on the mouse on her desk and, punching in a password, studied her screen. 'Both ladies are on duty. Do you want to interview them here?'

'Could I see the room Rex occupied? I appreciate someone new may have moved in . . .'

'No, it's empty. We'd normally have it occupied. We have a waiting list, but there's a problem with the en-suite and we're waiting for a new shower tray. Our staff do a thorough clean between patients, but we're waiting until we get the work completed. If you need to check for forensic evidence . . .'

'No, we're not looking for forensic evidence.'

'Oh, good. I'll get one of the girls who looked after Mr Gunnerson to take you up. You can speak to her then. Do you want me to tell her you're investigating Mr Gunnerson's stay?'

'I'll broach the subject. We'll also need to see the record of the drugs you administered to Mr Gunnerson.'

'Is there a suggestion we've made mistakes?'

'None, but it pays to be thorough.' The thought of requiring an exhumation order for Rex didn't bear thinking about.

'Good. I'll get hold of Ivana.' She summoned the carer, and they drank their tea and made awkward small talk while they waited.

Ivana arrived and Chapman accompanied the petite uniformed woman to the second floor. While Ivana unlocked the bedroom, the door next to it opened and a man carrying a pile of sheets and towels backed out before scurrying away. The bedroom looked much like the ones Chapman had visited in the care homes both his parents ended up in. The memory of his bewildered mother sobbing as he abandoned her following his father's death hit him like a punch.

'Are you okay, Mr Chapman?'

'Yeah, fine thanks.' He strode across to the window and stared out at a patch of lawn surrounded by a path bounded by flower beds as he gathered himself. Despite the weather, a woman pushed a man in a wheelchair round the path.

Once he'd recovered, he asked her about her work and her involvement with the patients. Not wanting to ask her if she'd sent the anonymous note straight out, he broached the subject of assisted suicide.

'Yes, I think maybe they allow for people suffering.'

'What would you do if you overheard a relative discussing ending the life of a patient with them?'

She focused on the stripped bed. 'I know is illegal, so I should report.'

After a few more questions, Chapman decided she'd almost certainly not sent the note and asked her to fetch her colleague. While he waited, he checked the drawers in the chest under the window, surprised to find it contained shirts and underwear. This must be Rex's stuff. A cough from the door made him jump.

'Hello, Inspector Chapman.' He offered his hand to the jolly-looking woman in the doorway. Older, with streaks of grey hair, she'd make two of her colleague.

He asked the same question about assisted dying and received an unequivocal reply.

'I think it's a disgrace it's not allowed, especially in places like this. People should have the choice to end their lives with dignity.' She held his gaze, challenging him to contradict her.

That told me. 'I noticed one of your patients down in the garden. Did Rex go down there?'

'He wasn't well enough to leave the room. He needed help breathing, and we put a ventilator in the room.'

'Who else might come in here when Rex had visitors?'

'Nobody apart from the care staff.'

'What about the guy I saw with the towels and sheets?'

'No, he wouldn't be here during visiting hours.'

Yasmin wouldn't have discussed something so sensitive with the door open. He went back to the window. 'Do these open?'

'Only a small amount. We have air conditioning and it's a long way up.'

Anyway, she would have been near the bed. She wouldn't stand here and shout it halfway across the room. 'Thanks, you've been very helpful.'

He left the room and waited for the carer to lock the door behind them. Neither of the women caring for Rex Gunnerson could have written the note. He'd leave for the weekend and start again on Monday.

A familiar voice approached from the lifts. Gunnerson. Panic paralysed him for a second and he cast around for an escape. The door to the linen store remained open. With a gesture to the carer to say nothing, he ducked through it.

Open wooden shelves, with piles of clean linen stacked on them, lined one wall of the small room. Chapman leant against the blank wall and waited, his heart racing. Voices carried from the back of the room, and he listened.

Pipes passed through the wall at the rear of the linen cupboard and, as he examined them, he noticed a small gap round them. If he moved nearer, he could hear the people speaking in the next room. Gunnerson spoke, her words clear, and the carer he'd just questioned replied.

The door opened and the man he'd seen earlier stood in the opening. Chapman had found his whistle-blower.

◆ ◆ ◆

Erika hadn't been impressed when Grainger told her he'd cancelled their visit to the new restaurant they'd finally managed to book. He hoped she'd have calmed down by the time he got back from interviewing Bucklin tonight. The satnav barked its instructions, and he focused on the road. The lane leading to the mews Antonia lived on looked too narrow to allow two-way traffic, but the parked cars pointed in both directions. He'd been surprised at the address. It was very handy for her office but houses round here didn't come cheap. Antonia had told him she inherited it from her predecessor, but then cut him off when he'd probed. A tall, slim figure waited in an opening on his left and he pulled over. He'd told her what he drove, and she intercepted him as he pulled up.

She got into the passenger seat, accompanied by a subtle scent, and examined the interior as she fastened her seatbelt. 'Very smart, Rick. I've not been in one of these before.'

'It's my wife's, but she doesn't drive much, so I end up with it.'

'I thought the doors lifted, like the car in *Back to The Future*?'

'Yeah, the back ones—' The satnav interrupted, announcing a change in direction. The journey time showed just over an hour.

Antonia looked over into the back. 'You got a dog?'

'Yeah, does it smell?' He should have cleaned it before setting off.

'No, I just noticed the blanket on the back seat.'

'Oh, right. He's a big softie, a cross between a chocolate Lab and ridgeback. Looks fierce, but more likely to lick you to death than bite you.'

During the journey, he grilled Antonia. He'd researched her background and knew she'd come over from South Sudan while still a child and endured the UK care system before Mrs Curtis adopted her. But the bare skeleton needed more flesh.

'Do you still have family in Malakal? I did a short stint there in 2016.'

She studied him with interest. 'Most people can't even find it on the map.'

'Advantages of working as a foreign correspondent.'

She stared into the distance. 'You'll know it better than I do. I was nine when I left.'

'Nine? I thought you were twelve when you . . .' How do you describe someone's escape from child slavery?

'I was.'

Bloody hell, those barbarians kept her in captivity for three years. He'd heard enough horror stories about them to know how hellish it must have been. He didn't know what to say, and an awkward silence filled the car. Then his reporter's instinct kicked in. 'You've not answered my question. Do you have family there?'

'Not any I know. They killed my mum and my siblings. Mum had a sister we used to visit, but I lost touch.'

The finality of her answer ended the conversation. How could you begin to imagine what she'd gone through? Discovering she was only twenty-four, and managing editor of such a prominent news outlet, had surprised him. He'd assumed Eleanor Curtis still kept a hand on the tiller, but she seemed happy to stay in the background. What Antonia must have suffered as a kid would certainly age you. He'd get a better handle on things when he'd worked there a while.

For the rest of the journey, Antonia turned the tables, asking him about his life and background. An unmistakable sadness gripped her when he described the happy, hectic childhood he'd shared with three brothers and two sisters in Derbyshire.

As they neared their destination, they fell silent. He checked on Antonia, who looked as tense as he felt. What if Bucklin had arranged a welcoming committee for them? Bucklin did need them on her side, but he didn't trust her. The fact Antonia had told Eleanor where they'd be going should ensure she didn't do anything stupid.

Bucklin lived in a village that looked like an advert for the English tourist board. Ornate street lamps illuminated a high street lined with tea rooms, antique shops and picturesque period houses. He cancelled the satnav. Bucklin had given detailed directions on how to get to the back entrance of her house. They drove past the huge ornate gates guarding the front entrance, glimpsing a magnificent manor house through trees.

'Why does someone who can afford a place like this need to take bribes?' Antonia voiced a question he'd often asked.

'They mix with others in a similar position and try to outdo each other. They don't see how perverse it is.'

'Maybe, but I see it as an illness which we should treat. It would make the world a much better place.'

The short stretch of street lamps ended, and the houses became less desirable. Despite Bucklin's reassurances, he couldn't suppress a sense of unease. Next to him, Antonia seemed unfazed. He put on his high beams, and they illuminated a bus stop followed by a telephone kiosk. Just beyond it, a gap in the hedge led to a narrow lane. The smooth surface led in a straight line between fields. Without warning, the road took a sharp turn. Water glinted beyond the roadway, and he braked and changed down. It straightened again and led through woods.

They crossed a cattle grid and passed through an open five-barred gate into an illuminated courtyard. Ivy-covered walls surrounded them on three sides. Two figures detached from the shadows, and one used a torch to direct them into a space next to a Land Rover and a mud-spattered pickup with enormous wheels. Their reception committee didn't exchange pleasantries but led them to a doorway.

It opened on to a gravel path surrounding the house they'd seen from the road. Floodlights illuminated it and Grainger recognised their guides, two of the goons from lunchtime. The bigger one kept giving Antonia sidelong glances she ignored. Their guides led them to the back door of the house, which opened before they reached it.

A man and woman waited inside and searched them, taking Grainger's phone off him.

The woman finished searching Antonia, letting her keep her notepad and pen. 'Where's your phone?'

'I haven't got one.'

The woman stared, as if the reply didn't compute. The two guards then led them through a gloomy, flagged corridor, the woman exuding stale cigarette fumes. A door at the end opened on to a parquet-floored hallway and another led them to a large room overlooking the back lawn. Four tall windows down to floor level overlooked a floodlit expanse of grass. *How much electricity did they waste?* Book-filled shelves lined the other three walls, and a desk sat in one corner, opposite a seating area clustered round a fireplace. Grainger exchanged a look with Antonia, who rolled her eyes.

When it became clear they'd have to wait, she wandered off to examine the books while he looked at the photos arranged on the desk. Bucklin with various celebrities and business leaders. He didn't spot any of the CEOs of the companies expected to get the nuclear contracts. Twenty minutes later, the door opened, and Bucklin came in with a small man of about sixty holding a blue folder. He wore a lived-in tweed jacket and mustard cords, and his white hair hung down to his shoulders.

'My husband, who's a lawyer and will act as my legal advisor.' She swept past them, and the couple occupied a sofa in the seating area.

Grainger gestured to Antonia, and she took one armchair facing it and he the other. They'd decided he'd take the lead. 'Thank you for agreeing to see us this evening, Minister. We'll both make notes while we question you. Your security detail have confiscated my recording device.'

'There's no need. My husband has documents.'

He opened the folder and waved a sheaf of papers in the air between Grainger and Antonia.

Antonia took them and skimmed the pages.

Grainger said, 'I'm sure these are very helpful, but what if they don't address the questions I'm going to ask you?'

'My wife has no intention of saying any more than is on those documents.' Her husband's plummy voice fitted his appearance.

'I can read them now and ask clarifying questions, or I can ask the questions I intended to, and we get out of your hair.'

Bucklin waved a dismissive hand. 'Let him ask whatever he wants. We can decide which to answer.'

'Thank you.' Grainger glanced at the list he and Antonia had compiled. 'Do any of your family own shares, or have a beneficial interest in, any of the other companies bidding for the Trident contracts?'

Bucklin cut her husband off. 'How should I know which companies my family own shares in?'

'Okay, we know about Ajax Engineering. That's enough to sink you. If you come forward as a whistle-blower, and other transactions come to light, it won't look too impressive.'

The couple exchanged a long look and held a whispered conversation, then the husband produced another sheet of paper. 'These are other shares the family benefits from.'

Grainger took it and glanced at it before passing it to Antonia. *Bloody hell!* The Ajax shares comprised just a fraction. 'Thank you. Can we now move on to the other co-conspirators—'

'I object to you using such a term to describe my wife.'

'What would you rather I called them? Co-accused?'

He glared at Grainger, but let his wife reply. 'We don't discuss it in cabinet, but I'm aware of seven other cabinet members who *may* benefit from a similar arrangement.'

93

Grainger held his pad, pen poised. Antonia held a similar pose, and they waited for Bucklin to speak.

'You realise you'll leave yourself open to legal challenge if you publish any of this without evidence.' Bucklin addressed Antonia.

'Let me worry about that. You worry about making sure you don't end up losing this lot under the Proceeds of Crime Act.' Antonia indicated the room.

Her husband's expression confirmed to Bucklin this wasn't an empty threat.

'Okay.' Bucklin took a deep breath and named seven cabinet colleagues, including the Prime Minister.

Grainger wrote them down. He already knew of three and suspected two others she'd not named. 'You've not included the Defence Secretary.'

'We rarely speak, so if she's involved . . .'

'Okay, let's concentrate on the ones you know about.' Suppressing his excitement, he questioned her about the colleagues she'd betrayed. As he worked his way through the questions, more papers appeared from the folder her husband clutched to him.

'Why don't you just give us everything in there, instead of making us draw it out of you?' Antonia said. 'Rick's got plenty more questions, but I'm sure you'd much rather we left.'

Another whispered conversation between the couple ensued. 'We give you this, but no more questions,' the husband said.

Antonia held his gaze. 'Carry on, Rick.'

'Okay, okay. This is everything we know.' He thrust the folder at Antonia.

She removed the documents and skimmed through them. She and Grainger had the same question list, but he wanted to check they'd got all the information he needed. Resisting the urge to take the pages off her, he waited until she'd looked at each one.

Antonia returned them to the folder. 'Just one piece of information missing. Who instigated this?'

Bucklin laughed. 'Who do you think? The PM, of course – nobody does anything without his say-so.'

Grainger could well believe it. He exchanged another look with Antonia, who nodded. He closed his notebook and stood. 'Thank you, Minister.' He nodded at Bucklin's husband, who scowled back, and let Antonia lead him to the door.

The two who'd escorted them in waited in the corridor and, returning his phone, led them back to their car. The pickup had gone, and only the Land Rover kept his car company. Eager to go, he reversed out of the parking space before Antonia had finished securing her seatbelt. As they left the courtyard, he let out a rebel yell.

'Ow, my ears.' Antonia covered her right ear, a big grin on her face.

'Bloody hell, we got a lot more than I expected.'

'Yup, well done, Rick.'

'You mentioning the Proceeds of Crime Act swung it. I forgot they could confiscate multiples of the money stolen.' He gestured at the document folder in her lap. 'What did they give us?'

'We've got enough. There's information on who got shares in which company on which date. I assume it was some sort of mutually assured destruction plan so anyone blowing the whistle would end up destroying—' She reached across and snatched the steering wheel. 'Look out!'

'What're you doing?' They'd almost reached the dangerous bend and Grainger slammed the brakes on, fighting to regain control of the steering wheel. Two wheels left the blacktop and bumped along on the grass, pulling them towards the river. Something disappeared under the car, then a tyre blew. They left the roadway. The headlights illuminated a fence. Behind it, water glinted. *Shit!*

CHAPTER 9

Chapman cleared away the remains of the pizza he'd shared with Abby as the credits scrolled up the screen, surprised at how much he'd enjoyed the film she'd chosen. He'd have liked to pour himself a large Scotch, but he'd promised Rhona not to drink anything stronger than beer in front of their daughter. At her age, he'd already experimented with spirits, and it had taken a few messy hangovers before he learned to temper his drinking.

He made the hot chocolate his daughter asked for and, deciding to have one himself, took them through to the living room. *Bloody hell, look at me. Friday night and I'm curled up with a hot chocolate.*

'Daaad.'

'Yes, darling.' *What now?*

'Can I stay here?'

'You are. You're not going back till Sunday.'

'No, I mean, can I move in?'

'Why?'

'I hate it at home—'

'I know you and your mum are having differences of opinion, but it will pass.'

'It's not just Mum, it's that new bloke of hers—'

'He's not touched you, has he?'

'No. Eeeugh. You lot think we're all being molested. I'd kick him in the balls if he tried anything. No, he's just such a lamebrain. He's always there—'

'Has he moved in?'

'Almost. He's there all the time, and now Mum's talking about us moving in with him.'

'And you don't want to?' Although he no longer contributed to the mortgage, Chapman was fighting for a share of the increase in equity since he and Rhona had bought the house sixteen years earlier. If she sold up to move in with this new guy, he might even afford to buy a flat.

'He lives on one of those "executive estates" with noddy houses where everyone washes the car on a Sunday. At least here I'm among real people.'

Rhona went on about how much this new guy earned developing software. 'I'm sure you'll have a lot more room there than here. Your room's tiny.'

'But you've made it really nice since last Christmas.'

So much for his fear his daughter wouldn't want to stay with him in the less-than-spacious flat he lived in. 'We've only got one bathroom. I bet you'll have your own if you move. And the Wi-Fi here's crap.'

Doubts crossed her features. 'I'm sure you could get a better router.'

'You'd have to think about school. You're starting your GCSEs soon, so changing school could cause problems.'

'Don't you want me here?'

'Of course I do, but you've got to consider the practicalities. Shall we discuss it with your mum on Sunday?'

'Okay.' She sipped her drink and checked her handset.

Glad of the reprieve, he drank his own hot chocolate. Much as he enjoyed spending time with Abby on his days off, he wasn't ready to have a stroppy teenager living here. He had no illusions that once she moved in, he'd become the parent putting up with her tantrums. And the flat *was* too small. The doorbell pulled him out of his reverie.

He exchanged a look with Abby. 'Probably a takeaway delivery pressed the wrong bell.' He strode into the hall and took the entryphone off the hook. 'Yep?'

'Russell, it's Yasmin.'

'Yasmin?' *Shit, what does she want?*

'I know it's late, but can I please talk to you?'

'Sure, yeah.' He pressed the buzzer.

Abby watched him from the door to the living room, a question in her body language.

'It's Yasmin.'

'Oh. Okay. Give her my love. I'll leave you to it.' She gave him a hug and wandered off to her room.

Abby had insisted on coming to the funeral and must have assumed his boss needed a shoulder to cry on. He put some shoes on and stepped out on to the landing. The numbers on the lift display counted to five and stopped. He swallowed as he waited for the doors to open. Yasmin, wearing a coat over the clothes she'd worn to work, nodded a greeting and left the lift.

He waited until she got closer. 'Yasmin, you okay?'

She shook her head. 'Can I come in?'

'Of course.' The odour of alcohol wafted off her as she passed him.

'You didn't drive?'

'Do you think I'm an idiot?' She closed her eyes and took a deep breath. 'You obviously do, but no, I got a cab.'

He guided her into the living room, and she stopped in the doorway. 'You've got visitors. Sorry, I'll go.'

'It's just Abby. She's gone to bed. Please, sit.' He took the dirty mugs to the kitchen. 'Can I get you a drink?'

'No, best I have no more. I've polished off most of a bottle of Malbec.'

'Do you mind if I have one?' He put three ice cubes in a glass, took them to the drinks cabinet and poured a generous measure from the bottle of Black Label he'd got for Christmas. He suspected he'd need it.

Gunnerson waited until he'd sat and taken a long sip. 'So, what were you doing there?'

'Was it the car?' He should have known Gunnerson would have noticed his presence at the hospice. She might spend most of her time behind a desk, but she was still an excellent detective.

'I wasn't a hundred per cent sure, but when I saw Ivana at the reception, she described you.'

'We received an anonymous letter.'

'Saying what?'

Chapman took another sip. 'They overheard you and Rex discussing ending his life. Harding told me to investigate.'

She absorbed this information for a few seconds. 'Why not Professional Standards?'

'He wanted to spare you – in case it wasn't true.'

She snorted. 'And you believed him?'

'An investigation always reflects on the top guy, even though he's new. He'll cover it up if he can.'

'You believe there's something to cover up?'

He swirled the ice around and focused on it. 'I don't know, Yasmin. No idea how *I'd* react in the same position, let alone guess how you behaved.'

'Thank you for your honesty. Which of the carers do you think it was?'

'What will you do if I tell you?'

'I'm just curious.' Gunnerson looked exhausted.

'Neither.'

'Who else could it be?'

'I hid in the linen cupboard when you arrived.' His face grew warm. 'A pipe in the back passes through the wall. I could hear you speaking to the carer.'

She smiled. 'It's always the little things that trip you up, isn't it?'

'Often.'

'What will you do?'

'It could be one of two people who look after the linen cupboard. I'll speak to them Monday morning and tell Harding what I've found. I suspect whichever sent the letter made a mistake.'

'Be careful, Russell.'

He looked at her quizzically.

'I told you to look out for Harding. He hasn't asked you to investigate because he thinks you're the best person for the job. He's got his own agenda.'

'Don't worry about me, Yasmin. I've got some shit on him.' The problem was, the footage he had of Harding at the site of a quadruple killing, *before* its official discovery, would also bring down Harding's wife, and he didn't want that.

She raised her eyebrows. 'Don't wrestle with a chimney sweep . . .'

'No, I don't plan to.' The fact he and Antonia had caused at least three of the deaths made it even more complicated, which was why he'd not used it before. What a mess.

◆ ◆ ◆

The fence loomed in the windscreen and beyond it the river. Antonia braced herself for the impact. The seatbelt bit into her shoulder and then, before they tore through the barrier, they came to a halt.

'Why the hell did you do that?' Grainger demanded, his voice high.

She unclipped her seatbelt, threw the door open and got out. She peered into the darkness but couldn't make out much.

Grainger's door opened, and he joined her. 'Are you going to answer me? You could have killed us.'

'I saw something on the road, that's what took out your tyre. I also saw someone there.'

She made her way over the damp grass towards the road twenty metres away, wary of any obstacles until her night vision improved. Behind her, Grainger's footsteps swished as he followed. Once on the tarmac, she speeded up. By the time they covered the ninety metres to where they'd left the road, she could make out the surrounding shapes. Across the dark ribbon of road lay a pale shadow.

'What's that?' Grainger came up behind her.

'It's a stinger. I just saw it in time.'

'Bloody hell.' Grainger picked up one end of the latticework frame and examined the spikes. 'They're solid.'

'What does that mean?'

Antonia scanned their surroundings. The stinger lay at the edge of the forested section, and she peered into the darker patches. She'd seen movement by the roadside before they left the road.

'It means whoever laid this trap didn't care what happened to us.' Grainger came alongside her. 'Shall we check the damage? Whoever put it there's gone.'

'Yeah, okay.' Antonia gave the wooded shadows a final examination.

'HEY!' Grainger let out a shout.

Antonia spun round. A figure crouched in the open doorway of Grainger's car, illuminated by the interior lights. 'The folder!'

Grainger ran, and she followed, racing along the blacktop. She overtook Grainger. The figure detached from the car and sprinted. From the way he moved, he held something in his hand. How had she been so stupid? Ahead, a dark outline waited on the road. A vehicle with huge tyres. The bloody pickup.

The man moved towards it, picking his way across the grass, running in a straight line rather than using the road. She must stop him before he reached the car. She put on a burst of speed, her lungs burning. The gap between her and her quarry closed. A hundred metres became seventy, then fifty. Would she catch him before he made it to the pickup?

He stumbled, almost overbalancing. A surge of adrenaline energised her. She would catch him. Then lights flickered and a powerful engine burst into life. She closed the gap. The man had made it on to the tarmac, and he speeded up. But not enough. She would catch him.

Gears crunched and reversing lights came on. The pickup whined as it came towards them. Antonia pumped her arms and pushed her legs. He reached the door but struggled to open it. Brake lights flared, and the door opened.

Her shoulder smashed into his back as he threw something on to the seat.

Ribs crunched, and the air left his body with a loud, 'Ooofff!'

Antonia clamped her arms round his torso and tucked her chin in. He bounced off the door pillar and they both fell on to the road. Antonia twisted, but not fast enough, and he landed on top of her, emptying her lungs. She rolled, pulling him with her. Rough tarmac ripped skin off her ankle as she did so. She ignored the pain and pushed her right hand into his face. Then, with all her strength, she slammed his head on to the road surface.

He stopped moving. Relieved, she rolled away from him and fought for breath. A door slammed. She pushed herself to her knees.

A shout of, 'LOOK OUT!'

Then her head exploded.

'Antonia, are you okay?'

She opened her eyes. Grainger's face loomed over her. She lay on her back. The side of her head and her right cheek hurt like hell. In the background, an engine idled. They hadn't gone. She couldn't have been out long. She attempted to rise.

'Don't get up. Your neck—'

'Let me go.' She pushed him away and sat. Her head swam and points of light flashed. Where was her attacker?

She looked towards the engine sound. The driver was struggling to push his unconscious colleague through the passenger door. She got to her knees, still groggy, as he managed it. He slammed the door, then ran round the front of the cab to the other side. He had the papers. By the time she scrambled to her feet, he'd made it to the driver's side and got in. Without thinking, she launched herself at the load bed of the pickup.

She landed as it moved away and slammed into a box bolted to the bed behind the cab, almost losing consciousness again. She gathered herself and tried to rise. The vehicle bucked and jerked, almost dislodging her. In the distance, Grainger shouted her name.

She flew across the load bed and slammed into the side. Her hand searched for a hold, but as she gripped the side, she flew across the floor, leaving half a fingernail behind, and slammed into the opposite side. She searched for something to hold on to but saw nothing except the bar above the cab. Way out of reach. As they drove over another bump, the lid of the box lifted and slammed down.

She crawled over and pushed it open. In it lay a large tarpaulin, tied in a bundle. They hit another bump, but she gripped the edge of the box and held on. She pulled the bundle out and lay it across her feet. When they hit the next bump, she held tight, flicked it up and kicked it over the side, letting out a fading scream as she did so. With any luck, he'd think she'd been thrown out.

The car continued to buck and rear. Unable to use her arms to protect her head, she pressed her shoulders against the side of the box, hoping she didn't jerk her head against metal. She held on, digging her fingers into the edge of the box. After a few more lurches, the ride smoothed. They must have returned to the road.

Antonia lifted her head above the side of the truck. Darkened fields flashed by as they moved in a straight line. Her ruse must have worked, but she'd better keep her head down. Lying on unyielding metal slats, she took an inventory of her injuries. Her head, where the driver hit her, hurt like hell. He must have kicked her. Her cheek had swollen, and her temple felt tender.

Her other injuries, from further blows to her head and various bangs to her limbs and body, weren't serious. She needed to come up with a plan to get those papers back and escape. Could she get them to crash and then recover the documents? But being exposed up here meant any smash would do her far more damage than the two in the cab. She'd have to wait until they stopped.

But they'd see her when they got out. Could she fit into the box? She lifted her head and peered inside. A musty, damp odour enveloped her. The rolled-up canvas sheet she'd discarded had been the only item in it. The vehicle stopped. Were they at the junction with the high street? She'd better get in the box before anyone saw her. She scrambled over the side. The box was shorter than she, and when she lowered the lid, it rested on her shoulder.

By scrunching herself over, she could just close it. A wave of claustrophobia triggered panic, and she pushed the lid up, leaving a gap. Lights flashed by as they passed street lamps, then the car slowed and turned left. They must be returning to the manor house by the front entrance. What had happened to Grainger? Did he have a spare so he could drive away? She recalled an acquaintance who drove the same model of car complaining it didn't have one. And if they'd burst two tyres, it wouldn't make any difference. At least he had a phone to get help.

The car braked for a minute, then it moved off. They must have gone through the gates. The crunch of gravel announced their arrival at the house. The car manoeuvred, then stopped and someone got out. Antonia scrunched herself down until the sliver of light disappeared. Focused on not panicking, she made herself listen.

Two doors slammed, then a voice, high. 'What happened to you?'

'The girl caught him.' The driver? It sounded like the man she'd confronted at lunch.

'Oh dear, how careless.' Bucklin didn't sound full of sympathy. 'But did you get it?'

'Yes, ma'am. And the notebooks.' Was he the one she'd hit? He still sounded groggy.

Blast! Antonia had hoped at least Grainger had somehow kept his notes. She must get their stuff back.

'Take them to the library. What have you done to the two meddlers?'

'The other two should have picked them up. The girl jumped in the back and flew out when I "accidentally" drove over a ditch.'

'Oh dear, hopefully she's not too undamaged. Did you check she was incapacitated?'

'Err, yes ma'am. She's going nowhere.'

Thank God he hadn't checked. Grainger must have called for help by now. The voices faded and, despite a rising sense of panic, she waited, counting to two hundred before lifting the lid. A quick scan told her she'd returned to the courtyard. Someone had taken the Land Rover. Still out collecting Grainger? Would they get him before he called for help?

And when they couldn't find her? *Blast!* She'd better get a move on. She clambered out of the box, ignoring her stiff and aching muscles. Her left hand cramped as she lowered the lid, which fell with a clang. She held her breath, but nobody reacted, so she crawled to the edge and dropped to the ground. She rushed to the doorway they'd gone through a few brief hours ago.

Nobody waited for her this time, and she replayed the route they'd taken when they arrived. Once the guards had searched them, they'd walked almost straight to the library. They'd gone left. Staying in the shadows, bent almost double, she did the same, running past darkened windows. She gave thanks they'd turned off the floodlights illuminating the lawn. Lights showed at an upper floor window and, four windows over, a faint glimmer at ground level. She reached it without incident and peered in.

A bulky figure stood at the desk, reading by the light of a lamp. The thug she'd embarrassed at lunchtime. He finished and, sliding the papers into the folder, left the room. She ran to the nearest window and tried the handle. Of course, it wasn't open, and a substantial lock mocked her optimism. By the time she checked the other three, she'd resigned herself to finding another way in.

She hadn't paid close attention to the other windows on her way. Now she retraced her steps, examining each frame. She'd heard no signs of the police. Had they overpowered Grainger before he called for help? If he'd been watching her when she leapt into the back of the pickup, he wouldn't have noticed anyone sneaking up behind him. Although he'd have smelled the tobacco wafting off the woman.

At the next window, she noticed pale slivers on the ground. A quick check confirmed they were cigarette butts. The window looked closed, but when she pushed against it, it sprung out a centimetre. She pulled at it, wincing as her broken nail caught on the wood. Then, with a jerk, it swung open. She opened it wide and reached up to grip the frame.

Stepping up on a nearby shrub, she eased her torso in, then the rest of her followed. She landed on a toilet seat before sliding to the floor. She uncoiled herself and, stepping to the door, listened. Conscious she didn't have long, she eased the door open and listened more. The dim lighting and flagged floor told her where she'd arrived. The door to the parquet-covered hall stood two paces away and without hesitating, she went through it and raced into the library, closing the door behind her with a click.

A pair of chairs flanked the door, and she wedged one under the door handle. The folder lay on the desk where the goon had left it. Next to it lay her notebook, but she couldn't find Grainger's. She checked the desk and the top drawers, but nothing. She'd have to leave it.

The door handle rattled. *Damn!* She slid her notebook in the folder and, gripping it, ran to the nearest window and tried the handle. It didn't move. She searched for a key but saw none. Raised voices came from behind the door. She rushed to the next one. No key there. She checked the shelves nearest, dislodging leather-bound tomes. The door shook. She checked the last two windows with the same result.

With a loud crack, the door gave way. Three figures stood in the opening. Bucklin, her husband, and in front of them, the goon who'd kicked her. With surprising speed, he crossed the floor, fists raised. With a tight hold of the papers, Antonia feinted, then met him head on with a front kick.

Despite his surprise, he twisted away, but the kick caught his thigh. Although hurt, he slid out of range. She mustn't underestimate him. Antonia attacked, but her kick missed, and his punch caught her a glancing blow. She stumbled as if hurt, and he came in for the kill. As he came closer, she kicked him in the same place, catching him square. He staggered, his leg useless. She spun, aiming a roundhouse at his head. If she missed, she would pay. But she didn't, and his jaw broke with a loud snap. As he slumped to the floor, Bucklin shouted for help.

'. . . and bring your gun!'

More adrenaline flooded Antonia's system. She looked for a way out. Two more chairs, sisters of those by the door, sat near the desk. She ran to the nearest, grabbing it, with the folder crushed in her grip. It wasn't ideal, but she wasn't letting it go. Bucklin and her husband cowered by the door. As she ran to the window, steps slapped on the parquet.

'Get the bitch!' Bucklin's husband shouted.

No time to smash the window. She changed her grip on the chair and charged.

'Stop or I shoot!'

Antonia tucked her head into the crook of the chair and launched herself.

CHAPTER 10

When he saw the body fly out of the back of the pickup, Grainger's pulse had spiked. Retrieving his phone from his pocket, he jabbed the emergency number and ran to where he thought Antonia had landed. His relief at the discovery of a bundle of canvas instead of a broken body had lasted until he realised his phone didn't work. The power came on and he could use the flashlight, but no signal and no saved numbers.

He'd bought a backup, so wasn't worried about losing data, but the ambush and now this made Grainger panic. They shouldn't have survived the stinger. It meant somebody would come to clear up. He ran to the stinger, and grabbing one end, dragged it back towards the house. Whoever came would expect it at the end of the wooded straight.

He reached a section of road that dipped, and he laid it in the dip, the thought they'd arrive any minute making him breathless. He ran back to his car and, wiping sweat out of his eyes, examined the tyres. He'd only burst one, thanks to Antonia. Where was she? *Don't worry about her, get out of here.* He sprung the boot and retrieved the scissor jack and extendible wrench he'd insisted on getting when he'd bought the spare wheel for Erika. He loosened the nuts and inserted the jack. The ground wasn't too soft and soon, the side of the car lifted.

Years of working in countries with dodgy roads meant he'd done this countless times, but never when terrified a group of assassins would be arriving any moment. A sound made him stop, and he listened. A car. Headlights flickered, coming from the house. *Shit!*

He finished loosening the nuts and took them off, throwing the wheel aside. He slid the spare out of its valise. It looked too narrow, but he had no choice. A bang, and then the lights jerked. They'd hit the stinger. Great. But how long to get here on foot? Two minutes, tops.

He held the wheel against the axle but couldn't get it on. Three panicky turns of the jack and it slid on. He inserted the nuts, tightening two at a time by hand. By the time he'd put all five in, sweat made him clammy and his breath caught. He lowered the jack and, after tightening two nuts, grabbed his tools and threw them in the boot. He checked the road. Was that a figure running? Without waiting to check, he closed the boot and ran to the driver's door. He glanced in the mirror and started the engine. He couldn't mistake the figure, now less than a hundred metres away.

The new wheel spun, too narrow to get a proper grip, then it caught, and the car moved forward. Careful not to put too much power on, he eased over the rough ground. The figure got closer, but then he reached the blacktop and hit the accelerator. The car shot forward. Behind him, the figure had reached his discarded wheel.

He reached the main road. Although tempted to get help straight away, he couldn't leave Antonia. He hoped she'd remained in the pickup, but where was it going? Back to the house? He couldn't just rock up and ask to see her. But he headed towards it, then screeched to a halt at the telephone kiosk. He checked behind him but reckoned he had at least three minutes.

He ran to the phone box, planning what to say to the police. *The Home Secretary is trying to kill me.* Maybe not. He pulled the door open, and the light came on to reveal neat rows of books, but no telephone.

'Shit!' He slammed the door and ran back to the car.

He remembered he'd not tightened all the wheel nuts and did so. They'd passed a pub. They'd have a phone. He drove through the village and as the main entrance to Bucklin's place came up, he tensed. The gates lay closed, but someone moved behind them. Despite wanting to get away, he paused. A tall, slender figure ran down the drive towards the gates. It came closer, and he recognised Antonia.

He jumped out of the car and ran towards the gates. 'Antonia!'

She reached the gates, breathing hard, and thrust a folder towards him. 'Whatever happens, keep these safe.'

Behind her, a man came round the side of the house. She reached up and pulled herself up, climbing the gate.

'Go!' she shouted.

He ran to the car, keeping a tight grip on the folder. Headlights approached along the high street, and a van raced past. Had the guys he'd evaded called for reinforcements? He wouldn't wait to find out. Grainger threw the folder in the footwell and started the engine. He checked Antonia's progress. She'd reached the top and now swung her body over it and fell, landing on her feet. Although she stumbled, she stayed upright and limped to him. She jumped in, and Grainger put his foot down.

The manufacturer claimed under three seconds to reach sixty for the car, and even with the spare wheel, it felt fast. Once they'd gone a few miles, he slowed and glanced across at Antonia. Blood smeared her arms and face.

'What happened?'

'I escaped through a window. Just got a few cuts. They're not deep.'

He activated the voice-controlled satnav. 'Nearest hospital with an accident—'

'No, just take me back to my place. I've got a first aid kit.'

'You really should get them seen—'

'Please, Rick. I don't want to argue.'

'Okay. What happened?'

She told him. 'I couldn't find your notebook, but we should have enough in this.' She gripped the folder.

How much blood had she lost? 'My notebook's in my jacket.' He told her what had happened to him, and they drove on in silence. As they entered the outskirts of London, he relaxed, but only a bit. As Home Secretary, Bucklin had enormous powers. She'd already tried to kill them. How much more would she use to stop them?

The buzzing broke through Chapman's dream. He'd stood in the dock, Gunnerson the judge, and his colleagues, plus several of his almost forgotten schoolteachers, made up the jury. Sanchez rose to deliver the verdict when the sound woke him. Without checking the caller, he answered.

'Chapman here, what's happened?' He fumbled for the light. The bedside clock read twelve. He must have just fallen asleep.

'Russell, I need your help.'

Antonia's voice banished sleep. 'Yeah, okay, where are you?'

'I'm at a petrol station, but can you meet me at the office?'

'Now?'

'We'll get there in half an hour.'

He'd have to do something with Abby. 'Yeah, I'll see you there.'

'Great, and, Russell, be careful. Remember our last nocturnal visit?'

How could he forget? He'd ended up shooting two men, something he still had nightmares about and hadn't paid for. Who'd she upset now? Someone powerful and ruthless, without a doubt. But Abby gave him an immediate problem to focus on. He couldn't leave her, but taking her was out of the question.

Who could he ask to come over? There weren't many who'd do it, and nobody who'd get there in time. He had one possibility. As he dressed, he remembered the whisky he'd drunk. He found one of the breathalyser kits he'd bought for a trip to France and used it. Under. Just.

He finished dressing and banged on Abby's door. 'Come on, Abby, we have to go out.'

After a long minute, she came to the door. 'What, Dad?'

'Get dressed. You're staying with Nadimah.'

'Why, what's happened?'

'Get dressed and I'll tell you on the way.'

He made a strong coffee, added cold water and drank it while he spoke to Nadimah's mum. Once he told her Antonia needed their help, Sabirah didn't ask questions.

'Okay, Dad, I'm ready.' Abby stood in the doorway, dressed and carrying her weekend bag.

They took the lift down and got in the car. As they pulled away, Abby fastened her seatbelt. 'I thought you weren't on call?'

'I'm helping Antonia. She's . . . She needs my help.'

'Is she . . . Are you an item?'

He laughed. 'No, she's just a friend.'

'Right, and you drop everything for *all* your friends?'

'Yeah. I've not got many.' He winked at her.

'I don't mind, you know. I think she's pretty cool. She'd make a kick-arse stepmother.'

113

'I'll let her know she's got your seal of approval.'

'It would make Mum jealous.'

It would make most of the blokes he knew jealous.

'You're going red, Dad.' She prodded him in the ribs.

'Right. When we get to Nadimah's, we need to make sure there's nobody dodgy waiting. I'm going to drive round the block, and you check the cars on your side and I'll do this side.'

'How will I know they're dodgy?'

'If someone is sitting in a car at this time of night, they're dodgy.'

'Even if they're snogging, and they don't want their parents to know they're an item? Or their daughter—'

'Just let me know, and I'll decide.' *Bloody kids these days.* He concentrated on driving.

They circled the block round Antonia's office twice but saw nothing untoward. 'Ring Nadimah and let her know you're here. Go straight in. Okay?'

'You're scaring me, Dad.'

'Sorry.' *Well done, you idiot.* He found a parking spot, and they left the car, Abby clutching her bag and looking about her. The front door of the house containing Sabirah's and Eleanor's flats opened before they reached it, and Nadimah stood there with her mother. 'Thank you, Sabirah, and Nadimah.'

'No problem. Welcome, Abby.'

'I'll pick you up in the morning.' He kissed his daughter and had fallen back to scanning the street before the front door closed.

He jogged down to the basement of the house and checked the main entrance of *The Electric Investigator* before returning to pavement level. As he walked past the nearest cars, peering in, head-lights swept the trees separating the house from the Regent's Canal. A top-of-the-range electric SUV pulled into a space. An emergency spare and mud-caked wheel-arches suggested it wasn't your usual Chelsea tractor.

Antonia got out of the passenger side and limped round the front of the car, carrying papers. A man he didn't recognise got out of the other side and locked the car. Younger than Chapman, he was a bruiser, stocky with greying cropped dark hair and big features. Chapman checked the shadows but as they got closer, he saw the blood.

'What the hell happened to you, Antonia?' Blood smeared the side of her head, which looked swollen, and more had soaked through the sleeves of her jacket.

'Thanks for coming, Russell. Meet Rick Grainger. He works with me.'

'Shall we go inside?' Chapman felt exposed.

He greeted Grainger while Antonia unlocked the front door and turned off the alarm. Close up, he thought he recognised him. In the light, he could see Antonia's injuries. Her face had swollen, but the blood came from a slight cut above the swelling.

'Take your jacket off and sit down in there.' He gestured to the staff kitchen.

'Where's your first aid kit, Antonia?' Grainger said.

She told him as she placed the papers on the kitchen work surface and removed her jacket. Dried blood discoloured the right forearm of her blouse, but the other didn't look too bad.

'Let's get these soaked in warm water.' Chapman led her to the sink and ran the tap. She winced as he ran the water over the bloody material. 'You should get these seen to properly.'

'That's what I told her.' Grainger came in holding the first aid kit. 'I'll set up a treatment station here.' He placed the bag on a table and unzipped it.

'I'm fine. You two stop fussing.'

'You'd better wash your hands before you touch those.' Chapman gestured at the array of sealed bandages and dressings.

Muttering to himself, Grainger went through to the toilets while Chapman led Antonia to the table. 'Let's get your sleeves rolled up.'

'Hadn't *you* better wash your hands?' She gave him a mischievous smile.

'Good point.' He washed them in the sink and dried them on a clean tea towel.

Grainger returned with his sleeves rolled up and forearms damp. Chapman ignored him and peeled back the left sleeve of Antonia's blouse. A thin red line showed where she'd cut herself. 'What happened?'

'I took the short way out of a room in Jilly Bucklin's house. Didn't have time to open the window.'

'Bloody hell, you were lucky.' He checked for any glass but couldn't find any. '*The* Jilly Bucklin, Home Sec?'

'Afraid so.'

'And the reason for your abrupt exit?' He took cotton pads and disinfectant from Grainger and cleaned the cut.

Antonia winced again and gestured at a bloodstained folder he'd not paid attention to. 'I wanted to recover that, and they didn't want me to have it. It contains evidence she and seven colleagues are on the take—'

'Antonia.' Grainger frowned at her.

'We can trust Russell.'

Grainger didn't seem convinced.

The declaration gave Chapman a warm glow. 'Why did you take it with you?' He placed the bloody, disinfectant-soaked cotton in a bag and took a bandage from Grainger.

'We didn't,' Grainger said. 'They gave it to us, but changed their minds, and recovered it after trying to kill us.'

Chapman's mind whirred. He'd guessed Antonia was in serious trouble, but not this serious. He bandaged her forearm and peeled the right sleeve back. This cut still oozed blood, but the warm water had done its job and freed the fabric. A piece of glass stuck out of the skin. 'You got tweezers in there?'

Grainger unwrapped a pair and passed them to him.

'I'm assuming they gave it to you for a reason.'

'Rick had enough to sink her *and* drag her kids into it. She was selling the others out to save herself.'

'Sounds par for the course.' Chapman removed the glass. Blood seeped out of the resulting crater. He closed the cut with butterfly stitches, cleaned it up and checked for more as Antonia and Grainger told him what had happened. The latter, reluctant to say too much. By the time he'd finished bandaging her arm, he knew enough. 'Okay, I get why you're avoiding hospitals, but what's your plan?'

'I'm going to copy everything in the folder and save it online. I plan to work on the story tonight and have it ready just in case they come looking for us. You up for that, Rick?'

'I'll let Erika know not to expect me.'

'I'll stay on site until you've finished,' Chapman said.

'No need. I just wanted you here until we got in. The reinforced doors and enhanced security we installed after Reed-Mayhew came for me last year should keep us safe.'

'What if they send someone official? I'll run interference.'

'You'll get into trouble. She's your boss.'

'I'm in the shit at work already, or I'm about to be. Anyway, Abby's sleeping upstairs, so I'd need to come back later.'

'You should have told me. I didn't expect you to bring her.' She took his hand in hers. 'Thank you, Russell.'

A shock travelled up his arm. 'Do you want to clean that yourself?' He pointed at the cut on her forehead.

'I'll do it in the loo, then change my top. I've got one in my office.'
She took cotton pads and disinfectant from the first aid kit and left.

After a brief silence, Grainger stood. 'I'll make a start scanning those in.' He took the folder and left Chapman to his thoughts.

Chapman bagged the rest of the litter and made a note of the first aid items they'd used. He'd leave it on Jean Sawyer's desk. The fact Bucklin sent her guards to kill – he had no doubt they intended to kill – them told him how desperate she was. He suspected the other seven would be as motivated, and any of them could do them serious harm.

Once she'd cleared the blood from her forehead, Antonia could see the cut wasn't serious. The swelling from where the goon had kicked her wouldn't clear up as fast. At least he'd need much longer to recover from his injury. The headache competed with the soreness from her cuts, especially her right arm. She'd better get the paperwork and make a start.

Grainger sat at the desk he'd used on his last visit, the phone clamped to his ear and sounding like he was having a difficult time. He gestured at a pile of printed documents. Scans of the papers from Bucklin and both his and Antonia's notepads. She mouthed, 'Thank you,' and left him to it. In her office, a mug of strong coffee steamed. She looked for Chapman to thank him and found him in the kitchen.

'I found some stuff in the fridge. Do you want toasted sandwiches?'

'That would be fantastic and thank you for the coffee.'

'I'll bring them through. Let me know if there's anything I can do to help. Some research?'

'I'll have a think and let you know when you bring the food.'

Grainger was still on his call. She returned to her desk and, using one of her large pads, sketched out a spider diagram for the story. She still hadn't finished when Grainger came in.

'Sorry about the delay. I had to explain to Erika about staying out all night and losing her wheel without giving too much away.'

'Everything all right now?'

'Once I do some more grovelling.' He studied the spider diagram. 'What's this?'

'It's how I plan out my stories.'

'Hmmm. But it's *my* story. We're clear?'

'I appreciate that, but I'm doing this to make sure *I* miss nothing.'

'I *don't* miss anything, and I've got my own system.'

'Great. You use it to structure your story. I'll work on individual sections, as you direct, and you can stitch them together.'

'Oh, right?'

'And once you've finished the story, you can bring it to your editor, and she'll edit it.'

'Look, I don't want you chopping—'

'I'm the editor. It's your story, but my paper. We'll work together.' She held his gaze.

Chapman backed into the room with a small stack of plates and a platter of toasted sandwiches. 'Cheese and mushroom, cheese and ham and plain cheese.' He pointed at three piles.

The smell made her stomach rumble, and taking a plate, she helped herself. 'Let me know which bits you want me to work on, Rick, and I'll make a start. Russell's offered to do some of the research, so it should speed things up.'

'Yeah, sure.' Grainger took a small pile and left.

Chapman removed the remaining food. 'Everything okay?'

'Yeah, just setting boundaries.'

'Good for you.' He left, closing the door behind him.

She sat for a few moments, drained by the experience. Had she overstepped the mark and stood on Grainger's toes, or had he overreacted? She wasn't sure, but didn't have the time or energy to deal with it now. She'd speak to Eleanor in the morning. But she wouldn't always be there to hold Antonia's hand. She forgot about it and concentrated on finishing her spider diagram.

She'd just completed it and was contemplating another coffee to stave off growing fatigue when Grainger came in with a tablet. 'You got a minute, Antonia?' He placed the device on her desk so she could see it and stood at the corner. 'I'm focusing on the PM. He's in charge and, according to Bucklin, he's the instigator. I already had him on my radar, but the info she gave us puts flesh on it.' He spent twenty minutes outlining the information he'd uncovered.

Antonia had seen some of it already, and the information Bucklin had given them. The way he'd used the two sources to draw conclusions, most of which he then found evidence for, impressed her. Her excitement pushed tiredness and pain away.

'And we're going for Bucklin?'

'Oh, yes. Any agreement we had with her is out the window. She's number two on my list. I've already spoken to my contact in Cayman and given him the company names and numbers of shares involved. He already had the names, but the extra evidence makes his search easier.'

'Okay, who do you want me to look at?'

'Having read your article on his attempts to interfere in your stories, I know how much you like the Culture Secretary. I'm pretty sure he's got shares through a holding company his wife's family own. Bucklin gave us details of the shares. Can you chase them up?' He gave her two more names, and leaving the tablet, returned to his desk.

Antonia took her mug through to the kitchen. In the main office, Chapman sat at a desk opposite Grainger, tapping on the keyboard. He looked up. 'Rick asked me to do a bit of background for him.'

'Great. I'm getting a coffee. You two want one?'

They both accepted, and grateful they seemed to get on, she made a large pot. The next four hours passed in a blur. The worry Bucklin would send someone to block them kept her at an exhausting level of concentration and she jumped every time someone came to her door with either more refreshments or work. She planned to spend the rest of the weekend sleeping.

She backed all her work on to her laptop and a memory stick and told Grainger to do the same. At five, Grainger came through with his final article. Antonia uploaded it on to her devices and read it. He sat in her visitor's chair, looking as exhausted as she. The front door buzzed, and they both froze.

'Upload it on to the cloud,' Grainger said.

Having covered a story where a contractor working for the National Security Agency had accessed several cloud providers' servers, Antonia didn't want to risk it, but knew she had no choice. Voices came from the main office as she clicked on the link. Nothing happened. 'Damn! We've lost Wi-Fi.'

'You got wireless?' Grainger's voice rose.

'It's down.'

The door burst open. She slid the memory stick off the desk as she rose, but it slipped through her tired fingers and fell to the floor.

A stocky woman in a dark suit stood in the doorway. 'Ms Conti, we have a warrant for your arrest—'

'On what grounds?'

'We've also got a warrant for Richard Grainger. Is that you, sir?'

'And what have I done?' Grainger scowled at her.

'We've also got warrants to search these premises, both your homes, and any vehicles you own.'

She placed the warrants on the desk. Antonia read the grounds. *Failure to inform the authorities of information pertinent to national security.* Both she and Grainger had written blistering articles criticising the legislation on its passage through the commons, but despite a public outcry and friction in the Lords, it had passed.

It meant they could keep her and Grainger locked up and isolated for sixty days.

CHAPTER 11

After spending the rest of the morning calling in favours and ringing contacts, however tenuous, Chapman had almost given up trying to locate Antonia and Grainger. Nobody knew where they'd
gone, and his friend from Special Branch gave him the worst news.

'They can hold them incommunicado almost indefinitely.'

'Is that legal?'

'I'm afraid it is. They need a judge to sign it off, but if you get
one who's swallowed the "it's all for the common good" bullshit,
they'll keep doing it. You need to make enough noise until the
Home Sec takes notice.'

Chapman's gloom deepened. 'She signed the paperwork.'

'Oh, shit. Sorry, Russell, if that's the case, your friends are
fucked.'

He ended the call and sat for a long moment. This sort of thing
didn't happen in civilised countries. *How the hell did we get here?*

He yawned and checked the time: gone eleven. He just wanted
to sleep but didn't expect Sabirah to look after Abby all day. After
sending his daughter a text, he left the flat. The reply arrived while
he drove, and he waited until he'd parked outside Sabirah's flat to
check it.

Can I go skating with Nad?

If he'd waited at home for a reply, he could have gone back to bed now. But he couldn't expect Sabirah to pay for his daughter.

Abby and Nadimah came to the door, followed by Sabirah.

'Can I, Dad?'

'If Sabirah doesn't mind.'

'It would be a pleasure.' Sabirah looked far more chilled than he'd ever seen her.

'Please let me pay, and why don't you take them for a pizza afterwards?'

'There's no need.'

'I insist.' He thrust a roll of twenties at Sabirah. She barely made enough to pay for her family.

'Thank you.' She slipped the money into her pocket.

'Someone broke in downstairs, Dad. We didn't hear a thing.'

'Mrs Curtis is very upset,' Sabirah said. 'She's down there now.'

He agreed to pick Abby up later and went down the steps to ring the doorbell. Jean, Antonia's PA, let him in. They must have got all hands on deck. The computers in the main office sat like eviscerated animals, their insides exposed and wires spilling out like guts. The old lady slumped in her wheelchair and studied Chapman.

'As you can see, Inspector, we've had visitors.' Eleanor Curtis looked near to tears.

'I was here when they came.'

'What happened?'

'Antonia and—'

'Hang on. Geoff, can you come through?'

Geoff Stokes, *The Electric Investigator*'s solicitor, came out of Antonia's office. 'Inspector Chapman, good to see you.'

'Mr Stokes.' Chapman took his hand. Apart from knowing him through Antonia, he'd crossed swords with the lawyer in a few interview rooms. With his expensive suit and a touch of grey at his temples, Stokes looked like the corporate lawyer from central casting, but Chapman had a lot of respect for his intellect *and* integrity.

'Russell was here when the thugs arrived.'

She must be rattled. He couldn't recall the last time the old lady had used his first name.

'Shall we use Antonia's office? I can make notes.' Stokes gestured at the open door.

'Have you checked the office for bugs?' Chapman had saved the paper from legal action after someone planted a bug in Antonia's office.

'Jean's swept the place.' Eleanor waved a hand round the room. 'And she's trying to get the network back running.'

Chapman followed the other two. Antonia's computer had received the same treatment as the others, and both her laptop and tablet weren't in their usual places. Once they'd sat down, Stokes turned on his voice recorder.

'Antonia rang me just after midnight and asked me to meet her here.' Chapman then told them what he'd done and what Antonia and Grainger told him.

'Antonia needs medical treatment,' Eleanor said.

'We don't know if she's received any,' Stokes said.

'Even if she has, they can't use anything she says if she's suffering from concussion.'

'Antonia has always taken my advice – to say nothing until I get there.'

'But in this case,' Chapman said, 'she won't get legal representation.' He still couldn't believe it.

'Then she will say nothing. What happened when they arrived with their paperwork?' Stokes tapped the copy of the warrants they'd left behind.

'Grainger had finished his article and took it through to Antonia. I was on my own in the outer office, so I answered the door. I showed my warrant card and told them I'd come to investigate a suspected break-in—'

'If they check, Inspector, you could get in real trouble.'

'I hope you'll represent me if it happens.'

'If I'm allowed. Why did you take such a risk?'

Chapman produced the memory stick he'd taken off Grainger's desk. 'I didn't want them to find this.'

'What have you got there?'

'I presume it's the story they worked on?' Eleanor held out her hand, and he passed it to her.

'I made copies in case . . . I lost it. It's the final version Rick saved just before we got raided. Rick also scanned in the documents he had and they're on there.'

'Can I check it, Eleanor?' Stokes took it and plugged it into a compact laptop he took out of his briefcase.

'I suggest you publish it straight away,' Chapman said. 'Once it's in the public domain, they won't have any reason to hold Antonia.'

'You're assuming they've arrested her to prevent this from coming out?' Stokes tapped his laptop.

'I have absolutely no doubt that's why they've grabbed them. They tried killing them first.'

'I suspect you're correct, but I can't let Eleanor publish anything which might endanger her licence, and maybe even the continued existence of her—'

'Compared to Antonia's freedom, I don't think it matters.'

'I'm sure Antonia wouldn't agree. And it's my job to protect Eleanor's baby.'

'So, *we* do nothing. I'll put it out there myself.'

'And achieve what? They'll dismiss you as a crank with a grievance, especially with you targeting the Home Secretary.'

Chapman caught himself before snapping a reply. 'What do you suggest?'

'I'll read it and take a view on which parts, if any, you can publish. Then, if you can' – Stokes gestured at Antonia's cannibalised desktop – 'I recommend you publish it.'

Chapman realised it made sense. 'Okay. How long?'

'However long it takes, Inspector. I suggest you take a rest. You look shattered.' He tapped his keys and focused on the screen.

Eleanor reversed away from the desk and wheeled herself out of the room. Chapman followed, his body heavy. Eleanor offered him a coffee.

'I doubt there's any left. We hammered it last night, and I'm jittery already.'

'Do you want to lie down, Russell? There's a spare room made up in my flat upstairs. You'll need to watch out for Max. He's getting cantankerous in his old age.'

Who said pets get to resemble their owners? 'Thank you for the offer, Eleanor, but the sofa in there is plenty comfortable and I could sleep on a clothes line.'

'As you wish. I'll tell people to keep out.'

'Thanks. Can you wake me if anything happens?' He jerked his head at Antonia's door.

Despite his assertion, he didn't sleep for ages. The thought of Antonia in the hands of kidnappers – he could think of no better word – and the fact that he'd let them take her haunted him. He'd checked the ID of this morning's visitors, but the people who'd tried to kill Antonia last night would have had genuine IDs too. At least he'd remembered their names and checked on them through his contacts after they'd left with Antonia and Grainger. If they were ringers, someone had found very close lookalikes.

'Mr Chapman?'

Someone shook him and he lashed out.

'Good thing I moved.' Jean Sawyer peered down at him through her milk-bottle-bottom lenses.

'Sorry, Jean.' His mouth tasted full of stale cotton wool. 'What's the time?'

'Three minutes past two.'

Couldn't be. He'd only just fallen asleep. 'Thanks, I'll get a wash.'

'Antonia keeps a new toothbrush under the sink. I'll replace it for her when I get the first aid supplies. Were they for her?'

'I'm afraid so.'

'I know she's tough, but she needs to take care of herself.'

'That's what I tell her every time.' He swung his legs off the sofa.

'I'll make you a coffee.'

'Thanks, Jean.'

A wash and brush of his teeth made him feel more human. He found Eleanor, Sawyer and Stokes in Antonia's office. Someone had shoehorned another chair into the space and a coffee waited for him.

Stokes waited until he'd lowered himself into the chair. 'I've gone through the article and supporting documentation. It would have been a devastating demolition of the government.'

'Would have been?'

'I'm afraid so. Based on the supporting evidence I found, we can't substantiate the bulk of the accusations.'

Chapman reacted like someone had punched him. 'How much can we publish?'

'We, Inspector? I wasn't aware you'd joined the staff.'

'No.' Chapman hesitated. 'I helped with some of the research and feel invested.'

'Hmmm.' Stokes didn't seem convinced. 'I've asked Eleanor to rewrite it. My prose would, I suspect, not be to your readers' liking.' He passed Chapman his laptop.

Chapman read the article in silence. It read like a thriller, and Bucklin wouldn't survive, but all too soon, he reached the end. 'Where's the rest?'

'We can't substantiate it.' Eleanor sounded as upset as he. 'Once we do, we'll have a brilliant follow-up.'

'But by then, the others will have covered their tracks. Rick thought he could get the evidence he needed for most of it by Monday, Wednesday at the latest. It gives us time to prepare a defence.'

'Mr Grainger isn't here, Inspector,' Stokes said. 'And on a story like this, I've strongly advised Eleanor to gather the evidence *before* she publishes, however certain you are of getting it.'

'We can always get the others later,' Eleanor said.

Chapman wasn't so sure. Antonia would have hated having to do this, and from what he'd gleaned, so would Grainger.

'I can see you're as upset as me about this, Russell, but our priority is getting Antonia and Mr Grainger out.'

'There's no guarantee this will succeed.'

'No. No, you're right. But I suspect her colleagues will turn on Bucklin. They'll hang her out to dry in the hope they escape scrutiny.'

'But they know we've got all this stuff. Look at what they took.' He indicated Antonia's desecrated computer.

'Bucklin knows. I suspect she has no desire for her colleagues to find out she betrayed them – however temporary she intended the betrayal to be.'

'I concur with Eleanor's assessment, Inspector. She's a very shrewd woman and an avid student of human nature.'

They outnumbered him, not that he had a vote. '*Can* you publish it?' He pointed at the gutted computer. 'And I think they took down your broadband.'

'And the backup,' Eleanor said. 'But Jean has patched us up to the website—'

'It's still up?' Chapman remembered a previous Home Sec taking down their site.

'Oh yes. After the last incident, I made sure we use backup servers out of our government's clutches.'

'I didn't hear that, Eleanor,' Stokes said. 'It's a condition of your licence that you don't.'

'Poppycock. Anyway, it's ready to go.' Eleanor looked at Chapman for his assent.

It wasn't his decision, but he nodded anyway, and Sawyer pressed Enter with a flourish.

Everyone seemed to exhale.

'I'd normally break out the bubbly on a story like this, but we'll keep it on ice until Antonia and Rick get out.'

Chapman sipped his coffee. There was no guarantee this would work. If Bucklin took the reporters who'd brought her down with her, he might never see Antonia again.

◆　◆　◆

The boredom preyed on Antonia. How long had she been here? It felt like days, but she suspected it wasn't. She'd even welcome being questioned again, just for some stimulation. At least it offered a change of scenery. She replayed her interviews, trying to guess from the questions they asked how much they knew and what they wanted. Despite wanting to tell them what she thought of them, she'd said nothing during her three interrogations.

She hoped Chapman had done something. Why did they let him go? If only she'd been able to give him her memory stick. The recollection of the moment one of the search team found it under her desk still sickened her. They'd turned over every part of the office and seized everything they'd got on the story. Losing all the work upset Antonia more than being cooped up. She lay on the bed, her feet overhanging the end, and stared at the ceiling, thinking how close it was. In fact, apart from the length, which had room for a bed and washbasin, she could touch the opposite surface on all sides. The sense of the claustrophobia she sometimes suffered bubbled under. Had they chosen this cell on purpose?

Think of something else.

Her headache and the pain from her cuts became pervasive. Her right forearm, in particular. Was it infected? Even though she hated taking drugs, she'd welcome painkillers now. She'd told the medic who'd examined her she needed nothing. Not only did she not trust them, but she had no intention of showing any weakness.

She'd not seen Grainger since they left the office. They'd separated them straight away and transported them in different vehicles. How would he feel? It was his story, and he'd spent months on it. She knew the disappointment. But they would get them, every one, especially Bucklin. She'd gone over the evidence in her head and memorised most of it. Grainger must have his own notes, but they'd have seized any at his house. Surely he'd have hidden them.

The thought of strangers searching her little house made her nauseous. *Stop torturing yourself, Antonia.* She dealt with stress using exercise, but not only didn't she have room, but any sudden movement exacerbated her headache.

How long would they keep her here? How long could she stand it? *Don't dwell on it, girl.* She went over the exercises her psychologist and mental resilience councillor had given her. She closed her eyes and took deep breaths. Her heavy body sank into the thin mattress, and she imagined herself falling all the way to the centre of the earth.

Footsteps echoed in the distance, and she focused on them, imagining she could see their owner. She'd heard the distinct pattern before. They came closer and halted outside her door. Keys didn't jangle, but with a loud click the door opened.

'Get up.'

The guard she'd visualised. The one who'd collected her for her first interrogation. She unfurled her legs and sat up. 'Get out so I can stand.'

He waited just long enough to save face before stepping back to stand in the doorway.

Antonia rose in a fluid motion and moved as if to headbutt him. It hurt like hell, but it was worth it to see his fear as he stumbled back. She smiled, and he returned a hate-filled glare that should have felled her. She'd make sure never to turn her back on *him*.

'Come on, you know the way.' He reached for her arm but changed his mind on seeing her expression.

As usual, two more waited outside, bigger than him and less insecure. Antonia fell into step between them and strode towards the interview rooms. She walked past four other doors like those on her cell. Did they have Grainger behind one of those?

They arrived at the interview room and a distinctive scent triggered a memory. Sure enough, instead of her usual interrogators, an old adversary, Millie Forman, waited for her. Last time they'd met, two thugs had flanked Forman. Chapman had killed one and Antonia the other. This time, the senior civil servant sat alone. She'd worked at the Ministry of Patriotism the last time they crossed swords. Why was she here now?

'Please sit, Ms Conti.' She dismissed the guards with a wave. 'Do you want some water?' She poured from an insulated flask into two glasses and drank from one.

Antonia drained the other. The interview room, like the rest of the building, felt too hot. Antonia guessed they could also make it too cold. She placed the empty glass down and studied Forman. One of her plucked eyebrows had a hair out of place. She sported the same diamond stud earrings she'd worn last time. They studied each other for a long moment, neither prepared to speak first. Antonia had done this for three hours in the last interview.

Forman's voice broke the thick silence. 'Jack Bucklin was twenty-three.'

Antonia recognised the name and waited for the question.

'He rode his motorbike into the support of a bridge. It wasn't an accident. Witnesses saw him throw off his helmet and swerve into it.'

Antonia waited. Why had he done such a thing? Had someone else broken the story?

'I hope you're proud of what you've done.'

Antonia uttered the first words she'd spoken in this room. 'You've kept me here for I don't know how long. I've done nothing but stare at walls and ceilings. Now, ask me some questions so I can ignore them.'

'Your scurrilous rag published a defamatory story about his mother. Now, not only have you smeared her, but she's also mourning her only son.'

What had happened? Had her attempt to upload the documents worked? Eleanor must have found them and published. A rush of relief made her smile.

'I'm glad you're happy about it.' Forman's usual icy expression slipped for once.

'Are you saying *The Investigator* published a story about the cabinet?'

'No, just the Home Secretary.'

Why had Eleanor only published part of the story? Antonia detected the cautious hand of Geoff Stokes behind this. But why hadn't Bucklin resigned?

'I'm here to tell you we're removing the licence from *The Electric Investigator*—'

'You can't.'

'We have. And we're also charging you with malicious misinformation. The Home Secretary has asked me to inform you she will push for the maximum sentence. As you know, because you caused someone's death, it's life.'

'And as *you* know, I was in here.'

'It didn't publish itself, Ms Conti. We will charge everyone responsible for this abomination.' She pressed a button under the table and the door opened.

CHAPTER 12

The light and noise woke Antonia, and she lifted her head off the pillow she'd rolled up under her head. Unable to lie full length on the narrow bed, she'd curled up on her side. Frigid air attacked any exposed flesh, and she shivered.

'Get up. Now.' An unfamiliar guard waited in the doorway.

'What's the time?'

'Just get dressed.'

'Get out, first.' She suspected they had hidden cameras, but she wasn't letting him stand there, watching her.

The door closed, and she threw the rough blanket off. Goose pimples exploded on her exposed skin as she pulled her tracksuit bottoms on. The bandages on her arms looked grubby, but they'd not offered to change them. She'd tell them now. The tracksuit sleeve, too short for her, caught on her right forearm, and a sharp pain made her wince. It should be healing. The other arm itched like hell. As she fastened the zip, the door swung open.

'You ready?'

'I need my bandages changing.'

'Not my problem. Come on, let's go.'

The usual three-man escort now comprised two men and one woman. The change in routine made Antonia uneasy. After Forman left, they'd questioned her once more. They'd given up after less than an hour, far quicker than in the previous sessions. They led her past the interview rooms.

'Where are we going?'

A prod in the back was the only response. She glimpsed a watch. It showed five, but morning or afternoon? The soft lighting in the corridor suggested the former, but she wouldn't put it past them to mess with her mind. They turned a corner and came to another door. This one, wider than those on the cells or interrogation rooms, swung open before they reached it.

Harsh white light made her squint. Several people waited for her in a vestibule, and she recognised the stocky figure of the woman who'd produced the warrants. She looked uncomfortable. Her escorts stopped at the doorway, as if crossing the threshold would harm them.

'Ms Conti,' the woman said, 'we're taking you back. Where do you want to go?'

'What's the time?'

'Oh five oh three.'

'Day?'

'Monday.'

She'd been here forty-eight hours. It felt much longer. 'Take me home.' She wanted to ask why they were releasing her but didn't want to burst the bubble. Unless this was a dream.

'Your clothes are in the cubicle.' The woman pointed to a narrow door in the wall behind her. 'You can change and leave what you're wearing.'

She didn't need a second invitation. Her clothes smelt of disinfectant and someone had unpicked the seams and then not-so-expertly resewn them. A clear bag held her keys, money and half a pack of chewing gum she forgot she had. She left the tracksuit in a heap on the floor and walked out of the cubicle.

The woman held a clipboard, which she offered to Antonia.

She skimmed it. 'What's this?'

'You're indemnifying the government, and specifically the Home Secretary, against any legal action you may wish to take.'

Was this an admission they'd broken the law? 'What if I don't sign?'

She stared. 'Are you?'

'Where's Rick? Rick Grainger?'

'Are you going to sign this?'

'No.'

She sighed and took the clipboard. 'These gentlemen will take you home.' Then she left.

'Where's Rick?'

She continued walking.

The two men left behind gave 'I've no idea' shrugs.

'Can you tell me where we are?'

They exchanged a look.

'Unless you intend to put a bag over my head, I'll see in a few minutes.'

'Battersea,' the younger-looking of the two said.

'Let's go then. I presume you know where I live.'

Reluctant to obey her, they waited several seconds before leading her to the lift and then into an underground car park. They put her in the back of a people-carrier, and she sank into the seat. At this time of the morning, she would get home in less than half an hour. The sun glinted off the Thames. They weren't too far from the park. She had a good idea in which building they'd held her. It belonged to a party donor, and she'd heard rumours the government had taken a long and expensive lease out on it.

She tried to relax, but her mind raced. Why would they try to get Bucklin off the hook? Whatever Eleanor published pushed the son to kill himself. It should have brought the mother down. Why hadn't it? She was too tired to work it out.

The car stopped, and the engine cut out. She jerked awake and recognised her neighbour's window.

'Did you guys search my house?'

They looked sheepish, and the younger one nodded.

'What state did you leave it in?'

'Tidy. We don't make a mess. Most people don't realise we've been in.' He sounded proud.

At least that was something. She slid the door open and got out, stumbling on the damp cobbles. 'See you around.' She slammed the door and fumbled for her keys.

The unset alarm gave the only indication she'd had unwanted visitors. She rang work and left a message, and after wrapping her forearms in bin liners, showered and fell into bed.

The incessant bell woke her almost immediately. Who'd call so early? She checked the time: nine thirty, but she couldn't have slept four hours. She put on a vest and knickers, then wrapped a big dressing gown round her. Chapman waited outside, a bakery bag in his hand.

Despite her exhaustion, she returned his smile. 'What's in there?'

'Two each of cheese and bacon savouries, almond croissants and pain au chocolat.'

'Okay, leave the bag and let me get back to sleep.'

'I'm afraid I can't.' He nodded at the stained fabric showing at her wrists. 'Do you want me to change your bandages?'

'Come in.' She took the bag off him as he passed.

'Coffee and pastries first, or bandages?'

'Food. I was hungry at five this morning.'

They drank coffee and ate at the breakfast bar in her compact kitchen, sitting in companionable silence. She'd eaten two pastries and finished one coffee before she felt ready to speak.

'Okay, what do I need to know?'

'You eaten enough?'

'No. But I can listen and chew now.'

'Okay.' He wiped his fingers on a tissue and drank some coffee. 'Bucklin's son killed himself yesterday.'

'Forman told me.' The thought that a young man, a year younger than her, had killed himself, haunted her.

'Millie Forman, the new Permanent Secretary?'

'Is she?'

'Announced this morning. Home Office.'

'She's working with Bucklin?'

'Nope. Bucklin resigned last night.'

She'd missed a lot. 'Who's the new person?'

Chapman mentioned the previous Education Secretary.

'But he's involved.'

'I know, but your Mr Stokes wouldn't let Eleanor publish everything.'

'I need to read the article. What reason did they give for Bucklin's resignation?'

'Her son's death. Some of the other papers mentioned your article, but caveated it with "she denies any wrongdoing". She did an interview. I'll see if I can find it.' He scrolled through his phone and found the footage.

A distraught-looking Bucklin, husband beside her, spoke into the camera, anger at Antonia and *The Investigator* the overriding theme of the interview. Antonia reminded herself the woman had tried to have her and Grainger killed.

'Have we heard from Rick?'

'Not sure. Eleanor didn't mention it when she rang this morning.'

'*Eleanor*, now. When did you two become pals?'

'I wouldn't say pals.' He gave her a smile. 'I was there Saturday when we published the story.'

'Did my version back up, then?'

'I don't think so. I took Grainger's memory stick—'

'And they let you?'

'I told them I'd come to investigate a reported break-in. They didn't suspect I had anything to do with you.'

'Thank you.' She hugged him and kissed him on the cheek, leaving a greasy smear on the reddening skin. 'I was sure we'd lost the lot.'

'Well, you can repay me by giving me a job if I get fired.' He wiped the mark with a piece of kitchen towel.

'Deal. I'd better ring Rick. Can I use your phone?'

'Sure. I've saved Rick's number on it.'

The mobile went straight to voicemail, so she rang the home number. 'Hello?'

'Erika?'

'Yes, who is this?'

'Antonia. Can I speak to Rick?'

The silence dragged on. 'He's resting.'

'He's home then.'

'I'll tell him you rang.' The line died.

Antonia resisted the temptation to ring back. She wanted to speak to Grainger and find out what he'd said. At least they'd released him.

They finished eating and Chapman removed the dressings on her arms. The left looked fine but the right still showed an angry scar, which he rebandaged.

'Thanks, Russell. Now, why couldn't you let me rest? And why did Eleanor ring you this morning?'

'To tell me they'd released you, and also' – he studied her, looking troubled – 'they suspended your licence this morning.'

'*The Investigator*'s?'

'They sent a load of people to the office.'

'Blast! Forman said they would. I thought she was just trying to soften me up. I'll have to go in.'

◆ ◆ ◆

'Come on, Hakim, we need to go.' Sabirah stood in the hallway of their first-floor apartment, waiting for her son. She checked her reflection in the antique mirror. She wasn't sure the shoes went with the 'new' suit she'd bought from the charity shop, but she had lots of walking to do today, and these were the most comfortable of her three pairs.

Nadimah, still in her dressing gown, came out of the kitchen with a glass of oat milk in one hand and her phone in the other.

'And you, young lady, make sure you get dressed and don't spend all day on the phone. Your friends will be in class, and you have all that work to do. I don't want you falling behind.'

'It's only one day, Mum—'

'On top of the two you missed last week. And since when did you call me Mum? Is Mama no longer good enough?'

'I'm thirteen now. Most of my friends call their mothers by their first name.'

'Not in this household.' She and Rashid had agreed they would never be the type of parents who imagined themselves as their children's 'pals'.

Hakim's arrival ended the argument before it started. Hakim needed new trousers, and she'd get him some shoes as well. At least she'd receive good money for the next few months.

The laptop bag lay in the hall by the front door, where Sabirah had left it since last night, in case she forgot it. After saying goodbye to Nadimah, they left. Two vans pulled up outside as they reached the street, and dark-clad people made their way to the basement offices. They looked like secret police and Sabirah hurried past them, dragging Hakim with her. They'd swarmed round the basement yesterday, and she'd taken the children out until they left.

She hadn't seen Antonia yesterday. Although it wasn't unusual for her to stay away all weekend, she'd expected her friend to check on the intruders. Come to think of it, she hadn't come on Saturday, when her friend Russell had called. Sabirah rang her, but only once, and got no reply. Antonia wasn't the most diligent at taking her phone with her, but Sabirah hoped her friend was okay. She'd try her later.

With those secret police around, she wasn't comfortable leaving Nadimah at home for the day. Although they shouldn't go anywhere near their apartment, the memory of the secret police raiding their home in Idlib still gave her nightmares. Hakim kept glancing backwards, and she hurried him.

'I don't want to be late. I'm presenting my plans to Mr Innis.'

'He'll love them, unless he's an idiot.'

She could always rely on Hakim to raise her spirits. 'I've told you, don't call people idiots.'

'And if you included a retractable roof terrace, like I told you . . .'

'Maybe on my next project.' Would she get another? Mrs Curtis had given her this job, but would a stranger trust her?

'That a promise?' He gave her a smile, showing where the last of his baby teeth left a gap.

'It's an aspiration. Now, come on, we'll be late.'

She left him at the school gate and hurried to work. The practice office, above a betting shop near Islington Green, would only take ten minutes on foot. She carried the laptop bag self-consciously. The thought she'd go to work in an office, and not to clean it, had become an alien concept, but she intended to get used to it.

Brody Innis was already in his office. Tall and stooped with shoulder-length white hair and bright round-framed glasses, he looked the part of a 'creative'. Even though they were due at the town hall, he wore his usual cords, scuffed brogues and a safari jacket.

'Ah, good morning, Mrs Fadil. How are ye today?'

'Good morning, Mr Innis. Very happy to be here.' She sometimes struggled to decipher his Scottish accent, and Mrs Curtis confessed she had the same problem.

'Brody, please.'

'Sabirah.'

'Okay, Sabirah, I've arranged for us to meet the planning officer at twelve to go through your proposals. You think you'll be ready for then?'

No! She'd expected to spend the day polishing her concept with input from Mr Innis. *Come on, Sabirah, it can't be worse than the evil gnome of a man in the Idlib planning office who didn't believe in women architects.* 'Of course. Can I show you first?'

'I've allowed two hours from nine thirty. It should give us plenty of time. I'm not expecting it will need much.'

Buoyed by this vote of confidence, Sabirah made her way to her desk. *I am an architect.* In the time before her conference with Mr Innis, she checked her plans, making sure she'd not made any silly mistakes, and by the time she showed them to him, she felt positive about her plans. He suggested some technical changes, so it would have a better chance of acceptance. Although she'd read up on the regulations and had gone over them during her work experience here, she'd never worked on a building in London.

'I'm very impressed, Sabirah. Excellent work.' He checked the time. 'Shall we go? It's only a ten-minute walk, but they've got all these security checks we'll need to go through. A right pain in the arse, pardon my French.'

Sabirah's anxiety levels increased as they neared the town hall. Despite Mr Innis's encouraging words, she wouldn't be happy until she'd got the okay on her plans. As he'd predicted, the security checks caused them delays. Her laptop, a new one Antonia had given her, needed three attempts to get through the scanner.

She took her shoes out of the tray, embarrassed by the worn heels, and slipped them back on. Mr Innis didn't seem at all discomfited by his worn and scuffed brogues. They arrived at the planning office with a minute to spare, but then waited ten minutes. She tried not to let this bother her and focused on her presentation as they sat in two low chairs in reception.

'Mr Innis, sorry to keep you waiting. My meeting overran.' A tall, elegant woman in a stylish suit stood over them.

'Ms Rani.' Mr Innis struggled to his feet.

Sabirah joined him, knocking her laptop case over as she did so. 'Hello. Sabirah.' She offered her hand.

The woman looked at it and then at hers, one of which held a tablet and the other a takeaway coffee from the concession in the foyer three floors below. 'Shall we go through?'

She strode down the corridor, her heels clicking. As he drew level with Sabirah, Mr Innis said, 'Don't worry, her bark's worse than her bite.'

Sabirah wasn't sure what he meant but, face hot, she followed. They entered a large room with a whiteboard at the front, and tables and chairs arranged in rows. Rani put her coffee and tablet on one and sat. Sabirah sat opposite, next to Mr Innis.

'This is my colleague, Ms Fadil. She's produced the plans we're submitting.'

Rani raised an eyebrow. 'You're a qualified architect?'

'Yes.' The defensive tone embarrassed Sabirah further. 'I have practised for nine years.'

'Where?'

'Two years in Aleppo and seven in Idlib.' Sabirah's voice dropped to a whisper.

'You've had your qualifications accepted by the ARB?'

She couldn't speak.

'Not yet, but I have full confidence in Ms Fadil.' Innis gave her a smile.

'We can't accept—'

'My practice will submit the plans and our insurance will back them.'

Rani pouted. 'Okay, let's see them. I will expect them to be to your usual standard, Mr Innis.'

'Of course.'

Sabirah got the zip of the laptop bag stuck, adding to the time to get the device up and running. Hot and wanting to hide, she reminded herself of the people depending on her. She'd given a presentation to a room full of middle-aged men, most of whom believed she should have cooked or served the meal they'd just eaten, when her practice entered her design for a prize. And she'd gone through a lot since then. She could do this.

'We're very keen to preserve the look of the building and all the work will remain in sympathy with the period, from retaining or even recreating the original features, to using the same colour paints and similar papers.' Once she started, Sabirah's concerns fell away.

She finished and glanced at Mr Innis, who looked like a proud father. Rani had a different reaction. She'd tapped out sheaves of notes as Sabirah spoke, pausing only to sip her coffee. Now a frown creased her forehead.

'We obviously expect you to preserve the character of our old buildings. However, I have misgivings about some of your proposals. You show a lift in the building. It will have a major impact—'

'Mrs Curtis needs a lift.'

'That's our client,' Innis explained.

145

'Not my problem.'

'There's a lift next door.' Sabirah reminded herself not to raise her voice.

Rani studied her tablet. 'Not according to our plans. I'll need to see plans and evidence you received permission to put it in.'

Sabirah looked at Innis. Had she done something wrong?

Innis gave Rani a smile. 'I'm sure Mrs Curtis will have gone through the proper channels. I'll make sure we get something through to you.'

Rani listed her other objections, but Sabirah couldn't focus on anything other than the thought she'd got Mrs Curtis into trouble.

CHAPTER 13

The National Security Agency staff who'd searched the offices of *The Electric Investigator* had gone by the time Chapman accompanied Antonia to the front door.

'Ring me if you need anything.'

'Thanks, Russell. For everything.' She gave him a hug.

He returned to his car. He should go to the hospice and finish his investigation, but his heart wasn't in it. Gunnerson had more or less admitted she'd helped Rex on his way. Would they let her take early retirement? She must have twenty-five in. *Come on, Russell, Harding will push for the maximum sentence. Even if the CPS doesn't proceed, he'll want her to lose her job and her pension.*

'Fuck!' He slapped the steering wheel. 'Let's get this over with.'

The car park at the hospice teemed, and he drove round it twice before getting a space. Small groups sat in the garden, the patients standing out from their guilty-looking visitors. How many of them would help a loved one end their life to save them from suffering? The receptionist recognised him with a look of panic before giving him a fake smile.

'Mr Chapman, good to see you again.' She spoke in an over-loud voice as a family wheeled their relative out. She picked the phone up and whispered into it before he could respond.

The manager took him straight into her office and closed the door. 'Inspector, I thought you'd finished Friday. Has something else happened?'

'No, but I need to speak to whoever has access to the linen cupboard on the top floor.'

'Why?'

'Are they here?'

She checked the clock on the wall in front of her desk. 'They're both in today. Do you want to speak to them upstairs? I'm not sure where they'll be. It's a busy time.'

'Is there an office where I can speak to them, one at a time?'

'You can use this one. I have to speak to the catering staff before lunch, anyway. I'll get the first one sent down and they can fetch their colleague once you finish.'

'Thank you, I really appreciate this.'

He'd finished arranging the seating when a faint knock on the door announced the first arrival. At his invitation, a small man stepped into the office, confused on seeing the manager's seat empty.

'Come in and close the door. I'm Inspector Chapman.'

The man froze.

'You're not in trouble. I just need to ask you a couple of questions. Please sit.'

He made his way to the chair Chapman had positioned. He'd placed it at an angle to him, so they weren't confronting each other. The man moved like someone apologising for occupying space, recalling Uriah Heep, and slid into the chair. He sat hunched over, his arse barely on the seat and his hands gripping the arms, ready to launch himself out of it.

Chapman asked him a few general questions to put him at ease, but soon decided he was wasting his time.

'I'm here because we received a letter about a patient.'

The man licked his lips and glanced at the door.

'Do you want to know what the letter said?'

His eyes flickered from side to side, and he swallowed.

'Did you write it?'

'There's no law against writing a letter.'

'I'm not here to get anyone into trouble. I just want to make sure we haven't misunderstood what the letter's saying.'

The man's grip on the arms tightened.

'Did you write it?'

'There's no law—'

'Can we discuss the circumstances under which you heard what you claim?'

'I *did* hear it.'

'I'm not doubting you. We just need to clarify how you over-heard what you did and what they said.'

As Chapman had suspected, he'd been near the pipe when he'd overheard Gunnerson and her husband talking.

'Did you often listen there?'

'I wasn't listening.' His voice rose, and a flush travelled up his scrawny neck. 'I was collecting bedsheets.'

'Okay. What did they say?'

'The husband asked her to kill him, and she agreed. That's not right, is it?'

'What exactly did he say?'

'I couldn't make it all out. He had one of them funny computer voices, like the scientist. But he said he was sick of all this and couldn't wait until he went.'

'Are those his exact words?'

He looked uncertain. 'Yeah, I'm sure.'

'You said you couldn't make out everything he said.'

'Well, not everything, but I heard that.' His mulish expression suggested he'd stick to this version.

'Okay, I'm just trying to get to the truth. What did his wife say?'

'She said, don't worry, it won't be long now. I promised I'd help you on your way.'

'Those are her exact words?'

'Yes.'

'Couldn't she have meant she'd stay with him on his journey? Many people here are near the end of their lives.'

'I've heard no one say that before.'

'So, you do listen.'

The flush deepened. 'You're just covering up for her because she's a policewoman. They said – you're all the same.'

'Believe me, I don't want to cover up for anyone. She's my boss. Would you cover up for your boss?'

He looked unsure, but subsided.

'I want to make sure there are no doubts about your story.'

'I know what I heard.'

'Would you make a statement?'

'Why do I need to? You can check his body for poison.'

'Is that a no?'

'I'll do it if I have to.'

I'm sure you will, and you'll make it as damning of Yasmin as you can. 'Thank you for your time and your honesty.'

'Shall I send—'

'No need, thanks.'

He'd tell Harding he saw no reason to take this further. He doubted whatever he said would influence the chief superintendent. The bastard would have already made a decision that suited his agenda. He should have recorded the witness, captured his evasiveness. The realisation he'd not handled it well preoccupied Chapman as he returned to the car.

◆ ◆ ◆

The offices of *The Electric Investigator* looked like a computer repair shop when Antonia walked in. A pile of hard drives lay on two of the desks in the main office. A distraught-looking Sawyer and Miles sorted through the hardware. Antonia needed a double take to recognise Sawyer. She'd changed her thick-lensed glasses for a stylish frame with thin lenses. She'd also had her hair cut by a professional and wore a smart suit.

'Antonia, how are you?' Sawyer put the hard drive she held on to the desk.

'Fine thanks, Jean. What's happened?'

'Our hard drives. They've returned them. Me and Miles are sorting through them.'

But they'd suspended their licence and were still investigating them. Weren't they? 'When did they bring them back?'

Sawyer exchanged a look with Miles. 'About two hours ago. They were already here questioning us—'

'What did they ask you?'

'If any of us had worked on the story about the Home Secretary. They came back Sunday.'

'Have you been here all weekend?' How had she had time to get her haircut and visit the optician?

'I came Saturday when Mr Chapman brought the memory stick back, but I didn't come Sunday. Mrs Curtis told me about it.'

'Where's Eleanor?' Antonia needed to speak to her.

'She's gone to see Mr Stokes. They've disabled the website.'

'They've suspended our licence, but we can still publish without a licence. It just reduces our credibility.'

'But we can't edit it or add anything.'

'They've left the story about Bucklin up?'

'I don't think they've changed anything, but nor can we. I've brought my laptop in. It's on my desk.'

151

Antonia checked it, relieved to find the site up and looking intact. They'd even left up the logo confirming its status as a verified Licenced News Enterprise. She checked the comments but found nothing since early this morning. They must have disabled it before releasing her.

Sawyer's wasn't the only laptop on view. 'Have you restored and checked all these?'

'Mrs Curtis asked everyone to bring their own. Ours are in there and need checking.' Sawyer pointed at two boxes under the desk. 'We've prioritised the server and desktops.'

'Good idea. Have you done mine yet?' Antonia wanted to check what they'd removed.

'Not yet.' Miles furrowed his brow. 'We didn't know when we'd see you again.'

'Understandable. Can you do it next?'

Sawyer held up a hard drive. 'This one's yours. I'll put it in and check it works. We've checked ours. Everything seems to be there.'

'Can't we back up from our cloud server?'

Sawyer didn't look happy. 'It's a local company, and they forced it to let them have access, so the security services may have wiped stuff off it.'

They'd discussed using a backup in another jurisdiction but had stayed local because of the enhanced security of the company they used. They might protect them against hackers, but not the government.

'Is there any way we can check what they've copied?'

'I'm afraid not, Ms Conti. We're running checks to find out if they've put on any spyware.'

Antonia expected them to. 'Have they returned my laptop from home?'

'We found two extra, so I guess one's yours. Do you want to check while I sort this out?'

Antonia sorted through the boxes and found both her and Grainger's laptops. The doorbell rang while she got them out. Two technicians wearing the uniform of their cyber security provider stood at the doorstep. Eleanor had asked them to check the building for bugs. They used more specialised equipment than Sawyer. By the time they'd finished, Sawyer had set Antonia's computer up.

She sat at her desk, feeling like she'd been gone for weeks rather than a long weekend. She found nothing relating to the article they'd written through the night. Someone had removed every trace. She checked other articles about the government but didn't notice any missing. Now they'd got the all-clear from the bug team, she rang Grainger.

The phone went to voicemail, and she left a brief message. Was he still asleep, or on the way here? She tried his mobile, with the same result. Nothing she could do but wait for him to get in touch.

She didn't have to wait long. Sawyer put him through twenty minutes later. 'How are you, Rick?'

'Been better. Can you meet me in forty minutes?' He sounded on edge.

'Yes, where?'

'Do you remember where we first met? By the exit? There's a café across the road.'

Which buildings had they passed when he'd helped her see off those undercover troublemakers? She didn't remember, especially with the ranks of security guards surrounding the protest. Then she realised he must mean the exit they'd escaped through.

'Okay, I'll set off now.'

'Don't be late.'

◆ ◆ ◆

Grainger woke, and the clock on his bedside cabinet read eleven thirty. His mobile showed two missed calls, one from the office and an earlier one from Chapman. Nothing from Antonia. Hadn't they released her yet? He unmuted it and got up. A shower revived him, and he searched for something to eat. A note from Erika on the kitchen table told him Antonia had rung.

He retrieved his laptop from the same hidden compartment under his dressing room floor where he'd left his phone and fired it up while he made himself a coffee. He wondered if they'd ever return the old machine they'd found in his study. Good thing he'd used it a few days ago, otherwise they'd have guessed he had another and come back.

Although hungry, he couldn't face cooking anything and poured out a large bowl of cereal. He'd read the report in *The Electric Investigator* when Erika told him about it first thing this morning, but wanted to check the reaction. He read the account in his old paper. The sketchy and guarded references to the story where they downplayed *The Investigator*'s claims told him the government remained in cover-up mode and were hoping it would go away before anyone else thought to investigate. He could imagine the conversation between a Number 10 spokesperson and Elfyn.

Other papers used the same language. He could predict how the story would play out. Bucklin's 'grieving mother' status would protect her for a few days, enough time for the others to cover their tracks. He still had his files but didn't have the information Bucklin had given them. Whoever wrote the article on Bucklin, and he assumed it was Eleanor, must have had the same information he had here. Antonia's backup must have worked.

He finished the cereal and made himself a second coffee while he checked his emails. One grabbed his attention, and he opened it first. His contact in Cayman had sent him a cryptic message via an encrypted server.

Lots of cleaning going on but spoke to a contact keen to show you what's under the carpet. Mention my name and request a deep clean.

The message ended with a hyperlink. Grainger avoided them, but he trusted his contact and clicked on it. It took him to a very amateurish website for domestic cleaning services. Few details. But a mobile number. He opened an encrypted app and punched it in.

A man with a mellifluous, educated voice answered. 'Domestic cleaning services. Can I help you?'

Grainger requested the deep clean.

'Hang on.' The phone died but reconnected in a few seconds. 'Mr Grainger?'

'And who am I talking to?'

'It doesn't matter. I can meet you and your editor in an hour. Name a venue.'

'I can't guarantee my editor can get there—'

'Make sure she does. This is a one-time offer. Where are we meeting?'

Grainger's mind whirred. He needed to choose somewhere both he and Antonia could reach in an hour, and somewhere that meant something to her. 'Okay, I'll meet you near the Henry Fawcett Monument in Victoria Embankment Gardens.'

'Very appropriate, considering the inability of our current politicians to see what's in front of them.'

'How will I recognise you?'

'I'll recognise you, and I'll definitely recognise your editor. I trust you'll ensure I'm not compromised by leading nefarious types to me. Fifty-seven minutes.' The line died.

A mixture of excitement and apprehension energised Grainger. What if he couldn't get hold of Antonia? Would the guy blank him if she wasn't there? No time to waste. He rang the office.

'*The Electric Investigator*, how—'

'Jean, is Antonia there? It's Rick.'

'Ooh, she's been trying to get hold of you.'

With a sense of relief, he waited for Sawyer to put him through. He dispensed with the pleasantries and once sure Antonia knew where to meet him, he set off. The café they'd agreed to meet in was a ten-minute walk from the rendezvous, but they should have plenty of time. As he made his way to Clapham Common tube station, he considered the potential risks of this meeting. The park would be busy at lunchtime, so he doubted anyone would try something there.

The main worry was this plummy-voiced stranger wouldn't show, and they'd waste a couple of hours. It didn't surprise him people were covering their tracks in Cayman. In other circumstances, he'd have waited until they had enough on all of them before publishing, but Eleanor had done well. Her publishing the story must have precipitated their release from custody.

The Northern Line took him straight to Charing Cross, and he made his way to the café. He waited for Antonia outside. If she walked, she'd come down The Strand, and three minutes later, her distinctive figure strode towards him. Something told him not to wave. She made fleeting eye contact but carried on past him.

Then he noticed her tail. A stocky man with a rucksack, trying not to run as he shadowed her. They'd have put at least one more tail on Antonia, and he saw her on the other side of the road, mobile held to her ear, but an earpiece in the other. How the hell would they get out of this?

Too focused on getting to their rendezvous on time, Antonia hadn't picked up the tails until she reached The Strand. In the short time she'd known Grainger, he hadn't struck her as someone to exaggerate, so if he said it was important, she believed him. And she had a good hunch about this, once she lost her tails. She considered options on how to do it.

By the time she reached Grainger, she'd formulated a plan. She just hoped he'd guess it. After identifying the man with the red rucksack, she'd looked for his backup and spotted a woman in jeans and a black leather jacket. Antonia passed Grainger, making minimal eye contact, and headed for the building they'd both escaped through following the riot.

She ducked into the alleyway they'd come out of and ran, hoping she'd guessed right. Up ahead was a door they'd passed after they got down the external fire escape. As she'd suspected, it wasn't closed. The pile of discarded cigarette butts outside it had suggested a favoured smokers' rendezvous. She pulled at the edge of the door and it resisted for a moment, but opened. As she slipped in, she spotted her tail at the entrance to the alley.

She pulled the door shut and lifted the push-bar to lock it. Now to find her way to the door they'd escaped through. Ten paces in, she ran across a woman with a pack of cigarettes in her hand. She must stop her opening the door.

'Excuse me, I need to get out on the Craven Street side.'

'Over there.' She pointed over her left shoulder.

'Can you show me?' She shot a glance over her own shoulder at the alley door. 'There's a guy I'm trying to get away from.'

'Ooh . . . Okay.' The woman retraced her steps. 'If you go down here to the T-junction, go left, second right and then second left.'

'Thanks. If you could give me a couple of minutes before opening the exit?' Antonia ran and a minute later passed the vertical ladder her rescuer had escaped up when she and Grainger ran from the faux protestors. The brand-new fire exit door opened, and Grainger waited outside.

'You lost them?'

'I think so,' she said. 'Which way?'

'Embankment Gardens. We'll go through the station just in case. We'd better hurry.'

They marched towards the station, Antonia's longer stride taking her away from Grainger, but at least he wasn't limping. Looking like they had a train to catch, they pushed past slower commuters and crossed the concourse. Grainger's fast breathing and apologies reassured her she'd not lost him, and at the far side, she waited to let him catch up, using the opportunity to check behind her. Neither of her tails appeared, and she relaxed.

They came out on Villiers Street, and Grainger took the lead. 'We've got two minutes.'

She followed, her easy stride keeping up with his half-jog. At the Fawcett Monument, he stopped. A bench facing it sat empty and, looking disappointed, he slumped into it. After letting him catch his breath, Antonia questioned him.

'Who are we meeting?'

'I'm not sure. I got a message from one of my contacts. This guy's keen to "do some spring cleaning". I'm assuming he's got some dirt on our targets.'

'I'm not sure we can use it—'

'What do you mean?'

'I mean, we can't update our site. Eleanor's trying to get it overturned, but I don't know how she got on.'

'Fuck!' A passing couple glared at Grainger. 'What happened to you in custody?'

'I got questioned by the spooks three times, asked for a solicitor and gave them the silent treatment. Then I got Millie Forman—'

'You were honoured. She's going places. What did she want?'

'She told me about Bucklin's son and told me they'd close us down. Something she's threatened before.'

'She was all sweetness and light to me. Offered me untold riches if I agreed to tell them all we knew and spied on you.'

'And?'

'I wouldn't tell you if I'd agreed to do it.'

They sat in silence for a moment.

Antonia checked their surroundings. The numbers thinned as lunchtime ended and she could see nobody promising as a contact. 'What time's your guy showing?'

Grainger checked his phone. 'Ten minutes ago.'

'You think he'll show?'

'Your guess is as good as mine. He might want to check nobody's followed us.'

It made sense. They'd not seen either of her tails, but there might be a third one she'd not spotted. 'Shall we give him a few more minutes?'

'What time does the café shut? I'll get coffees.'

She scanned the park while she waited. Birdsong and the scent of blossom suggested a tranquillity at odds with her mood. Most of the lunchtime visitors had gone, except for a woman with a pram.

Grainger came back with two steaming cups. 'Shall we finish these and go?'

'Yeah, I'll check if Eleanor's got anywhere.' Antonia shared his obvious disappointment.

The pram drew level, and something dropped from it. Expecting a dummy or child's toy, Antonia leant forward to pick it up. A pen. The woman bent down to her level.

'Try not to lose it.' Then she set off at a brisk pace.

Antonia examined the pen. Under the cap, a USB connector.

'Antonia, let's go.'

She looked up. The man with the rucksack walked towards them. From the opposite side came his female companion, with two men flanking her.

CHAPTER 14

Chapman studied the chief superintendent while he read his report. Harding had been a slim, fit-looking inspector when he'd first crossed Chapman's path. Now, his puffy cheeks and ruddy complexion made him look like someone heading for an early heart attack. Was it married life or too many rich dinners at his Masonic lodge?

'You're saying there's nothing to investigate?' Harding looked disappointed. 'I disagree.'

'The guy who wrote the letter changes the bedding and claims he heard a conversation through the wall. I've transcribed what he told me. It's very thin and you could interpret it—'

'I disagree. It needs proper investigation.'

'The guy isn't even sure what he heard.'

'You press him on it?'

'Of course.'

'He sounds certain.'

'You know what some witnesses are like. He's dug his heels in and will say he definitely heard it.' Chapman again wished he'd recorded the interview.

'And you can't prove he didn't.'

'The guy knows Yasmin's police, and he clearly doesn't like us.'

'Lots of people don't like us, Russell, but it doesn't mean they're lying.'

'You asked me to check and tell you if I think it needs further investigation. I'm telling you it doesn't. Do you know how many of these cases go to court and result in a prosecution?'

'That's not the point. If one of our officers has committed a crime, we must show no favour.'

'And I'm telling you, I don't think anyone has committed a crime.'

'I'm very disappointed, Russell. I assumed you'd approach this with an open mind, like you would any case. You've clearly decided to protect—'

'Bullshit!'

'Remember who you're talking to, Inspector.'

'I haven't forgotten, Ian. And you don't forget why we're here. To catch crooks, not climb the greasy pole by shitting on our colleagues.'

'That's enough.' Harding's complexion had grown darker.

'The woman's just buried her husband—'

'And there's a possibility she might have put him there.'

'He was in a hospice receiving end-of-life care.'

'It's our responsibility to protect everyone, not just those with a long life ahead of them.'

'You're unbelievable. You've got my report, do whatever you want.' Chapman pushed his chair back.

'Inspector!'

Chapman spun on his heel and strode to the door. He needed to get out before he smacked him.

'INSPECTOR!'

Chapman slammed the door behind him and marched down the corridor, expecting Harding to follow him. He resisted the urge to keep walking to the entrance and either go home or to the pub.

He'd missed too much work already with this bullshit investigation and helping Antonia. Well, he didn't regret the latter. He returned to his office to catch up with his admin. Harding, true to past form, produced a blizzard of paperwork, which every officer under his command had to read and acknowledge.

Unable to face it so soon after his run-in with the man, he checked his emails. One from the officer dealing with Hughes lifted his spirits. The case linked to his incarceration had moved up, and the courts would deal with it sooner. It meant he might have good news for Antonia. When he could finally face Harding's memos, he made good progress, but a visit from Sanchez gave him a welcome respite.

'Boss, can I have a word?'

'If you call me boss, I know I'm in trouble.'

'I always call you boss, in front of the troops.' Her demeanour suggested he'd guessed right.

'Okay, what's up?'

'Professional Standards are investigating the DCI over her husband's death.'

'Shit!' He hit the desk. 'The sneaky bastard.'

Sanchez looked even more unhappy. 'That's what they're calling *you*.'

'What?'

'There's a rumour Harding asked you to look into it—'

'Yeah, he did.'

'Why did you take it?'

'Orders are discretionary now?'

'No, what I meant was . . .' She took a deep breath. 'Why did you recommend suspension?'

'I didn't. Told him not to.'

'Sorry, you said they *shouldn't* investigate her?'

'Of course. Not enough evidence. The "witness" couldn't even swear to what he heard.'

'The talk is, you recommended it, and it's coming from Professional Standards, and you approached them because you thought Harding might protect her.'

'What? He accused *me* of doing that.' He needed to speak to Yasmin. Tell her he'd not stabbed her. Once he'd done so, he'd deal with Harding.

◆　◆　◆

At the entrance to the park, they split up and Grainger went to Embankment tube while Antonia headed back to Charing Cross. Antonia had passed him the lid to the pen drive before she left, hoping to confuse their pursuers. Although he took evasive action, he'd seen nobody following him, or if they had, they'd given up early.

He got the cab to drop him at the pub on the next block and walked to the office, keeping a lookout for any unwelcome attention as he made his way to the entrance. Jean Sawyer greeted him, looking ten years younger than she had on Friday.

'Hair looks great, Jean. And the glasses. Super trendy.'

She blushed as she let him in. 'Is Antonia with you, Rick?'

'No, we got split up. She's coming later.' How much did Sawyer know and how much should he tell her? Everyone must have heard of the raid on Saturday morning, but he didn't want people worrying.

Miles stood in the main office, a hard drive in his hand and a pile of laptops on the desk in front of him. 'Rick, glad to see you. Do you want a coffee?'

'I had one with Antonia, thanks.' Although he'd abandoned most of his. 'They've returned the hard drives?'

'This is the last one. We've checked them all—'

'For spyware?'

'Of course.' Sawyer sounded affronted. 'And we've swept the place for bugs.'

'I can see you've done this before.' He wondered how quickly his last paper would have got this organised. He'd made an excellent decision coming here, despite the drop in money. And the attempts to kill them, the arrests and being followed by spooks gave him a buzz.

He spent thirty minutes following up some leads he'd sounded out on Friday when Sawyer let out a yell.

'What's up, Jean?'

'We're live. I've just updated a report. Mrs Curtis must have got the block removed.'

A buzz circulated, elevating Grainger's mood further. He logged on to check the site. The feedback streams started filling, most commenting on Bucklin's story. A couple criticised *The Investigator* for the way they'd reported it, accusing them of causing her son's death, but most praised their coverage and thanked them for restoring faith in the mainstream media.

He wouldn't class *The Investigator* as mainstream yet, but didn't doubt they soon would be as influential as their rivals. A headline ribbon at the bottom of the screen caught his attention. 'Ex Home Secretary under the cosh.' He clicked on it. The Fraud Squad had opened an investigation of Bucklin for corruption. The others must have decided to throw her overboard. Once they realised she'd betrayed them, it wouldn't have taken much. But if she decided she had nothing to lose, she'd become a dangerous adversary.

'Shit!'

'Is that a considered critique of the story?' Eleanor gestured at the screen.

'Mrs Curtis, welcome back and well done.' Sawyer led a round of applause from the staff, and Miles led three cheers.

Eleanor, part gratified, but as much embarrassed, called for silence. 'Thank you, everyone. The real thanks must go to our solicitors, in particular Geoff Stokes, who's been a tremendous warrior on our behalf. Let's kick ass.' As the room erupted, she looked surprised she'd said the last phrase. 'Where's Antonia?'

'I left her at Victoria Embankment when we split up.'

'Did you? And what were you doing there?'

'We'd arranged to meet an informant with important information.'

'And they didn't show?'

'I'm not sure. Someone gave Antonia the other half of this.' He placed the cap of the memory stick on the desk. If he'd kept the other half, they could have read it by now.

'And the reason she's not here with it?'

'We thought we spotted a tail, so we split up.'

'I'd suggest Antonia's more than able to take care of herself. So, let's not worry about her. Now, your expletive when I walked in. Does it have anything to do with our former Home Secretary?'

He scanned the busy office, everyone engrossed in their work or indulging in chatter to neighbours, doubtless planning a celebratory drink later. 'They've obviously decided she's toast, but she can take them all down.'

'Do you think they'll give her a way out if she keeps quiet?'

'I'm more inclined to suspect she won't make it to court alive.'

'That's the other option.' She studied him. 'You've met her more than once. Do you think she'll talk to us?'

'After your piece? No chance. It was very good, by the way.'

'Thank you, but I had to do *you* justice. It's your story.'

'Thanks for putting my name on the by-line. But you should have included Antonia. She wrote much of it.'

'I'm sure Antonia will have plenty of opportunities to bask in her own glory.' She looked towards the door, her expression at odds with her words.

Grainger shared her anxiety. He'd seen how desperate cornered politicians could be.

◆ ◆ ◆

Within fifty metres of leaving Grainger, Antonia realised their pursuers had decided to tail her. The two she'd seen earlier, plus the two new ones, all followed her. It wouldn't surprise her if they'd put more on Grainger. Would he spot them?

She should forget Grainger and focus on herself. For all she knew, they had more people on her and intended driving her into a trap.

Not thinking they'd still keep track of her, she'd not even worn any ghost powder. They'd have access to the face recognition cameras, which is how they'd found her in the park. *Stupid! Stupid!* A faint whirring from above made her glance up. A drone. It might not be theirs, but she needed to get off the street. She walked up Villiers Street, fast, but not quite a jog. Ahead, the entrance to the underground. A train must have arrived, as a horde of people poured up the stairs.

She dived into the crowd, elbows and hands creating space as she barged past those leaving, a smile and apology defusing many angry retorts. She'd seen a shop selling ghost powder in the concourse and hoped it hadn't closed. Although it wasn't yet illegal, they got harassed, and many had stopped stocking it. She jogged away from the stairs, checking if she could see her pursuers.

She reached the shop and charged into it. A well-dressed man stood paying the young woman behind the counter, struggling to get his contactless card to work. The woman gave Antonia a sympathetic smile.

'Do you have any ghost?'

'Sure, fifty mil or a hundred?'

'Fifty. How much?'

'Fourteen pounds.' She gave an apologetic smile. You could buy five times as much online for the same money.

'I'll take one.'

'Young lady, I'm still getting served.'

Antonia smiled at him. 'Sorry, a strange man's following me.' She checked the entrance and through the stickers and signs, she saw the woman who'd shadowed her. 'You got another way out?'

'We're not supposed to let customers . . .' She held the tube of ghost powder in her right hand.

'Please.'

'Okay. Through there.' She pointed at a narrow doorway almost hidden behind racking.

'Thanks.' Antonia slipped a twenty into the woman's hand and took the powder.

'Don't you want your change?'

She waved a negative and eased her way through the opening. After negotiating a short corridor and a kitchenette, she came out behind the shops. She scanned the passing travellers but didn't recognise any of her pursuers. A sign for toilets led her into a tiled corridor with barriers across the entrance. She paid her fifty pence and wandered into the deserted ladies. Using the pockmarked mirror above the last sink in the row, she applied the make-up using broad strokes.

It looked obvious and would attract attention close up, but would do the job of hiding her from the face recognition cameras. Someone else came in, their reflection familiar. Antonia spun round, and the woman pulled the mic dangling from a cable across to her mouth. Without thinking, Antonia ran at her and launched a flying side kick. The woman lifted an arm to defend herself, but Antonia's foot smashed it into her torso and knocked her off her feet. She flew into the wall behind, where she slumped to the floor.

Antonia ran, vaulting the barriers at the entrance, and headed towards the nearest platforms. She used a travel card she always carried and jumped into the first train, not caring where it took her. A couple of passengers checked out her make-up and muttered to themselves, but a glare kept them silent. The recent government campaign, suggesting only people with something to hide would wear the powder, seemed to have gained traction. The train arrived at Leicester Square, a teeming station at almost any time of day. She changed lines, travelled to Covent Garden and left the station. When certain she'd lost her shadows, she found an internet café catering to tourists.

A cubicle at the far end of the room gave her a view of the entrance and quick access to the emergency exit. She held her breath as she opened the memory stick. A brief inspection showed what looked like financial records, share certificates and contracts. Names she recognised flashed across the screen as she checked the cache. She logged into a cloud server she sometimes used and uploaded it. Once she'd finished, she took the drive out, cleared the memory and left.

She walked to Russell Square, taking quieter back roads so she'd spot any tails, then got the tube to Kings Cross. She bought a bright red hoody on the concourse and set off back to the office. On the walk back to Vincent Terrace, she formulated a plan. The memory stick contained the information the plummy-voiced man had promised. If they hadn't regained access to the site, she'd share the article with a network of blogs she'd worked with before. It wouldn't bring the kudos of breaking the story, but once the information was in the public domain, it should get these goons off their backs.

She swung by a hotel on Pentonville Road and took a cab with blacked-out windows. They arrived at Vincent Terrace and she made him drive round the block before dropping her outside. With the hood pulled over her head and hunched over to disguise her height, she made her way to the entrance and let herself in. A buzz around the office alerted her to something momentous.

Miles noticed her return first. 'Antonia, you're back.'

The door to her office opened, and Grainger appeared. The fact she'd not thought of him since they'd split up filled her with guilt.

'You got away then.' He stepped aside and Eleanor joined him.

'Eleanor, I'm guessing you overturned the block.'

'Of course, with Geoff on our team. Have you got the rest of this?' She held up the cap of the memory stick.

Antonia produced it from her pocket. 'Shall we see what's on it?'

After checking with Sawyer that she was safe to use it, and disconnecting it from the internet, Antonia plugged the memory stick into her desktop. She uploaded the files on it and gave it to Grainger. As he looked at it on his laptop, she examined the documents.

Her excitement grew as she took in the detail. 'Who gave us these?'

A distracted Grainger didn't answer straight away. 'Erm . . . a contact of the guy I've spoken to in Cayman.'

'Bloody good contact. This will sink the lot of them.' Elation made her tingle as she read.

'You know they've turned on Bucklin.'

'It doesn't surprise me. How long do you give her?'

'If we can get this out, I reckon they'll back off. They'll be too busy defending themselves. If we don't, I'd say days.'

'You've got more faith in the Fraud Squad than I have,' Eleanor said. 'They'll take months, if not years.'

'We're talking about someone taking her out,' Grainger said.

'Oh. Right. You're both very blasé about someone's murder.'

'Maybe if she'd tried to have you killed, you'd feel as we do.'

Antonia wasn't sure how she felt. The fact they'd already brought Bucklin down felt like enough payback for trying to kill them. She focused on the others. Did they know what Antonia had? They'd put at least four operatives on her *before* she'd collected this. After the raid last time stopped them getting their story out, she decided they couldn't take any chances.

'Eleanor, can we get the rest of the staff out of here and lock the doors? The reinforcing we put on them at the end of last year should hold out for a while.'

'What do you want to do?'

'I want to make sure we can publish this. Rick, how long to get it into shape?'

He blew out his cheeks. 'I've got the original article Russell saved. I'd happily publish it in an emergency. There's more material here, but we can add it later.'

'I want Geoff to check it.' Eleanor wore a determined expression.

Antonia frowned. 'Get him to come over if possible. But I'm not delaying getting this out.'

'We'll see. I'll ring him and tell the others they've got the rest of the afternoon off.'

'You'd better keep Jean back. We might need her help, especially if they try to prevent us publishing. And why don't you give Miles the credit card and tell him to take them to the pub to celebrate your success?'

'Isn't that extravagant?'

'It's not every day we get a Home Secretary to resign, and if anyone's watching, it might throw them off.'

'You think they'll try to stop us?' Eleanor looked even more worried.

'Yes, I do.'

Eleanor left to speak to the others and Grainger said, 'If they knew we had this, they'd nuke the place.'

'That's what I'm worried about.'

Once the remaining staff had left, they set up the system so it would publish the original article at the push of a button. Eleanor, Grainger and Antonia worked on part of the new article, each focusing on a group of ministers. Antonia tried to remember the last time a corruption scandal had implicated so many senior ministers anywhere. But they still covered up so much stuff. Would this get published if it wasn't for *The Investigator*? How many other reporters and editors had they warned off?

At around six, the doorbell rang, and Antonia froze. She got up and strode into the outer office. Jean stood at the intercom screen. Antonia had told her to let nobody in, but after studying the visitor, she pressed the buzzer.

Geoff Stokes walked in and looked around. 'Antonia, glad to see you out. I trust you followed my advice.'

'Always, Geoff. Do you want a drink?'

'If you have a small sherry?'

'There's some left from Christmas.' Jean disappeared into the kitchen.

'Can you get me a coffee, Jean?' Although, despite Antonia's misgivings, they'd arranged to back up their work externally, she'd asked Jean to stay by her desk if they got any more callers, ready to press the 'publish' button in case of another raid.

They set Stokes up on a spare desktop and he read through the notes before examining the latest version of the article. Two hours later, he came into Antonia's office.

'Whoever gave you the memory stick has excellent connections. The evidence supports your article one hundred per cent. You could go further.'

'We're still working on it.'

'Do you want me to check it?'

'If you would.'

'I'm happy to stay. Off the clock, provided you can feed me. It's not every day you help bring down the government.' Stokes looked ten years younger.

She could eat but had ignored her hunger pangs. 'Will Thai do? I'll ask the pub if they'll deliver.'

'Marvellous, shall I speak to Jean about it?'

They ate at their desks, each of them working on their parts of the article until at last both Eleanor and Antonia delivered their respective sections to Grainger to stitch together. Antonia stretched. She'd sleep well tonight. Had they only released her this morning? Full night's sleep tonight and then gym tomorrow evening. Blow the cobwebs away.

Grainger finished and Antonia read it at the same time as Stokes. Although tired, Antonia focused on the article and completed her changes when Stokes finished.

'I'm happy, although many won't be,' Stokes said. 'I'm off to bed and I look forward to waking to the' – he hesitated for several seconds – 'shitstorm, I believe is the term.'

Jean stared at him, open-mouthed. 'Well, I never.'

Antonia finished and gave a copy to Grainger and Eleanor to read. The phone rang, making everyone jump. Jean answered in the next room, then came through, looking startled.

'The inspector, he's on his way.'

'Chapman, what does he want?'

'He didn't say. He asked if you're here, then said he'll get here in two minutes.'

With a growing sense of unease, Antonia waited in the main office with the others. Had he heard something they should know about?

Chapman arrived soon after and charged in, making sure the door closed behind him. 'Have you seen the news?'

'We're working on a story,' Antonia said.

Grainger opened a news browser on his laptop and turned the screen so they could all see it. Despite the damage, Antonia recognised the house straight away. The banner below read, *Former Home Secretary Jilly Bucklin and husband feared dead following a serious fire.*

'Shit! I was way out,' Grainger said.

Chapman turned on him. 'What do you mean?'

'We discussed how long before one of the others did something to stop Bucklin appearing in court. I guessed a few days.'

Antonia watched with horror. 'Why wasn't she in custody?'

'Courtesy afforded a former Home Sec, but I'm here to warn both of you, they're blaming you—'

'What do you mean?'

Grainger's mobile rang, and he answered.

'Malicious Communications Act,' Chapman replied. 'You're both named as people involved in inciting a person or persons unknown to start the fire. I got a call from a friend, so tried ringing your house then called round, but found the police already there. Which is why I came here.'

Grainger ended his call. 'Erika said the police have arrived at our place.'

The doorbell rang and someone hammered on the door. Antonia's mind raced into overdrive. 'Russell, go upstairs with Eleanor. They can't find you here. Jean, let's get this story up—'

'You think that's a good idea?' Chapman said.

'They're only here to stop it. Once it's up, they'll have to back down.'

Chapman accompanied Eleanor to the lift. Hoping she was right, Antonia returned to her desk. They didn't have time for a last check. It would have to go as it was. The banging continued and someone shouted through the door. Her hand trembled as she pressed Send.

'Jean, make sure it uploads.'

CHAPTER 15

Rushing because she'd overslept, and feeling guilty at not having the time to take Nadimah to school on her first day back, Sabirah steeled herself for something she needed to do. She should have done it yesterday. Mrs Curtis was already in the office when Sabirah went down to apologise, using the lift that had caused the problem. She found Mrs Curtis watching the news on Jean's computer. Everyone in the office sat glued to their screens or devices and a funereal atmosphere permeated the office. What had happened?

'Good morning, Mrs Curtis.'

'Hello, Sabirah. Aren't you working with Brody today?'

'I'm going later. Please, can we talk?'

The old lady studied her from her chair. 'Shall we use Antonia's office? She's . . . not in.'

'Jean said they released her yesterday morning.' Sabirah still felt guilty that Antonia was in a cell when she'd gone skating and eating pizza with the children.

'She was. Shall we go through?'

Sabirah followed her and closed the door. She didn't want witnesses to her betrayal. Mrs Curtis waited for her to sit.

'Okay, dear, what's troubling you?'

'We went to a meeting at the town hall about the proposed plans.'

'Did it not go well?'

'I'm so sorry, Mrs Curtis . . .' Her throat closed up.

'Don't upset yourself. I'm sure it's nothing we can't overcome.'

'No, it's not the new place. I'm so sorry.'

'What happened, Sabirah?'

'The lift. They said they won't allow—'

'We'll manage. I'll stay in the cellar. I've worked down here for thirty years.'

Sabirah wasn't doing well. 'The lift here from your apartment. They said you don't have permission.'

'Of course I do. I remember going to the planning appeal.'

'You have permission?'

'Yes. I know I have little respect for our leaders and some of their stupid rules, but I wouldn't flout the law.'

'Do you have papers?'

'Geoff Stokes will. The company who installed insisted on it. I'll ring him.'

Sabirah waited in relief as Mrs Curtis used the phone. The woman at the council must have made a mistake, or had she done it deliberately? Mrs Curtis spoke for a minute or two and then placed the phone down.

'Geoff, I've put you on speaker, Sabirah's here.'

'Sabirah, good morning. I can assure you Eleanor had permission to put the lift in. She made an impassioned speech to the planning committee. I'll get a copy of their letter emailed.' He hesitated. 'Are you two watching the news?'

Mrs Curtis switched on Antonia's screen. 'What's happening?'

'It looks like we might see each other before too long.'

The screen came on and Mrs Curtis clicked the mouse until a news bulletin came on. A woman's voice called Mr Stokes.

'I need to go. I'll let you watch it, Eleanor. Sabirah.'

The line died, and Mrs Curtis replaced the handset, her attention on the screen. It showed a well-known black door with reporters gathered outside. A lectern waited on the pavement. The door opened and cameras flashed. Shouted questions rained on the Prime Minister.

'Is it true . . . ?'

'What have you got to say . . . ?'

'Are you going to resign . . . ?'

He held a hand up for silence, his usual ebullient manner replaced by a downbeat, defeated air.

'I wish to make a statement and will not take questions.' He scanned the sea of faces in front of him, not exchanging the usual friendly greetings. 'You'll be aware of the scurrilous allegations made about me and many of my cabinet colleagues. I wish to state emphatically, there isn't a grain of truth in them. I intend to fight and clear my name and make sure those making these allegations pay.'

Mrs Curtis jabbed a bony finger at the screen. 'Go on then, you phoney.'

'As a first step, we're closing down the site spreading the lies—'

'Jean!' Mrs Curtis muted the sound and shouted through the closed door.

After a few seconds, it opened and Miles appeared. 'They've shut us down.'

'How? We're using the backup servers.'

'I don't know.' Miles looked distressed. 'Jean's looking into it.'

The figure on the screen retreated into his lair.

'What's happened, Mrs Curtis?' Sabirah said.

'We published an article last night, exposing the PM and seven of his cabinet as criminals, illegally profiting from their decisions.'

Even in this country, exposing corruption must be dangerous. Sabirah waved at the screen. 'Is that where Antonia is, asking questions?'

'They arrested her and Rick Grainger last night—'

'Arrested again? But why?' The memory of her arrest still gave Sabirah nightmares.

'They wanted to stop her, but I'm sure they'll release her soon. Don't worry.'

But Mrs Curtis looked anxious. Sabirah's relief she'd not caused her any trouble evaporated.

◆ ◆ ◆

Cowering with Eleanor while colleagues arrested Antonia and Grainger hadn't sat well with Chapman, but he realised it made sense. He'd resisted the temptation to make calls to find out where they'd taken her until this morning and had gone in early.

The discovery of Gunnerson's suspension when he arrived at the station added to his concerns. He'd not expected Professional Standards to move so fast. It wasn't as if she'd do it again. At least he'd told her he'd not dropped her in it. Looks and muttered comments behind his back suggested the rumour that he'd instigated her downfall had travelled as quickly as he'd feared. He'd need to deal with it, but not now. Ignoring them, he made his way to his office.

At eight, he tracked Antonia down to his own station. His initial elation that another dodgy government agency hadn't taken her to a secret location lasted until he learned Harding had taken personal charge of the case. What was he up to? He rang the custody suite and spoke to a sergeant he'd known since he joined.

'Inspector Chapman, I'm surprised you're not in hiding.'

'You as well? How long have you known me?'

'Yeah, I thought it odd. So, what's the story?'

Chapman told him what Harding had done.

'Sounds par for the course. I'll make sure word gets out.'

'Thanks.'

'You won't thank me in a minute. He's left explicit instructions. Nobody's allowed to speak to either prisoner without his permission.'

'What? Even to take them food?'

'Russell, don't even think about it. He'll check the CCTV—'

'He said that?'

'Yus, mate.'

Chapman realised Harding had said this for his benefit. Bastard!

'And, Russell, don't even think about pissing him off. He got his arse kicked for delaying the raid.'

'Do you know why?'

'Cock-up with the paperwork. Blames his inspector, but I heard he'd done it himself and messed up the details.'

Chapman couldn't suppress a chuckle. 'Couldn't have happened to a nicer guy. Thanks for letting me know.' Harding was usually shit-hot on paperwork. His elevation to senior rank must have made him sloppy.

Sanchez's arrival let him know he had more to worry about.

'Morning, Alice. I'm going to have to avoid you if you keep bringing me problems.'

'Sorry, Russell. You heard the mutterings outside.'

'Of course.'

'Well, it's in here as well.'

'Don't tell me. Sanderson.'

'He's not the only one. And they've got good reason—'

'What?'

Sanchez looked uncomfortable. 'I'll let them tell you.'

The chill atmosphere as he walked into the main office told him Sanchez hadn't exaggerated. 'Right, guys, gather round.'

They gathered in a horseshoe.

'You've obviously heard the bullshit rumours. I can assure you, they're not true. You all know me and it's not my style.'

After an awkward silence, Louisa Walker spoke. 'Yeah, that's what I thought, boss, but then we heard Harding offered you her job.'

'What?' Harding! 'The sneaky bastard. I'm not taking it. He can shove it where the sun don't shine.' He turned about and headed for the door.

'Boss, don't do anything stupid.' Sanchez followed him out of the office. 'Russell!'

He ignored her and marched to Harding's office, ready to rip his head off. The chief super's secretary also tried to impede him, but he ignored *her* and barged into the station commander's office. Harding sat talking to two uniformed officers. Chapman recognised his ex, now a chief inspector with Professional Standards. He didn't recall meeting the other one.

'What the hell are you doing, Inspector?' a red-faced Harding demanded.

'I came to tell you, you can shove the DCI's job.'

Harding's expression changed. 'I don't know what you're talking about, Inspector, but you're already in enough trouble without adding insubordination.'

'I'm in trouble? What are you talking about?'

'These officers are investigating DCI Gunnerson and spoke to the witness who claims you tried to bully him into changing his story.'

'Bullshit.'

'That's enough, Inspector!' Harding slapped the desk, his face crimson. 'Now get out of here before I suspend you. And don't even try to speak to the witness. He's given us a statement and if you so much as ring him, I'll make sure you're charged with perverting the course of justice.'

'Excuse me, sir.' The officer Chapman didn't recognise spoke to Harding.

'Yes?'

'What we spoke about before, Inspector Chapman speaking to the suspect?'

'Oh, yes. Have you spoken to DCI Gunnerson since I asked you to investigate her?'

'She's my line manager. Did you want me to blank her?'

Harding ground his teeth. 'Apart from at work.'

'Why would I?'

'Answer the question.'

'Am I under caution?'

'Not yet.'

He left before he said anything that could come back to bite him. When had they interviewed the witness? Chapman hadn't told Harding his findings until yesterday. The bastard must have already called these vultures before he spoke to Chapman. He'd been set up, and he'd fallen for it. *Stupid idiot!*

Without warning, two officers collected Antonia from her cell and told her they were releasing her. Why? They still had another ten hours they could hold them, and the red-faced creep who'd interviewed her had suggested he'd request extra time to hold her, although she wasn't sure why. He seemed to be going through the motions rather than seriously interrogating her. She understood why Chapman hated him so much.

An unsmiling constable took her to the custody desk where the sergeant greeted her. 'Ms Conti, I'm pleased to let you know we're releasing you on pre-charge bail.'

'On bail? Are you serious?'

'Don't you want to go?'

She'd sort it later. 'Where do I sign?'

He placed a tablet on the desk and passed her a stylus. 'Please read and sign here.'

She checked what it said and scribbled her signature. 'Where's the stuff you took off me?'

'Here it is, miss.' The custody sergeant passed her a plastic envelope. 'Can you please check it and sign here?' He swiped the tablet to produce a second form.

It didn't take her long to check her things. 'Where's my tube of powder?'

He revealed a disclaimer. *We may not return some items if possessing them is illegal, or we have concerns about their use.*

'It's not illegal to own or use ghost powder.'

'That's why they add the second bit.'

'I need it for my self-protection, so dodgy people can't track me down.' She intended to go straight to the office, so didn't care if they tracked her, but it was the principle.

'Sorry. You can make a claim.'

'Forget it.' She used the stylus to scrawl her signature.

'Antonia, did they say why they're letting you go?' Grainger came out from the cells.

'No. Have they told you?'

'Nope.'

They both regarded the desk sergeant. 'Sorry, just told to release you both. You're on pre-charge bail as well, Mr Grainger. Here are your belongings.'

She waited for Grainger to check his property. Chapman worked at this station. Had he taken the day off? 'Is Inspector Chapman on duty?'

'He did ring earlier, miss, but the boss restricted visitors. I'll let him know we've released you.'

'Thanks.' She'd wondered why he'd not even called to see how she was.

Once Grainger finished his checks, they made their way out of the station.

'God, what an arsehole Harding is,' Grainger said.

'Russell has a particular antipathy to him. I hadn't realised he worked here now. Poor Russell.'

'Boss from hell or what? But your Mr Stokes tied him up in knots. He didn't like that. I thought he'd explode.'

'Geoff's excellent. He charges plenty, but worth every penny. Are you getting off home?' Although her body needed rest, her mind fizzed with energy, elated to be released.

'I wanted to see what's happened with our story first. Erika doesn't know I'm out, so won't worry if I don't go straight home.'

They flagged down a cab on Edgware Road and sat in comfortable silence as it took them to Vincent Terrace. Antonia realised something wasn't right as soon as they arrived. A dour dullness had replaced yesterday's bubbling enthusiasm.

'Miles, what's up?'

'Antonia. They've released you. What happened?'

'We're on bail. What's gone on here? You all look depressed, and it can't be just because we've returned.'

His smile faded. 'They've accused us of spreading misinformation and closed the site down.'

Her elation following her release evaporated. 'Closed down. Don't we have a server they can't reach?'

'Their president's a mate of our PM, so they pulled strings.'

'What time?'

'Around four this morning.'

'So, nobody's reading our story? Nobody will have seen it so early in the morning.' She slumped in the nearest chair.

'Some people have picked it up.' Miles injected optimism into his voice. 'A Chinese news website has copied some of it and broadcast it.'

'How many people will see it?' *Don't snap, Antonia, it's not his fault.* 'Sorry, I'm just disappointed.'

'I understand, and I'm worried about Eleanor.' Miles's demeanour became mournful. 'Spreading misinformation is a serious charge. She's still the publisher. She could end up doing ten years.'

'Where is she?'

'I'm here.' With a whirr, she wheeled herself out of Antonia's office. 'I'm trying to see if we can get someone else to pick the story up, but everyone's too scared or doesn't want to believe it.'

'Who have you tried?' Grainger asked. 'I could ask Elfyn.'

'I thought you came here because he wouldn't touch it,' Antonia said.

'That's before we'd collected all this evidence. Shall I try him?'

'I didn't think it's worth bothering, but he might listen to you. What do you think, Antonia?' Eleanor sounded defeated.

Antonia hated the thought of handing the story to a rival, but did they have a choice? 'Go on. Do you want to use my office?'

Eleanor and Antonia followed him and waited in silence while Grainger rang his old employer. The feeling of helplessness, of having to rely on another, gnawed at Antonia. Grainger negotiated the labyrinth of gatekeepers until he got through to his old editor and put the phone on speaker.

'You phoning for your old job back?'

'Hi, Elfyn, why would I do that?'

'Because the shitrag you've joined has gone under. I warned you not to touch the story.'

Antonia wanted to tell Elfyn where he could go. She exchanged a look with Eleanor. This wasn't going well.

'It's a good story, Elfyn. Have you read it?'

'Yeah. And by good, do you mean something which will get your arse sued? I don't know what possessed you.'

Antonia didn't need to hear any more and signalled to Grainger to cut the call.

'You used to have balls, Elfyn, but the lure of a knighthood must be—'

'Don't talk to me about balls. You're letting an old cripple and her piccaninny boss—'

Antonia snatched the handset from Grainger. 'Do you want to call me that to my face?'

After a moment's silence, the line died.

'I guess it's a no, then.' Eleanor gave a rueful smile.

'Sorry, Antonia, Eleanor.' Grainger sat red-faced.

'Not your fault your old boss is an arsehole.' Antonia's eyes prickled with tears of anger and frustration. 'I'll ring a few people.'

Grainger got up. 'I'm really sorry.'

Antonia waved his apology away as she took her seat. She'd try those blogs she'd considered when the government locked their site.

'I need a drink. Do you want anything, Antonia?' Eleanor said.

'Coffee please, thank you.' She looked up the contact details for the blogs and sent each an email outlining the story and what had happened. She got one reply straight away.

Thanks for the offer but we've heard there are issues with the veracity of your article and can't risk publishing it as it could adversely affect our application for a licence.

Eleanor returned with the drinks. 'Bad news?'

'From one.' Antonia showed her the email.

'How many more did you approach?'

'Four.'

By the time two more had replied with similar responses, Antonia knew they'd not get any positive answers. 'Someone's got at them.'

'Hasn't Rick got contacts in Europe?'

'France and Germany, I think. Rick!' she shouted through the open door.

He appeared in the doorway. 'Have you seen this?' He held up his laptop and placed it on the desk between Antonia and Eleanor.

It showed a headline on *The Washington Post* website.

British government implicated in corruption scandal.

Explosive allegations made by influential London-based, anti-corruption news outlet, The Electric Investigator, *exposing the extent of corruption at the top of British politics.*

They summarised the allegations and ended with a report confirming the UK government had taken down *The Investigator*'s website.

'They must be interested in printing our story,' Grainger said. 'We used to share stories with sister papers at my last place.'

Why didn't I think of that? 'I'll ask. I've got the email for the editor somewhere. They did our story on memory replacement.'

Her phone rang. 'Antonia, it's a man from America—'

That was quick. '*Washington Post?*'

'*New York Times*, I think.'

'Put him through.'

'Hi, am I speaking to Antonio Conti?'

'Antonia. How can I help you?'

'Sorry, Antonia,' a throaty transatlantic voice said. 'I'm foreign news editor at *The New York Times* and wondered if you'd be willing to let us publish your article on the UK government corruption. We'd offer the usual terms.'

Antonia had no clue what these were. 'Sure, let me have your email.' She noted this down and ended the call. '*New York Times* wants to do the story.'

'That's fantastic.' Grainger wore a huge smile.

Over the rest of the afternoon, a series of US outlets contacted *The Investigator* wanting to share the story. The funereal atmosphere changed – it became more like the office of a news outlet that had broken an enormous story. Nobody wanted to leave, and by seven, when *The Los Angeles Times* got in touch, a party atmosphere pervaded the main office.

'We've still got to get our site back up.' Antonia hated every minute *her* site remained down.

Half an hour later, a cheer in the outer office dragged her from her desk, where she composed an email to yet another Canadian newspaper. Sawyer stood surrounded by clapping colleagues.

'Jean's got the site back up,' Miles announced.

'How?'

Pink-cheeked, Sawyer waited for the applause to end. 'We'd backed everything up, so I found a server which would host us in Vilnius.'

'Well done, Jean.' Antonia returned to her desk and clicked on the site.

There it was, without the official Licenced News Enterprise logo, but their site, and people were already commenting on the headline story. Would they come down harder on Eleanor because she'd put it back up? She guessed it wouldn't bother her. She'd want it back, broadcasting, at least as much as Antonia did. The breaking news banner at the bottom of her screen caught her attention.

Eleanor wheeled herself into the office, two glasses of Prosecco on the tray clamped to her wheelchair. 'I thought we should celebrate Jean's success.'

'You know this could make it worse for you.'

She waved a hand, almost upsetting the glasses. 'Who cares?'

Antonia laughed. 'There's a story breaking.' She clicked on the banner and a street scene opened. A reporter spoke to camera.

'The Prime Minister's official spokesperson has confirmed the rumour the PM has resigned. There's no news on whether he'll make a statement, but it's believed the resignation is linked to serious allegations made in an article in The Electric Investigator *in the early hours of this morning. We believe other ministers have also resigned and we'll bring you more on those stories later.'*

A black limousine sped past with the Prime Minister's grim-faced wife in the back.

Antonia and Eleanor looked at each other for a long moment. Taking care not to upset the drinks, Antonia stood and hugged her adoptive mother.

CHAPTER 16

'Jean wanted to know if you'll have time to go through her investigation today, Antonia. She's concerned about something she's discovered.'

'Can you not discuss it with her?' Antonia dragged her attention from her screen and studied Eleanor.

'You're her editor.'

'Yes, you're right. Sorry, I'm up to my eyes. I've got an interview with *The Sydney Morning Herald* to prepare for.'

'It's all very well being the darling of the world's press, but we've got to focus on our output. How many new stories have we broken in the four weeks since the PM resigned?'

'We've done follow-ups and profiles of all the politicians in the new cabinet.'

'Fluff and window dressing.' Eleanor waved a dismissive hand. 'We're investigative journalists. We tell the truths about powerful people that they don't want told. That's our purpose and we're not doing it.'

The barb hurt because it contained the truth. 'Okay, I'll go through it with her this afternoon.'

'Don't forget, Sabirah's going over the plans for your new office suite this afternoon.'

She had forgotten. 'Of course not.'

'And when's Rick back from Paris? We need him working on something substantial, not swanning around the continent giving interviews.'

'He only left this morning.'

'Yes, but he went to Frankfurt last week and only came back two days ago.'

'He's raising our profile in Europe. We've increased our reader-ship in France, Germany and Italy.'

'They won't stay with us if we don't give them more meat. We've broken big stories before, but we can't afford to sit on our laurels.'

'Okay, I hear you.'

After extracting a promise to get Grainger back in harness, and to progress Sawyer's article, Eleanor left Antonia in peace.

The proposed questions from the Sydney paper followed a familiar pattern, and Antonia rehearsed her replies in the lead-up to the interview. Although she'd been terrified before the first interview she'd given, on the day after the story exploded across the globe, she'd done so many in the last month they'd become almost routine. Careful not to become blasé, Antonia took the interview in her stride and presented herself and *The Investigator* in a good light.

After the interview, she made careful notes about the people she'd spoken to. She now had an excellent network of professionals who worked for publications around the world. Previous stories had generated international interest, but nothing on this scale. Mindful of Eleanor's criticism, she made notes on stories that could become bigger investigations. None would be as big as the last one, so few were, but she needed to make sure she kept the publication interesting.

Sabirah knocked on the door and came in, her smart suit a world away from the baggy tracksuits she'd worn when Antonia first met her and they both cleaned the offices of GRM.

'Are you ready to look round next door, Antonia?' Her enthusiasm made her skin glow.

Antonia couldn't help but respond. 'Sure, shall we go?' She followed her friend out into the bright sunshine. An eight-foot-high fence separated the neighbouring house from the pavement and a large sign on it announced Sabirah Fadil as the architectural consultant on the project. Behind the fence were a half-empty skip and a site office where each of them signed in and collected a bright yellow hard hat and high-vis jacket. Neat scaffolding sheathed the building up to roof height.

Antonia followed Sabirah up the steps and into the house. The builders had removed the rubbish and graffiti they'd encountered on Antonia's last visit and left bare tile, floorboards and brickwork. The odour of fresh-cut timber pervaded the atmosphere, and the hum of voices and whine of power tools filled the air.

She followed Sabirah into the front room where three electricians attached ducting to the bare bricks and passed cables through openings in the floor. 'I can't believe the difference in the place.'

'We've worked hard. They're starting the first fix. These cables lead down to the server, which will be in a temperature-controlled chamber. We'll have a high-speed fibre-optic system to connect the computers, for speed and security. Do you want to see your new office upstairs? We've finished the structural work.'

They walked into the hallway and up the elegant stairs. The lift engineers worked on the framework of the lift, which would enable Eleanor to access her new empire. 'I thought you had problems with the planning for a lift.'

Sabirah smiled. 'They tried, but Eleanor and Mr Stokes argued we needed it. We will hide it behind panelling, so they agreed.'

They reached the landing and teams of tradesmen filled the reclaimed rooms. As soon as they saw Sabirah, they swarmed round her, firing questions and demanding decisions. Antonia watched her friend, amazed and happy to see her transformation from a timid and uncertain refugee to a confident professional woman happy in her environment.

She finished answering queries and led Antonia into the back room. Light flooded in through two large windows.

'Do you remember the kitchen here?' Sabirah walked over to the window. 'The partition here down the middle of the window and the bedroom on the other side?'

'How could I forget?' When Sabirah outlined her vision for the room, Antonia had found it impossible to believe that the pokey rooms with ill-fitting partitions and false ceilings would one day become the light, elegant space Sabirah had described and Antonia could now see.

Sabirah pointed out of the window. 'We'll landscape the garden and install seating areas linked to the server. On days like today, you can work down there.'

'Instead of a gloomy cellar.'

Sabirah smiled.

Antonia indicated the wire mesh attached to the brickwork. 'What's this on the walls?'

'It will shield this room from electromagnetic radiation. You can't use a mobile without an external aerial, but it protects everything said in here from anyone listening. We discussed?'

'Yeah, sure.' Antonia hadn't realised it would include her entire office, but she could live with it.

They continued the tour into the second floor and attic space. Not only would they have plenty of room for existing staff, but they could double their number without getting crowded. The thought daunted Antonia. She couldn't manage much more than she did now. Twice the work would mean she'd have no time to do her own investigations. Not something she intended to give up.

She left Sabirah talking to two workmen installing a replacement window. Something about one of them struck her as familiar, and not in a good way. Antonia wracked her memory to recall where she'd seen him, but with her mind on her forthcoming meeting with Sawyer, she couldn't remember. The signing-in book wasn't much help. Maybe it was someone she'd encountered in passing. There were plenty of those.

She rushed back to the office. Desks sat too close together, and it looked too full and gloomy. Now she'd seen the new offices, she couldn't wait to move in.

Sawyer waited in Antonia's office.

'You're late, Antonia.'

'Sorry, Jean, Sabirah took me next door to look at our new offices. You'll have twice as much room, at least. And the cyber-security should satisfy even you.'

'Sabirah took me round last night, in my *own* time. I didn't keep people waiting.'

'Okay, Jean, what's the problem?' She obsessed over punctuality, but it had never manifested in such overt hostility.

'I've investigated the insider dealing for six weeks now and I've accumulated a huge amount of evidence.'

'That's why we're sitting here. I'm going to go through it with you and we can outline the story so you can focus on filling in any gaps.'

'But Rick said *he* wants to investigate it.'

'What do you mean? We've not discussed anything about his next project.'

Sawyer looked uncomfortable. 'I don't enjoy telling tales, but I found him looking at my laptop this morning—'

'You always lock it.'

'I popped next door to show Tomasz something he wasn't sure about. I didn't expect anyone to go snooping.'

'Okay, I'll speak to him on his return.'

'He said he was working on the story now. But you gave it to me.'

'I did. He must have misunderstood. I've not discussed it with Rick once.' In fact, she'd not discussed any stories with Grainger, and hoped he'd come to her with his own. It was one reason they'd taken him on, and why he got paid so much.

'You want me to carry on?'

'Of course. You've done such a lot of excellent work on it. Shall we see how far you've got?'

'If you say so.' Although mollified, Sawyer remained upset.

Antonia would need to speak to Grainger. Although he'd do a better job than Sawyer – in addition to his years of broad experience, he'd bring a personal touch to the article Sawyer couldn't match – Antonia wasn't prepared to let him take stories off her other reporters.

An email arrived in Chapman's inbox reminding him of something he'd almost forgotten. Wanting to make sure he'd not misunderstood it, he rang the inspector who'd sent it.

'Yeah, we got the verdict yesterday and the two guys are going down for extortion, demanding money with menaces, kidnapping and torture. They'll be away for a very long time.'

'What if they appeal?' Chapman said.

'They're bound to, but it could take years. We can't justify keeping Hughes in remand until they've exhausted the appeal process. We've got the witness statements into the court. I doubt Hughes will bother trying to intimidate them now. No point. Anyway, once the guys are off the streets, replacements will move in. Within six months, people will forget who they are, and they'll have no status. We're going to seize their assets, so someone like Hughes won't work for them. That's if he's around in six months.'

'Doesn't it depress you?'

'What?'

'This endlessness. You take one down and within six months, another's doing the same.'

'You reckon we should just leave them in place?'

'No, I heard it from one of my bosses. He kept the kingpins in place to keep the others under control and snitch on the newcomers. He got plenty of arrests, but I discovered he was also on the take.' And it almost cost me my job, Chapman could have added.

'If we got rid of them once and for all, we'd be out of a job.'

'One way of looking at things. When will you let him go?'

'Anytime, but I thought if you saw him, tell him you've sorted out his release, he'll be more likely to speak to your contact.'

'Great, I'll get down there soon as and let you know. And thanks for this, I won't forget it.'

Chapman ended the call and checked his diary. He had a meeting with the temporary DCI, still covering for the suspended Gunnerson, at four, but he should get to see Hughes and get back in time. He buzzed Sanchez, who came through.

'What's up, Alice?'

She checked she'd shut the door behind her. 'That bloody arsehole Harding brought in to replace the boss. He's got me analysing how much time we spend on paperwork and how we can cut it down with better training.'

'Why don't you tell him you'd spend a damn sight less time if he didn't ask you to do his stupid projects.'

'Shitty, pointless paperwork. I wish I'd applied for the Child Protection job now.'

Chapman didn't want to lose Sanchez, especially if she only got a transfer to avoid this Harding-clone. If she applied for a sideways move, he knew of a dozen teams who'd snap her up. 'I've got a meeting with him at four, so I'll bring it up.'

'Don't make it bloody worse, Russell.'

'How dare you, Sergeant? I've never made things worse.'

'Sure you haven't. Have Professional Standards lifted their investigation yet?'

'Not yet.' Although he ignored the threat of it hanging over him most of the time, he should speak to Gunnerson, find out how she was coping, but hadn't so far. He'd go and see her soon and sod them. 'I'm popping out to Bradwell.'

'You can't stay away from the place, especially after what you said last time you went. I'm assuming the boss is happy about it.'

'He'll only find out if you tell him.'

'What if he asks?'

'He won't. He'll be counting paperclips. And if he does, I'm sure you'll come up with something.'

'Aren't you interviewing those witnesses to the lorry hijacking?' She winked.

'I spoke to them yester— Cheers, Alice, of course I am. Ring me if anything happens.'

He made good time. Some schools had already broken up for the summer and this reduced the traffic. In three weeks, he'd take Abby and Nadimah to Northumberland. He'd wanted somewhere hot, but Nadimah still didn't own a passport. A week in this country with two teenage girls would present enough of a challenge.

Even the desolate landscape as he approached the prison didn't seem as grim in the sunshine. He'd hoped the last-minute nature of his visit would mean they hadn't prepared a reception committee for him this time. The fact they took him straight to the interview room suggested they hadn't. Hughes looked more ragged and bedraggled than ever. His oft-broken nose bore signs of recent violence and his wiry arms evidence of defensive cuts on the forearms.

'You upset someone in here?'

'What's it to you?' Hughes thrust his jaw forward.

'I'm the person who can get you out.'

'So you said, but here I am.' He waved an expansive hand around the small room.

'If I recall, you couldn't give me an assurance you'd give us the information we need.'

'I told you, I'm not a snitch.'

'Okay.' Chapman reached for the buzzer to summon the guards.

'I'll speak to the girl, but not you cu— lot.'

'When?'

'You get me out of here and I'll talk to her the next day.' He grinned. 'Better give me a couple of days to sleep it off.'

'You mess me about . . .'

'And what?'

Chapman held his glare. 'How do you think your mate got his limp?'

Hughes unclenched his fists. 'Get me released, and I'll give you the rest of him.'

Still wary from his last visit, Chapman didn't relax until he reached the car park. His stomach rumbled as he started the car. He'd missed lunch. One thing about coming here, the sea air made him hungry, but he didn't have time to stop. The petrol-station sandwich and crisps he ended up with, washed down with an energy drink, weren't what he needed, and Abby would certainly have an opinion if she found out.

He made the station with ten minutes to spare and rushed up to the office. Greville Sanderson, counting down his last few months before retirement, sat on his own. Had Chapman missed a shout? He'd kept the radio on. He checked his phone. Nothing.

'Where's everyone, Grev?'

'Training on using the new reporting system. They decided I wasn't worth training.'

'You'll have gone before it comes in. I'm off to see the DCI if anyone asks.'

'No problem, boss.'

Deciding he didn't have time for a coffee, Chapman retrieved a couple of mints from his top drawer. He needed to get rid of the taste of the crap he'd eaten at lunchtime. He arrived dead on time, but the TDCI made him wait. Chapman listened at the door but heard no voices. Five minutes later, he heard, 'Come,' through the door.

The TDCI sat behind his desk, his thin face topped by a high forehead winning the battle with his hairline. 'Sorry to keep you waiting, Russ, I got a call from the chief super, and you know what he's like.' He gave a 'we're-all-in-this-together' grin.

'It's Russell.' He sat without waiting for an invitation.

'Of course, Russell. Take a seat.'

They looked at each other for several seconds. 'You called me in?' Chapman said.

'Where have you been?'

'We had a nasty hijacking over the weekend. Driver and his mate are still in hospital. We needed a statement.' He doubted he'd check the dates on the statements Chapman took yesterday.

'Oh, right? They okay?'

'They'll live, but the driver probably won't work again. Did you want to see me about something else? You arranged this yesterday.'

'Sorry, yeah. As you know, we've had issues with officers getting too close to the press and leaking stuff.'

'Yeah, Leveson identified it ten years ago, and it went on long before then.' *I bet you weren't even in the job ten years ago.*

'Of course, but more recently, some officers have forgotten which side they're working for.'

'I thought we worked for the public.'

'Of course we do. But sometimes law enforcement means we must make tough decisions. You know, people who'd normally be on our side aren't any more.'

'Not sure I'm following you.' Chapman had no intention of giving him an easy ride.

'Right, well, it's a hard concept for some people to grasp. Here's a memo the chief super has prepared. You're to sign one copy and keep the other.'

> *Let all officers be in no doubt. Sharing police intelligence with members of the public, and in particular, the press, without my express permission, will be a disciplinary matter.*

Underneath, they'd printed the relevant sections from the disciplinary code, leaving a space to print and sign your name.

'This is all covered by our contract.'

'Of course. Mr Harding wants everyone to be aware of it.'

'I'm aware of it.'

'Great, you won't mind signing it then.'

'I don't need to. As I've explained, I signed a contract with this clause when I joined. You're not changing anything, so why do I need to sign it?'

'Because Mr Harding wants to make sure everyone is—' He gave an exasperated sigh. 'Look, everyone else has signed it.'

Chapman fixed him with his gaze. 'If you want to insist, I'll speak to my rep and see what the Fed have to say about this.'

'Look, Russ. Russell. It's no big deal.'

'Okay. Can I take a copy to show my rep?' Chapman took one before the DCI could object. 'Who else have you asked to sign this?'

His eyes darted. 'Nobody's refused.'

'Okay, if that's all, I'll see you.' He got up and walked out. Had Harding somehow discovered he'd warned Antonia and Grainger of the impending raid? They could have tracked his car using the camera system. But it had been five weeks ago. Why bring this up now?

CHAPTER 17

The fact *The Investigator* was looking into the company his wife worked for preyed on Grainger's mind during his stay in Paris. And the summons back to London had really pissed him off. He'd planned to stay for the weekend and have Erika join him, but he'd had to go into the office on a Friday.

Did Antonia know his wife worked for JN Partners? He'd said nothing to Erika, but that couldn't continue, especially if the article implicated her. But in what? He'd known Jacinda Nieto had ruffled feathers in her rise to the top, but who in her position hadn't? But she didn't warrant a full investigation.

The workmen next door had already started when he arrived at the office and so had Antonia. He took his coffee and knocked on her door. 'Can I have a word, Antonia?'

'Come in. How was Paris?'

'Interesting. They asked if they can interview you for a profile piece. They're impressed by what you've done here.'

'This is Eleanor's baby. I'm a newcomer.'

'Sure, but what you've done since you took over is impressive. There's also your background – ex-refugee rising to the top.'

She looked uncomfortable. 'I've no interest in becoming the story.'

'I told them you wouldn't want to do it, but said I'd ask.' An awkward silence filled the room. 'Antonia, I appreciate you're my boss, but did you need to summon me back?'

'I asked when you're planning to return to work.'

'You implied I wasn't pulling my weight. I was promoting *The Investigator* on French TV. I wasn't on a jolly.'

'Yes, I saw your interview, but I need you working on the next story.'

'Yeah, I *do* know how this business works. I'm not a newbie—'

'And I am?'

'No, that's not what I meant.'

She seemed to search for what to say. 'You're our senior reporter and I need you working on a new story. You made a fantastic start, but we need to move forward.'

'Like a shark.'

'Sorry?'

'Elfyn used to say a newspaper is like a shark. If it stops going forward, it dies.' He shouldn't have mentioned Elfyn.

Antonia glanced at her screen. 'Can we discuss your next project? I've prepared a list of stories I want you to consider—'

'I've got my own I wanted to work on. We discussed it when you took me on. I thought you wanted me to generate my material.'

'Yes, we did. Have you got something in mind?'

'I'm looking into a couple of lines of enquiry.' He wasn't ready to discuss the story a conversation with his wife had put him on to. Especially as Antonia was already investigating Erika's employer.

'Can you tell me what they are?'

'I've been following the developments in Zungharistan. We could do the story behind this dispute with the UK government. I went there with my wife last year and made a few contacts.' He hated lying to Antonia, but he could do this story while working on the other one and keep her off his back.

'We rarely focus on foreign stories. Is there anything else you're working on?'

He hesitated. 'A couple of items, but I'd rather not go into details. At least not until I know there's something to investigate. I'm superstitious about these things. I don't discuss them until I'm sure there's a solid story there.'

'Do they involve insider dealing?'

'I'd rather not say.'

She frowned. Had she made a mistake taking Grainger on? 'How long will it take to have something you can show me?'

'I can't say. I'm seeing people and gathering information all the time. You can't hurry these things. The last one took six months to get to the point I knew I had a story worth pursuing. Sometimes you have to accumulate the evidence.'

'Of course, but we've got a small team here and I can't afford to have anyone, let alone someone of your profile—'

'And salary?'

'Yeah, that as well. I'll email you the list of stories I want you to work on. You tell me which you want to do, and you can work on it while you gather information for your own project.'

'Yeah, okay.'

'There's something else I want to talk to you about.'

'Same here, but you go first.'

She looked ready to argue, but didn't. 'You told Jean you intended to take over the story she's working on. That will not happen. I decide who works on which story and she's already done a lot of work on it.'

'I didn't say I'd be taking it over.'

'It's the impression Jean got.'

'Yeah, sorry, she sometimes gets the wrong impression.'

'Jean's very literal. I thought you'd have spotted that by now.'

'Yeah, I have.' He cast around for a way to broach his concerns. 'I'm worried what Jean's working on will affect me and my family.'

'What do you mean?'

'My wife works for JN Partners.'

Antonia's eyes widened. 'I didn't know. What does she do?'

'Financial director.'

'Right. What's her name?'

'Erika Voight.'

'I've not seen her name in the investigations. Hang on, I'll do a search.' She punched the keyboard, then read from the screen.

Grainger wanted so much to crane round and read with her but restrained himself. 'Is she mentioned?'

'Hang on . . . No. No evidence of her involvement.' Antonia bit her lip. 'This goes no further—'

'If it affects my wife, all bets are off.'

'What about if it affects her boss?'

'Jacinda Nieto is tough, but I don't think she's a crook.'

'What do you know about her?'

'She comes to our house, and we go to hers, but we're not bosom pals or anything.'

'You wouldn't feel obliged to warn her if we're investigating her?'

'It's obvious you are. Do you want to tell me what you're looking at?'

'Does this name mean anything?' Antonia glanced at the screen and read out a name.

'Yeah, he was Erika's predecessor, but died in a skiing accident. Why?'

'Jean thinks they killed him because of a disagreement over some of Nieto's deals.'

Grainger's insides chilled.

'You okay, Rick?'

'Yeah, sorry. Erika had some issues with accessing some of his records. Jacinda told her not to worry about it. They had rows. Erika's very conscientious and is still pushing to get them.'

'Are you going to tell her what I've told you?'

'I don't know. I can't just leave her there, knowing what you've told me.'

◆　◆　◆

Following his run-in with the TDCI, Chapman took every opportunity to get off station. A comment he overheard in the canteen, where most people now accepted he hadn't stabbed Gunnerson in the back, got him thinking. Back in the office, he addressed the team.

'I want us to re-examine the spate of hijackings we looked at after last weekend's attack.'

'We have, boss, and found no links.' Louisa Walker sounded frustrated. 'We looked at the freight companies, depots used and the companies sending or receiving the goods. There's no link. There isn't even a common denominator with the type of cargo.'

'But where did the drivers come from?'

'Most of them were local,' Sanchez said, 'but you'd expect that. Why?'

'No, I mean, who employed them?'

'What you thinking?'

'What if the agency supplying the drivers is tipping off the robbers?'

'Bloody hell, what a scam.' Darren Baxter leant back in his chair, which let out an ominous creak.

'Right, I'll get the list and share it out.' Sanchez returned to her desk.

'Can you also look at lorries stolen from services and car parks?'

Sanderson winced. 'There will be loads, boss.'

'You'd better make a start then, hadn't you, Grev?' Chapman returned to his office and checked nothing urgent had arrived.

The email confirming Hughes's release included contact details, as he remained on licence for a previous sentence. The phone went straight to voicemail, so Chapman left a message. He checked the address. Not somewhere you'd want to visit on your own. If he didn't get a reply, he might take Darren Baxter with him and pay a visit.

He told Sanchez he needed to see the driver of the hijacked lorry, to find out which agency he worked for. The man lived near Gunnerson, so he intended to see her on the way home. It didn't take him long to confirm the driver worked for three agencies. A pain, but they should narrow it down as they spoke to more drivers. At least his theory had legs. He texted Sanchez the details before going to Gunnerson's house.

'Russell, what a pleasant surprise.' She looked ten years younger, as if her suspension had taken a weight off her shoulders.

He followed her into a kitchen they'd extended into a conservatory overlooking a neat lawn. 'Is this new?'

'We got it done when Rex got diagnosed. We'd always wanted one, and we needed a downstairs bathroom, so did it together. Coffee?'

He stroked a sleeping cat as he waited for his drink. After an awkward silence, he said, 'How are you coping?'

'Fine. The clowns from Professional Standards have interviewed me twice. But apart from that, I'm enjoying the sunshine and the garden. No end of visitors. I'm treating it like a rehearsal for retirement.'

'Are you coming back?' How many people would visit him in the same circumstance?

'If they clear me.'

'They will, won't they?'

She held his gaze. 'You never know. But if they do, I need another thirteen months to get the maximum pension, so I intend to return.'

'Thank God. They've put a Harding clone in your place.'

'I heard. You didn't think anyone could be worse, did you?' Her smile faded. 'When I learned about Harding's games, to get you ostracised. I've told everyone it wasn't you.'

'It's helped. Nobody's given me a hard time about it.'

'You once said you had something you could use to get back at him.'

'Did I?' He'd considered it more than once but decided it could blow back on him *and* Antonia. 'Just bravado. You know what blokes are like.'

'Bullshit, Russell. I told you I helped Rex on his way. Now spill.'

'You didn't actually tell me, and I'm assuming you're teasing me now.'

'Maybe I am. What *have* you got on Harding?'

He'd give a much-edited version, one that didn't implicate him and Antonia in murder. 'He and his wife processed a crime scene before we got notified about it. And I'm talking about a serious crime.'

Gunnerson whistled. 'She's a senior CSI, isn't she?'

'Yep, and I'm pretty sure they did it for Gustav Reed-Mayhew.'

She whistled again. 'Bloody hell, Russell, you don't mess about.' She sipped her drink. 'How's Reed-Mayhew linked?'

'He owned the building, and he'd visited it earlier. Also, two of the people who turned up with Harding have close links to Reed-Mayhew.'

'You're saying Reed-Mayhew committed the crime?'

'Not that one.'

'What have you got on Harding?'

'Footage of him and his wife arriving at the scene with the two people I mentioned and leaving three hours later.'

'If you're sure it won't touch Reed-Mayhew, then I'd use it now—'

'Why?'

'I've heard he's determined to do you, and he's got something planned.'

'Yeah, he tried to set me up with your case—'

'It's something else, something he's found out recently. Watch your back, Russell. I'm looking forward to seeing your smiling face when I come back.'

Much as she loved what she did, Sabirah sometimes wished she could return to the simplicity of working as a cleaner. No worrying if a particular contractor would get his job done in time to enable the next step to progress, or if the suppliers would let you down. And having time to spend with the children would be a big bonus. She'd not been able to take them to and collect them from school, but still ate meals with them twice a day, even if she no longer had time to cook their favourite Syrian treats. Even something as simple as manakish took too much effort.

She made her way down from the attic of the new house. She'd arranged a meeting with Nadimah's headmistress in half an hour and she didn't want to be late. It clashed with the delivery of the steel for the framework of the lift mechanism this afternoon, and she wanted to oversee it, but the Head refused to reschedule. Obviously annoyed Sabirah had forced her hand. She wasn't too worried. Their foreman was excellent and so were the lift engineers.

She reached the ground floor without too many interruptions and, leaving her safety clothing in the hut, signed out and left the site. The crane had arrived in Vincent Terrace and the crew manoeuvred it into position outside. She expected a few neighbours would complain, but Mrs Curtis would deal with them.

She arrived at the school, warm from having hurried but with time to spare, and reported to reception. The difference in how she felt compared to the first time she came astounded her. She came to assert her rights, not beg acceptance. Nadimah waited outside the Head's office and Sabirah couldn't resist straightening her tie.

'Mum. Mamma, please.'

'Don't fuss. Are you ready for the meeting?'

'I suppose so.'

She sat next to her daughter. 'Always prepare for meetings. Make sure you anticipate everything which might happen.' She'd not articulated Rashid's advice to her for a long time, and the reminder of how much she missed him hit her like a blow.

Nadimah slipped her arm through hers. 'You okay, Mamma?'

She blinked and took her hand. 'Of course I'm fine. Just thinking about work.'

A tall bald man she didn't recognise came into the waiting room and gave them a disapproving look. Nadimah untangled her hand as the man knocked on the Head's door and entered.

'He's in charge of the exams,' Nadimah whispered.

Two minutes later, the Head called them in. The bald man sat on her left, still scowling.

'Please sit, Mrs Fadil, Nadimah.'

Two chairs sat in front of the Head's desk, both lower than those of the two teachers'. Sabirah couldn't suppress a smile as the Head introduced her colleague.

'We've decided about the boy your daughter punched—'

'The boy who sexually assaulted her,' Sabirah corrected her.

'That's an unproven allegation.'

'Other girls have told Nadimah it happened to them.'

209

'That's as may be. As you know, we've excluded him and the other boys involved since the incident. We've decided he will not return next year.'

'What about the other boys?'

'We excluded them until the end of term, and we think it's enough punishment.'

'Only because I threatened to tell the police. They helped their friend carry out a sexual assault.'

The bald man spoke. 'These boys are in the top set and will sit their GCSEs next year.'

'I don't care if they're geniuses getting degrees at fifteen. They took part in an assault on my daughter.'

'What my colleague meant is they have never been in any trouble before.'

'What does zero tolerance mean to you?'

The Head blinked behind her glasses. 'I'm sorry?'

'In your letter, telling me you have excluded the boys, you said you have zero tolerance for that behaviour.'

The Head turned pink and, following a short, whispered conversation with her colleague, addressed Sabirah. 'We'll make sure they don't return to this school.'

Sabirah exchanged a look with her daughter. 'Thank you.'

'Your daughter, on her part, must undertake never to punch another child—'

'She was defending herself.'

'We can't have pupils assaulting each other with impunity.'

'She didn't assault—'

'Mamma, it's okay.' Nadimah addressed the Head. 'I promise not to hit anyone.'

'Thank you, Nadimah, it's very mature of you. I'll confirm everything in writing.'

Sabirah left the office, and her thoughts turned to the site.

'What happened to you, Mamma?'

'What?'

'You're like a pit bull.'

'I'm your mother. That's what we do. Now you'd better go to your class.'

'Class finished. Didn't you hear the bell?'

She'd heard nothing outside the bubble of the Head's office. She checked the time. 'Shall we collect your brother?'

'Can we go for an ice cream?'

'Maybe later. I need to check the site.'

Nadimah rolled her eyes. 'Always the site.'

'It's very important. Mrs Curtis has trusted me, and I won't let her down. Now, let's collect Hakim before he goes home without us.' At least today, she'd fought for her daughter, and it felt good. Her son greeted them with a huge smile, which made her feel even better.

'Mamma, can I go camping with the scouts?'

'When?'

'In three weeks, when Nadimah goes away with Abby.'

She'd fretted about what to do with her son that week. The project would be in full swing, and she'd need to spend a lot of time on site. She'd hoped Nadimah would mind her brother, until Russell's invitation. This could turn out a godsend.

'Who's going?'

Hakim mentioned three of his closest friends.

'I meant, who's in charge?'

'Oh, yeah. My form teacher.'

Sabirah liked him, a man you could trust. 'We'll see.'

'Yay.' Hakim gave her a hug, their first in public since he became self-conscious over a year ago.

'Scouts have to wear uniform, like the army,' Nadimah announced.

'We have uniforms, but it's not like the army.'

'Will you need a uniform to go away with them?' The extra money she now earned meant she didn't have to worry too much, but she wanted to save for an uncertain future.

'They have plenty I can borrow. I tried some on, and they fit me.'

'Hmmm, okay.' Was she such a pushover?

They made their way home, the two children excited by the prospect of their adventures. These would be the first holidays since fleeing their home. For her, it meant she could throw herself into the project for an entire week, not having to worry about the children.

The top of the crane had gone from above the roofline. They must have finished. She'd check what the steelwork looked like.

As they turned into Vincent Terrace, her insides knotted. An ambulance with a blue light flashing sat outside the house and in front of it, a fire engine.

'Children, go home. I'll join you soon.' She rushed to the site, and the ambulance pulled away before she reached it. The foreman stood, ashen-faced, in the gateway.

'What's happened?'

'The steel fell on one of the lift engineers, smashed his leg.'

'Which one?' Sabirah's stomach churned and her heart raced.

He told her. The older one, a nice man with a new granddaughter.

'Which floor?'

'Top, but you can't go up there. The health and safety guy has cordoned it all off.'

She stopped at the top of the steps. Heavy treads sounded on the stairs and through the open doorway she saw a team of fire-fighters descending. She waited for the one with the stripes on her helmet to reach her.

'What happened? I'm the architect.'

'They hadn't secured the steel and when he tried to climb on it, it fell.'

'Will he be okay?'

The fire officer blew out her cheeks. 'A broken femur is serious, but they'll take care of him in hospital.'

Sabirah moved to one side and let them pass. She needed to sit. Before she could move, more steps and a lone figure with a tablet came down.

'You shouldn't enter the site without safety clothing.'

'Yes, of course. I'm the project manager and I just want to find out what happened.'

'So do I. We'll be here for a couple of hours. I'll impound your logbook and seal the site until we give you permission to go back in.'

'You can't say what happened?'

'Who are you?'

She told him.

'You'll get a report. Give me your contact details. I might also charge you with running a dangerous site.'

'It's not dangerous.'

He looked at her. 'One man's gone to hospital. He might lose a leg. And you're trying to enter the site with no protective equipment.'

She wanted to argue but realised the futility and trudged away.

CHAPTER 18

'You're looking fed up. I told you, a weekend in Paris would have been lovely, but we'll go another time, when I'm not knackered. I'd have spent all weekend on my phone, anyway. It's full on at the moment.' Erika sipped her wine.

'I'm just disappointed for you.' Grainger had spent the journey home thinking of Antonia's accusations. Jacinda was a tough cookie, but could she kill her finance director of over ten years?

'Don't be. We'll go for a week, on your birthday.'

'Yeah, okay.'

'Anyway, what did the African Princess want?'

'Who calls her that?' Antonia better *never* hear it.

'Jacinda. She saw one of her interviews after *your* story brought down the government.'

'*Ours*. I started it, but without her, it would never have seen the light of day.' Not to mention the pair of them nearly ending up at the bottom of a river, but Erika must never find *that* out. 'Talking about Jacinda. How long did your predecessor work for her?'

'I don't know, years. They worked together before Jacinda set up on her own. He'd worked with her at least since she set up JN Partners. Why?'

'Just curious. His name came up during the week.'

'In Paris?'

'Was he close to Jacinda?'

'Very. He owned shares in the business.'

'Like you do?'

'No. I own a tiny number. He owned at least ten per cent.'

Even four years ago, it would have been a sizeable chunk. 'And who got those after he died?'

'Not sure. His family? He and Jacinda went on holiday together. In fact, she was with him when he died.'

'What, literally, with him?' Had she killed him herself? Although a powerful woman, he couldn't imagine her killing anyone.

'No. Luckily for her, she had a hangover so didn't go out. He and his guide got caught in a rockfall and both died.'

Not so lucky for them. 'A guide?'

'Yeah, they were off-piste. Jacinda's into loads of extreme sports.'

Including murder? 'She seems to like risk.'

'Only in her leisure activities. She makes sure she doesn't take chances in her business, which is why she's so successful.'

'Does she load the odds?'

'What do you mean?'

'Make sure she's got a better chance of winning. Lots of businesses do it.'

'God, no. Jacinda would regard it as cheating. She's just very thorough, and works bloody hard to understand all the odds, so she overlooks nothing.'

'I'm sure she does. But she's always on the profit side. That's some winning streak.'

'Are you saying she's bent? Do you think I'd work for her if she was?'

'Of course not. I'm just saying she's lucky.'

A dangerous glint appeared in Erika's eyes. He'd drifted into perilous waters.

'You're becoming very cynical. Some people are successful because they're more talented and work harder.'

'Like you.' That didn't come out how he meant it to.

She studied him and drained her glass. 'I'm off to bed.' She stood, swaying, righted herself and pecked him on the forehead. 'Don't forget the dishwasher.' She stopped in the doorway. 'Bugger, I've left my laptop on in the study and I'm still logged in at work.'

'I'll shut it down.'

She hesitated, then yawned, 'Thank you,' and left.

Grainger took the glasses through to the kitchen. He binned the remains of the takeaway, loaded and started the dishwasher, and checked all the doors. The thought Jacinda Nieto had arranged the death of her former partner wouldn't leave him. It would make a great story, but would Antonia think it too close to Sawyer's article? Too tired to think now, he'd join Erika. But he would check who inherited those shares.

He reached the third step and remembered the laptop. He'd better do it. Erika would give him hell if he didn't. A sudden urge to see what his wife was working on came over him. He'd closed her computer down countless times, but never had the desire to check it. It felt like a betrayal. He entered her password, feeling uneasy that although she trusted him with hers, he'd recently changed his to one she didn't know.

As he disconnected from her work server, he noticed a new folder – not that he read them, but he recognised the familiar pattern, and this one broke it. He clicked on it. More sub-folders. A name he'd seen a lot of recently caught his attention. With a guilty start, he checked the door. But Erika would be fast asleep.

He opened the sub-folder. A spreadsheet and dozens of PDFs. He opened the spreadsheet and the first document. Share certificates for the company he'd recognised. Not a huge number, but more than he could afford. He checked the spreadsheet and found it listed. The price looked too low. His tiredness evaporated as he checked the certificates. They were in ten names, none of which sounded real.

He finished checking the certificates and examined the spreadsheets. How much did these shares represent? He clicked on the browser, then stopped himself. He didn't want to leave a footprint, so used his phone to check. The totals on the spreadsheet equalled almost sixty per cent of the company, but no one shareholder held more than the reporting threshold, so they could remain anonymous.

Was this insider dealing? Why had Antonia asked him if his new story involved insider dealing? *Shit!* That was why they were investigating Nieto's company, not the murder of Erika's predecessor. And she must know about it. It was on her laptop. He wanted to throw up. As he closed the files, he spotted another he'd not seen before. Five minutes later, he gave up trying to open it. Why the hell did Erika have an encrypted file with her predecessor's name on it?

The sign on the closed gates to the building site next door, a contrast to the bustling scene she'd encountered every morning for the last month, reminded Antonia no work would happen on their new headquarters building for the foreseeable future. She'd done her best to comfort Sabirah over the weekend, but her friend remained inconsolable and blamed herself for not being on site when the accident happened.

The incident cast a pall over the office, where Sabirah had become a popular visitor as she oversaw the work. Even the normally ebullient Miles exhibited a downbeat air. Antonia contemplated what she could do to raise morale before Eleanor's arrival. Her expression when she did arrive made Antonia fear more bad news.

'What's happened, Eleanor?'

'Nothing since Friday, but I've been wrestling with the fallout.'

'The HSE are still investigating, aren't they?'

'Yes, but it's the financial implications I'm concerned about.'

Antonia hadn't concerned herself with the budget, content to let Eleanor deal with the money. 'I assumed we had the budget sorted. What's the issue?'

'We'd already dipped into the contingency fund to do the additional work linked to the lift. The panelling and extra restoration work we agreed to.'

'I didn't know.'

'I saw no need to worry you.'

'Maybe you should have.' In some ways, Eleanor still treated her as a child. 'What's the situation now?'

'Each day's delay costs us at least ten thousand.'

'That's a lot.'

'We must pay the subcontractors, otherwise we'll lose them to another job. We've also got to get the crane back to sort out the steelwork and find another company to finish the lift installation.'

'Why?'

'They called over the weekend. They've said they haven't got the staff, but it sounded like an excuse. I've started ringing round, but I'm struggling to find anyone. And it'll be expensive.'

'Do you have a ballpark figure for the total cost?'

'It depends on how long we're delayed, but I'm expecting it to cost over a hundred.'

Antonia did a quick calculation. 'The increase in subscribers in the last month has brought in a lot. By the time the project finishes, we should have enough—'

'But we need to spend it on content, otherwise we'll lose these new subscribers and some of the existing ones. They're not paying us out of affection. If we're not delivering, they'll just leave.'

Was that a barb? 'I'm on it. Jean's story's turning into a biggie, and Miles is putting the finishing touches on his investigation.'

'What about Rick? He's our most expensive asset.'

'I'm expecting him to tell me what he's working on later. He's working from home this morning. But, Eleanor, I wouldn't worry too much about the money. We'll get through it.'

'There's also the small matter of the HSE investigation and the fine—'

'They've not fined us yet.'

Eleanor produced an envelope, which she slid across the table. 'We'll pay for the investigation, regardless of blame and whether there's a fine.'

'No.'

'They slipped the legislation through just before the Christmas break.' Antonia checked the amount. 'I didn't realise HSE inspectors got paid so much. But, Eleanor, I still think you're worrying too much—'

'Then there's this.' Eleanor produced an envelope with the familiar logo of a very expensive firm of solicitors printed on it.

'What do they want?' Antonia took it and slid out the thick cream paper.

'Bucklin's daughter is suing us for emotional distress and financial losses—'

'She got the insurance money from the house and the life insurances, plus she inherited whatever her parents owned.'

'According to her solicitor, the losses when the shares in the nuclear contractors plummeted wiped everything out.'

'That's not on us. Well, it is, but they were committing a crime and we prevented it.'

'I know, but we've got to fight it, and it will cost money. And our energy.'

'If we have to, we have to.' Antonia wondered how she'd fit it in.

'Don't worry, I'll organise the defence. I'm looking forward to it.' A glint in Eleanor's eyes reminded Antonia that although in her seventies, she still had plenty of fight in her.

Antonia tried to put the concerns behind her and focus on her primary job. A comment from Zabo when he brought her the fourth coffee of the day interrupted her.

'What's that? Who's saying we're responsible for reducing pension payments?'

'Two or three papers on their financial pages. Sorry.' He pushed his glasses back up his nose in a gesture so reminiscent of Alan, her predecessor, it took her breath away.

'Thanks for telling me.' Aware she'd regret it, she checked the usual suspects.

A partisan headline screamed.

Are unpatriotic news outlets harming the British economy?

Underneath, a table showed the share price of the companies the cabinet members had bought shares in, showing the price on the Friday before their story broke and comparing it to the day before the new cabinet cancelled the Trident replacement. By judicious use of doctored scales, it made it look like *The Investigator's* story had destroyed most of the value of the companies.

The rest of the article mentioned the negative impact they'd had on some pension funds, making it seem as if this included the entire market, and asked pointed questions about the patriotism of the journalists involved. Uncomfortable, Antonia searched the other papers and found three more who trotted out a similar line. She was reading the last one when Grainger arrived.

'Take a seat, Rick. I'm just reading about how we're responsible for the collapse of the London stock market.'

'You've not read Elfyn's contribution, have you?'

'Just reading it now.'

'Oh, I hoped you'd not seen it.'

'Too late.' She read the last paragraph.

The editor, Antonia Conti, who we took in as a desperate child refugee, nurtured and educated, has repaid us by turning on the civilisation that made her. She's spent the last month since she brought down the government, and made the UK the subject of ridicule, swanning round TV studios slagging off the country.

A familiar roofline she'd hoped never to see again made her scroll down. A group photo at The Towers Children's Home, with her, a skinny black girl with angry eyes, at one end. At the other, Larry Mishkin, her abuser, wearing a big grin. His hand rested on the shoulder of a young girl. Antonia looked closer and saw the terror in her eyes. Six weeks after this photo, Mishkin had killed her while Antonia hid in an airing cupboard in the same room. She swallowed the bile filling her mouth.

'You okay? Elfyn can be a real arsehole.'

'Yeah, I spotted that the other day. Where did he get the photo?'

'I'm not sure. That's the pervert you killed on the left, isn't it?'

Antonia closed the screen. 'What have you got for me?'

'I've got something big which I've spent the weekend on.'

She waited for him to continue. 'And?'

'It will take me a couple of weeks to determine the extent of the story, but I can give you an outline then.'

'I need to know what it is.'

He spread his hands. 'You don't mind if I don't say. I can assure you, it will be worthwhile. I haven't let you down so far.'

'No, you haven't, you're one from one, so far. But I can't afford to have someone of your calibre not producing work. We've used your name to leverage subscribers, and I need you to give me stories.'

'Of course. I'll work on anything you want me to in the meantime.'

Still thinking of the photo, Antonia couldn't focus. 'I've sent you the list, have a look and tell me which one you want to work on.'

'Great.' He stood, and Antonia's attention drifted back to the photo.

She'd never seen it but remembered the day. She'd once fantasised about tracking the other children down, but the first two she'd found had led such broken lives, she'd lost any impetus.

'I wondered if you'd seen it.'

'Eleanor. I didn't hear you.'

'No, I'm not surprised. I'm going to speak to the editor and tell him what I think of him.'

'The editor wrote it. The one who called me your "little piccaninny" on the phone to Rick.'

'Oh, him. What an obnoxious shit.'

'It's a sign we've got them rattled.' Antonia smiled. 'You're not here with good news?'

'Afraid not. I've just received a call from the subcontractors doing the plasterwork. They're pulling out.'

'Why?'

'He said the guys don't feel safe because of what happened on Friday.'

'We don't even know what happened on Friday.' Antonia exhaled in frustration.

'I doubt we'll change his mind. They'll be difficult to replace, it's a specialist job, but at least we'll save money not having to pay them while we're waiting to restart.'

Antonia suspected any replacements would cost much more. 'Okay, thanks for letting me know.'

Eleanor didn't move.

'What else?'

'The plumbers texted to basically say the same.'

'Have you spoken to them?'

'He's been in meetings for the last hour.'

Antonia took a deep breath. 'I'm going to ring the others.'

'Why?'

'Someone's got at them. First, we have a concerted media blitz. Each of those stories came from the same source. And now, our contractors are jumping ship.'

'The papers I can believe, and I'm sure friends of those who resigned will want revenge, but the builders? How would you get them to comply? These are tough guys and won't appreciate threats.'

'There's one way to find out. The joiner is Darius and Milo's uncle. Nobody will intimidate him.'

He answered on the first ring.

'Mrs Curtis?' his baritone boomed.

'It's me, Antonia.'

'Antonia. The boys said I should give you a map showing the location of the gym next time I saw you.'

She laughed. 'Tell them I'll come over in the next few days.'

'Milo says the young girl you brought to the gym is almost ready to kick your arse next time you come. She almost broke the guy who takes the women's advanced self-defence class in her last lesson.'

The way Nadimah had grown in confidence amazed Antonia. 'I'll bear it in mind. Look, I'm ringing because some of the other contractors have—'

'I'll stop you there. My guys on site weren't happy about Friday.'

'I can assure you we take safety—'

'No. No. That's not what I meant. They said there was something hinky about the accident. They weren't happy about the crane operator. I was going to ring you about it, then I got a call this morning. Some geezer told me it would be in my interests to find another site to work on.'

'He threatened you?'

'Not openly, but I got the hint. Then he offered the sweetener, the same as you're paying us, but for doing nothing. I didn't really have any choice—'

'Okay, I understand. Thanks.' The energy drained from her.

A deep laugh rumbled over the airwaves. 'I don't think you do. I told the lickspittle that if anything happened to my men, his own mother wouldn't recognise him when I've finished with him.'

'Oh. I can't thank you enough.'

'No need. I said we'd do the job, and we will.'

She put the phone down.

Eleanor smiled. 'I heard. He's the sort you want on your side.'

'Yes, but how many of the others can we rely on?'

'No idea, Antonia, but the ones we've already lost are proving difficult to replace.'

'I know. But who's behind this, and why?'

'You hurt a lot of powerful people a few weeks ago. Any of them could organise something like this.'

'The papers, maybe, but threatening contractors?' Antonia couldn't imagine any of the politicians they'd brought down having the contacts to do it.

The comment about the crane driver got her thinking. She called Sawyer into her office. 'Jean, have you got Friday's footage from the cameras we put next door?'

'Sabirah asked me, but they only show the front and back doors. We didn't put any in the building.'

'I just want to see the crane operator.'

'Do you think he sabotaged the steelwork?' Eleanor said.

'I recognised a tradesman the other day. I've been thinking about it, and it's bugging me.'

Sawyer returned with the laptop and played the footage. The camera positioned above the front door showed a front view of everyone entering the building. The crane drew up beyond the gates and Antonia fast-forwarded until it finished setting up its jacks. Then the operator climbed on to the turntable and his assistant came straight up the path.

'Shouldn't he sign in at the hut?' Jean said. 'Sabirah always makes me do it.'

'Yes, he should.' And having seen him preparing the crane, Antonia had already guessed who it was. As he approached the front door, she froze the image. A solid block of a man, his bandy legs the same length as his body and with long, greasy hair flowing from under his hard hat. 'Gareth Beynon.'

'Who?'

'He and his friend tried to bury me in the basement of a derelict house, then set it on fire because I escaped. He's put on weight and grown his hair and a beard, but I'd know him anywhere.'

Sawyer stared at Antonia, open-mouthed.

'Let me guess who he works for,' Eleanor said. 'Our old friend, Reed-Mayhew.'

'Right in one. And he's still smarting because he lost all those prison contracts when we exposed his lawbreaking.'

'Yes, but why now, Antonia? That happened six months ago.'

'I don't know.' But whatever the reason, it meant bad news for them.

CHAPTER 19

Chapman stuck his head out into the main office. 'Darren, we're going in five, okay?'

Sanchez raised her eyebrows. 'We're still busy checking lorry thefts.'

'We won't be long. I'm seeing a potential witness to a shooting.'

'And you need Darren because?'

He told her his destination.

'Sensible idea, I'd take Darren.'

Chapman returned to his desk to collect his jacket. His phone vibrated, and he checked the caller. Smiling, he took the call.

'I thought you'd be too grand for us now, after your TV appearances.'

'Not you as well.' Antonia sounded fed up. 'Have you got a minute?'

'What's up?' He sat.

'You know we're converting next door into our new offices?'

'You inviting me to the opening?'

'It could be a while.' She told him about the accident.

'You think this guy, Gareth Beynon, did it deliberately?'

'Bloody coincidence if he didn't. The joiners said there was something "hinky" about him—'

'You spoken to them?'

'Their boss, but I will, unless you . . .'

He remembered the warning Gunnerson's replacement had given him. 'I'm struggling at the moment . . .'

'Of course. And I saw another guy on the site I recognised. I think he worked in the maintenance team at the GRM building when I worked there.'

Where Chapman had first met her. And where she'd knocked him on to his arse when he'd tried to arrest her. 'Do you want me to run a check on Beynon?'

'If you could.'

He wrote the name on the back of a receipt. 'I'll send you anything I find.'

'Thanks, Russell.'

Baxter stuck his head in the door and Chapman signalled five minutes. 'By the way, Antonia, Hughes is out.'

'Great, have you got his contact details?'

'He's not answering his phone, so I'm going to pay him a visit.'

'Can you let me know how you get on?'

'Sure, do you want to meet for a drink later?'

'Can I get back to you? There's a lot happening today.'

He swallowed his disappointment. 'Sure.'

'This week, if you're free.'

Cheered by the prospect, he ended the call and collected Baxter. His car's suspension groaned when Baxter got in the passenger seat.

'How much do you weigh, Darren?'

'One thirty, boss. I've lost a bit.'

Chapman converted it. About twenty stone in old money. 'What's your BMI?'

'Thirty-five. They told me I was morbidly obese.'

Chapman joined in his laughter. Baxter's body fat levels were below ten per cent. About half a mile from their destination, Chapman pulled into the car park of a shopping centre.

He parked in sight of the security camera by the entrance. 'We'll walk the rest of the way.'

'Good idea, boss.'

He opened the glove compartment and took out an extendible cosh. 'You want one of these?'

'Don't believe in them.' Baxter winked.

If he was the same size, he wouldn't either. The properties they passed, already scruffy, grew more dilapidated. Graffiti tags covered any vertical surface and weathered plywood sheets covered broken windows. After five minutes, the flats Hughes gave as his address appeared. Low rise, with a staircase at each end leading to an open landing with the flats off it, they looked on their last legs. They approached a gaudy BMW with a bespoke paint job. The four lads in it stared at them with flat eyes.

The driver made oinking noises as they passed. Chapman gave thanks he'd brought Baxter. A group of young lads wearing hoodies gathered at the bottom of the nearest staircase.

'You lads know where thirty-six is?' Chapman had visited other flats here before and knew it.

Nobody answered.

Chapman stepped in front of the one he guessed was the leader. 'Third floor, you say, mate? Thanks.'

'I ain't said nuffink.' He looked at his companions, shaking his head.

Chapman winked and went to pass him. He saw the thought of blocking him occur to the lad, but on seeing Baxter, he moved aside, and his mates followed. The stink of skunk pervaded their clothes and followed Chapman up the open staircase. Even that couldn't disguise the stench of stale piss and vomit ground into the concrete.

Imagine having to live here and walk through this every day.

On the third floor, a woman holding a crying baby hawked and spat on the floor near Chapman's feet. He smiled at the baby, who stopped crying. Although none of the original plastic numbers survived, someone had painted numbers on the walls by each door. They passed thirty-one.

Baxter hung back while Chapman made his way to thirty-six. His skin tingled as he imagined the eyes watching him. By the time they left, every resident would know the police had visited Hughes. He knocked on Hughes's door until he got a response. A shadow moved behind the reeded glass, and he stepped back.

A bigger version of Hughes, more hair and more flesh on his skeleton, snatched the door open, accompanied by a cloud of pungent smoke.

'What?' He looked Chapman up and down.

'Where's your brother?'

'Fuck me. He's only just come out. Can't you lot leave him in peace?'

'He's out because of me. Now tell him I'm here.'

Another tough came to the door, his spliff hanging from his lower lip. He stared at Chapman, saying nothing.

Hughes appeared. 'The fuck you want?'

'I told you, I get you out, you speak to my friend. How you going to do that if you don't answer your phone?'

Hughes's eyes darted. 'I fucking told you, I'm not a snitch.'

'And I told you not to mess me about.'

'Oh, yeah, what you going to do?' He stepped out on to the landing and the other two joined him, studying Chapman like he was dinner.

Chapman resisted the impulse to swallow and kept his voice steady. 'You have two choices. Give me your phone number, your real one, and answer it. Or I turn your place over and do all three of you for possession.'

'Oh yeah, you and whose army?' Hughes's brother moved towards Chapman. Something glinted in his hand.

Full of adrenaline, Chapman reacted. His hands shot out. One grabbed his assailant's wrist. The other, he shoved into the side of the man's face and slammed it into the concrete wall. He did it again, roaring as he did so. He saw movement to his right and swung an elbow. Hughes grunted as it smacked into his face.

A large brown figure barrelled into Hughes and threw him into the wall as if he weighed nothing. Baxter. Chapman returned his attention to the brother and hit him again. A knife fell from his hand. Chapman cocked his fist.

'Boss, he's had enough.'

Chapman stopped, panting and blood pounding in his ears. He released Hughes's brother's wrist, and the man slumped to the floor. Blood poured out of the side of his face. Blood, bits of skin and flesh smeared the concrete wall.

Hughes crouched on all fours, wheezing as he fought to catch his breath. Blood dripped on to the floor from his nose. Chapman retrieved a card and shoved it down Hughes's shirt collar.

'If I don't hear from you in the next two days, I'll come looking for you.'

A mob of angry-looking men crowded on to the landing, blocking the route to the stairs.

The summons to an interview in the offices of *The Electric Investigator* filled Sabirah with panic. She knew both Antonia and Mrs Curtis, as directors of the company, had received summonses. She made her way down to the offices in good time.

Antonia sat in the canteen working on her laptop. 'Sabirah, can I get you a drink?'

'I shall make it. Do you want one?'

'No, thanks.' She pointed to a steaming mug next to her.

'Have they spoken to you?'

'Don't worry, it's just a formality. We know it was a deliberate attack on us. They're getting statements from witnesses.'

'Is Mrs Curtis . . . ?' Sabirah indicated Antonia's closed office door.

'She should finish soon.'

And then it would be her turn. Her stomach knotted. At least she would have Mr Stokes with her.

'Don't worry, Sabirah. You did nothing wrong.'

'I should have been there.'

'What could you have done? I spoke to the joiners, and they said the crane guy stayed up there when they had their break. He must have removed the bolts.'

Sabirah wasn't sure what she could have done, but she should have been on site. 'What did Mr Stokes say?'

'The usual advice. Answer the questions and no more. Stick to the facts. Are you happy with what you want to say?'

'Yes, I practise with Mrs Curtis this morning.'

'Good. You'll be fine, Sabirah.'

She wasn't too sure, and her doubts deepened when Mrs Curtis came out and a woman called out her name.

'Yes.' Sabirah stood.

'Come through please.' The woman gestured towards Antonia's office.

Sabirah nodded to Mrs Curtis as she passed her and stopped in the doorway. The man who'd reprimanded her for not wearing her hard hat on Friday looked up from Antonia's place.

She paused in the doorway. 'Where is Mr Stokes?'

'Is that your lawyer? You're not entitled to legal representation.'

She looked at Mrs Curtis. 'He's right. Just remember this morning and you'll be okay.'

The woman behind Sabirah frowned and gestured her to go in. She closed the door while Sabirah took her seat. She faced the two unsmiling officials.

'I hope you're not colluding,' the man said.

'My English isn't always too good, so I check with Mrs Curtis.'

'Do you need an interpreter?' He spoke slowly.

'No.'

'You are Mrs Sabirah Fadil, and you're the project manager for the construction site next door?'

'Yes.'

'Okay, Mrs Fadil, I have to warn you, you're under caution.'

Sabirah didn't hear the words, but they followed a familiar pattern and she agreed when he asked her if she understood. Could they arrest her for this? What would happen to her Leave to Remain?

'Mrs Fadil?'

'Yes?'

'Do you understand?' He slowed his speech again.

'Yes. I. Do.'

He didn't like her response, and asked for her personal details, speaking much too fast.

'Other witnesses state you weren't on site Friday afternoon. Can you tell me why?'

'I went to my daughter's school to meet the Head.'

'So, you prioritised a meeting at your daughter's school over your responsibilities and abandoned the site.'

'I did not abandon. Do I have to stay on site every minute?'

'We ask the questions.'

'You made a statement, I correct you.'

He turned pink. 'Why did you decide to leave the site when you knew a complex and dangerous operation would take place?'

She mustn't annoy him too much. What had they agreed she'd say to this question? 'I am architect and not required to perform the operation. We employ professional and qualified steel fixers and crane operators to carry out the task.'

'I presume that's one of your rehearsed questions.'

She held his gaze. 'It's the truth.'

'You claim you're an architect, but I can't find any record of you in the professional listings.'

Her face grew hot. 'I qualified at Aleppo University. Mr Brody Innis supervises my work here until I complete my Prescribed Qualifications exams.'

'So, you're not qualified to practise?'

'Is there problem with my designs?'

'I'm just trying to get a full picture, Mrs Fadil. Let's look at this crane company. Who appointed them?'

She still got a headache thinking about this. 'The original company cancelled our contract because of illness. I needed to find a replacement.'

'You chose them?'

'Yes.'

'And how did you find the company you appointed?'

'From the internet.'

'You used Google to find someone to carry out a dangerous operation on your site?'

'Mr Brody had a directory, but nobody was available. This company had the correct qualifications.'

'We'll come back to that.'

'What do you mean?'

He ignored her. 'Who appointed the Competent Person to supervise the lift operation?'

'The company. We booked a contract lift, so they arrange everything.'

He took his glasses off and placed them on the desk. 'Mrs Fadil. This company *you* appointed and trusted to carry out a dangerous task doesn't appear to exist.'

'But they have website and send certificates. We gave them to you.'

'Fakes. And there's no website. Not under the domain name you gave me.'

Sabirah's revelation the crane company didn't exist had spurred Antonia into action and she'd put both Grainger and Sawyer on the case. Both reporters had completed their investigations and sat in her office.

'Who wants to start?'

'I'll let Jean go first.'

'Thank you, Rick. I investigated the website first. Nobody has ever registered that domain name.'

'How did Sabirah find them?' Antonia said.

'The first time, on an internet search. They'd advertised, so came up high on the search engines, but they weren't using the domain name they claimed to be. On subsequent occasions, she used a hyperlink they'd inserted into the fake certification they'd sent her. Again, that didn't link to the domain it claimed to be.'

'Have you found the domain name they used?'

'I couldn't find it on Sabirah's search history, so searched for companies which advertised crane hire but cancelled the adverts once Sabirah contacted them. Most crane hire companies take out long advertising contracts, and only one fits that category. They've taken the site down now.'

'And who owns the domain?'

'Would you believe, a company in Cayman?'

Antonia exhaled in frustration. 'All too easily. What about the bank?'

'What they did was clever. They used an existing company name and copied their bank details. I spoke to their finance director, and he's sending our money back. They hire out scaffolding and access platforms and wondered about the payment since we paid the deposit. That's my bit. So over to you, Rick.' Sawyer sat back with a satisfied air.

'Well done, Jean, and even better getting our money back. Rick?'

'First, their offices. The address exists, but they've been empty for months. I've tracked the crane down. They'd given us the registration, which is legit, and the crane belongs to a leasing company.'

'Don't lease companies carry out due diligence?'

'They do, and again, the person contacting them claimed to work for the scaffolding company and said they wanted to expand into crane hire. The offer to pay a year's hire in advance and the promise of more orders in the pipeline swayed the decision.'

'How much did the year's lease cost?'

'Best part of forty K.'

'And they paid it?'

'Every penny.'

'Someone's spent a lot of money getting at us. Can we trace who paid it?' Antonia looked at Sawyer.

'It would take a while and might require a bit of rule-bending.'

'Don't bother, Jean. I suspect it will be another dead end, like the domain. Do we know where the crane is, Rick?'

'Yeah, in the back yard of the empty premises. I spoke to the guy who delivered it and he said they told him they were just moving in. There was a removal lorry and two blokes there. I showed him the photo of Beynon and he identified him. The estate agent dealing with the site said a prospective client borrowed the keys, so they could have copied them, but it's a dead end.'

'And what happened to the original company we hired?'

Grainger furrowed his brow. 'The guy was cagey, like the contractors who've dropped us, so I assume he's received the same call.'

'Okay, put it in your report. Doubt anything will come of it, but it supports our case. Well done both of you, and especially the speed at which you've done this. Can we send a copy to the supercilious HSE inspector and to the local police?'

She'd got the impression Chapman wouldn't want to involve himself in this. At least this would prove someone had targeted them and should enable them to get the work back on track, *and* get Sabirah off the hook.

CHAPTER 20

When Antonia got hold of Hughes, he'd reassured her he knew the man responsible for the murder of her friend Alan, but he wouldn't give his name over the phone. The man, who Antonia and Chapman named 'The Smoker', had also tortured Chapman and they were sure they could link him to Reed-Mayhew. Hughes boasted he met him for drinks in the King's Cross area and would tell her the next time he did. Then, after prevaricating and stringing her along for weeks, Hughes surprised Antonia by ringing her in her office.

'I'm meeting him on Monday.'

She'd almost given up. 'Great, can you tell me where?'

Hughes snorted. 'Do you know how hard it is when you get out of prison? No, of course not. You've had an easy life, haven't you? Nice home, with Mummy and Daddy, uni and then a great job falls into your lap.'

'Don't make assumptions, Mr Hughes.' *Would he have survived her childhood?*

'What, your parents divorced or something? Spare me.'

'Do you want to tell me what you want?'

'Yeah, I want some cash. Enough to make a start somewhere else.'

'I've already told you, we're not a big paper awash with funds.'

'Oh yeah, I saw you on telly when I was inside. They always have loads of cash.'

'They interviewed me; I wasn't working for the TV company.'

'Yeah, well. They've never even interviewed me.'

How much has he drunk?

'I want twenty grand.'

'You said you didn't want money.'

'I've changed my mind. Ten, then.'

'Thank you for taking the time to ring me, Mr Hughes. Goodbye.'

'Five, I'm going no lower.'

'We're not paying.'

The line grew silent. Had she lost him? They could pay him five. She'd happily pay that to find the man who'd killed Alan. Before she could say anything, he laughed.

'Worth a try. Okay then.'

Her relief made her tremble. 'Where are you meeting him?'

'I'm not telling you over the phone. You'll have to look me in the eye when I tell you.'

She'd expected this. 'What time's your meet?'

'One.'

'Okay, shall we meet at Granary Square at twelve? You can tell me then. I'll be on a bench between the fountains and the road.'

He covered the phone and mumbled something. *Is he speaking to someone else?*

'Yeah, okay.'

'Are you talking to someone? I'm not meeting anyone else, just you.'

'Nah, no problem. It's me mate asking me if I want a drink.' A glass clinked.

'How will I recognise you?'

He described himself, in more flattering terms than the mug-shot Chapman had sent her, and ended the call.

Antonia put the handset down and wiped her hands on her jeans. She felt like she'd gone three rounds. At least he'd agreed to the location. She got a glass of water and rang Chapman.

'Russell, I'm meeting Hughes in Granary Square, where you suggested. Monday at twelve. He's going for a drink with "The Smoker" at one, and he'll tell me where they're meeting.'

'He didn't tell you?'

'No, I didn't expect him to, although I asked.'

'Okay, we can work with that. We've got an outline plan which we can firm up. I'll have to familiarise you with it. When shall we go over it? I've got tomorrow afternoon free if you want to come over and meet the team, or maybe Friday.'

'We're "topping-out" the project tomorrow at three. It's not a real topping-out, but we're marking the completion for Sabirah. Why don't you come over if you're free? Be nice to see you.'

'Not a good idea. I'll still be on duty. What about Friday?'

'We're moving into the new place. I'm not expecting to have any time. Are you free tonight?'

'Yeah, but my team will have gone home.'

'I've met a couple and I can meet the rest Monday, after I've seen Hughes. Shall we eat? I'm sure it's my turn to pay. We can catch up over a meal and you brief me.'

'Yeah, sounds good.'

The rest of the day passed in a blur as she got the office ready for the move. At seven, she rushed home and changed, arriving at the restaurant five minutes late. The aroma of garlic and ginger enveloped her as she walked in. As usual, Chapman occupied a table near the back. He rose to greet her, and they hugged.

'You growing the afro again?' He indicated her hair.

'I'm getting it cut first thing for the photos in the afternoon. Anyway, why have you avoided us? No visits to the office?'

'I've been away.'

'Oh yeah, how did your week with two teenage girls go?'

'Hmmm. Better than I expected, although I spent a lot of time scowling at groups of boys who materialised wherever we went. Way more than when I'm just with Abby.'

'Yeah, Nadimah's growing into a bit of a stunner.' Sabirah had made a similar complaint. 'But that was only one week. We've not seen you for ages.'

He avoided her gaze. 'We've been really busy.'

'Oh yeah? You're not a great liar, for a copper.'

'I got warned off talking to the press by the temporary DCI.'

'Is Gunnerson still suspended?'

'She came back Monday, cleared of all charges.'

'Hence this meeting?'

'No. The warning came from Harding. He's still there.'

'Are you sure you can risk being seen with me now?'

'Yeah, I reckon so. Did Hughes say why he'd rung you?'

'He asked for twenty grand.'

'You're not paying him?'

'No chance. I told him to sling his hook, and he tried to laugh it off. What's the plan Monday?'

'You'll have your phone with you, and we'll be tracking it. There's a transmitter with a separate mini battery hidden in it, just in case. We've also got the cameras, so don't use the make-up stuff.'

'What if the cameras are down? They often get sabotaged round there.'

'We'll monitor them and if anything happens to them, we'll abort the mission. My team will monitor you while you're in the square. The forecast is good, so we can expect crowds, but we've got good vantage points in the art college and from an office across the canal. Before you meet him, ring me and keep the phone open. I'll turn my mic off so there are no mistakes. We'll also have a parabolic mic on you to listen in. As soon as he tells you where they're meeting, we'll send our armed response team there to set up a reception committee for "The Smoker".'

'You think Hughes is dangerous?'

'No question, but you'll be in a busy public space, and we've got you covered, don't worry.'

Although she'd missed the children and loved having them back home, Sabirah had appreciated the week when she had nothing to worry about but the project. Rashid used to tease her about her single-mindedness when she had a project to finish. The new sub-contractors she'd found to replace those they'd lost had been superb. They'd worked every day until dusk, and she'd worked alongside them.

Today, they would finish, and so would her work. She mustn't let the sense of panic whenever she considered her future spoil today. The children must still be asleep, unless Nadimah was back on her phone. She needed to wean the girl off it. It sounded like they'd both enjoyed a full week away. Would they ever forget the hardships they'd endured? She doubted it, but she could always hope.

The sound of steel against hollow steel told her the scaffolders had arrived to remove the last of their creation. A flatbed sat outside, layers of poles already filling it. She entered the site office and signed in for the last time. The contractors had removed almost everything not fixed to the frame, and it too would go on a flatbed.

She entered through the shiny black front door and into the hallway. Protective matting still covered the repaired and restored tiles. She followed the sound of hammering from the basement. The door to the computer suite had polythene sheeting taped across it. Behind the sheeting, a steel door with gas-tight seals would keep the room beyond it sterile. The new servers would arrive tomorrow, once the builders had finished and taken their dust.

The banging came from the party wall between this building and the existing offices of *The Investigator* next door. She found the joiners making final adjustments to the doorway, which would join the two spaces.

'Mrs Fadil, good morning,' Mr Decker's baritone rumbled. 'We're just adjusting the hang of this door.' He pointed at two of his men. 'These monkeys thought they'd get away with a rough job.'

She'd inspected the doors last night, and they'd looked perfect. 'I wanted to thank you for helping us find the workmen to finish the job.'

'Anything for Antonia. Has she found the rassclaats who tried to close you down?'

Sabirah guessed what the word meant from his tone. 'She knows who's behind it.'

'If she needs help to lick 'em down, she knows where to find me an' the boys.'

'I'll tell her.' Antonia hadn't told her who'd caused the accident and scared off the other contractors, but Sabirah had a good idea. And however big and strong Mr Decker and his 'boys' were, she didn't think they were big enough. The idea such an evil man remained obsessed with her friend frightened her. Last time, he'd dragged Sabirah in, and it almost destroyed her.

She left Mr Decker and his men and completed her inspection of the basement. Back on the ground floor, the contractors completed last-minute jobs and the cleaning team had arrived. Sabirah inspected every room in the building, picking up any snags she'd missed last night. She couldn't help a sense of pride as she passed through the restored, elegant rooms.

The scaffolding came down by midday, and the fencing and portable buildings soon joined it. Sabirah walked out on to the pavement and inspected the building. The paintwork and render gleamed in the sunshine. Next door, the matching new paintwork looked as magnificent. She paused for a few moments. She made all this happen, but the fact Rashid wasn't here to see it took off some of the gloss. At least their children would see what their mother could do.

Inside, she found Antonia, who'd come through the adjoining door. 'Sabirah, this is just fabulous. Do you want to show me round?'

Her friend's compliments as they inspected the rooms made her proud, but under Antonia's excitement, she sensed worry. 'Is everything okay?'

'Of course, why wouldn't it be? You've created a wonderful new headquarters for us.'

'Antonia, how long have I known you?'

Antonia held a palm up as if to push her away. 'Please, not today. I want to enjoy it and make it special for Eleanor. I'll tell you tomorrow.'

'Okay. Shall I show you your office?'

Antonia reacted like a kid given a fabulous present. 'This is so much more than I expected.'

'Once we get the new furniture in, it will look even better.'

Antonia almost ran to the window. 'I don't know what to say. Thank you.' She grabbed Sabirah and hugged her.

Sabirah blinked. 'Does this mean I get an excellent review in "How's my architecting"?'

She laughed. 'Five stars, highly recommended.'

Within an hour, almost all the workers left and the caterers arrived. They set up the main buffet in Antonia's new office suite. As the time for her to make a speech approached, Sabirah grew more nervous. She'd become used to avoiding attention but she knew she must stop hiding from people.

She made one last circuit of the site. The trades had completed the finishing touches and the skip lorry had arrived for the final load. She should go home and change. Time to rehearse her speech one last time and then come back with the children.

Hakim met her in the hall, looking very grown-up in his suit. 'You look very smart. Your dad would have been proud.'

He looked troubled.

'Are you okay? Where's your sister?'

'Nadimah's gone out. A boy phoned her.'

'Shall I come back later?' Grainger watched a harassed-looking Antonia addressing the two removal men loading one of her filing cabinets on to a hand-truck. Behind her, someone had wedged the double doors leading into the building next door open, turning her office into a corridor.

'I'm using Jean's office until we move next door. I'll see you there in a bit, okay?'

'Sure.'

The workmen hadn't touched Sawyer's office yet, unlike the canteen, which they'd stripped. Grainger had seen his new office, and although not as fancy as Antonia's, he liked it a lot. His move here felt more like an excellent decision every day, especially since Elfyn seemed to have become more hysterical and irrational.

The edge of a piece of paper stuck out of a drawer on the desk and he opened it and examined the paper. A large sheet folded in four. He unfurled it. Neat handwriting filled speech bubbles linked with lines and arrows. It looked like a tidier version of the mind maps Antonia used.

He read the title with a sense of foreboding. *JN Partners. Insider dealing.*

He recognised some names near the top of the form because of the size of the companies mentioned. Those nearer the bottom were companies Erika had mentioned. Companies JN Partners had done well from either short selling, just before the price collapsed, or buying early, just before a breakthrough in technology sent their shares stratospheric. Although Antonia said Erika wasn't involved, what he'd found on her laptop made him fear she was. The question was, would *The Investigator* implicate her in Nieto's crimes?

They'd visited Nieto's mansion on Tuesday, admiring the toys and gadgets she'd filled it with. She'd had a real go at him at one point, but that was Jacinda. And he'd got drunk on her twenty-four-year-old malt and dealt it back at her. Probably said something stupid. What had he said to annoy her?

He refolded the document, deciding to speak to Antonia about it. He couldn't let Erika get dragged into it. Most of the deals happened before her time. When her predecessor ran things. He still hadn't finished his investigations into the man's death.

God, he'd not mentioned his suspicions to Nieto, had he? The accusation you'd had your colleague murdered would have pissed off even a mild-mannered person. Surely he hadn't been that drunk. He slid the chart back into the drawer. Another one lay under a folder. As he pulled it out and opened it, Antonia's voice came closer. He folded it, shoved both in the drawer and slammed it shut as she came in.

'Sorry to keep you, Rick. It's non-stop today.'

'Sorry, I'll let you sit here.' He rose and walked round the desk.

'Thanks.' She slumped in the chair and opened a drawer.

He held his breath until she produced a flask and filled a small mug.

'I meant to warn you,' she said, 'no facilities in the canteen. Do you want some coffee?'

'I'm fine.' He'd tried her treacle-like brew before.

She gulped a mouthful and ran a hand over her face, smoothing her frizzy hair back over her skull. 'Right, you said you'd give me the rundown of what you've been working on.'

Flashes of what he'd seen on the two mind maps wouldn't leave him. 'Are you investigating my wife?'

'We've discussed this before. Did you speak to her following our last conversation?'

'No, I considered it, but didn't. You've not answered my question.'

Antonia laughed. 'You won't even discuss the *subject* of your investigation with me, yet you want me to tell you what Jean's working on?'

'That's twice you've avoided answering. I can only draw my own conclusions.'

Antonia drained her mug. 'You mention this to anyone, you're out. And I'll kick your arse, *and* make sure your name's mud in the business. Are we clear?'

'I think so.'

'Jean has discovered evidence JN Partners have used inside information since they started. They've made billions.'

'You think Erika's involved?'

'Do you?'

'Of course not. Have you found anything . . . ?' Would she tell him if she had?

'We haven't found proof, as I told you last time—'

'You didn't mention insider dealing last time.'

'No, I didn't. Although we don't believe your wife's involved, she must suspect. She's far from stupid. Her predecessor was up to his neck in it until someone broke it for him.'

'I've been thinking about what you said about that. Jacinda has a short temper. I should know, she blew her top on Tuesday night at her place. But—'

'What set her off?'

He shook his head. 'Some throwaway line of mine I can't even remember. But the point is, it takes a lot to get someone killed.'

Antonia took a deep breath. 'If you repeat what I tell you now outside this room, I'll not only kick your arse. I'll make sure our article smears Erika.'

'I appealed to our friendship earlier, and I owe you my life. I pay my debts.'

'Okay, Rick.' She lowered her voice. 'Jacinda Nieto has links with Gustav Reed-Mayhew, and we think he helped her get rid of her FD.'

'Can you prove it?'

'No. But I know he did it.'

'He caused the accident next door, didn't he?'

'We won't ever prove it.'

'Do you believe Erika's at risk?'

'We've found nothing to suggest that. But it could change.'

'You'd tell me if you heard . . .'

'Of course.'

His thoughts churned. 'I need to be with my wife.'

'And I've got a mountain of work next door. We'll go through everything Monday first thing.'

'Yeah, I'll see you in your new executive suite Monday, bright and early.' He almost ran from the room. But why hurry? He'd arrive home long before Erika. But he wanted to be there to meet her. Reassure himself she was okay.

CHAPTER 21

'Good morning, Antonia. Another coffee?' Tomasz Zabo held a steaming mug in his right hand.

'You're a mind reader. Thank you.' Antonia checked the time as he placed the mug on her desk. 'Have you heard from Rick? We're due a progress update on his latest project.'

'Nope, but that's not unusual. Do you want me to chase him up?'

'Don't worry, I'll give him a bell.'

Zabo left, closing the door behind him. If she hadn't known he'd lost most of his left leg, she couldn't tell from watching him. The memory of that night, when a van meant to hit her had ploughed him down, still made her feel guilty. The fact it had happened just outside the office made her wonder if it upset him every day, passing the place he'd lost his leg. She picked up her phone and called Grainger's number.

'You've reached the mailbox of Rick Grainger—'

Antonia left a message telling him to ring her and looked up his home number. She let it ring a dozen times before giving up. 'Blast!'

'Everything okay, Antonia?' Eleanor Curtis wheeled herself into Antonia's office.

'I can't get hold of Rick Grainger. He's due to give me an update on the story he's working on.'

'You've given him too much latitude. I warned you. It will be harder to rein him in now he's used to walking all over you.'

'He doesn't walk all over me. I give him the same freedom to follow his investigations as I give other experienced reporters.' Although she must admit, even Zabo, who'd just started, had noticed Rick Grainger's habit of not turning up.

'Name anyone else here who would work on a story for so long without telling you what they're working on?'

'He's a very experienced reporter. He's won awards—'

'And he's won those because he's had an editor making sure he's working on the right stories. Here, it's you.'

Antonia had to agree. She'd allowed him too much leeway. 'I'll have a word when I next see him.'

Eleanor's expression softened. 'It's not easy, but apart from your blind spot with Mr Grainger, I'm impressed by how you've done. And you've managed the move to bigger offices without too much disruption to our output.'

The unexpected praise gave Antonia a lift. She looked around her new office. 'A team effort, much down to Sabirah.'

'She did a splendid job. Anyway, what did you want me for?'

Antonia swallowed. 'I've found someone who says he can lead me to the men who killed Alan.'

The mention of her nephew threw Eleanor, who opened her mouth and stared for several seconds. 'Do you believe them?'

'I'll find out when I've spoken to him in' – she checked the time – 'about two hours.'

'Be careful.'

'Which is why I'm meeting him in Granary Square. It'll be packed at lunchtime.'

'If you're sure. Have you told Russell?'

249

'He knows. His team will be there.'

'If you find them, do you think they'd give Reed-Mayhew up?'

Antonia hesitated. 'I doubt anyone as low on the food chain would have an inkling of his involvement. I'm just hoping having their names will enable me to find the next link in the chain.'

'A slow process. How long since Alan died? Eighteen months?'

'Sixteen months and three days. I thought you'd be pleased.' The idea that Eleanor didn't know exactly when those men murdered her nephew irritated her. But why would she? Eleanor had been in a coma at the time and, unlike Antonia, hadn't witnessed the killing.

'I am, but I'm also conscious of my age. Will we get to Reed-Mayhew before I shuffle off this mortal coil?'

'You've got plenty more years in you. I'm more worried about his ever-increasing power making him untouchable.' Antonia's phone beeped, and she checked the message.

'Trouble?'

'My contact wants to change where we're meeting.' She slid the phone across to Eleanor.

Lks lke rain met in King's X caff on plat 10.

Eleanor frowned. 'Tell him no, original meet or nothing. Are we paying him?'

'I've said no but might go to five.' She pictured the new location he'd suggested. 'I'll agree. I don't want to put him off, and it's an open space, next to the main shops. I'll tell Chapman.'

'You're the boss.' Eleanor slid the phone back. 'I'll leave you to it.'

As she began to leave, Antonia realised what was different about Eleanor. 'Where's your electric chair?'

'I wondered if you'd notice. It's at my desk. I'm just getting used to this one, makes my forearms ache.'

Antonia got up and gave Eleanor a hug. 'Well done. I knew you'd do it.'

'Hmmm, I'd allowed myself a year, and as you observed, it's over sixteen months since those thugs put me in hospital.'

'Give yourself a break. Few seventy-six-year-olds would do what you've done.' Antonia returned to her desk and responded to the text before forwarding it to Chapman in an encrypted message.

An hour later she set off, taking just her phone, a burner she used to keep in touch with Hughes. Although in the habit of stripping her phone every time she left her office, she left this one live. The walk took her past innumerable cameras, whose intrusive surveillance she'd have usually resented, but today welcomed.

The long-promised summer heatwave had arrived, despite the clouds, and Antonia wished she'd worn shorts instead of her habitual jeans. Arriving early, she checked out her surroundings. A curved latticework of white steel supported the soaring roof, and a high yellow brick wall faced a modern curved two-storey complex of retail outlets where Chapman's crew waited. She avoided looking towards this and made her way into the vast space, parallel to the brick wall. The wait would give her time to cool off. As she'd recalled, the café occupied a busy corner near several teeming shops and close to the platforms.

She didn't see anyone who looked like Hughes and took a table near the back from where she could see most of the concourse. As agreed, she rang Chapman and, checking he could hear her, left the phone in her pocket. She'd almost finished her coffee and sandwich when Hughes strode into view. Tall and thin, he had a shaved head and a broken nose. Despite the warm weather, he wore a long jacket. A canvas courier bag secured by two leather straps hung off his left shoulder. He came straight to her and as he came closer, she noticed he wore tribal scars. After checking for possible accomplices, she stood to greet him.

'Mr Hughes?'

He nodded and ignored her proffered hand. 'Phone.' He snapped his fingers.

'I'm sorry?'

'Phone, or I walk.'

Antonia made a calculation. Assuming Chapman's team had the parabolic mic on her, they should hear what they said. She wasn't going anywhere with him. 'Here.' She killed the call in her pocket and handed it to him.

He switched it off, produced a Faraday pouch from his bag and slipped her phone into it. He then produced a short wand, which he ran over her body. The two couples on either side of them were either incurious or too polite to look as he checked her for bugs. She studied his tribal scars. She'd read about them and how effective they were at evading the face-recognition cameras. Maybe she should try them instead of the ghost powder she still used. She'd ask him about them later.

Once he'd finished, he put the wand back in the bag and sat. 'We can talk now.'

Antonia tried to get a handle on him as he studied her with cold grey eyes. His impatient manner suggested he'd appreciate her getting down to business. 'Can we clarify we won't pay you for any information you may give us?'

'I don't want money. That bastard owes me, and I want to see him taken down.'

Antonia got the impression Hughes, or whatever his real name was, would sort out his own payback. 'Are you going to tell me his name?'

Hughes nodded. 'The guy in charge, big bloke with a voice like gravel.'

Antonia and Chapman had dubbed him 'The Smoker'. He hadn't pulled the trigger, but he was the one they wanted, especially Chapman. 'Go on then.'

'Not yet.' The waitress wandered over, but his scowl sent her scurrying to another table. 'What will you do with the name?'

'I'll make sure he pays for his part in killing my friend Alan.'

'The police?'

'Of course.'

His harsh laugh stopped her. 'Why do you think they found no evidence at the house where they killed your friend?'

'Let me worry about that. By the time I've written the story, they won't be able to ignore it.' Although she and Chapman had witnessed the men employed to guard Alan kill him, they couldn't risk admitting it to the police and had made an anonymous call to report the murder. Something that still filled Antonia with guilt. 'How do you know him?'

Hughes leant back and folded his arms. 'Does it matter?'

'It gives your story veracity. How do I know you're not just trying to drop someone you don't like in the shit?' This felt wrong. Sources, especially those keen to do a hatchet job on someone, wanted to convince you of their credibility. Hughes seemed utterly unconcerned.

He shrugged. 'We're in the same line of work. I asked him about his limp, and he told me about the girl who gave it to him.' Antonia wished she'd done a lot more than smash his knee when he'd attacked her.

Despite Hughes's earlier eagerness to hurry things along, he now seemed to be stalling. 'Are you going to tell me?'

In the background, a train emitted a shrill whistle.

Hughes leant forward. 'The guy you want is called Danil Derenski.'

Antonia checked the two couples at the nearest tables, but they remained engrossed in their own business. Before she could respond, the train whistled again and then came a terrific crash. People screamed. Antonia followed the sound of the impact. The train had stopped a metre or so beyond the buffers, its front wheels off the track and the first carriage at an angle.

An excited hubbub filled the space as the racket faded and people streamed towards the platforms. She stepped towards the pile-up, the urge to help and witness it strong. Hughes also stood, but his focus remained on Antonia. He stuck an arm out, impeding her. She reached to push him away, then saw the automatic under his jacket.

'One word and you're dead.'

She checked the nearest couple. They'd also got up, but instead of focusing on the incident, came towards her, grim-faced. Antonia turned to the other pair, but they'd abandoned the pram they'd arrived with and now waited a couple of metres away.

'This way.' Hughes pointed at a door behind them. 'Come on, I don't give a fuck if I have to shoot you.'

She walked towards the door, which opened before she reached it. The two couples formed a wall behind Antonia and Hughes, shielding them from prying eyes. Would Chapman's team realise what was happening in time? The door opened wide, and Hughes shoved her in the back. She stumbled forward into the darkened opening. As she crossed the threshold, hands grabbed her, pulling her inside. The door slammed. Everything paused for a moment. No movement, no light, no sound. Just the smell of fried food and coffee.

Then lights flickered on, illuminating a stark service corridor. Two men she didn't recognise flanked her, holding her arms. They twisted them, trying to get them behind her. She resisted until Hughes aimed the automatic at her left knee.

'I hear it's very painful.'

She stopped resisting and a zip tie secured her wrists behind her back, then Hughes wound tape round her mouth. The two men grabbed her arms, and they half-dragged her down the corridor and into a service lift. It dropped several floors. The door opened, bringing the stench of vehicle fumes.

A large walk-in van the size of a small removal lorry waited, its side door open. The men pushed her towards it. Then they lifted her and threw her into the back, slamming her to the floor. Winded, she lay trying to gather her breath.

'Miss Conti, we meet again,' a gravelly voice she recognised said from outside the vehicle. The Smoker. Danil Derenski, if Hughes was to be believed. Antonia's pulse spiked. The last time she'd heard that voice, the man who owned it held an automatic to her neck. He'd also tortured Chapman and his men shot and killed Alan Turner.

'I'm looking forward to discussing our last meeting and what you did to my knee,' he said, 'but I'd rather do it somewhere more private. Until we meet again, Ms Conti. Soon.' His foot scraped on the concrete as he walked away. Then the door slammed, and the engine started.

DC Louisa Walker's voice came over the radio network. 'Where the fuck she gone?'

'What do you mean?' Chapman sat in the front of a lorry containing banks of screens linked to the city's surveillance system. Behind them, a second police vehicle, a minibus full of armed officers, waited for his orders.

'She's disappeared, boss.'

'Has she gone off somewhere?'

'She was here one minute, then she's gone.'

Chapman addressed another member of his team. 'Grev, what have you got?'

'Hang on a second, boss.' DC Greville Sanderson manipulated a mouse and studied one screen. 'Shit! There, she went off with the guy she met.'

Chapman got up and stepped through the narrow opening into the back of the lorry. The screen to Sanderson's left showed Antonia heading for the service door at the back of where she'd met Hughes. He'd followed her, and behind them, four people in a line.

'Louisa, she's gone through the service door—'

'Shit! Let's go, Darren—'

'No, you pick up the two couples who sat on each side of her. I'll send our teams in.'

'There's only two of us up here.'

'And one of you is Darren. Just do it.' He contacted the leader of the armed response teams. 'She's disappeared into a service door behind the café. Can you send a team to look for her while I speak to their control room?' He ended the call and returned his attention to the screens. 'We've got every exit covered, haven't we?'

The non-police surveillance technician next to Sanderson pointed to the bank of screens on his right. 'Each one.'

At least that was something. He retrieved his work mobile and punched in the number he had for the control centre at the station.

A harassed-sounding woman answered. 'Control room, King's Cross.'

'Hi, DI Chapman, Serious Crimes. Can I speak to whoever controls your surveillance—'

'Can this wait? We're a bit busy—'

'No, we've had a woman abducted from one of your platforms.'

'Okay, hang on.'

He waited. 'How the hell did you miss her, Grev?'

Sanderson indicated the screen above the one showing the exit Antonia left by. The damaged train sat alongside the crowded platform. Disorientated and shocked passengers mixed with eager spectators while officials and emergency workers tried to bring order.

'Coincidences make my neck itch. Find out who's investigating once we've sorted this out.' He could have done with Sanchez on site, rather than in the control centre of the company running the city's surveillance system. 'Alice, can we check every vehicle going into the complex since six this morning?'

'Already on it, Russell. I've gone from midnight last night.'

'Quick work.'

'Yep, Grev texted me.'

Great, you don't really need me, do you? At least they'd bugged her phone. He just hoped the kidnappers didn't dump it. He should have cancelled the meet as soon as Hughes changed the venue. But they would have been okay if the train hadn't crashed . . . *If, if, if. Idiot.*

A voice from his mobile broke into his thoughts. 'DI Chapman? What do you need me to do?'

'A young woman's been abducted from the café next to platform ten—'

'Where the train went through the barrier?'

'Yes. She's mixed-race, six feet tall and athletic build. She's wearing blue jeans, boots and a short-sleeved red and yellow top.'

'Short hair. Looks like she doesn't take any shit.'

'You found her already?'

'No, but I noticed her when she arrived. Okay, I'll start a search. Anything else?'

'If we give you the ID of every vehicle which leaves, can you speak to the person authorised to bring it on site?'

'I can try. It depends how many vehicles leave. Do you have any for me to check now?'

'Can I put you on to my colleague, DC Greville Sanderson?' He passed the handset to Sanderson and told him what he needed to do.

He checked the time. Antonia had gone missing eleven minutes ago. Anything could have happened to her. He returned to his seat in the front and checked the laptop linked to the tracker in Antonia's phone. Anticipating Hughes might remove the battery and SIM card, they'd inserted a low-energy tracker with its own power source. Good for twenty-four hours. However, they'd lost the signal as soon as Hughes arrived. He must have smashed the phone, but they'd not seen him do it.

Chapman resisted the temptation to chase Sanchez and Walker. After an interminable wait, Walker's breathless voice came over his earphones.

'Boss, we've got one couple and the bloke from the other couple, but lost the second woman.'

'Okay, get them picked up, then come and join us.'

'Boss?' Sanderson called from the back of the lorry, his tone warning Chapman to expect bad news.

'Go on?'

'A van left eight minutes ago. They've just got hold of the owner and it shouldn't be going anywhere.'

'Shit! Can we find it on the system—'

'Already on it.' Sanchez's calm voice broke in. 'We're doing an auto search for the plates.'

'Boss.' Sanderson held the handset out to Chapman.

'Inspector. We've found your young woman on the system, in a service lift. Taking her downstairs to the car park with three men.'

'Is she okay?'

'She looks fine. Arms behind her back, and she looks pissed off, but unhurt.'

Chapman could imagine how pissed off. 'Do you have any footage in the car park?' It would almost certainly show them putting her in the missing van.

'Sorry, cameras were pointed at the wrong areas.'

Not by accident. 'Can we get stills of the men from inside the lift?'

'Just one. The other two have their backs to the camera.'

'Okay, send it through to our guys for processing. Can we take the lift out of commission? We might get fingerprints.'

'How long for?'

'A few hours.'

'Ermm, I'll see.'

'Thanks.' Chapman suspected Harding would veto fingerprinting the lifts. They'd find dozens and the new contract they'd signed with the forensic lab meant they paid per set eliminated. What idiot had agreed it? Some bastard nearing retirement and due to take up a new job in the private sector.

Conscious of time passing, he wanted to chase Sanchez up, but she'd let him know once she had something to report. He didn't have to wait long.

'Russell, we can't find the van.'

'How far have you looked? Can you extend—'

'It's not been on the system since yesterday, seventeen hundred.'

His mind raced. 'So, they've changed the numberplate. Can we find it leaving the station and search for the new ID?'

'Sorry, boss.' Sanderson's mournful tone warned him of more bad news. 'Here's the van leaving.'

A still from the traffic camera covering the entrance to the staff car park showed a small removal lorry, the number plate pixilated and the windscreen an opaque sheet.

'They're using a screening device,' the technician next to Sanderson added. 'You'll never find them.'

Chapman, who'd once resorted to using one, didn't need telling.

CHAPTER 22

The zip tie bit into her wrists as Antonia lay on her back and pushed her arms down the back of her legs until her hands reached her heels. With a tremendous effort, she pulled her knees up to her chest and stretched her arms until the ties passed under her feet. Halfway through, her left leg cramped. She gritted her teeth and pushed, and then, when she thought she'd end up stuck, her toe slipped free. Her legs followed. She lay on her back, snorting, and tried to strip the tape off her mouth, but her hands weren't cooperating. As she flexed her fingers to get them to respond, she hooked a nail under the edge of the tape. Careless of what damage she did, she ripped the tape off and lay there panting. She'd have to make sure she spent more time stretching when she next got to the gym.

Although not accustomed to the gloom, she could tell the roof was way above her. It would easily be high enough for her to stand up in. She listened, fighting to bring her breathing under control. Above the vehicle and road sounds came the background chatter of the police radio they'd tuned to. Most messages referred to the crash Hughes, or whoever employed him, must have arranged. None of the messages mentioned her abduction, but the operation tracking her used another frequency. Chapman and his team must have noticed she'd gone by now.

One man spoke, and she listened. Had they heard her? But the laugh in response told her they hadn't. How many were in the front? If only two, even with her hands secured, she might overcome them. If she caught them by surprise.

As her vision became accustomed to the dim light, she checked her surroundings. Apart from the door they'd thrown her in, another door separated her from the crew cab. Long metal shelves lined the sides of the vehicle, leading to roller shutters at the rear. It looked new, so the shelves would have a few sharp edges. She flexed her legs, trying to restore her circulation, then rolled over on to her front and pushed herself on to her knees. She ran her fingers along the bottom shelf. At the edge where they met the upright, a burr nicked the ball of her thumb. Perfect.

She positioned herself so her wrists straddled the sharp edge and sawed at the tie securing her hands. Every time they stopped, she paused until they moved off. She'd not paid attention to the traffic and couldn't guess their destination. What if they arrived before she freed herself? She resumed her sawing, now energised by fear.

Then her hands parted. One hit the side of the shelf with a meaty clunk. She froze, waiting. They didn't react and, guessing they hadn't heard, she massaged her wrists. Her hands tingled, and she relaxed. Now, she could surprise them, but a weapon would even the odds even further. She checked under the shelves but saw nothing.

As they turned a corner, something slid along an upper shelf. She reached up and caught a strap. Hughes's courier bag. She seized it and, waiting for the vehicle to accelerate, pulled it off the shelf. Despite her efforts, it swung against the shelf below with a hollow clang. She stopped, holding her breath and listening. In the distance, a car horn beeped, and the driver swore in response.

She'd got away with it. She examined the bag. Hughes must be in the front. Damn! She'd assumed there would only be his two accomplices. She definitely needed a weapon. Fingers still not functioning, she fumbled with the bag's buckles until she got them open. The vehicle changed direction, and she braced herself against the shelf, waiting until it straightened to check the bag's contents. Nothing to use as a weapon. The wand he'd used on her wasn't robust enough. But she found the Faraday pouch. Her phone slid out. Could she switch it on without her captors hearing it? The weight when she picked it up told her Hughes had removed the battery. A search of the bag confirmed he'd taken it with him, or more likely binned it before they set off. At least the transmitter hidden in it should now give Chapman her location. Provided she wasn't out of range. Would they find her before it was too late?

Each time they slowed, she tensed. The shrill note of a mobile made her jump. She slid forward to the door separating her from the cab and listened.

'Yeah?'

Was that Hughes?

'Not far, about five minutes. See you then.'

Her pulse raced. She couldn't wait any longer. She got up, using the shelves to support her. A last check of the top shelf confirmed it contained nothing she could use. She grabbed the courier bag and screwed it up tight round the wand, wrapping the straps round it to make it denser. After stretching her muscles, she opened the door and launched herself through the opening.

She landed in the gap between two seats. To her left, scrunched up against the window, sat Hughes, and nearest her, perched on the edge of the seat, one of the men who'd dragged her down the corridor. She swung the rolled-up bag at his eyes. It hit him with a wet thud and the man cried out. Hughes, still holding his phone, opened his mouth. Antonia swung the bag at him. He dropped the mobile and raised his arm too late. The bag hit him high on the forehead.

He reacted fast to grab it. Antonia let it go, then hit him hard in the throat with the side of her fist, using it like a hammer. Hughes gagged and collapsed into the seat holding his throat. She cocked her fist to hit his companion, but a hand grabbed it.

The driver had released the steering wheel and seized her forearm. He spun her round to face him. She snatched her hand back, but he held on. A fist thumped into her lower back and a hand grabbed her jacket. More surprised than hurt, she swung her left elbow. A grunt told her she'd hit the target. The driver pulled on her right arm. Antonia didn't resist but used the momentum from his jerk to spin and punched him with her left fist. It cracked into his cheek with enough force to snap his head back. She prepared another punch, but he slumped in the seat.

The hand pulled at her jacket. She turned to deal with it, but froze when she saw what lay ahead. They'd entered a slip road in a concrete canyon, which took a sharp bend to their right, but they aimed straight ahead. At a solid wall. Antonia lunged for the steering wheel, but Hughes's companion wasn't finished and grabbed her round the waist. Before she could free herself, the van lurched and left the road. The concrete uprights loomed in the windscreen and Antonia searched for something to hold on to.

The queue at the checkpoint out of the tube station moved far too slowly and a sense of panic seized Sabirah. She mustn't be late for this interview. After a long wait, she reached the front of the queue. Three members of the Security Auxiliary Force looked her up and down.

'Papers?' the woman demanded.

Sabirah produced the pass she'd long dreamt of owning and still couldn't believe she possessed.

The woman frowned and held it up to the light before passing it to her companions, who subjected it to the same scrutiny.

Despite knowing she'd received it through legitimate channels, Sabirah couldn't suppress her anxiety. The people stuck behind her muttered, and she mouthed an apology. How quickly she'd fallen from last week's confident triumph.

The woman held the pass. 'How did you get Indefinite Leave?'

'I'm a person of good character who will make a positive contribution to British society and values.' She recited the wording she'd learned by heart for her hearing.

With a scowl, the woman returned the pass and Sabirah hurried away, alternating between relief and anxiety she'd arrive late. Should she phone to warn them, or just get there? She chose the latter and arrived at her destination, a smart office block near Waterloo Bridge, late and out of breath. Now she'd finished working as a cleaner, she did far less exercise. And the fact she'd worked next door to her home for the last three months meant she hadn't even got exercise on her walk to work.

She charged into the entrance, relieved to find a lift discharging people. After hurrying from the tube, she needed to cool down. It took her up to the fourth floor, and she checked her reflection in the mirrored walls. She wore her best outfit, although the skirt felt tight. She'd have to get Antonia to suggest an exercise regime. The one she'd devised for Russell seemed to have worked. She'd have to speak to him about what had happened on holiday. Nadimah came back changed. The lift stopped, and she put those thoughts out of her mind. She needed to get a job.

A sign directed her to Space Design Partners, and she followed it. They'd cleverly used light in the smallish reception area to give a sense of space. A woman of about Sabirah's age came from behind a desk to greet her.

'Hello, I'm Mrs Fadil, I'm here about the job—'

'You're early. Do you want to take a seat? Can I get you a drink?'

Early? Sabirah must have been mistaken about the time of the interview. Grateful for her mistake, she took the chilled bottle of water the receptionist offered her and perched on one of two sofas arranged either side of a coffee table. She picked up a copy of *Architectural Digest* and flicked through the pages. Too nervous to read, she checked the time and sipped her water.

She should ask the receptionist the time of her interview, but not wanting to disturb her, Sabirah waited. Growing ever more uncomfortable, she flicked through another magazine, then her phone rang. She opened the laptop bag Antonia had lent her and retrieved her phone. Good thing she wasn't in the middle of the interview. Her face hot, she took the call from a number she didn't recognise.

'Sabirah Fadil, can I help you?'

'Mrs Fadil, it's Tim Eve. Have you been delayed?'

'No, I'm here. I arrived half an hour ago.'

'Oh! Hold on, I'll be right with you.' He ended the call.

Puzzled, she switched the phone off and put it away.

A tall man with a high forehead and his shirtsleeves rolled up strode up to the receptionist and spoke in an urgent undertone.

'I thought she came for the cleaner's job.'

The man jabbed a finger at the screen and spoke, his voice low and angry.

'She didn't say.' The receptionist gave Sabirah an accusatory look.

Sabirah resisted the urge to apologise and take the blame, but she needed this man to believe in her. She'd rebuild bridges with this woman once – if – she got the job. She gave the woman a tight smile and got one in return.

Eve transferred his attention to Sabirah and rearranged his expression. 'Sorry, Mrs Fadil, there seems to have been a misunderstanding.'

She rose and took his large hand. He stood a head above her and his Adam's apple bobbed when he spoke.

'Please come through.' He gestured to the open door he'd come through.

Sabirah clutched her laptop bag like a shield and entered the room. A table big enough for a dozen took up the centre of the space and models of buildings lined the outside. Two people sat at the top end of the table, one on each side, not giving Sabirah a clue where they expected her to sit.

The woman, fifty and in a sober tweed suit, wore multicoloured reading glasses and short hair dyed in rainbow colours. The man, also wearing a tweed suit, looked older and wore a striped bow tie.

'Mrs Fadil, please meet Diana and Jeremy.'

The couple nodded.

'Please call me Sabirah.' She took the nearest seat, wanting to escape their scrutiny, although they continued to study her.

Eve sat opposite her. 'We're short of time, so please tell us about yourself.'

Sabirah, feeling the need to rush, started by recounting her time studying architecture in Aleppo University and raced through her professional life until it all came to a halt in 2013, nine years earlier.

Diana gestured at her bag. 'I presume you have a portfolio in there.'

Sabirah nodded and retrieved the laptop. Antonia had picked out one of their newest machines, and it started almost instantly. She slid it across to the three architects, who crowded round it like three teenagers and devoured its contents.

'Some excellent designs, but nothing recent.' Eve sounded disappointed.

'The drawings for the conversion I oversaw are there.' She directed them to the file she'd left open.

After studying them, Eve said, 'They have another name on them. I thought he'd retired.'

'I couldn't put my plans forward, so Mr Brody Innis, a friend of Eleanor, Mrs Curtis, the building owner, presented my designs.'

'Hmm.' Jeremy didn't seem impressed. 'You're allowed to practise now?'

'Yes, I have Indefinite Leave to Remain. I have to take some Prescribed Qualifications exams, but I can work supervised.'

'So, you're effectively a trainee. We need an experienced architect.'

'No, I am experienced architect. But I'm happy to take trainee salary until I finished my conversion.' She guessed it would be much less than the job they'd advertised, but still more than she earned doing two jobs before.

'But one who hasn't worked for nine years. I'm not even sure how architecture qualifications from' – Diana glanced at the notes she'd made – 'the University of Aleppo compare to ours?' She looked over her glasses at her two companions, who shrugged.

'I have applied to ARB for full recognition of my qualifications.'

'Applied, not granted?'

'No.' Sabirah's voice faded.

'Okay, Mrs Fadil. Thank you for coming in. We'll be in touch.' Eve stood and walked to the door.

Sabirah scooped up the laptop and her bag, stumbled to her feet and scurried out of the door, all the clever things she'd planned to say unsaid and humiliation making her hot.

◆ ◆ ◆

Louisa Walker led the way and Chapman watched her and Darren Baxter make their way to his vehicle. Darren limped. It would have taken a lot to damage the man-mountain. As Chapman waited for them, his laptop beeped. The tracker in Antonia's phone had reactivated. With a surge of excitement, he opened the map. The cursor flashed on Mare Street in Hackney, four miles away. They'd made good time. He picked up the handset as Walker opened the door.

He passed her the handset. 'Speak to Control. We need a drone near Hackney.'

'Right, boss.' Walker took it.

Chapman spoke into his headset. 'Alice?'

'I heard. What have you got?'

'The tracker we put in Antonia's phone has woken up.'

'Where?'

He gave her the address.

'Leave it with me. We'll find the right cameras and patch them through to your feed in the van.'

While he waited, Chapman spoke to Baxter. 'What happened to your leg, Darren?'

'The woman who got away, she had a pram, which she used to ram me. It's just a dead leg.' He looked embarrassed.

'And she got away with the pram?'

'Nah, she dumped it. They'd put the hood up, but there's no baby in it.'

'What did the other three say?'

'Not a lot. The first one we caught clammed up when the other two joined him. I told the crew who picked him up to keep them apart, but whether they do . . .'

'Boss!' Sanderson pointed at the screens, which now showed stretches of road around Hackney.

'Alice, what am I looking at?'

'The roads they *could* leave on. We're covering the bases until we spot the vehicle.'

Chapman leant over the front seat and checked the laptop. 'They're just turning into Well St.'

'Got them!' Sanchez let out an excited cry. 'I'll put it on the main screen.'

The large van he'd last seen leaving the station car park appeared on the screen in front of Sanderson. 'Right, don't lose them.' Chapman addressed Walker. 'Anything, Louisa?'

'There's a drone covering a multi-vehicle pile-up less than two minutes away.'

Chapman took the handset off her and spoke to Control. 'Have we got any vehicles in the vicinity?'

'The local vehicles are attending an RTC on the Westbound A12 in Leytonstone. The nearest is a car on the M11 just north of Chigwell. I'm sending it and checking if Essex has any nearby.'

Chapman did a quick calculation. They'd be going the wrong direction and would need to negotiate a couple of interchanges before they reached the van. 'Where's your car, Louisa?'

'Just over there.' Walker jerked a thumb over her shoulder.

'Get it.'

Her face lit up, and slamming the door, she ran.

'Inspector?' the Control operator called. 'The drone has a visual. I'll email a link to your laptop.'

By the time his email pinged, Walker had arrived. Chapman grabbed the laptop and retrieved his work mobile from Sanderson. He got an update from the operator in the station on his way to Walker's car. They still hadn't found Antonia in the complex. That made it almost certain Hughes and his cronies had taken her in the van. He got in the car, and it set off with a throaty roar before he'd fastened his seatbelt.

Bracing himself against the dashboard, Chapman opened the email and clicked on the link. The image came into focus. The white van moved along a ribbon of road in the centre of the screen. It slowed as it approached a five-way junction. They kept below the speed limit, not driving as if they'd spotted the drone. The van moved through the junction going towards the A12. Then it veered to one side.

'Alice, have you got a camera angle so we can see into the cab?'

'Sorry, no. It's no use, anyway. They've screened the van so we can't see in.'

Chapman swore. The van disappeared from the screen as the road it was on passed under the A12. The drone flew over the junction and hovered, waiting for the van to reappear. What the hell was happening?

'Alice, can you see into the tunnel?'

She didn't reply.

'Alice?'

'Sorry, Russell. The van has crashed. It's on its side. I've just notified the emergency services.'

Walker heard the message through her headset and increased her speed. Chapman placed the laptop on the floor and held on. Walker always drove like a rally driver, but this represented a step up. Chapman prayed and hoped they'd not join Antonia. He imagined her in the back of the van, being thrown about with whatever the owners kept there. The thought of tools and bits of machinery smashing into her body made him feel sick.

He opened his eyes and focused on their surroundings. He searched for a landmark and spotted a pub he'd visited. They approached Hackney, not too far now. Walker braked for a bus negotiating the bridge ahead of them. She beeped the horn, adding to the cacophony from the siren and screaming engine. Chapman realised they'd just crossed the Regent Canal, which passed in front of Antonia's offices. Less than a mile and a half to the crash.

Walker slowed as they came into Hackney's main street. She used the bus lane to make progress, siren blaring and blue lights flashing. Chapman held his breath as they passed a pub where a group of men making the most of the warm weather teetered on the edge of the pavement in front of them. Then Walker shot off the main road, down a one-way street. She accelerated, bullying a taxi off the road and missing a cyclist by inches. The road straightened, and although narrow, you could see a long way. She piled on the accelerator and almost too soon they approached the junction through which they'd seen Antonia pass. They didn't seem to slow through the chicane and then, at the slip road, everything stopped. Two lanes of stationary traffic.

Despite Walker's efforts, they made slow progress. As they approached the underpass, a gout of black smoke appeared from under it. Walker swore and Chapman's stomach cramped.

'Let me out.' He opened the door before they'd stopped.

He ran, weaving between stationary cars and their occupants getting out to have a look. The van lay on its side, occupying the hard shoulder and inside lane. Lazy orange flames accompanied by black smoke clung to the vehicle. Next to it, blocking the second and third lanes, sat a large pickup. As he got closer, he saw another vehicle beyond it. The stench of burning rubber and plastic assaulted his nose.

Heat and smoke pumped out from the van, and ducking to avoid it, he ran through the gap between it and the pickup. He could now see the second vehicle, a large people-carrier with blacked-out windows. Dark-clad people moved with purpose. Two of them picked up a casualty, and for a split second, Chapman mistook them for medics, but the way they carried the body told him they weren't.

The front of the overturned van looked like a giant had hit it with a hammer. Two men dragged out a body slumped sideways in the driver's seat.

'What are you doing?'

The men stopped, then one produced an automatic and pointed it at him. Chapman ducked back behind the van. *What if they've grabbed Antonia?* He edged forward and stuck his head out. They'd almost reached their vehicle. He ran forward, then out the corner of his eye, saw yellow fabric.

Antonia lay in a crumpled heap on the road in front of the van. He veered towards her, then he saw the blood.

CHAPTER 23

The stench of burnt hair filled Grainger's nostrils as his befuddled brain regained consciousness. He opened his eyes but saw nothing. The events of last night passed through his thoughts in a jumble. Had they happened? He attempted to get up, but couldn't lift his exhausted body off the bed. The dull ache in his left arm became a sharp pain and then increased in intensity until the agony became unbearable. Grainger couldn't suppress his moans.

A bright light penetrated his eyelids. He squinted until his eyes adjusted. A woman in medical scrubs leant over him. Where was he?

'Am I in hospital?' His voice came out as a hoarse whisper.

'You wish.' The sibilant voice brought back memories of another awakening.

The medic moved aside to reveal the leader of the team of kidnappers and the man Grainger had scarred with his bottle in his futile escape attempt. Terror seized Grainger, and he fought to get up. Three wide straps held him down, leaving his left arm free. He tried to move it, but the pain increased. Heavy bandages swaddled the limb.

The two men came forward and unbuckled the straps. Scarface pushed his left arm aside, making Grainger scream in pain.

'Shall I give him more painkillers? The others have worn off,' the woman asked.

'No. We've got more questions for him.' Scarface gave him a nasty grin.

A moan escaped Grainger's mouth. The two men dragged him to his feet, not caring if they hurt him. He wobbled but stayed upright. Instead of his T-shirt and boxers, he wore some institutional pyjamas.

Scarface noticed his reaction. 'You pissed yourself, didn't you, you dirty bastard.' He prodded Grainger in the back. 'Come on, Mr R – the boss wants a word.'

The slip earned Scarface a scowl from the team leader. The medic couldn't know who she worked for. Grainger thought of telling her but he realised it would result in her death. The men led him out of the room and through a bright corridor, Scarface in front and the team leader following. A sense of dread, increasing with every step, seized Grainger. He couldn't go through it again.

They reached a doorway at the end of the corridor and Scarface pulled the door open and half-stepped through. Grainger barged forward and pushed the door against Scarface with all his strength. Before he made his next move, agony swamped his system, paralysing him.

'Go on then.' The team leader squeezed his left wrist through the bandages.

Sobbing in pain, Grainger begged, 'Please, don't.'

A furious Scarface pushed Grainger and punched him in the face, but compared to the agony from his arm, it didn't register. Grainger fell to his knees, more to escape the pain than because of the punch, but he couldn't get away.

'Try that again, and I will hurt you.' The team leader grabbed his shoulders and pulled him upright. 'Now, let's go. Mr Reed-Mayhew doesn't like to be kept waiting.'

Grainger stumbled along behind Scarface, unable to think, just wanting the pain to finish. Another door ahead, reviving the memory of this morning. Was it still today? He had no idea. His steps faltered, but a prod of his bandaged forearm encouraged him to speed up. Scarface opened the door and led them into a large room, but no furnace.

The relief lasted until he saw Reed-Mayhew examining an expensive watch. He wore a different suit, but by the same designer. He must have bought the man's entire collection. The two men flanked Grainger and led him forward to a chair in front of their boss.

'Now you've had time to think. Will you tell me the truth?' Reed-Mayhew said.

'I told the truth.'

Reed-Mayhew gestured at Scarface, who seized Grainger's bandaged arm and squeezed. His scream echoed.

'Shall we try again?'

Sweat poured into Grainger's eyes, but not from any heat. Panting, he said, 'I can't change the truth—'

This time, he passed out. The terrifying sensation of drowning woke him. Spluttering, he sucked air into his lungs. The pain from his arm overrode all else. When he could sit up, he looked at Reed-Mayhew. The bastard didn't hide his enjoyment of Grainger's suffering. A surge of anger strengthened his resolve.

'I have told you the truth. Whatever you get your goons to do won't change that.'

Reed-Mayhew smiled. 'I've got to rush, but we'll have another chat tomorrow.' He addressed the team leader. 'The furnace room tomorrow, and tell the nurse he won't need pain relief tonight. Until tomorrow then, Mr Grainger.'

◆ ◆ ◆

'Antonia!'

She recognised the voice. Then doors slammed and a vehicle roared into life, then a second. The stench of burning oil filled her nostrils.

'Antonia!'

Someone lifted her shoulders off the ground.

'You shouldn't move her, guv.'

Gentle hands lowered her to the ground. 'Sorry.'

Chapman. *What is he doing here?* Then, with a rush, her memory returned. The concrete wall racing towards her, then grabbing the man who'd sat next to Hughes, using his body as a shield as they flew through the windscreen.

She opened her eyes, the lids sticky. Chapman stared down at her, concern etched on his features.

'Are you okay? I mean, where does it hurt?' He looked at someone standing behind her. 'Where's the ambulance?'

'I'll check, boss.'

Antonia recognised Walker's voice. She'd met her on a couple of occasions. She considered his question. Her shoulder, where she'd slammed into the man when they hit the road, and her head after his snapped back into hers, both hurt, but not excessively. She remembered the sound it made, a wet crunch.

'What's happened to the man?'

'What man? Don't worry about him.'

A dull ache infused her body, reminding her of the time a lorry smashed into the car she and her informant John were sitting in. The image of the top of his head, brain exposed, returned and with it, nausea. She attempted to rise.

'Stay still, you're hurt.'

'Help me up, I'm fine.'

'You're covered in blood.' Chapman sounded incredulous.

'Russell, please.' She let a note of exasperation enter her voice.

His arms gripped her shoulders and helped her sit. She checked herself. Blood stained her jeans and what remained of her top.

'Oh, God,' he said. 'Your back . . .'

Her face grew hot. 'Give me your jacket.'

'But you're—'

'Just do it.' She wanted to lie down, hide the hideous scars on her back.

Chapman took his jacket off and draped it over her shoulders. The smell reminded her of the last time she'd worn one of his jackets. She'd ended up killing a man, but she'd saved Chapman.

A distant siren sounded, and closer, a hubbub of voices. Had anyone else seen her scars? She wanted to get out of there and did a quick inventory. Nothing seemed damaged.

'Help me up, Russell.'

'But . . .' He gave a resigned sigh and helped her to her feet.

After a slight wobble, she steadied. Apart from her shoulder and aching all over, she felt well. Not even a headache, although she must have been out for a while. She slipped her arms through the sleeves of the jacket as Chapman watched her with a wary concern.

'This isn't mine.' She tapped her bloodied clothes. 'There were two of us in the front without seatbelts on. I— We got thrown out together. This came from him.'

Behind her, the remains of the van lay on its side, now engulfed in flames, but they didn't hide its smashed bodywork. She checked the cab, a mass of flame, and even from this distance, the heat made her skin crinkle.

'The driver, and Hughes, they wore seatbelts—'

'They've gone.'

'What do you mean?'

'Someone took them. Some blokes in a people-carrier and pickup collected the bodies. I thought they'd taken you.'

Chapman's tone provoked a wave of tenderness. 'Good thing you arrived.'

Danil Derenski and his henchmen must have followed the van. She'd had a lucky escape. She noticed the smear of blood on the road surface. And flesh mixed up in those pieces of fabric. She replayed the collision, relieved she could recall everything, including the impact and landing on the road, clamped to the man who'd saved her life but lost his, judging from what he'd left behind.

The sirens stopped, and an ambulance edged round the blazing van to come to a halt alongside Antonia and Chapman. A paramedic got out and studied Antonia, looking puzzled by how someone who appeared to have lost so much blood could stand unaided.

'It's not hers,' Chapman said.

'So, are you injured?'

'I found her unconscious, and she needs a check-up, her back—'

'I passed out for a brief spell.'

'Okay, let's check you out.'

A second paramedic arrived, gesturing to the burning van. 'Is anyone still in there?'

'They've gone,' Chapman explained as Antonia followed the first medic to the rear of the ambulance.

While she underwent checks, two fire engines arrived and dealt with the van. Antonia craned her neck to check the crews for her firefighter friend, Adam, but didn't see anyone she recognised. The paramedic finished his checks.

'If you survived that, you've been unbelievably lucky. I'd recommend an overnight stay for observation, but we're short of beds and unless you're at death's door, we won't take you in. You shouldn't be alone for at least twenty-four hours. He your boyfriend?' He gestured at Chapman, who stood talking to the fire officer.

'Of course not! He's a policeman. We're working together.'

'Oh, right. I'm trying to imagine you in uniform.' He grinned. 'I'm a reporter.'

His grin faded. 'Oh, right? You know the bit I said before about the bed shortage? We're not supposed to say . . .'

After reassuring him she wouldn't repeat his comment, she joined Chapman.

Chapman nodded at the paramedic. 'What did he say?'

'He said I've had a remarkable escape, to come out of that uninjured.'

'What about your back . . .' He saw her expression. 'What happened when they grabbed you?'

'They zip-tied me.' She showed the fading red marks on her wrists. 'But I got free and found my phone. He'd put it in a Faraday pouch. I presume you picked up the signal, to get here so fast.'

'Sanchez picked you up via the cameras and a drone followed you until . . .' He jerked a thumb up at the concrete underside of the road above. 'Why did they crash?'

'Hughes got a call, and I heard him say they'd arrive in five minutes. So, I stopped them.'

'You did that.' He gestured at the smouldering wreck. 'Sanchez is tracking the two vehicles that were here when I arrived. I'll warn her they may have turned off somewhere.' He spoke into his headset.

Antonia tuned him out and examined the wreckage. The fire-fighters had finished and made up their equipment. A police car had arrived, and two uniformed officers surveyed the site. An object glinted in the sunlight on the roadway ahead of the van, near the blood smear. She approached, stopping two paces away. A battered phone, its casing cracked, and the screen crazed, lay in the gutter.

'Russell?'

Chapman came over and she pointed out the phone.

'I think that belonged to the guy who got thrown out of the van.'

'Okay, well spotted. I'll get these guys to deal with it.' He approached the uniformed officers, and, after speaking to them, shouted to Walker, 'Louisa, bring the car.' He rushed back to Antonia. 'Alice has tracked the cars to an industrial estate near here, just off the next junction. The armed response team we had at King's Cross is on the way and I'm meeting them there.'

'Can I come?'

'The traffic guys will need a statement.'

'They'll be a while before they're ready to take one.' Antonia gestured to the incident, where the officers had set up a cordon. 'Anyway, I'll be with you. Imagine I've gone to hospital. What would they do then?'

'I'm in enough trouble with this mess.' He pointed over his shoulder.

'Please, Russell.'

He shook his head.

'I'm the only one who knows what they look like.'

He gave an exasperated sigh. 'Okay. But stay out of the way.'

She gave him a hug as an unmarked car roared to stop alongside them. Walker gave a big grin as she unlocked the doors. Antonia clambered into the back and fumbled for the seatbelt as they surged away. As someone who didn't drive, she admired the effortless way Walker handled the car. Maybe she should learn.

They covered the three miles to the junction in two minutes, taking advantage of the empty road. Then they hit the side streets. To Antonia's surprise, they didn't appear to slow, and a blur of green on one side gave the only clue they were passing a park. They changed direction, then passed a hospital.

A minute later, Chapman spoke. 'Slow down, Louisa. We need to wait for backup.'

They approached Siding Lane, a dead-end road that led to the industrial estate.

'Pull up on the left.' He addressed his headset. 'Do we know where they went down here, Alice?' He listened for a while. 'Right, okay, let me know if you see anything.'

'What's happened?' Antonia said, her leg cramping in the tight back seat.

'They lost them once they came down here. The cameras are out.'

'We need to identify where they've gone. Anything could be happening.' Antonia pointed at a large lorry, which lumbered towards them and drew alongside. 'They could even have their cars in the back of this thing.'

'You want me to stop all the traffic?'

'Why not? Danil Derenski, the guy behind Alan's death, is in one of those cars.'

'Hughes told you his name?'

'Didn't you pick it up with the mic?'

'Too much echo in the station. I'm surprised Hughes told you.'

'He didn't expect me to . . .' To live, she was about to say. The reality of how close she'd come to disaster sunk in and her hands trembled.

'Now we've got his name, we can track him down.'

'We don't need to track him down. He's down there somewhere.' She pulled the door handle. 'Let me out.'

Chapman turned in his seat. 'Not if you're going to do something stupid.'

'I'm getting a cramp in here. Can you let me out?'

Chapman opened his door and nodded to Walker. The locks clicked on the back doors and Antonia scrambled out.

'Can we just check?' she said. 'They could have parked outside a unit.'

Chapman thought for a few moments. 'I'll go. They'll recognise you.'

'Didn't they see you at the crash?'

'Shit. They did.'

Antonia wouldn't let Derenski get away if she could help it. 'I'm having a quick look. You don't have to come.' She strode off down Siding Lane. She'd gone a few paces, and Chapman's steps followed.

'Hang on, I'll come with you. Would you recognise their cars?'

Blast! She'd noticed no one following them. 'I'll recognise *them.*'

'Right.' Chapman walked alongside, hurrying to keep up.

Rows of mainly single-storey industrial units, mostly clad in steel, and with few windows, lined the lane. Many had their steel roller shutters open as the workers went about their tasks in the summer heat. Dumpsters, steel containers and piles of wooden pallets crowded the space between the units. With every unit they passed without seeing the cars, Antonia grew more tense. Had they got past them in the rear of a lorry? She hated the thought of being so close but missing them. As they neared the end of the lane, her steps faltered. Next to her, Chapman slowed. The road ended and opened out into a T and she stopped. There, up against the fence in front of the adjoining railway line, sat two vehicles – a black van and a pickup – their noses against the barrier.

'Are those the two?' she asked Chapman.

'I think so.'

She watched from the corner, not wanting to alert anyone in them. Because of their blacked-out windows, she couldn't see into the people-carrier or the pickup.

'What's that?'

Alerted by Chapman's tone, Antonia peered. Lights flickered in the back of the people-carrier. Then the windows exploded.

Orange flame filled the openings and a pressure wave hit her, hot and unyielding, as the explosion made her ears ring. A second followed, centred on the cab of the pickup. A cloud of dense black smoke mushroomed above the vehicles.

Antonia got closer, unable to see inside. Behind her, Chapman spoke in urgent tones. Something moved in the rear of the people-carrier. Could she see someone still in there? She moved up to the window. Yes, a body sat in the back seat.

'Antonia, don't go any nearer!'

Ignoring the warning, she crouched to avoid the worst of the heat and slid the jacket over her head.

'Don't be stupid,' Chapman shouted.

She peered into the flames, then the body moved. Before she could react, Chapman barrelled into her and dragged her back. Then, with a whoosh, flame exploded, knocking her and the policeman backwards. Antonia curled up into a protective ball and her ears popped.

CHAPTER 24

Her ears ringing, Antonia lay face down on the tarmac for the second time that day. Chapman's weight lay across her legs, and he struggled to get off her.

'Sorry, are you okay?' He sounded out of breath.

She pushed her torso off the tarmac and knelt, brushing her hands together. A thin ribbon of blood leaked from a puncture in the ball of her right thumb. 'I'll live.'

They both scrambled to their feet and retreated from the ball of fire engulfing the two vehicles.

'Thanks, Russell.' *What was I thinking?*

A crowd of around fifty had gathered, and she scanned them on the off chance Derenski hadn't left the estate. She saw nobody she recognised. Heavy boots clattered on the road and three armed officers arrived.

The crowd parted, and the inspector approached Chapman. 'I've blocked the road with our vehicle, so nobody can leave.'

'Leave the driver and one guy. The rest of you check each unit.' Chapman addressed the crowd. 'Can you all return to your place of work? We'll need to search each building to make sure the people responsible aren't hiding.'

A stocky guy with a big chin and sticking-out ears pointed to the building behind them. 'I'll get my guys to search our place.'

'Thanks for the offer, but let these guys do it. There's a good chance the fugitives are carrying firearms.'

An uneasy murmur greeted this observation, but the crowd melted away.

'I'll make a start.' The inspector started back to the entrance.

'I'll go with them.' Antonia followed.

'No way.'

'Why not? I know what Derenski looks like, and I expect he'll be with the other guys who murdered Alan.'

Chapman hesitated, then called the inspector. 'Can you take Antonia? She can recognise the men we're looking for.'

The inspector looked ready to argue, but nodded. 'You'll have to stay well back, miss.'

He trotted after his men, and Antonia joined him. After a few steps, the aches from where she'd hit the tarmac eased. They passed the units they'd have to search, many small, so wouldn't take long, but there were plenty of them. At the entrance to the lane, the minibus containing the rest of the armed response team and the car she'd arrived in formed a barrier.

Walker stood at the window of a van trying to leave, speaking to the driver, while two armed officers looked on. The driver got out and led her to the back. Antonia checked his passenger but didn't recognise him either.

She waited, impatient to make a start, while the inspector briefed his crew. As they checked the first unit, two fire engines arrived and within less than a minute, the thick black smoke rising from the wreckages of the two vehicles turned white. The police team moved through the units, working with practised efficiency, and soon cleared the first few, the occupants of each eager to show they had nothing to hide.

Antonia, who'd described Derenski to them, followed them into the units, checking the male occupants of the right age. By the time they reached the end of the close the firefighters had finished, and a forensic team had cordoned off the area round the two smouldering vehicles. An ambulance parked alongside the fire engines, much too late to help the occupants of the cars.

They reached the large unit next to them, the top of one of its walls blackened by the fire. Nobody answered when the inspector rang the doorbell. Even standing at the rear of the squad, Antonia could hear it echo within.

The empty unit they'd already encountered had roller shutters down over the openings. This one had them raised. A tension settled over the team and the inspector signalled her to move back. He gestured to the team members to check the other openings and two pairs broke off to check the side and back.

A minute later, the two who'd disappeared round the back jogged back, their body language telling Antonia they'd found something. She edged closer but couldn't hear them. After a quick briefing, they smashed the front door and charged in, shouting warnings.

The noise attracted a young man in overalls from a nearby unit. 'What's going on? Have you found someone?'

'I don't know.'

'That's where the blokes from the car went.'

'Which car?'

He pointed to the smouldering wrecks. 'They parked outside, all got out and then moved them there.'

A surge of adrenaline energised Antonia. She rushed to the open main door. From inside, the sound of the crews searching and clearing spaces carried.

'Hello, Inspector, can you hear me?' She waited, muscles tense, then a figure approached.

The sergeant appeared in the doorway. 'Please stay back, miss, we've not—'

'This guy saw the people we're looking for come in here earlier.'

The sergeant glanced at the young man. 'Right, stay back.' He disappeared back into the building, speaking into his mic.

Antonia waited, then a few minutes later, three armoured officers came out. Their body language spoke of disappointment.

The sergeant saw her. 'All clear, there's nobody in there.' A hint of accusation sounded in his voice.

'Can I have a look?'

He spoke into his head mic, then nodded. 'The guvnor's in the main area.'

Antonia walked into a corridor with three doors on the right and a single door on the opposite wall. Three open doors led into offices that looked abandoned. The lone door led into an enormous space that rose to the underside of the roof.

The inspector stood in the back corner with three of his team. 'Not a lot to see.'

'Why did you break in?' Antonia walked towards them.

'Two of our guys thought they'd heard someone. Obviously mistaken.'

Spots of fresh oil on the concrete floor showed where a large vehicle had parked. Antonia pointed at them. 'This must have come from the lorry they left the site in.'

'Could be. We'd better check the remainder of the estate.'

'Aren't you going to get forensics in here?'

'What for?' He swept an arm around the space. 'There's nothing here.'

'But they must have meant to bring me here.'

He shrugged. 'Have a look round and let me know if you find anything.'

One of his men chuckled, and they followed him to the exit. Antonia, annoyed at their attitude, followed, but stopped. This must be Derenski's destination. Why would he bring her to an empty industrial unit? Determined to find something, she returned to the offices, but the undisturbed dust on the surfaces told her she'd find nothing. Disappointed, she set off to catch up with the team, but something held her back.

She made her way to the large open space. It extended further back than the offices. Had she missed rooms off the ones she'd looked in? A check confirmed she hadn't. Not ready to give up, she returned to the open space. The plasterboard-covered partition separating it from the offices ended at the rear wall. Why would they block off part of it and not use it? It made no sense.

She walked along the plasterboard wall. Where the offices finished, she paid special attention. Halfway along this section, she spotted a mark on the floor. Although one of many, it stood out. She rubbed it with her toe, and it left a reddish smear. With growing excitement, she examined the adjacent wall.

The joints between the plasterboard sheets weren't perfect and whoever put them up hadn't taped them. The one nearest the stain had scratches at the edge. She checked the others, and they all displayed scuff marks, but these looked more uniform. Unable to get her fingers into the gap, she looked for a tool. In one office, she found metal bars slotted into brackets along the edge of a filing cabinet's drawers. She retrieved one and rushed back to the wall.

Should she get the team back before she did any more? The thought of them mocking her, if it turned out to be a false alarm, decided her. The metal bar slid into the gap. Why wasn't there an upright in the gap? She used the bar as a lever and although the plaster crumbled, the gap widened. Once she could get her fingers in, she dropped the bar and pulled.

The sheet of plasterboard swung open to reveal a normal-sized door. Antonia gripped the handle and turned. Sound insulation covered the back of the door. She poked her head into the pitch-black opening. An unpleasant odour like rotting meat filled her nostrils. Advancing into the room, she found a light switch. Strip lights flickered on, bathing everything in a harsh light.

Antonia blinked and examined the space. The same sound insulation covered all surfaces. Two chairs sat bolted to the floor in the centre of the room. Reddish brown splotches covered the floor surrounding them. She froze, and her insides churned. She'd once rescued Chapman from a room like this. Derenski's torture chamber, and this is where they'd intended to bring her.

Marks on the floor led to an open door in the rear corner. She walked towards it, senses on alert. Beyond the door was another, less than three metres away. Dark shadows showed at the bottom corner of this. She approached, pushed it open and peered through the opening. She should get the backup team, but pressed on. As her shadow preceded her into the opening, a cry made her pulse spike.

◆ ◆ ◆

Police tape formed a flimsy barrier across the open doorway and Chapman stared into the room beyond. The memory of being tied to a similar chair in a basement he'd still never located made him nauseous. Part of him didn't want to find it, as it could still contain evidence, not just of his savage beating, but also of Antonia's presence and where she'd killed one of his torturers. Who was the man who'd received the same treatment here? He and Antonia had helped the paramedics get the poor guy to the ambulance, and he'd left Antonia there with instructions to get checked out. He left the doorway and made his way outside.

The paramedic examining Antonia said something, and her reply made him laugh. He looked like the same guy who'd attended the crash. Antonia stood and, after another exchange, which again made the medic laugh, moved towards Chapman. She moved stiffly, but it wasn't surprising after being in a collision and then getting blown up. He ached where he'd smashed into her.

'You seemed to get on,' Chapman said. 'What did he say? You okay?'

'He said it's possible I've got bruised kidneys from where you hit me.'

'Shit, I'm sorry.'

She laughed. 'He said I'm fine and did I fancy meeting for a drink after he finished his shift.'

'Cheeky sod. I should report him.'

'Leave him alone, Mr Grumpy.' Antonia's expression grew sombre. 'Horrible, wasn't it?'

'Yeah. How do you feel?'

'Glad I found the bloke. He could have died in there—'

'I'm going to make sure whoever missed the room gets hauled over the coals. They should have found him, not you.'

'It wasn't easy to find. You're in an unforgiving mood. First the paramedic, then these guys.'

'I don't like sloppiness.'

'It's not just that. You'd normally just kick their arses, like you did, then move on.'

He took a deep breath. 'You're right. I'm annoyed we almost lost you and I blame myself.'

'You'll have to try harder if you want to lose me.'

'I suppose so. Even in London, losing a six-foot mixed-race woman with a shaved head isn't easy.'

She ran her hand over the fine fuzz covering her skull. 'As you said last week, I'd let it get long. Anyway, meeting Hughes was my idea.'

'I shouldn't have allowed you to put yourself at risk.'

'What makes you think I'd have listened? Imagine if I'd met him on my own.' Antonia winked and indicated the two cars. 'What's happening?'

Chapman turned his attention to the forensic team swarming over the two burnt-out shells. 'They've found two bodies in the rear of the people-carrier. I'm guessing they're two of the men from your van. They must have been dead already. One of the fire guys said the body might have moved because of the heat.'

'At least I hadn't imagined it. The one who accompanied me through the windscreen will be one and I bet the other one's Hughes.'

'Was he in the passenger seat?' As in most collisions, the near-side of the van suffered the worst damage.

Antonia looked distressed. 'He provided a link to Derenski.'

'Don't worry, now we've got Derenski's name we don't need Hughes.'

'I hope you're right. What's going on now?' The activity around the burnt-out vehicles increased.

'Looks like they're getting the bodies out.'

The uniformed officers sent to investigate called for a detective to take over when they discovered the bodies. To Chapman's relief, DI Stevie Gillich arrived and took charge of the scene. She came towards them now, wearing a thoughtful expression.

'Afternoon, Russell.' She studied Antonia, noting her blood-stained clothing.

'It's from the crash just over there.' Antonia waved towards Hackney Wick.

'Shouldn't you be in hospital?'

'It's not mine. It's from one of the other people in the accident.'

'He must be in a bad way. I didn't realise there were casualties.'

Chapman nodded at the burnt-out cars. 'I'm pretty sure he's in there.'

'Oh yeah, do tell?'

'My team has been working with Antonia and she met a suspect in King's Cross—'

'Anything to do with the train smash?'

'We think they arranged it as a diversion so they could snatch Antonia.'

Gillich studied Antonia with renewed interest. 'You've been involved in a trail of destruction this afternoon.'

Antonia shrugged.

'The kidnappers escaped in a van which crashed,' Chapman said. 'When I arrived, the occupants of these two' – he indicated the two vehicles – 'were scooping up bodies to get rid of evidence. Alice is at the observation centre and tracked them here.'

Gillich pointed to Chapman's headset. 'Are you in contact with her?'

'The cameras are out on this bit, which is why we came down on foot and arrived as they burst into flames.'

'Right, so we're looking for timers.' She spoke into her radio.

'It looks like they were coming here.' Chapman pointed to the building where they'd found the injured man.

Gillich nodded. 'I've asked for another forensics team to deal with the building. I don't want any accusations of cross-contamination.'

'We think they got away in another vehicle,' Antonia said.

'Makes sense. Did Alice get anything on the cameras?'

Chapman said, 'She's got twenty-one vehicles leaving the site between these two arriving and us setting up a roadblock.'

'That's quite a few.'

'I've asked her to focus on bigger vehicles. There would have been a few in the cars, plus guards for the poor guy we found.'

Antonia's attention switched as the first body bag came out of the people-carrier. 'Do you have any ID for those two?'

'Nothing obvious, but their clothes had melted to the bodies, so we'll have to wait for the post-mortem. It looks a nasty one.'

'I'd suggest both were dead before the fire started.'

Gillich studied Antonia. 'Why would you think that?'

Chapman stepped in. 'It's possible one body is a guy called Hughes. We've got his details. The other guy is almost certainly the one who bled all over Antonia.'

'We need to speak to you, Ms Conti. Don't go anywhere.'

Chapman stepped in before Antonia could respond. 'No problem, she's in my car. We'll grab drinks. There's a trailer back there doing refreshments.'

He guided Antonia away, and she let him, as Gillich returned her attention to the body bags.

Antonia waited until they moved out of earshot. 'She's full of herself, isn't she?'

'She's very good at her job and she dealt with paedophiles and child traffickers for six years.'

Antonia digested this revelation. 'Poor woman.'

They joined the short queue at the trailer, Antonia causing a stir with her bloodied clothes, which looked like a costume from a zombie movie.

Sanchez's voice came over the earpiece. 'Boss, we've identified the getaway vehicle.'

'Hang on.' He told Antonia what to get him and stepped away. 'Where is it?'

'We tracked the five most likely and have eliminated four. The fifth one has disappeared.'

'What do you mean?'

'They drove towards Brentwood, came off the main road and stopped at a retail park. They parked out of sight of the cameras and just stayed there. We sent a patrol from Essex, and they said it's empty. I'm pretty sure they've just melted away and joined the other customers.'

'Shit!'

'Sorry, Russell.'

'Not your fault, Alice. You might as well get back to the station. Stevie Gillich is investigating our car fires, and she wants Antonia to give a statement.'

'You'd better not upset Stevie. Give her my regards and I'll see you back at the ranch.'

He ended the call and went looking for Antonia *and* his coffee. As he found her, two patrol cars arrived, blue lights on and in a hurry. They screeched to a halt and four officers poured out, heading for Antonia. He arrived as the lead officer read out her rights.

'What's going on?'

'Do you want to stay out of this, sir?' A constable stepped towards him.

'DI Chapman.' He showed his ID. 'What are you doing?'

'She's wanted for questioning—'

'I know, and I told Inspector Gillich I'd make sure she gave a statement.'

'Our orders come from higher up,' the lead officer said. 'She's a suspect in kidnapping and torture.'

'What? She's the *victim* of a kidnapping.'

'Some of our guys found a kidnap victim in a unit here—'

'Antonia found him, and I helped her.'

'So, she found him, did she?'

'I just told you.' The officer's attitude irritated Chapman.

'The guy named her as the person who lured him there.'

'What?' Chapman exchanged a look with Antonia, who looked resigned as they put on handcuffs. 'There's no need to cuff her.'

'I'll decide what's appropriate, sir.'

'Where are you taking her?'

'Leyton Custody Centre.'

He watched them lead her away. Whatever the story there, there's no way Antonia would be involved. He just hoped he could prove that.

CHAPTER 25

Like every interview room Antonia had been in, the one in Leyton Custody Centre smelt of desperation and fear. They'd left her in a cell for two hours and then brought her here half an hour ago. Despite the warm weather, they'd put the heating on, making the room stifling and dry. She desperately needed a drink, which of course had to have been their intention. The papery disposable jumpsuit they'd provided her with stuck to her damp skin. The door opened and Geoff Stokes came in, carrying a sheaf of papers.

'Good evening, Antonia.'

She stood to greet him and the constable watching her stiffened. What the hell had they told them about her? First sending four heavies to arrest her, then watching her like she was Britain's most wanted.

'Geoff, am I glad to see you.' As usual, Stokes wore an immaculate suit and exuded an air of calm competence which immediately lessened the stress of her situation.

Stokes addressed the uniformed constable. 'I need to confer with my client in private.' Once he left, Stokes took the seat facing Antonia. 'I'll get you out of here in no time.' He placed the papers on the table between them, a copy of her charge sheet on top. 'The charges are pretty serious. They claim you helped to lure

Abel Latif to a meeting in Unit 23, Siding Lane, where someone tortured him.'

The name jolted Antonia back eighteen months. 'I remember a Latif framed for murder by Gustav Reed-Mayhew, but I helped get him released, and last I heard he'd left the country.'

'So, you *do* know him?'

'I saw him at the hearing where they released him, and he thanked me for uncovering the evidence exonerating him.'

'According to the police, he's back.' Stokes read from the charge sheet. 'He claims to have contacted you looking for work and agreed to meet you this morning.'

'None of that ever happened. I thought he'd got a big pay-out and sold his story to a tabloid.'

'Let's examine the substance of this. You're certain you haven't met or spoken to him since the date of his hearing?'

'Yes.'

'When did that hearing take place?'

'Sorry, Geoff, I don't recall the exact date. Sometime in May last year. I'm sure we can find it in the court record.'

'No problem. Let's go over what you want to say.'

They spent twenty minutes refining Antonia's statement. They sat side by side, ready to face her accuser. The door opened and Harding walked in with a female officer. Antonia suppressed the mixture of irritation and anger seeing him again so soon provoked. Chapman believed he was in Reed-Mayhew's pay and his involvement suggested the corrupt businessman was the power behind her arrest. She needed to focus.

The two police took their seats, and the woman officer started the recording equipment, after which Harding introduced himself and his assistant, Inspector Koval.

Antonia concentrated on the ill-advised moustache Harding sported as the inspector read out the charges.

'My client denies all the charges. You have nothing but baseless accusations which you can't substantiate.'

Although his inspector gave the impression of professional detachment, something about Harding's reaction made Antonia wary. She focused on reading him as he began the questions.

'Do you deny knowing Mr Latif?'

'I met him once at his acquittal in May last year. You can check the date from the court records.'

'And you don't recall ever speaking to or meeting him at any other time?' Harding's manner increased her unease.

As always advised by Stokes, she kept her answers short. 'No.'

'What, no you haven't, or no you don't recall?'

'If you can't remember the question you asked me, write it down.'

Two spots of colour appeared on Harding's full cheeks. 'Well, which is it?'

'No, I've had no contact with Mr Latif since the meeting in May last year.'

'What do you say to the fact a witness saw you meet Mr Latif?'

'I'd say you're lying.'

Harding's jaw tightened, and he glanced down at his notes. 'You met him for a coffee on Monday, first of August.' He gave a name of a café in Islington.

Antonia cast her mind back ten days. She'd gone to Islington that morning and *had* gone for a coffee, but on her own. Had someone followed her? 'I was there, but Latif wasn't.'

Harding seemed disappointed she didn't deny being there. 'You're saying you don't recall meeting Mr Latif?'

'I'm saying I didn't meet him.'

'You've had issues with your memory, haven't you?'

Stokes leant forward to intervene, but Antonia stopped him. 'I have no issues with my memory.'

Harding checked his notes again. 'Are you saying the Syrus Clinic didn't treat you last November?'

'Are you asking me if they treated me?' The experiments they'd carried out on her had almost broken her and left scars still not healed.

'Yes!'

'I investigated the clinic and because of my investigation, they closed down.'

'Only because someone murdered the owners.'

'Well, it wasn't me.' The ease of her lie surprised Antonia.

'So you say.'

'Chief Superintendent, are you accusing my client of murdering somebody? I can't find any reference to it on the charge sheet.' Geoff Stokes's calm tone lowered the temperature of the interview room.

Harding held his attention on Antonia. 'Not at the moment.'

She wouldn't look away. *I know you were there, investigating their deaths for your crooked boss, Reed-Mayhew, before the police arrived.*

'Back to your meeting with Mr Latif—'

'There was no meeting.'

'Not one you can remember.'

'There. Was. No. Meeting.' Chapman described Harding as a man who abused the right to be irritating, and she knew what he meant.

'We've got you on CCTV.'

This time, Stokes silenced *her*. 'My client doesn't deny being there. Does your footage show her meeting Mr Latif?'

Harding's blue eyes clouded. 'Mr Latif tells us you phoned him this morning at—'

'No, I didn't.'

Stokes intervened again. 'Mr Harding—'

298

'Chief Superintendent,' Harding cut in.

Stokes gave a dismissive wave. 'Can you produce any evidence to justify continuing with this charade?'

'Your client faces very serious charges—'

'Completely unfounded. Either produce something or let my client go.'

Harding swallowed his irritation and continued to question Antonia. She couldn't get a handle on him. He acted like a person waiting for something, but what, and why? The longer she remained here answering pointless questions, the sooner he must release her. She could see Stokes was ready to intervene again, but a uniformed officer knocked on the door and stuck her head in. Inspector Koval took a document from her and passed it to Harding.

He read it and whatever he read elicited an unpleasant smile. 'You claimed you didn't phone Mr Latif this morning, Ms Conti.'

'I didn't. I told you, I prepared for a meeting with an informer.'

'Do you recognise this number?' He recited a familiar landline number.

'Of course, it's *The Electric Investigator*, the news outlet I work for.'

He slid a piece of paper across the table. 'Here's a printout of Mr Latif's phone log. Someone from your office contacted him this morning at nine twenty-three.'

Determined not to let her disappointment show, Sabirah took the children to Regent's Park. At least Nadimah had stopped sulking about the telling-off she'd got for almost missing Sabirah's big moment. What made her behave in such an uncharacteristic way, agreeing to meet a boy when she was due next door for the ceremony?

Sabirah had planned a more exciting outing if she'd got the job, but thought it so unlikely, she needed to consider going back to cleaning. She spent the afternoon with her cheerful face on as they avoided the hordes of tourists enjoying the sunshine. Maybe she should apply for acting jobs. She'd had so much practice pretending since arriving in the UK, and not just to her children.

'Are you okay, Mamma?' Hakim said.

'Of course. I'm just thinking of what we can eat tonight.' Maybe she wasn't ready for Hollywood yet. But Hakim was always perceptive. 'Shall we start for home? Where's your sister?'

'There.' He pointed to a group of boys surrounding Nadimah.

The smart pastel shades they wore marked them out as tourists. Sabirah attempted to attract her attention and drew closer. A couple of them looked almost men. Although tall and elegant, her daughter was only thirteen. Trying not to appear annoyed, Sabirah called Nadimah. Her daughter delayed just long enough before leaving her admirers. She swung her hips in an exaggerated sashay. Sabirah veered between amusement and anger at the boys' reactions.

'Who were those boys?' Although she knew she shouldn't, Sabirah couldn't help interrogating her daughter.

'Just boys.'

'They're much too old for you.'

'They're fifteen.' Nadimah rolled her eyes. 'Sixteen at most. I'm not talking to thirteen-year-old boys.'

'Even me, when I'm thirteen?' Hakim said.

'Especially you.' She gave him a playful cuff.

Sabirah couldn't stop herself. 'How do you know them?'

'I don't. They just started talking to me.'

'I've told you about talking to strangers—'

'They're not strangers.'

'Oh, so you know them?'

'No.' Nadimah folded her arms. 'But "strangers" means old creeps.'

'You don't even know where they're from.' *Why did I say that? As if it matters.*

'They're from Antwerp. It's in Belgium.'

The vivid memory of planning to visit Antwerp with Rashid and bringing their young family on a European trip hit her. She walked on in silence, fighting to control her emotions. Her children, seeming to sense her mood, exchanged a look as they walked alongside her.

Torn by guilt, she said, 'Shall we get a takeaway tonight?'

Nadimah studied her. 'There's no need, Mamma. I can cook something.'

Sabirah reached up to put her arm across her daughter's shoulders. 'We'll have pasta.' She now cooked far more European dishes as her children's tastes changed. The thought of no longer eating Syrian food saddened her.

When they arrived home, Sabirah again gave thanks they lived in such a wonderful house. She couldn't help looking at the house next door. She might not get a job as an architect, but at least she'd shown her children and her friends what she could do.

Mrs Curtis waited at the bottom of the stairs. 'I've been dying to find out how you got on.'

Sabirah hesitated. 'Do you two want to go upstairs and get cleaned up?' She waited for the children to clear the half-landing on the next floor and let her true feelings show.

'Oh dear, shall we go through to the kitchen?'

Sabirah followed her landlady's wheelchair into her kitchen at the back of the house. Max, her cat, came to greet them. He still limped, the result of his encounter with intruders who'd almost broken his back as he fought to defend his mistress.

'Do you want a coffee or tea?' Mrs Curtis gestured at her steaming mug.

'Tea, please. I'll make—' The look from the old lady stilled her, and she sat, gathering her thoughts.

Mrs Curtis wheeled herself across the room, a mug of fresh tea on the tray on her chair. After handing it to Sabirah, she took her place opposite. 'What made you think you won't get the job?'

Where to start? 'I arrived late because of the security checks and then the receptionist thought I came for the cleaner's job, so she made me wait and I became even later—'

'That's not your fault.'

'I should have made it clear. I didn't.'

'They won't reject you for a misunderstanding. Did you tell them why you arrived late?'

Sabirah shook her head. 'They would think it's a problem if I'm stopped every day.'

'Are you?' Mrs Curtis looked angry.

'No, not *every* day.'

'Apart from being late, what else persuaded you you'd failed?'

Sabirah couldn't point to any one thing. 'They said I couldn't practise until I finish my tests, so I would be like a student.'

'Did they see your work?'

'Yes, but most is old.'

'What about the excellent work you did next door? Did you show them my comments?'

Sabirah took a sip of her tea. She didn't want this post-mortem. She'd failed, and nothing they said would change it. 'I have to feed the children.'

'Sabirah, I think you've underestimated how you did today, but even if this practice doesn't offer you a job, you're a brilliant architect and you will get a job.'

Tears stung her eyes. 'Thank you.' She bent over and hugged the old woman. Although she looked frail, she felt solid. Sabirah rushed away. She needed to straighten herself before the children saw her. The desire for Rashid to hold her hit her like a physical pain. She couldn't do this on her own any longer.

◆ ◆ ◆

The officer in charge of Leyton Custody Centre had refused to give Chapman any information when he'd enquired about Antonia. He'd reluctantly gone home after ringing Stokes, her solicitor, who told him she'd be kept in overnight. Why would Harding question her? Someone so senior wouldn't normally question suspects, and it wasn't even his station.

He parked his car in the station car park and got out. His shoulder had come up a delightful shade of purple overnight. He'd forgotten how running into Antonia could hurt. What had she been thinking, trying to get into a burning car? As he entered their office, Sanchez signalled she wanted a word.

He mouthed, 'Give me two minutes,' went into his office and took off his jacket. He mustn't forget to get the one he'd lent Antonia back. By the time he'd made two coffees and sat down, Sanchez joined him and closed the door behind her.

'You look like shit, Russell.'

'And good morning to you as well. To think I was about to recommend you for the inspector's vacancy in Special Ops.'

'You weren't?'

'I quite fancied it, but they said they wanted someone with "enthusiasm and drive".'

'What's wrong with my enthusiasm and drive?' Sanchez sat opposite him.

'It's ten years too old. I made a few enquiries.'

'They're bastards, aren't they? Thanks for recommending me, although it might be better if you didn't. No offence.'

'I haven't done it yet, and if I do, Yasmin will put her name to the report.'

'In that case, thank you very much, boss. I'll do my best to not let you down.'

'That's better. Now, what did you want?'

'First, I want to update you on yesterday. The truck we found at the services is the one from the unit where you found the casualty. Its tyres match and they're checking the chemical composition of the oil drips to make certain. The bad news is they wiped the inside clean with bleach, so no forensics.'

'What about the two bodies in the burnt-out cars?'

'Stevie Gillich has identified one, and they should identify the other early today. The one she identified is a small-time thug with a long list of convictions for violence.'

'Why do I have the feeling you've got bad news for me?'

'We've nothing on Danil Derenski, the guy Hughes claimed killed your friend.'

Although Alan Turner had sacrificed his life to help Chapman, he didn't know him, but he'd been Antonia's boss and friend. 'No police record or no sign on any database?'

'Both. I think Hughes gave Antonia a bum steer.'

'We have to hope Hughes got away and we can pick him up.'

Sanchez didn't seem convinced. 'How's Antonia, by the way?'

'A bit bruised and battered, but they've kept her in Leyton overnight after Harding questioned her.' He wasn't looking forward to telling her they'd lost Derenski.

'Harding? Why's he involved?'

'I thought it strange. I'm going to investigate the train smash. It can't be— Oh, hello, boss.'

'A word in private, please, Russell.' DCI Yasmin Gunnerson looked at Sanchez, who made her excuses and left.

'I take it this isn't a social call.'

She looked uncomfortable. 'I've had my ear chewed off about yesterday's debacle—'

'None of it was our fault.'

'You almost lost Ms Conti and left a trail of destruction across south-east London. We've got two bodies in the mortuary, a victim of torture—'

'Hang on, we found him *because of* our "debacle". If we hadn't lost Antonia, we wouldn't have gone anywhere near there.'

'I'm not disputing that, but the fact is, you and your team let her meet a known violent criminal who kidnapped her.'

'Only because they crashed a train to distract us.'

'You can't be certain.'

'Come on, Yasmin. You think it's a coincidence? He changed the venue at the last minute and a train crashed on the next platform.'

'You should have aborted the mission when they changed the venue.'

'Have you tried stopping Antonia from doing anything she wanted to?'

Gunnerson sighed. 'How is she?'

'Sore after being kidnapped and in a serious RTC but, well, considering they arrested her—'

'What?'

Chapman explained what had happened.

'Leave it with me.' Gunnerson stood. 'And I'll need your report by close of play today.'

Chapman gave a mock salute. Gunnerson should have more joy finding out about Antonia's situation than he had. Talk of the train crash reminded him he still had to speak to the investigating

305

officer. Four phone calls later, he spoke to the head of the Specialist Response Unit of the transport police at King's Cross.

'How may I help you, Inspector?'

'I'm trying to discover the cause of the crash on platform ten yesterday.' He explained why.

'The Rail Accident Investigation Branch will investigate the mechanics of exactly what happened, but it looks like the automatic braking system on the train failed.'

'Failed or someone sabotaged it?'

He laughed. 'That's the question. But we've had information suggesting it was deliberate.'

A frisson of excitement stirred Chapman. 'Do you have a suspect?'

'Not an individual, but an organisation we've only recently heard of claimed responsibility. The South Sudan People's Front. No idea where that is, somewhere in darkest Africa, I'll bet. Why do they have to come over here and cause trouble? They should stay in their own countries.' He tutted. 'Don't get me started.'

'It's below Egypt and above Uganda. If we hadn't gone over there and colonised their country, they wouldn't come here.'

A long silence greeted this. 'If that's all you wanted, Inspector.'

'How did they claim responsibility?'

The delay in getting a reply made Chapman think he'd not get an answer. 'Anonymous call from a mobile we couldn't trace.'

'Have you recorded the message?'

'Of course, I'll get it sent to you. Did you want anything else?'

Chapman ended the call, guessing he'd not be on their Christmas card list. Before he met Antonia, he didn't even know where to find South Sudan, and might even have sympathised with the man's views. He couldn't dismiss his unease at the link to Antonia via her country of birth. He spoke to a contact in

Special Branch to discover more about the organisation behind the attack.

'Funny you should ask about them. They're new to us, but we've received intel from a couple of sources suggesting we monitor disaffected members of the diaspora.'

'How recently?' Chapman didn't like the sound of this.

'It's come across my desk in the last few days.'

'And your sources?'

'Come on, Russell, you don't expect me to reveal those.'

'Of course, but how reliable are they?'

'Let's say we're not dismissing them. Anyway, why do you want to know?'

'I attended King's Cross yesterday on a surveillance and . . . let's say the incident there caused me serious problems.'

'Right. Do you mind telling me who told you about it? It's not meant to be circulated.'

Chapman considered for a moment. Should he drop the guy from the railways in it? 'Sorry, I can't reveal my sources.'

A brief silence greeted this. 'Okay, mate. But keep it to yourself.'

With a promise to meet up for a pint, they ended the call. Chapman wasn't sure he could keep the promise not to tell Antonia. Apart from her obvious interest, he suspected this wasn't a coincidence.

Sanchez arrived, her demeanour suggesting she brought more bad news. 'They've identified the other body in the burnout. It *is* Hughes. I know you hoped to pick him up.'

'Not realistically. I'd guessed he'd have taken the brunt of the impact, having been in the passenger seat . . .'

Sanchez took a seat. 'I spoke to someone about why Harding's involved. They've called him in because of his experience with Financial Crimes.'

'What's it got to do with Antonia?'

'Sorry, Russell. They're investigating money laundering linked to terrorism.'

'But why question— Shit! Is it linked to South Sudan?'

Sanchez's eyes widened. 'How did you know? They swore me to secrecy.'

'Yeah, same here. Bugger!' If they dragged Antonia into a terrorism investigation, they could hold her for sixty days without charge.

CHAPTER 26

Antonia finished her hundredth squat when the cell door opened. The big, beefy inspector in charge of the cells watched her.

She wiped her forehead with the back of her hand. 'What do you want?'

'Your lawyer brought these.' He threw a carrier bag containing a change of clothing on to the bed.

She picked it off the bed without breaking eye contact. 'I'll need you to leave so I can get changed.'

He loitered for an age. 'I'll wait outside until you're ready.' Then, with a leer, he backed out of the room.

Antonia made sure the observation port remained closed and got changed. It felt good to get out of the jumpsuit they'd lent her and into her own clothes, although they'd removed the laces from her trainers. She'd have preferred a shower to get rid of the stink of smoke and sweat, but that would have to wait. She rapped on the door to inform the inspector she was ready and after making her wait, he let her out.

Stokes waited in the interview room, his usual comforting presence. The news that Chapman had arranged for his superior to contact the Custody Centre raised her spirits. No sooner had she sat than Harding and Koval barged into the room. The chief superintendent looked pleased with himself, and the inspector carried an evidence bag with a mobile phone in it.

Once they'd got the preliminaries out of the way, Stokes said, 'You've almost had your twenty-four hours, Chief Superintendent. Are you here to release my client?'

Harding ignored the question and placed a tablet on the desk in front of him. 'Our investigations confirmed that your receptionist' – Harding glanced at his screen – 'Tomasz Zabo, rang Latif's phone in response to an email he received.'

Relief flooded through Antonia, and she exchanged a glance with Stokes.

'I'm glad you've got that cleared up. So, you *will* be releasing my client.'

'On the contrary. I'm here to inform you we're investigating your client under the Border Protection Act.'

Antonia leant forward. 'You can't—'

Stokes cut her off. 'On what grounds?'

'We suspect your client's involved with the South Sudan People's Front.'

'You have no evidence of any link. I'm sick of you officers who use this pernicious legislation to target people like my client, because they're born in other countries.'

Antonia had never seen Stokes so angry, and even Harding seemed shocked.

He fidgeted for a few seconds, then snatched the evidence bag from his assistant. 'This phone connects your client to a terrorist incident.'

'I doubt it very much, Chief Superintendent, but I'm sure you'll enlighten us.'

Harding slid a piece of paper across the desk. 'Here's a screenshot of a message your client sent.'

Antonia reached for the sheet, which showed her message agreeing to meet Hughes at King's Cross. She put it down.

'Well?' Harding demanded.

'I'm waiting for a question.'

'Do you deny sending this message?'

'No.'

A gentle laugh from Stokes filled the silence that followed Antonia's reply.

Harding's cheeks reddened. 'You admit you arranged to meet a known criminal at King's Cross Station, and minutes after you arrive, a terrorist group linked to you—'

'There's *no* link to my client.'

'You're from South Sudan.' Harding jabbed a finger at her.

'Mr Harding. You're making offensive claims about my client, with no evidence. Your superiors led us to believe these outdated attitudes are in the past. Is your commissioner misleading us?'

Harding took several breaths. 'Ms Conti, do you deny arranging to meet a known criminal at King's Cross?'

'Yes.'

'You sent this message agreeing to meet him.'

Antonia didn't wait for a question. 'He sent the message changing the venue for our meeting. I agreed. That's the message you showed me.'

'It's the only message on this phone.' Harding tapped the evidence bag.

'Then somebody has wiped the others. I texted him details of our original meeting venue and then he replied, asking me to change the venue because it "looked like rain".'

'We only have your word.'

'It's on my phone.'

'And where is it?'

311

Antonia replayed the previous day's events. She hadn't seen the phone since she caused the accident. She pictured the aftermath. Would it have survived the fire?

'Well, Ms Conti, where is this phone?'

'I left it in the vehicle the kidnappers took me in yesterday. It crashed and caught fire.'

'How very convenient. I presume it was incinerated, so we can't check.'

'The impact threw several items clear, including a phone. Why don't you check the items recovered by your accident investigation team?'

Koval made a note, but Harding frowned. 'When I need advice about investigating crimes from an amateur, I'll tell you.'

'As a non-amateur,' Stokes said, 'I suggest you investigate if this person my client met had a hand in the train crash, as it seemed to facilitate his plans.'

'He's dead, and your client hasn't explained why she met him.'

'My client's a reporter. She meets many people, some of them unsavoury.' He gave Harding a long look.

'I met him because he knew the whereabouts of a murderer. A team of police were tracking my phone and kept me under surveillance from the moment I left my office.'

Harding's eyebrows shot up. 'You realise I can check?'

'I'm banking on it. It's DCI Gunnerson you want.'

'It can't be. She's under my command and I would know of such an operation.'

Had she dropped Gunnerson in it? 'I agree, you should. A competent commander would.'

He gave her a venomous look and stomped out of the room, his inspector in his wake. The two officers returned twenty minutes later.

Harding's expression suggested an unpleasant odour lay concealed in his moustache. 'You must surrender your passport and report to Shoreditch Police Station every day at zero nine hundred hours until further notice.'

'My client has done nothing to justify—'

Antonia stopped Stokes with a gesture. 'Eight. I have work to do and often have meetings at nine.'

'Okay, eight it is.' Harding left, and Koval hurried to keep up.

'I would have fought your corner more, Antonia.'

'I just want to go. We can argue later.'

'Yes, of course.'

The beefy inspector waited outside and led them to the custody suite where the sergeant had Antonia's belongings in a small pile on his desk. He slid a tablet across to her. 'Please check you've received everything you arrived with. Are you aware of your conditions?'

'Yes, thank you.' Antonia took the stylus and signed the form.

'If you fail to surrender your passport or check in every morning, we will arrest you,' the inspector said.

'Yes, your colleague explained, thank you.'

'If I had my way, you'd stay in our cells until we deported you.'

'If I had my way, you'd be cleaning toilets in a refugee shelter with your toothbrush, but there you go.'

His face turned beetroot red, but before he could reply, Geoff Stokes stepped in. 'Shall we go, Antonia?'

As she followed him out, the inspector grabbed her arm and whispered, 'Watch yourself.'

The contrast between this building and the one she'd visited for her interview two days earlier depressed Sabirah. Set in a scruffy and dirty yard with overflowing bins in one corner, an air of dilapidation hung over it. The urge to turn tail and go home seized her, but she needed to work, and with luck, she'd find something better soon. She'd saved from the generous fee Mrs Curtis had given her, but she didn't want to spend it, in case anything happened. And the Border Force regularly checked her employment status as part of her right to stay in the country.

An intercom box to the left of the double doors didn't seem to work. After waiting a minute, she pushed at the door, which swung open. An unpleasant stink, a mixture of mould, rotting food and air freshener, assailed her nostrils.

'Hello?' She paused in the corridor until her eyesight got used to the gloom. It needed a good clean, or better still, a complete refurbishment.

A man wearing a baggy beige suit stuck his head out of a door in the corridor. 'You here about the job?'

A startled Sabirah said, 'Yes.'

'Well, come in. I don't bite.' He showed yellowed teeth and waved her into the room.

She squeezed past him into an office, which continued the theme from the corridor. The smell in here comprised stale tobacco and body odour. Papers lay strewn over every surface, including the chair he directed her to.

'Just put them on the floor, but don't mix them up.'

She lifted the stack of papers and files and placed them on the cleanest piece of carpet she could see behind the seat. She perched on the edge of the less-than-clean chair, not wanting to get her best suit dirty, her handbag on her lap.

He took a seat behind the overflowing desk. 'As you can see, we've not had anyone cleaning for a while.' He sipped from a large mug. 'What do you want to ask me?'

This didn't resemble any interview she'd ever had. 'Can you tell me about the job?'

'Cleaning.' He waved a hand around the room, dislodging a cigarette butt from an overflowing ashtray perched above a 'NO smoking' sticker on the desk to join a small pile on the floor below.

'Is it the whole building?'

'Yup, I own all of it.' He looked very pleased with this. 'We don't use the top floor much, so just tickle it once in a while.'

'What hours will I work?'

He blew air through loose lips. 'The last woman did three hours every morning.'

It wasn't too far to get here, but the prospect of coming here every day would soon depress her. 'Can I do five every three days?'

'Well, I wanted someone to come in five days.' He scratched his unshaven chin.

Sabirah surprised herself by saying, 'I have other commitments.'

He contemplated the contents of his mug. 'I wanted someone every day.'

She stopped herself from replying.

'Okay,' he said with a sigh. 'When can you start?'

'Do you want to ask me questions? My work experience, references?'

He looked surprised. 'You've got a family?'

'Yes.'

'There you are. You must be able to clean. How hard is it?'

She looked around.

'You need to do a few extra hours the first week. Do you have a work permit?'

'I have Indefinite Leave to Remain.' She reached into her handbag for her documents.

'No need, I believe you.' He waved a hand. 'We pay cash every Friday. You sort out your own tax and insurance.'

'The advertisement said PAYE.'

'Well, you got this other job as well, so you can be self-employed. It's easier for everyone.'

'I need a proper contract for my Leave to Remain.'

'Do you want the job?'

This had been the only suitable job she'd found within reasonable distance of home. 'Okay, how much?'

He mentioned a rate below the minimum wage, a challenge in his tone.

She would find another job as soon as she could. 'When do you want me to start?'

'Tomorrow?'

She looked around. Could she bear coming here? *Come on, Sabirah, you've faced worse.* 'Okay.' She stood, eager to get out.

He rose and offered a hand. 'Welcome aboard.' His clammy palm held on too long.

She untangled it. 'Thank you.'

'What does your husband do?'

She replied without thinking. 'He's dead.'

'I *am* sorry.' But the small, hooded eyes lit up. As he escorted her from the room, his hand pushed into her lower back. She resisted slapping it away. 'I hope you won't wear shapeless coveralls like the last woman. I like a woman who knows how to dress.'

'Thank you.' *I will wear the most unflattering clothes I own, covered in a sack.*

'I'll see you tomorrow.'

'Yes, thank you.' She resisted shuddering or running. She couldn't come back here. But she needed to work. She would look for another job and hope to get one soon. As she reached the gates, she glanced back. He stood there, watching her. The thought of the next morning filled her with dread.

◆ ◆ ◆

The smell of paint and fresh plaster permeated Antonia's new office. She still hadn't got used to the size and the height of the ceiling. Light flooded in through the two enormous windows overlooking the back garden. Her old office in the basement now formed a corridor, joining the two buildings, and part of the communications hub. Antonia stared at her screen, not taking in anything as she reflected on the last twenty-four hours.

'Why don't you go home, Antonia?' Eleanor's voice startled her. At least when she'd used an electric wheelchair, you could hear her coming.

She tapped the screen. 'Too much to do.'

'Nonsense. Not only were you involved in a nasty car crash, but the police kept you in a cell overnight. You must be shattered.' Eleanor studied Antonia with a concerned expression.

'I'm fine.' Despite her ordeal, she felt well after a night in her own bed. Tired and stiff, but nothing serious. 'I'm worried we haven't heard from Rick.'

'So am I, but Tomasz contacted every hospital within twenty miles and nobody has a patient matching Rick's description.'

'If he's just injured.'

'What do you mean?' Eleanor looked alarmed.

'The last story he worked on upset some powerful people.'

'But now the story's out there. Why would anyone bother?'

'Revenge?'

'Hmm, it's possible he's just taken a few days out—'

'And not mention it? He's only been with us for a few weeks, but he worked as a top professional for years. Do you think his last employer would have just shrugged their shoulders if he'd have gone AWOL while working on a story?'

'No, dear. But maybe he thinks he'd get away with it here.'

'I know you think I give him too much leeway, but suggesting he has no respect for me—'

'I meant we'd be more forgiving. Maybe he came here to get away from the pressure.'

'So, he only took this job because he's washed up?'

'I didn't say that, Antonia.' She exhaled in frustration. 'Would we treat anyone like those big tabloids do?'

'No, I suppose you're right. He seemed stressed last week.'

'Do you think he'd take his own life?'

'It hadn't occurred to me. I thought he may have gone walkabout.'

'Like John Stonehouse?'

Antonia stared at Eleanor. 'Who?'

'Before your time, a politician disappeared and turned up the other side of the world. Mind you, he staged *his* suicide.'

The more she considered this, the more worried Antonia got. 'I'm going to see his wife.'

'You sure it's a good idea?'

'Why not?'

'What will you say? "I think your husband's hiding from me. Where is he?" Or even worse, "I think he may have harmed himself. Where is he likely to go so I can look for the body?"'

'It's not funny, Eleanor.'

'I'm not being funny, but consider the consequences before you wade in.'

Antonia stopped herself from snapping. Eleanor was right, she needed to take care. 'I'll speak to Russell, find out if they've found . . . If he knows anything.'

'I'll leave you to it, then.' Eleanor wheeled herself out.

Antonia took a deep breath. Although tired, she'd do this and go home early. She rang Chapman's mobile.

'Antonia, where are you?'

'At work, why?'

'They've let you out?'

318

'Yep. You okay, Russell?'

'Yeah, sure. Just worried about you.' He took a deep breath. 'What happened?'

'Your friend Harding tried to link me to the train crash.'

'No way.'

'A South Sudanese terrorist group claimed responsibility, and with my background . . .'

'He could have locked you up for months.'

'Yeah.' How could a civilised country lock you up and nobody know where they'd taken you?

'Had you heard of the group who attacked the train?'

'No, but it's not something on my radar. I'll look into it now.'

'Did he have any evidence apart from you being born there?'

'A message agreeing to meet Hughes at King's Cross.'

'But he sent the message changing the venue.'

'Yeah, but Harding only had my reply. And the phone I used has gone missing.'

'You forwarded the message to me.'

Antonia cast her exhausted mind back to yesterday morning. 'Oh, God, how did I forget forwarding it to you?'

'But he still let you go?'

'Gunnerson told him I was working with you. Before I forget, he got furious when I told him I was. He said she should have informed him. You'd better warn her. I suspect me goading him about it didn't help.'

'Yasmin would have informed him. I bet he didn't read it. I'd have liked to have seen the smug git have to release you.'

'Well, I'm not free. I still had to hand in my passport and report in every morning at eight.'

'He's a shithouse. Do you want me to see if I can do anything about it? I've got the message you sent and we can say we need you to help us find Derenski. He's now linked to two more deaths.'

'Thank you, Russell, I'd appreciate it.' She already regretted asking to change the time she needed to report to the police to eight, especially tomorrow.

'Leave it with me. Did you want anything else?'

'I'm worried about Rick Grainger. He's gone missing.'

'What's happened?'

Antonia told him.

'He's just missed three days' work?'

The way Chapman said it made it seem she'd been worrying over nothing. 'We can't get hold of him on his phone. He's supposed to brief me on his latest story.'

'What's he investigating? His last story pissed off some powerful and wealthy people but none of them would take direct action.'

'They're pissed off with me as well. I'd imagine more than with Rick. It could be his new story that's set them off, but I don't know what he's working on . . .'

'He hasn't told you?'

'You're sounding like Eleanor.'

'God, no.'

An idea occurred to Antonia. 'Blast!'

'What?'

'Could they have arrested Rick in a terrorism investigation, and be keeping him incommunicado?'

'It's unlikely. He's a well-known reporter.'

'Unlike me, you mean?'

'I didn't mean it like that . . .'

She imagined him going red. 'I'd appreciate it if you could check.'

'No problem. If he was investigating terrorists, there's more chance they'd have— You know.'

'Yeah, thanks.' She imagined Grainger captured by a load of fanatics.

Chapman broke the silence. 'Have you spoken to his wife?'

'No answer from home, but she works long hours. I meant to ring her last night, but never made it.'

'I'd speak to her, find out if she knows, or can point you in the right direction.'

'You're right. I'll ring her.'

'I'd go round. You can tell if she's spinning you a yarn. If he's on a bender, she might not want you to know. You know what these reporters are like.'

'Were. The drinking culture died out last century. I'll think about going round.'

'In the meantime, you want me to check he's not ended up in a body bag?'

The realisation Hughes and his companion were both dead, and she'd come so close to joining them, hit her like a blow. 'Thanks, Russell.'

'You've got one more.'

'What?'

'Wishes. You get three, don't you?'

'Can I leave the last one in the lamp until I need it?'

He laughed and ended the call. Antonia checked the time. She wanted to go home, but Chapman's suggestion she should see Grainger's wife nagged at her. After checking his address, she ordered a cab and left the office. The drive to Clapham Common took forty minutes in rush hour traffic, and Antonia spent the time catching up with the emails she'd downloaded on to her laptop. Feeling motion sick, she arrived at the street Grainger lived on.

Victorian terraced houses lined the narrow lane off The Common. The road widened, and the houses changed to larger detached properties set further back. The taxi dropped her off opposite the house she wanted. Carrying her backpack, she approached.

Unlike the houses at the other end of the street, substantial gardens surrounded these.

Although nice, and beyond the means of the vast majority, they weren't the sort of grand place you'd expect to find someone making millions from insider trading. Reassured by the thought, Antonia ascended the steps to the front door and rang the bell. A dim light showed behind the stained-glass panels in the door. As she waited, she glanced down the road. Movement from the front of a parked car caught her attention and, as casually as she could, she checked it. Two men sat in the front, and she imagined them watching her.

The door to the house opened and a woman of about forty peered out through the narrow gap. A solid bar prevented the door from opening further and cut her face in two. 'Can I help you?' Her eyes said, 'Go away before I call the police.'

Antonia glanced at Erika's left hand, which held a panic alarm. 'Erika, it's Antonia.'

After a long pause, she replied, 'Sorry. I didn't recognise you.'

'Can I come in?'

Erika swallowed and looked past Antonia. 'Okay.' So quiet, Antonia wasn't sure she'd said it until the door pushed shut before it opened wide.

Antonia stepped into a hallway with blue and cream tiles on the floor. Erika wore low heels and stood ten centimetres shorter than Antonia. In the dim light, her expensive-looking peach trouser suit almost blended in with her tanned skin. She wore her thick brown hair in a razored bob and her bloodshot, big brown eyes suggested she'd been crying.

'Do you want to go through?' Erika gestured to a door ahead of them.

Antonia tried to place her accent as she offered refreshments. They settled in a pair of canework armchairs at the back of a huge kitchen and living room overlooking the back garden.

'Do you know where Rick is, Erika?'

Although she must have expected the question, Erika reacted as if Antonia had slapped her. 'Rick. He's . . . He's not here.'

'He's not come in to work for three days. Is he ill?'

'No, he's fine.'

Antonia waited, then said, 'Do you know why he's not come to work?'

'Erm, he went away. Family . . . His dad's ill.'

He'd told Antonia his dad died two years ago. 'I've not been able to get hold of his mobile.'

'The reception is awful there, so he'll have turned it off.'

She had no doubt this woman was lying. 'How can I get hold of him? It's very important.'

'He should be back soon. I'll tell him when he rings me.'

'You can ring him, then?'

Erika studied the half-finished glass of red in front of her. 'His parents have a landline but they don't like people ringing it. Rick rings me every evening, so I'll tell him you need to speak to him.'

Antonia sipped the mineral water she'd asked for and held her right hand vertically, palm forward, before folding her thumb over and gripping it. Erika concentrated on the violence at home hand signal. Her eyes widened, but she gave a small shake of her head.

After a few moments of perfunctory small talk, Antonia left. What the hell had happened to Grainger? She'd put any money on him not being at his dad's. The car with the two men in it hadn't moved, and she examined it as she ordered a cab to collect her by The Common. She decided to walk past them, and as she got closer, focused her attention on the car, letting them know she'd seen them.

Derenski recognised her the instant she identified him.

CHAPTER 27

Chapman's computer pinged to announce a new email. He clicked on the screen. DI Stevie Gillich's name in the sender's box told him what to expect. Before he could open it, his phone rang. Gillich was ringing him, too.

'Chapman.'

'Russell, I've just sent you an email.'

'Just opening it now.'

'Hughes, the one you asked about, was still alive when they set the fire and died of smoke inhalation.'

'Murder then?'

'Technically, but they say it's doubtful he'd have survived his injuries.'

'I imagine that's why they left him. What about the other one?'

'Dead before the fire. "Catastrophic injuries consistent with those received in a serious RTC and being dragged on a roadway."'

'Sounds painful. Did they say how they think it happened?' Antonia had given Chapman an account of the crash and her actions before she got arrested.

'It's linked to the RTC your friend survived.'

'Do you know what they think caused it yet?' Chapman knew the answer but had no intention of dropping Antonia in it, even though they'd probably accept what she did as justified.

'Not yet.' Gillich hesitated. 'I wondered if you could persuade your friend to talk to us. Her solicitor sent us a statement, but . . .'

'What did she say?'

'They'd tied her up in the back and she saw nothing.'

'Yeah, that's what she told me.'

'Did you have to untie her when you found her?'

He hesitated. 'They'd used zip ties round her wrists.'

'You don't think she's covering something up?'

'Like what? There were three of them and they'd tied her up. Do you think she had anything to do with them crashing?'

'If you put it that way, no. Okay, thanks, Russell.'

He relaxed and opened the email. At least he hadn't lied. He'd just finished reading it and his mobile buzzed, signalling an encrypted voice call. 'Antonia, we were just talking about you.'

'In what context?'

'Stevie Gillich rang, asking me about your role in the RTC.'

She didn't reply straight away. 'What did you say?'

'I told her the account you gave me tallied with the statement you'd given, of course.'

'Oh, right? Thanks. I've got a favour to ask.'

'It depends what it is.' He'd avoided Harding, but suspected he'd be fuming because he'd had to let Antonia go. If he caught Chapman doing her a favour, he'd go ballistic.

'I took your advice and visited Erika Voight last night – Rick's wife.'

'Oh yeah, and what do you think?'

'She's hiding something. I shouldn't tell you this, but we're investigating the company she works for.'

'You think that's linked to his disappearance?'

'Rick's not involved in the investigation, but he found out and I told him in no uncertain terms I'd sack him if he said anything.'

'But if his wife's involved, he's likely to disregard any threats.'

'I didn't get the impression she knew we're investigating her, but something's wrong. She behaved like someone hiding something but wanting you to discover it. She said Rick was visiting his sick dad, but he told me his dad died a couple of years ago. I've just found his obituary online.'

Chapman's mind made the obvious connection. 'You think someone's kidnapped him?'

'Don't you?'

'I can't instigate an investigation unless someone either witnessed the kidnap or his wife comes to us with evidence.'

'I know, that's not the favour.'

'Go on then.'

'I caught Derenski watching the house. I walked towards his car and they drove off, but I got the number.'

'That was bloody stupid. You should have kept your distance and phoned—'

'I didn't recognise him until I got up close.'

'What's the number?'

She gave it to him. 'Okay, I'll put it through as an anonymous tip, keep you out of it.'

'Is Harding still pissed off?'

'I'd guarantee it. Someone in the corridor overheard him tearing a strip off Koval for not highlighting Yasmin's memo about our operation.'

They ended the call, but before he could instigate the search, Sanchez knocked on his door. 'Come in, Alice. I've just spoken to Antonia. She saw Derenski last night. I've got the ID for his car.'

'I wouldn't tell Harding you've spoken to her.'

'Don't worry, I'll avoid him for the foreseeable.'

'Good luck. Koval's just rung. The chief super requests your presence.'

'Shit! Couldn't you say I'd gone out?'

She raised her eyebrows. 'Do you want to give me the car reg? In case you don't return.'

Chapman wasn't sure if she was joking.

Harding made him wait outside before letting him into his office. He continued the act by ignoring him for several minutes while he checked a document. Chapman refused to let this needle him and adopted as relaxed a pose as he could.

'What did I tell you about talking to reporters?' Harding spoke without looking up.

'Are you talking to me?'

'Do any of my other officers consort with reporters?'

'Do you want to tell me what you've invited me here for?'

'Yes, Inspector. I told you that if you leaked information to the press, I'd discipline you, yet you continue to do so.'

Were they bugging his office? 'I haven't.'

'Have you read this?' Harding activated his tablet and slid it across the table.

The screen showed the familiar *Electric Investigator* site and a story about Antonia's kidnapping. She hadn't mentioned she intended to write one, but he'd not asked her not to.

Chapman read the article and pushed the screen away. 'So?'

'You deny giving them the information to write this report?'

'She witnessed everything she's written about, including the RTC, which I never saw.'

'What about the search of the industrial estate? Only someone who witnessed it could have written her account.'

'She did. I didn't. I investigated the vehicle fire where we found two bodies. There's nothing in the report about them.'

'You let her follow an armed response team on operations?'

'It wasn't my decision, but she was the only person who could identify the fugitives. Did you want anything else?'

'Your phone.'

Chapman put his work mobile on the desk.

'Your personal phone.'

He swallowed. 'Do you have a warrant?'

'Why would I need one if you've nothing to hide?'

'You show me yours first.'

'What?'

'If you let me examine your phone, you can look at mine.'

Harding reddened. 'Don't be impertinent.'

'If that's everything, I've got work to do.' Chapman stood and walked out. He wouldn't put it past Harding to get a warrant. He'd need to get a new phone.

The unwelcome alarm woke a still-exhausted Sabirah. The prospect of having to work at *that place* had kept her awake until the early hours. After forcing herself to get up, she showered, grateful she had her own bathroom. When she came out in her dressing gown, she found Hakim in the doorway to her bedroom.

'Mamma, can I use your bathroom?'

'What's wrong with yours?'

'Nadimah's using it. She's been in there ages. Please, Mamma, I'm desperate.'

'Okay, and make sure you put the seat back down.'

With a cry of thanks, he ran past her and closed the door. How quickly they'd got used to living here after moving from the horrible flat with one damp and draughty bathroom between the three of them. Mind you, compared to the refugee camp, it had seemed like a palace.

She continued dressing and went down to the kitchen to prepare breakfast. By the time the children arrived, she'd arranged her features into the semblance of happiness.

'Are you starting your new job today, Mamma?' Nadimah said. It looked like she'd put on make-up.

'What's around your eyes?'

'Nothing.' She focused on her bowl.

'Look at me, darling.'

Nadimah hadn't done a bad job of applying eyeliner.

'It will have to come off.'

'But, Mamma, all the girls wear it.'

'I'm sure they don't. And anyway, even if they do, you know it's against the rules.'

'But, Mamma—'

'No, do it now.' She wasn't in the mood to be messed about and watched her daughter trudge from the room.

'Are you okay, Mamma?' Hakim asked.

'Of course, now finish your cereal.' She needed to improve her act, but the idea of having to go to that place three times a week made it difficult. At least it wasn't five.

She didn't have time to take them to school and saw them off before changing into her work clothes. Was she so ashamed of what she wore she didn't want her children to see her? She didn't care what her new boss said about how she dressed, she wasn't doing it for him. She left the house, making sure nobody saw her, and hurried to the bus stop in the dismal rain. How appropriate.

Not having time to take the children to school made her feel guilty, but she'd not taken them when she worked the job where she'd met Antonia. They started so early. She glimpsed her reflection in a shop window as she rushed by, determined not to get there late. Maybe she'd overdone the shapeless rags look, but at least he'd get the message.

The bus dropped her three hundred metres from work. She had ten minutes to get there, plenty of time. But each step she took felt like wading through treacle. Fighting the urge to walk past, she entered the courtyard. In the dull drizzle, it looked even worse than yesterday. Had it only been sixteen hours since her interview? She forced herself to go in. She pushed the door, which opened with a groan. *I know how you feel.*

A young woman wearing heels and a too-short skirt looked up from the reception desk. 'Can I help you?'

'Sabirah. I'm the new cleaner.'

'Oh, right, the boss said you're starting today.' She looked at Sabirah's outfit with obvious distaste. 'He's out, but here's your rota.' She handed Sabirah a fan of laminated sheets held together with a red treasury tag.

It held five sheets, designed to suit the previous cleaner's rota. 'I'm doing three days, so if I change this, can you type it up for me?'

'Three days?' This sounded too difficult to compute. 'The boss wrote it. He won't like you changing it.'

'Don't worry, I'll make sure I cover all the jobs he wanted done, but in three days, not five. Do you have a locker for me?'

'Staffroom's there.' She pointed at a door ten paces down the corridor. 'But you're supposed to start now.'

'Okay. Where do you keep the cleaner's equipment?'

'Next door, along from the staffroom.'

'Thank you.' Sabirah headed towards it.

'Hang on, you need the key.' She produced a key chained to a large circular piece of plywood with 'CLEANER' painted in Tippex across the centre. 'Bring it back when you've finished.'

Sabirah took it and set off again. Two labelled doors led off the staffroom, a depressing place with too few windows and too much cheap furniture. In the ladies', a grubby sink stood next to two cubicles facing the door. At the right-hand end of the room, a row of tiny lockers lined the wall. Sabirah counted twenty-five, and each bore signs of damage from break-ins.

Her spirits falling further, she headed to the cleaner's store. The huge 'keyring' made opening the door a struggle, but she got into the cupboard-like space. The stench of mould and stagnant water hit her. She found a switch and a yellow light flickered on. Two mops sat in a bucket of water with thick scum on it, next to a stained sink. A small metal cabinet contained some half-empty bottles of bleach and cleaning liquids. An ancient vacuum cleaner with grey tape round the hose and more round the flex leant against the opposite wall. The walls and floor looked like someone had last cleaned them the day they bought the hoover.

Although nearly overcome by the urge to run, she looked for rubber gloves and found a pair, not new, but serviceable. She hung her coat and handbag up behind the door, carried the contents of the room into the corridor, and an hour of intense work later, she ached, but every surface gleamed, and the room smelled of bleach and pine cleaner. Light-headed, she left to get fresh air.

As she walked past the reception, the woman said, 'You'd better put all that stuff away before the boss gets here. And where's the key?'

Pointing to her streaming eyes, Sabirah walked past her. 'I need fresh air.' She let the rain wash her face and went back in as the damp penetrated her top. 'Who do I see about getting more materials?'

'What about the key?'

'I need to go back in.'

'Okay.' The woman didn't hide her displeasure. 'What do you need?'

Sabirah gave her a list.

'I can see two mops from here.'

'They're rotten. Someone left them in water.'

'Well, the hoover still works.'

'It's not safe. You can see the wires.'

331

'I'll have to ask the boss.'

'Okay, you ask him. I'll start on the work routine and write the new one at lunch.' Which she intended to have far from here.

'Haven't you started the routine?'

'Did you see the state of the cleaner's cupboard?'

The receptionist sighed and returned her attention to her screen.

A loud bell clanged, and figures swarmed into the corridor.

'Is that the fire alarm?' Sabirah had left her handbag and coat in the store.

'Morning break.'

A few smokers braved the rain, but the rest poured into the staffroom. The women all wore outfits Sabirah would have regarded as daring even for a night out, and the men looked beaten. Sabirah forwent her break. She doubted she'd fit in the room, anyway.

She'd put away most of the items when a familiar voice demanded, 'Who the fuck left this shit in the corridor?'

'The new cleaner, boss.'

Sabirah stepped out. Her new boss wheeled from confronting the receptionist, red-faced in his damp overcoat.

'Get this crap put away, now.'

Sabirah grew hot and fought the urge to apologise.

'I hope you haven't moved my papers.'

'I haven't cleaned your office.'

He spun back to the receptionist. 'I told you to get her to clean my office.'

The woman turned red. 'I told her, sir, but she gave me a list of what she needs.'

Sabirah bit back her protest. 'I'll do your office now.'

'No, I've got important calls to make. You can stay afterwards and do it.'

'I have to meet my children.'

332

'No, clean my office.' Shouting, he'd approached to within two paces.

The hubbub from behind the staffroom door died. Sabirah's pulse raced and acid filled her throat.

He jabbed a finger at her. 'And what the hell are you wearing?'

The door to the staffroom opened and a wall of faces appeared. Sabirah couldn't breathe. She ducked back into the store and pushed the door shut. She leant against it, ignoring the shouting and banging behind her. Memories of trying to escape the gang of women attacking her in the prison showers returned. But she also remembered the sensation as she fought back.

Uplifted by the memory, she put her coat on, picked up her bag and opened the door.

'Don't ever fucking shut the door on me.'

Sabirah ignored him and as she walked past, kicked the mop-bucket over, sending a deluge of soapy water over his shoes.

'You fucking bitch—'

She spun to face him. 'You are a bully who harasses women. You are a—' Her English failed her for a moment. 'You should be ashamed.'

Heart pounding and eyes blurring, she stormed out of the building into the rain.

Even on a dismal day, light flooded into Antonia's office and the pale-yellow paint cheered her up. Following last night's visit to Grainger's house and near encounter with Derenski, she needed cheering up. Although relieved when his car drove off, she'd also experienced disappointment he'd got away. Her phone beeped.

'Russell, you found it?'

'Not good news, I'm afraid.'

'Cloned plates?'

'Got it in one. Sorry.'

'Well, I feared as much. Thanks for checking.'

'The question I'm asking myself is why watch Grainger's house?'

The question had kept Antonia awake. 'Unless he'd followed me, and I'd led him there.'

'Could be, but why would they follow you? If they're after you, they wouldn't have run. You think his wife's lying, so what if they've got him and are monitoring her so she keeps quiet?'

'I signalled to her, but she dismissed it. I'm still trying to work out why anyone would kidnap him and who it might be.'

'Find out what story he's working on. I bet they're linked.'

She exhaled in frustration. 'I wish I could. Anyway, I'd better go. Thanks for checking.'

'No problem. And, Antonia, there's a strong possibility they were following you, so be careful.'

Promising she would, she ended the call. She opened her laptop and checked her emails. Another bundle she'd have to wade through. Jean had arranged for most to go to Zabo to filter, but he still forwarded ninety per cent. She'd have to spend some time with him to explain she didn't need to see every email from a reader suggesting she investigate a particular government official.

The file of emails coming directly to her held far fewer new messages, and she concentrated on those. One, from an unfamiliar email but purporting to come from Grainger, grabbed her attention. She opened it, disappointed it just contained a hyperlink. Instead of deleting it, she called Jean Sawyer.

Antonia still hadn't got used to Sawyer's new look of smart, modern outfits, trendy glasses with high-index lenses and professionally cut and styled hair.

'Jean, I've received this. It claims to be from Rick, but I suspect a scam.'

'Ooh. Let me see.' Jean wheeled the visitor's chair alongside Antonia and slid the keyboard and mouse towards her. She opened a new page on the browser and typed in a web address. After performing a dizzying series of checks, she returned to the email and clicked the link.

'What are you doing? You're always telling us to never click on those links.'

She tapped her nose. 'If you know what you're doing, like I do . . .' The link took them to a page like the one she'd first opened. An orange button bore the word *DOWNLOAD* on it. She clicked on it. 'It's a dead delivery device. You set it up to send a message to chosen targets. You must report in with a code every few days, but if you don't, it sends the message.'

'Like an "open if anything happens to me" letter?'

'Yes. I use the same one.'

Antonia's concern for Grainger rose a dozen notches. 'Why do you need one?'

Jean fixed her with her gaze. Although much thinner, her new lenses still magnified her eyes. 'You never know what might happen.'

Antonia reminded herself how little she knew about Sawyer as she opened the downloaded document. 'Hang on.' Antonia turned the screen away from Sawyer.

'What's wrong?'

'Sorry, Jean. I need to know what's so important Rick couldn't just tell me.'

'Don't you trust me?'

'Rick feared something would happen to him and my guess is, it's because of something he was working on. Anyone else who knows it will run the same risk.'

Jean's mouth formed an O, and she blinked. 'Oh, right. I'll leave you to it then.'

'Thanks, Jean.' Antonia waited until she'd left and studied the message on the screen.

Hi Antonia, if you're reading this, it means something's happened to me. It will be because of the story I'm working on, and I'd really like you to finish it. If you continue to work on it, I don't need to tell you to be careful. I've seen you in action, so I know you're more than capable of taking care of yourself, but I'm still worried about exposing you to this level of risk. Which is why I haven't told you anything yet. Now, I don't have a choice. Sorry.

You MUST make sure you only use an air-gapped computer whenever you work on the story and never discuss it with anyone. Remember, Air-gapped. You'll find everything you need on my laptop. Good luck, and it was a pleasure working with you.

Rick

Underneath, two lines of what looked like passwords, followed by a cryptic message:

You will know a chap who can help you find one. If not, ask a man.

Please delete this permanently, for your own safety.

She scrolled down the message but found no more. She checked in her downloaded messages file but found no other documents. Antonia stared at the message for a long time. What the hell did he mean? Then she put it together. Of course: chap and man.

336

She rang Chapman. 'Russell, did Rick ever—' She stopped herself. It wasn't long ago someone had bugged her other office.

'Did Rick ever what?' Chapman sounded stressed.

'Can we meet?'

'When?'

'Lunchtime?'

He covered up the handset and spoke to someone in his office before replying. 'Sorry, no can do. What about early doors after work? Six thirty at—'

'How about the place we met for lunch near the British Museum?' She hoped he'd remember.

She ended the call with mixed emotions. The likelihood something had happened to Grainger had increased significantly, but the thought of finding out what he was working on excited her, and she couldn't wait. Mind you, she would then be as much a target as he'd been.

CHAPTER 28

The rain, which cast a pall over the earlier part of the day, cleared, leaving a bright summer's evening. The grass in the park in Russell Square glinted with water drops like tiny diamonds. Antonia walked round the perimeter path, glancing behind her to make sure she'd not picked up any tails. She'd arrived early and didn't fancy waiting on her own.

At six twenty, she headed towards the British Museum and the bar where she'd arranged to meet Chapman. She made her way in and wove between the milling office workers, looking for him. The aroma of alcohol and coffee combined to confirm the mixture of clientele. As she pushed her way through, the words of Grainger's message wouldn't leave her.

She'd finished a circuit of the room and returned to the entrance by the time Chapman arrived. After greeting him and buying him a drink, she led him to the back corner where, despite the place being busy, a few tables remained unoccupied.

Chapman sipped his drink and saluted her with the glass. 'What couldn't you say in your office?'

'I got an email from Rick.'

'Where is he? Somewhere sunny?'

'What we suspected seems to have happened. It came from a dead delivery service.'

'What's one of those, a firm of trendy undertakers?'

'Ha, ha. It's a service enabling you to send an email if anything happens to you.' She explained what Sawyer had told her.

'Did he say what he thinks might happen to him?'

'Bucklin tried to kill us. He didn't tell me what he's working on now because he didn't want to expose me to the risk.'

'Shit! What you going to do?'

'I'm going to find out what he was working on and, if I can, publish the story. I'm hoping we can either use the information to find who's holding him and get him released, or whoever has him might release him once the story breaks.'

'You think he's still alive?'

'I don't know, Russell. I hope to God he is.' Had he taken chances because she pushed him for a story?

'Have you got the email?'

'Why?'

'I presume you want me to instigate a kidnap investigation. I'll need it as evidence.'

'Not a good idea.'

'Look, the team the Met has is very good. It would amaze you to discover how many relatives of oligarchs and sheikhs disappear for ransom every year. Most return alive and unharmed.'

'And in how many cases did a ransom get paid?'

Chapman didn't answer.

'Exactly. There's nobody wanting a payoff here.'

'We still can't leave him in the hope your story gets him released.'

'Two problems. The first is I've destroyed the message—'

'Why? It's evidence. We'll have to recover it from the server.'

'I asked Jean to make sure nobody can recover it.'

Chapman blew out his cheeks and took a deep drink from his glass. 'And the second problem?'

'You're named in the email.'

'What?' A couple at the next occupied table looked at Chapman and he leant towards her. 'What do you mean?'

'Everything he's worked on is on his laptop. He left a cryptic message suggesting you know where it is.'

'Me?'

She'd scribbled the codes and the last lines Rick had appended to his message on a piece of notepad and handed them to him. 'Does this mean anything to you?'

He frowned, studying the figures for a long time. Then he smiled and looked around before leaning into her. 'He asked me if I know the most secure self-storage units in London. This place has never reported a break-in and has a reputation for discretion. No cameras or surveillance.'

'How come?'

'They're owned by heavy-duty crooks. They wouldn't report a theft, but nobody would dare rob them. I suspect half the units are full of swag.'

'So, this is where he's got the laptop.'

'Sounds like it.'

'Can you take me there?'

'Now?'

'What time do they shut?'

'They don't. They have twenty-four-hour access. You just need the codes, and bingo you're in.'

Antonia wanted to find out what Grainger had been working on, but even if they recovered what he kept in the unit, trawling through it would take hours. 'Shall we eat and then go, or do you need to shoot?'

'My social life doesn't exist and Abby's away with her mum and the "new" bloke, so I'm all yours.'

'Are you okay with that?'

'No social life? I'm used to it.' He winked.

'I meant the new bloke.'

'Good luck to her. We're never going to get back together.'

'How about Abby calling him Dad?'

He laughed. 'She calls him David Brent, amongst other names. She's only going on the holiday because they're staying in the Burj Khalifa, and her friends will be "insanely jealous", according to her.'

'He must have a few quid.'

'Yeah, partner in some hedge fund. Anyway, enough about him. Shall we eat here or go somewhere else?'

They ordered and enjoyed a relaxed meal. Their friendship had gone through a rough patch six months earlier but had recovered. At nine, they set off for the storage units. Once they left central London, they made good time and arrived in Tottenham at quarter to ten.

The storage depot lay just off the main road on the edge of an industrial estate. A three-metre-high fence with coils of razor wire on top and tower lights at regular intervals suggested a prison. Two guards in a kiosk watched Chapman as he punched a code into the keypad by the gate.

'I'm impressed you memorised the entry code.'

'It's the same as mine. Where do you think I keep the stuff from my divorce? I've got enough furniture in there for a house I can't afford unless I move to Yorkshire or somewhere just as godforsaken.'

'Why don't you get rid of it, save the rental for this place?'

'You're probably right, but I've got furniture my dad made. I could just keep those bits, but it would feel like giving up.'

Antonia owned nothing of her dad's, not even a photo, and although she knew his family came from Palermo, she'd not tried finding anyone who might know him.

'You okay?'

They'd pulled up next to three other vehicles. 'Yeah, sorry, I was miles away.'

She followed him to the main building, a huge steel-framed structure lit by floodlights and painted in black and white squares. The entrance doors swished open, and she followed him into a bright but stark reception area. Two more guards sat in a glass-fronted kiosk. Hard-faced young men with the bulk of steroid users. They wore dark uniforms with black and white shoulder flashes.

Chapman waved a greeting they ignored and glanced at the paper Antonia had written the codes on. A large board listed three-letter codes next to floor numbers.

'Third floor.' Chapman entered another code into a keypad by the lift controls and the doors slid open.

The huge lift car with battered sides crawled up. 'There's a lot of guys on duty for this time of night.'

'Yeah, more than usual. Something's going on. Let's get this stuff picked up and get out of here.'

Antonia's neck prickled. 'We can come back later. Tomorrow morning?'

'It would have to be evening. Let's just get this stuff and go. We're here now.'

The lift stopped, and the doors opened on to a stark corridor illuminated by strip lights. Signs with more three-letter codes and arrows hung off the wall opposite.

'This way.' Chapman walked off to the right, and she followed.

Her sense of danger grew as their steps echoed. Steel doors, painted with the same black and white squares, lined the corridor. Each door had a keypad lock, but many also had padlocks through a hasp. What if Grainger's unit had a padlock? He'd said nothing about a key.

They rounded a corner and almost barged into two security guards. The nearest scowled at them. 'What you doing here?'

'We're picking up our stuff.' Chapman pointed at a unit ten metres down the corridor.

The guard stepped aside. The one behind him turned away as they walked past. Where did she know him from? Her pulse racing, Antonia followed Chapman to the unit. She saw the padlock from five paces away and let out a groan. Conscious of the guards watching and listening, she said nothing. *Blast!* What could they do?

Chapman, seeming unperturbed, held the padlock in one hand and removed it.

'How'd you get it open?' she whispered.

'There are too many figures for the keycode, so I guessed the extra numbers were to open the padlock.'

He handed her the padlock, then entered a code in the lock. With a click, the door swung open, and a light flickered on in the unit. A two-metre cube, it contained a small stack of document boxes with files in them. Sensing a change, Antonia checked behind her. The guards had gone.

Chapman stepped into the unit and checked the first file. 'What do you make of this?' He handed it to Antonia.

Copies of share certificates, and the names made her insides knot. 'Let's find the laptop. He'll have scanned everything on to it.'

Chapman found a courier bag containing a small MacBook and gave it to Antonia. 'Let's go.'

She didn't need persuading and waited in the corridor while he reattached the padlock. As they neared the lift, Antonia in the lead, men's voices reached them. The security guards? But two men in jeans and leather jackets lurked by a large trolley, waiting for the lift. The nearest one faced them, and Antonia yelped.

'Hughes?' But he was dead.

He studied her, and she realised her mistake. Despite a strong resemblance, he was bigger and beefier than Hughes.

'Do I know you?' He looked her up and down with a leer.

Fresh scar tissue criss-crossed his cheek. Then recognition bloomed in his eyes as he looked behind her.

'I fucking know you though, don't I?' He jabbed a finger at Chapman, then reached inside his jacket.

Antonia didn't think. She punched him in the throat and as he reared back, launched a kick at the side of his knee. It snapped, and he fell, screaming. His companion pointed an automatic at her head. The stink of weed came off him in waves, but the pistol remained rock steady.

Waking from yet another short but merciful escape from the pain, Grainger lay in the dark, trying to ignore the agony of his burns. He recalled interviewing a yoga guru who espoused embracing pain and using it to strengthen your core. Had someone thrust the guru's arm into a furnace and then left him without painkillers? Grainger tried to recall the lesson the guru had given him on how to do it, but he couldn't focus.

How long had he been here? The pain from his arm made every minute like an hour. When he'd begged the nurse for painkillers, she'd regarded him like a specimen in a zoo. But he thought he heard a whispered, 'Sorry' as she changed his dressing.

He'd made the mistake of looking at it when the bandage came off. The mess of suppurating and swollen flesh became a monster that tried to devour him in the fleeting moments he lost consciousness. The wish for death grew stronger. He'd always believed he had a strong will to live, but now he just wanted death. The light came on, and Grainger screwed up his eyes. Voices entered the room.

'Mr Grainger, how are you today?' Scarface, with a mocking tone.

Grainger opened his eyes. Next to Scarface, the team leader, the pair seeming joined together.

They undid the straps. But he didn't have the strength to lift himself off the bed, let alone try to escape. They dragged him to his feet, the pain every time they touched his left arm making him whimper. He no longer cared if they saw his fear. After two halting baby-steps, he almost fell. Scarface held him up by his bandaged arm and he screamed, almost fainting.

Sweat poured down his back, and he panted. 'I can't walk.' He sounded drunk.

'We know. They never can.' The team leader pointed to a wheelchair beside the bed.

Grainger almost fell into it, and they wheeled him out of the room. 'How many times have you done this?'

Scarface laughed. 'Enough. But don't worry, you only have to do it once.' He pushed the chair through the corridor, but not the way they'd gone last time.

With a sense of foreboding, Grainger waited for them to arrive. The air grew hotter and drier. Or was he imagining it? He'd heard more than once, from victims *and* exponents of torture, that a man with an imagination suffered far more than one without.

The door ahead opened, and a wave of hot dry air belched out. An acrid smell and damp sensation told him he'd pissed himself before Scarface's mocking jeer confirmed it. The third thug waited in the room and closed the door behind them.

Scarface couldn't help gloating. 'Fucking pissed himself again, hasn't he.'

Reed-Mayhew, also waiting in the room and wearing the same suit he'd worn the first time, studied Scarface. 'Maybe we can arrange for you to discover what it's like. See how long before you soil yourself?'

Scarface paled and mumbled an apology.

Reed-Mayhew ignored him. 'Mr Grainger, I'll ask you one last time if you've told anyone else what you were investigating.'

'No.' The smart answer he'd imagined giving would have taken too much energy.

'A pity.' Reed-Mayhew nodded at the team leader.

They lifted Grainger out of the wheelchair and dragged him to the powered chair they'd placed him in last time. Determined to fight with all his strength, he cried in frustration as they transferred him to the other chair with minimal inconvenience. By the time they'd finished, he realised they'd reversed the brackets on the chair. This time, his right arm, almost undamaged so far, protruded before him like a short, blunt lance.

'No. Please, leave one arm.'

'Why would we?' Reed-Mayhew looked puzzled.

With a click, a motor started. A sound that visited Grainger in his waking nightmares. The chair jerked into motion and slid forward.

'Please, don't do this.'

'Just tell me the truth.'

'I have.' Would Antonia have received his message now? And if she had, could she decipher it? Would she even download it? He should have told her to expect a message if he disappeared. As the heat increased, he remembered something Reed-Mayhew had said.

'What have you done to my wife?'

'Don't worry about your wife, Mr Grainger. Just think about yourself and your arm.'

The stink of burning hair filled his nostrils, and the heat grew unbearable. His eyeballs dried in the heat.

'Please stop.'

'Who have you told?'

'Nobody.' His eyebrows went, then his shirt burst into flames as intense heat consumed his arm.

'I shall have to assume you've told the interfering busybody you work for and deal with her.'

'No!'

'What about the policeman who's always sniffing round her?'

'Nobody.'

'Your loyalty does you credit, Mr Grainger, even at the expense of your common sense.'

He screamed, then the pain infused every cell until he blacked out.

The thrumming of wheels on tarmac seeped into his senses, then voices, muffled and distant. Pain permeated every part of him. The car went over a pothole, magnifying his agony. A sixth sense told him he must be quiet. Where was he? His eyes couldn't penetrate the gloom, however wide he opened them. Did they think him dead and had buried him already?

Of course not. He was in a car. Reed-Mayhew had finished with him. They must have a place to dispose of their victims. He remembered Antonia uncovering a mass grave under a house. They must be taking him somewhere similar. Reed-Mayhew's comments about Antonia came back to him. How could he warn her? Would she have got his message now? And Erika. Had they already killed her? Something about the night they snatched him still confused him. She'd seemed not terrified but resigned, like she did when they attended social functions she didn't want to go to. Had she expected the men? No, he couldn't think that.

The pain pressed on him again, but he couldn't let it win. Not yet. When he'd breathed in, fabric brushed against his face. Had they wrapped him in a shroud? He moved his right arm. The agony when it brushed against the wrapping almost made him pass out. They'd not bothered bandaging his right hand, so he used his left, now his 'better' hand. The bandages on that hand slipped over the surface of whatever contained him. A polythene bag? Yes. But he could breathe, so they hadn't sealed it.

He found the opening and slid out of it, moving his body like a fish. Not using his arms. Once free of the bag, he lay on the plywood floor of a van. He crawled towards the voices, and they grew louder until, after listening, he identified Scarface and the team leader.

Light flickered in a small gap on his right. The road flashed by. He lay beside a door in the side of the van. Could he reach the handle? He sat up, agony every time his arms or hands touched anything. He'd hired one of these to collect a bed for a friend. The side doors in these vehicles slid to open. Did he have the strength to open it? He doubted it, but had an idea. He waited until the vehicle slowed.

Then, ignoring the pain, he grabbed the handle and pulled. It slid a few centimetres, but his strength ebbed. Then, as they accelerated, it gave and opened. Panting with effort, he leant against the bulkhead separating him from the cab. A cool breeze eased his pain as he rested. The vehicle braked, and the door slid forward. *NO!* He threw himself at it. Then they accelerated, and the slide stopped.

He must get out before they reached their destination. It meant leaping out of a moving vehicle. The fall would kill him, but he didn't think he'd survive, anyway. He could lie down and die now, but he wanted them caught. He poked his head out, and the breeze on his neck made him shiver. No streetlights and no lights behind him. He turned round and saw none ahead. Where in London would they find no other traffic?

He must have dozed because when he next looked, red tail-lights showed up ahead. Close. The van had pulled out to overtake a car. It drew alongside a camper van. A couple in the front. They saw him, mouths opened in shock. They flashed their headlights.

'No don't, they'll kill you. Call the police.' He shouted the warning, despite knowing they couldn't hear him.

With the last of his strength, he threw himself out of the opening. Lights came at him and brakes squealed. Then darkness.

CHAPTER 29

The insistent trilling broke through Chapman's nightmare. In it, he'd run and left Antonia to face the gunman. He'd turned on hearing a shot and Antonia's accusing glance as blood gushed from the hole in her forehead had punctuated the dream.

At least he could remember what had actually happened. The two security guys had come from behind the gunman and overpowered him. He doubted either he or Hughes's brother would trouble them again.

Light leaked in through the edge of the curtains, but the clock on his phone showed before six. He pressed reply and clamped it to his ear.

'DI Chapman?'

'Go on,' he said.

'I've got an RTC, three fatalities—'

'Why are you ringing me?'

'We found your name and address on the scene.'

His tiredness evaporated. 'Where is it?'

He wrote the address down. It took him over an hour to reach the site. The road passed through bucolic countryside with a golf course on one side and fields of ripening rapeseed on the other. A portable sign warned him of a road closure ahead. A patrol car with its blue light flashing sat in the middle of the road. The incident remained out of sight, round a bend.

Chapman introduced himself and the constable directed him to park beyond the patrol car and make his way to the incident. Chapman retrieved two disposable gloves and got out of his vehicle. Police cars, ambulances, a mortuary hearse and two fire engines lined the road, the firefighters getting ready to leave. A shocked-looking couple of elderly hippies sat on the grass at the back of one ambulance.

Chapman arrived at the scene. A body bag lay on the verge, ready for removal. Past it, an ancient but well-maintained camper van had landed with its nose in a ditch on the left side of the road. On the other side the remains of a mangled Transit van, its cab cut open, lay upon its roof on the grass verge behind it. The lorry that must have ploughed into it sat in the opposite ditch, the front offside crushed.

He found the officer in charge, a young uniformed inspector, and introduced himself. 'What do you reckon happened?'

She pursed her lips. 'The van tried to overtake the camper, but it braked as it passed and couldn't pull in when the lorry came round the bend.'

'Do we know why?'

'The couple in the camper saw someone trying to get out the back through the side door. I reckon the driver saw him in his mirrors and braked, not realising the lorry was there.'

'Ouch.' He gestured at the mangled van. 'Who are your fatalities?'

'Both the people in the front, and the guy who jumped out the back.' She nodded at the body bag.

'And where did you find my address?'

'One guy in the van had your details on a sheet of paper. You and someone called Antonia—'

'Conti?' Chapman's blood chilled.

'Yeah, you obviously know her.'

'I spoke to her last night. Who had it?'

'If it's his wallet we found in his jacket, he's a nasty piece of work. Not someone you want knowing where you live.'

'Can I have a look at the other guy?'

'Not pretty. The camper ran over him.'

'Poor couple. No wonder they look shocked.' Chapman walked to the body bag, pulling on the disposable gloves.

The inspector unzipped the bag.

A battered Rick Grainger stared up at him through sightless eyes. Even though he'd expected it, bile rose in Chapman's throat.

'You recognise him?'

'Yeah. Rick Grainger. He's a reporter.'

'Shit, I read his stuff. I didn't recognise him.'

Cogs whirred in Chapman's brain as he pieced together what he already knew with this new information. 'Can you pull the zip down a bit more?'

'It's not pretty,' she warned him again, then exposed his torso.

His shirt had disintegrated, but the remaining bits bore scorch marks. His swollen and misshapen arm looked like a piece of cooked meat. Strips of bandage clung to similar burns on the other arm.

She straightened. 'Not sure how he got the burns. None of the vehicles show signs of fire and the underside of the camper's engine wouldn't have got hot enough to cause those injuries.'

'They're the results of torture. You can see they've treated his left arm to keep him alive.' He wanted to heave. Antonia, he must warn her. 'Excuse me.' He called the number. *Please answer.*

'This better be important, Chapman. I was fast asleep.'

'I've found Grainger, what's left of him.' He didn't have time to break it gently.

'Where—'

'The guys transporting him had your address and mine. You need to get out of there.'

She hesitated for a second. 'Okay, I'll go to work—'

'I'll send a car to sit outside, and we'll find you somewhere to stay tonight. You don't have to worry about the guys who we found with your address, but whoever they're working for . . .'

He ended the call and arranged for a patrol car to meet her at the office. The inspector had resealed the body bag and two undertakers waited with their trolley.

'Have you finished with him?' She looked shaken.

'Yeah, take him away please, guys.'

The young inspector waited until they moved out of earshot. 'This is my incident. It's not even your force area. I informed you as a courtesy.'

'Sorry. Habit. Though I think we'll end up taking this off you. It's not just an RTC, it's a kidnapping. I'd like you to treat the van as a crime scene. Grainger has been missing since Monday morning. We think they took him from his home in Clapham.'

'Right, I'll inform our control.'

Wanting to make sure he got the case, Chapman rang Gunnerson.

'Russell, I presume you're not ringing to wish me an early good morning.'

'I wish. I'm at an RTC in Essex.' He gave her the details.

'And you want the case?'

'It's linked to our operation in King's Cross.'

'How?'

'A message from the victim sent us to an address in Tottenham. There we encountered two thugs, one of whom is Hughes's brother. The guy Antonia met at King's Cross.'

Gunnerson pondered for a moment. 'I'll see what I can do. You in Essex now?'

'Yes, we've got the van they transported Grainger in, which I'd like to bring back to our lab, plus the three bodies.'

'Okay, I'll arrange for the vehicle to be brought over. You finish up and we'll talk when you get here.'

He ended the call and stared at the van. He'd worried something had happened to Grainger but had imagined nothing as bad as those horrific injuries. The thought of the person who'd caused them hunting Antonia sickened him.

◆ ◆ ◆

The news of Grainger's death knocked Antonia sideways. She'd accepted the possibility someone might kill him, and his email message emphasised the fact, but she'd hoped she could free him by publishing his story. Her determination to get his last story out there grew with every step she took to the office.

Chapman had told her the men with Grainger were out of action. Arrested or dead? She still hurried and checked for anyone dodgy. Grainger's laptop sat in her backpack, and she clutched it to her, conscious of the value of its contents. Or, more precisely, the price Grainger had paid. She replayed the brief conversation with Chapman. She didn't like the sound of 'what's left of him'. What did he mean?

She let herself into the new offices. The bright open space, which she'd so welcomed, now made her feel exposed and she longed for the more defendable basement. She'd not considered if anyone overlooked her windows. Out of habit, she kept any screens she used away from them, making sure nobody could see what she was reading, but people could still see *her*.

She didn't want the blinds down. The memory of a thirtieth-floor apartment with blacked-out windows made her cringe. She'd been investigating a memory clinic, and they'd convinced her the people protecting her were enemies and took her there, she'd thought, to keep her safe, but they'd made her their prisoner.

Antonia took a coffee into her office and placed it on her desk alongside the backpack. Grainger's laptop fired up in seconds, battery ninety-seven per cent. When had he placed it in the storage unit? He must have another he worked on and backed up to this one every few days. Going to the unit too often would increase the risk.

The machine asked for a password. She retrieved a copy of the paper she'd given to Chapman. Working on the assumption he'd included the password in the two sets of codes he'd sent her, she studied them. How many characters did a MacBook require to unlock it? And did it lock out after too many failed attempts?

Sawyer stuck her head in the door. 'Morning, Antonia. Oh, you've got Rick's laptop. Is he in?'

'How do you know it's Rick's laptop?'

'There's a scratch on the case. I suggested he changed it, but he didn't care.' Antonia had given up reprimanding Sawyer for refusing to use notebooks with 'wonky' covers, or pens whose caps weren't square.

'Do you know much about these? I need to work out the password.'

'Hasn't he given it to you?'

Antonia tried the numbers Chapman had used to open the padlock. A warning in large red letters flashed across the screen.

'Ooh. Not good.' Sawyer pointed at the screen. 'He's booby-trapped it. If you mess up the next two goes, it will wipe the contents.'

Damn! 'Can we override it?' Antonia stared at the jumble of letters and numbers on the paper. Which ones formed the password?

'I'm sorry, if we have access to his iCloud account, we might. Are you sure he didn't give you the password?'

Antonia resisted the temptation to snap at her. He must have given her a clue sometime. She replayed the message. He'd reiterated the need for her to use an air-gapped computer. But he'd written it with a capital once and then without. Which way round? She had two attempts, so just try one. She typed it with the capital first, then hesitated over the enter button. Sawyer stared with her big brown eyes.

Antonia pressed the button, and the screen went blank. 'Blast! I thought I had three goes.'

'You do. You're in.'

Antonia exhaled. 'Thank God.'

'Where is Rick?'

Antonia didn't want to give the bad news, but she didn't have a choice. One burden of leadership. 'I'm sorry, Jean. Rick's dead.'

'Dead? What's happened? I was talking to him last week.'

'I'm not sure, but Russell rang me. There's been a car accident, and they found him dead at the scene.'

'Oh my.' Sawyer wobbled and Antonia grabbed her before easing her into her chair.

'I'll get you some water, Jean.'

She came back with a glass and Sawyer gulped some down. Tears tracked down the powder on her cheeks. 'Thank you.'

Despite her eagerness to check the contents of the laptop, Antonia hovered over Sawyer until her colour improved. 'Are you going to be okay?'

'Has someone told his wife?'

She'd not even thought of her. 'I'm sure Russell will tell her.' Would he? She'd better check.

With a promise not to mention it until Antonia told the staff, Sawyer left, shutting the door. Antonia would have to announce it once everyone arrived.

The laptop had locked itself, but with the code, Antonia reopened it. She found a series of folders that recalled the last investigation, labelled with the familiar names of the companies they'd looked into when they'd brought down the government. Each contained dozens of copy share certificates.

She found the main file and opened a document entitled, *Read me first.*

Antonia, I'm hoping you never read this, but if you are, I wanted to say how much I enjoyed working with you and Eleanor. You restored a cynical old hack's faith in the press. Keep doing what you're doing. You will shake up the world.

OK, enough of the bullshit. Now is where you earn your corn. You'll find a series of share certificates for all the companies we investigated, plus a few more. They're the companies which will prosper if we ever renew Trident. But I can't see it ever happening. Although I've gathered lots of data, I don't know the following.

1/ Who's buying the shares? I've discovered whose names are on the share certificates, entities controlled by the company my wife works for, JN Partners. If you can, please keep her out of this.

2/ Why are they buying them? At first, I thought it was more insider dealing by Jacinda. But the scale is too great. I'm sorry I misled Jean to get her to tell me more about the story she's working on. Jacinda doesn't take risks, not with her company anyway. The amount committed to paying for these shares is £43 billion, far greater than the net worth of her fund, and she would never take such a risk.

If it's not insider dealing, then it's something else. And here's where I'm stuck.

As you know, the value of the companies plummeted following our report. I've calculated the value they lost in total from the day they announced the deal. £37 billion.

It made me blink. If someone had shorted those shares, they would now be hugely wealthy. But nobody did. People like Bucklin bought most, and they expected to become very rich by holding on to them.

The reason I've become paranoid is because two of my sources in Cayman have had 'accidents' in the last week, after I asked them to investigate who'd bought the shares. I also posted some questions about those shares on a very discreet chat group. Anticipating trouble, I did it from an internet café outside London, used a VPN, and bounced the signal via seven servers around the globe. I got out and watched from a discreet distance. An hour later, some very nasty-looking men came to the café searching for me.

That's GCHQ-type tracking, but these men didn't work for our security services.

I've also been thinking about what caused Jacinda to blow her top last week. I made a crack about how I could have fed my wife the information on the crooked politicians so she could benefit from some insider dealing – stupid,

I know, but I was very, very drunk. Although I'm pretty
sure it wasn't the trigger, as I also mentioned how much
someone could make if they bought up those shares and
Trident went ahead. That could have been when she got
angry. Or maybe she didn't like me drinking so much of
her best whisky.

I've left you all my notes and all my contact details and
discoveries. I suspect some contacts will blank you, but
many will prove useful, if not now, later in your career.
Maybe you'll see what I couldn't. There's something going
on, and someone powerful and very ruthless is determined
to hide it, but I don't know what it is. But I know, if
anyone can get to the bottom of this, it's you.

Rick.

'Antonia, why are you crying?'

She gathered herself and wiped her cheeks. Tears dripped off her chin on to the desk. 'I didn't realise I was.'

A blurred Eleanor studied her from the doorway. 'Jean can hardly talk. Has something happened to Rick?'

'Do you want to come in and close the door?' Antonia retrieved a tissue from a small pack she'd had since Alan's death. 'Russell rang me from the site of a road smash. They found Rick's body.'

'Oh my. Did he say what happened?'

'No, but I think someone hurt Rick before they killed him.'

'Killed?'

'This is his laptop. I recovered it from a storage unit last night. We bumped into the brother of Hughes, the man who lured me to King's Cross, and another man. I overpowered him, but his friend produced a gun.'

'What happened?'

'They, and some others, had been hanging around all day and the owners of the site got nervous. They brought their own guys in, and they intervened.'

'What happened to the gunman?'

'I don't know and don't want to.'

'Didn't you call the police?'

'Russell was with me, and one guy who intervened is Mr Decker's nephew, the joiner who helped us out. He's also a cousin to my friends who run the gym.'

'But he might have caused the deaths of those two men.'

'Men linked to Rick's death.'

'So, it's an eye for an eye?'

'Sometimes it has to be, Eleanor.' How many men *and* women had Antonia killed? 'I'd better tell the others about Rick. Then find out who killed him.'

CHAPTER 30

The offices of JN Partners occupied the tenth floor of a smart office block overlooking Cabot Square in Canary Wharf. Chapman and Sanchez took the lift in silence. Neither loved this part of the job. The minimalist but expensive furniture in the reception area suggested they'd used the services of a competent interior decorator. The young receptionist wouldn't look out of place on a catwalk. He quickly recovered his surprise when the two police officers asked to see Erika Voight.

He checked their ID and returned with an elegant woman in her forties. Tall, with an athletic build, she wore an understated business suit with an expensive label, and an equally expensive scent. Her hazel eyes appraised them as Chapman stood.

'Ms Voight, can we—'

'Nieto. I'm Jacinda Nieto, the owner.'

'We're here to see Ms Voight.'

'And I need to know why you're harassing my staff at work.'

Chapman kept his tone even. 'We're not harassing anyone. But we need to speak to Ms Voight on a personal matter.'

'What personal matter?'

'Do you understand what personal means?' Sanchez said.

'And you are?' Nieto turned on Sanchez.

'Are you going to let us speak to Ms Voight or not? And my name is Chapman, Inspector, if you have an issue with us.'

She held his gaze. 'I'll let you speak to her, but I'll stay with her.'

He attempted to read her. What the hell was going on? 'It's up to her. As we said, it's a personal matter.'

'Follow me.' She turned and strode away without waiting for them.

They followed her to an enormous office on a corner with a curved window overlooking the fountain in the square. It contained three distinct zones: a work area with an imposing desk at its centre, a meeting area round an oval table and a comfortable seating area. She left them standing in a no-man's-land inside the door and used a handset on the desk to summon Erika Voight.

Voight arrived, looking alarmed when Nieto introduced the two officers. Younger than Nieto, she looked under strain and displayed the nervy behaviour Antonia had described.

Sanchez spoke first. 'Ms Voight, we're here on a personal matter. Are you happy for your boss to listen in?'

'Yes, I've nothing to hide from Jacinda.' Her voice didn't rise above a whisper.

Sanchez looked to Chapman. *Cheers, Alice.* He cleared his throat. 'I'm sorry to tell you, your husband died this morning in a road traffic accident.'

Voight didn't react for a few seconds, then the colour drained from her, and Chapman feared she'd faint.

Nieto reached her first and put an arm around her shoulders. 'Oh, Erika, I'm so sorry. What happened, Inspector?' She led her to a chair at the oval table and fetched a bottle of water from a fridge hidden behind a wooden panel.

'Please sit.' Nieto gestured to chairs opposite Voight and sat next to her with a hand on her shoulder. 'Drink, Erika.'

Chapman signalled Sanchez to take the lead. 'Ms Voight, I realise it must be a shock, but we need to ask you a few questions.'

Voight wiped at a few drops of water she'd spilled on the pale table. 'Okay, I'll try to answer.'

'Your husband hasn't gone to work this week. Can you tell us where he's been?'

Voight looked at Nieto before answering. 'He decided he needed a few days off. He'd been working very hard on a big story and after it broke, he had lots of follow-up media engagements. They took their toll.'

'Do you know where he went?'

'He didn't tell me.'

'Did he often go away without telling you where you could contact him?'

Nieto leant forward. 'Some women aren't so insecure they need to keep tabs on their husbands, Constable.'

Chapman didn't wait for Sanchez to reply. 'It's Sergeant, Ms Nieto, and can you let Ms Voight answer? This must be distressing enough without your intervention.'

'It's fine, Jacinda. He often just took off with no plan and ended up where his fancy took him.'

Sanchez gave Nieto a glare before turning back to Voight. 'And when did you last speak to him?'

'Sunday night, before he left.'

'Weren't you concerned when he didn't contact you?'

'No. He often went days without contacting me. In war zones, he couldn't.'

'Do you think he'd gone to a war zone?'

'What she means, Sergeant, is she didn't go to pieces if she didn't hear from him every night.'

'Why don't you let Ms Voight tell me what she means?'

'Jacinda's right. I had complete trust in Rick.'

Chapman took over. 'Do you know anyone who wanted to hurt your husband?'

'No, why?'

'There was' – he'd thought hard how to phrase this – 'a suggestion he might have been mistreated before his death.'

Voight looked alarmed. 'What do you mean, mistreated?'

'Can you think of anyone he might have upset?'

'The dead Home Secretary's daughter is suing the outlet he works for. He's upset a few people in the past, because of his line of business.'

'Nobody more recent?'

Voight hesitated. 'Not anyone I'm aware of.'

'Do you know what he's working on?'

'Why don't you ask the African princess?' Nieto folded her arms.

'Who?'

'The girl he works for.'

He decided not to react. 'We're speaking to everyone who we think can help us.'

'Well, she's got some funny friends, hasn't she?'

'What do you mean?'

'Don't they tell you anything, Inspector? Some of her friends are terrorists.'

'Who's saying that?'

'I have my sources.'

Sanchez cleared her throat. 'Can we check Mr Grainger's room—'

Nieto laughed, a throaty sound. 'They're married and, like any normal couple, they share a room.'

'Are you familiar with the sleeping arrangements of all your staff?'

Nieto reddened.

Chapman leapt in. 'I'm sure Mr Grainger will have a study and documents which might give us a clue what might have happened to him.'

'Yes, yes, of course.' Voight acted as if in a trance. 'When?'

'As soon as possible. We could take you there now. I'm sure Ms Nieto won't expect you to stay here.'

'Of course not,' Nieto said, 'but I'll take her. Shall we say four?'

'The sooner we do this, the better.'

'Can't you see Erika needs some time to compose herself? She's not one of the habitual criminals you're used to dealing with.'

'Ms Voight, it's crucial we see it as soon as possible.' Why was Nieto stalling them?

Voight studied him with a look of panic, then glanced at Nieto.

'You can see she needs time, Inspector,' Nieto said. 'I can't see how an hour or so will make any difference.'

Chapman wanted to insist, but on what grounds? 'Four then.'

Nieto caught up with him as they waited for the lift. 'Sorry, I gave your assistant a hard time. It's very upsetting for us, Chief Inspector.' Her smile was a credit to her orthodontist.

In the lift car, Sanchez rolled her eyes. 'Your assistant, *Chief* Inspector?'

'She's a piece of work, isn't she?'

'And why do they need so long before we can check out his "room"?'

'I wondered as well, but short of getting a warrant, there's not much we can do.' He hoped the laptop Antonia recovered would help them discover what had happened to Grainger.

◆ ◆ ◆

Antonia told the staff about Grainger and, after fielding questions and offering counselling to anyone who wanted it, returned to her desk. Compared to Alan's death, this seemed less traumatic. A car crash was less shocking than being shot. And Alan had been a friend and close colleague for years. Grainger was a newcomer and not all the staff knew him.

A reminder from Miles prompted her to ring Chapman. 'Can you talk, Russell? It sounds like you're driving.'

'Hands-free. I'm here with Alice on our way back from speaking to Erika.'

'Oh, good. I rang to ask if you'd told her. How did she take it?'

'Shocked, but I wouldn't say surprised. I told her he'd died in an RTC, but she didn't ask where or what had happened— And up yours.' A horn beeped. 'Sorry, some arsehole made his own lane.'

'If she was in shock . . .'

'You could be right, but her boss was something else. I thought she'd stop me speaking to her.'

'She's got a history . . .'

'Of what? She'd not got a record.'

Antonia didn't want to say too much with Sanchez listening. 'We're looking into her business practices.'

'Okay, that's something we might end up doing. Did, erm, the items you recovered last night bear fruit?'

'I'd rather not discuss them over the phone.'

He said something to Sanchez she didn't catch. 'We'll swing by in half an hour.'

'See you soon.'

She asked Sawyer to come through with what she'd already discovered about JN Partners.

Sawyer looked worried. 'There's a police car outside, Antonia.'

It couldn't be Chapman already, but of course, the police escort he'd arranged. 'They're here to keep an eye on me. I'll ask Tomasz to offer them refreshments. What you got for me?'

Sawyer obviously wanted to know more about the police guards, but she didn't ask. 'The investigation of JN Partners. It's almost ready. I should finish by lunchtime.'

'Great. What did Rick ask you about it?'

A pink line crawled up Sawyer's neck. 'I didn't tell him much. Nothing about his wife.'

'I'm sure you didn't. What did he ask you?'

'If I had any information on the first finance director.'

'What, exactly?'

'What happened to his shares in JN following his accident.'

'And *what* happened to them?'

'Under the terms of their agreement, Nieto had first option on them.'

'His heirs got nothing?'

'Oh no, she had to pay, but she fixed the price at nine, on the morning they announced his death. The market reacted to a rumour he'd killed himself because they discovered a black hole in the accounts. The shares fell forty per cent. By the end of the day, they'd recovered, but she got them at the discounted price.'

'And who started the rumour, I wonder?'

'His son wondered the same in a press interview and ended up paying Nieto half a million plus costs.'

'What a lovely woman. Okay, let me have the finished article and I'll get Geoff Stokes to go over it.' Antonia wouldn't risk any possibility of someone like Nieto taking legal action over a minor mistake. 'Have you looked into the shares she's involved in buying now?'

Sawyer blinked. 'The article focuses on historical transactions, like we discussed.'

'Don't worry, I'm not criticising you, but can you see what involvement they have in these shares?' She gave her the list of

367

companies Grainger had investigated. 'Can you also find out who, if anyone, could cover purchases of forty billion plus?'

'UK or worldwide?'

'Start with the UK, then Europe.'

'There won't be many.'

'I'm hoping not. Thanks, Jean.'

A text announced Chapman's arrival and after giving him a quick look round the new offices, he and Sanchez sat in Antonia's office.

Chapman looked around the imposing room. 'I'm impressed, Antonia. You'll be too grand to speak to me soon.'

'All because of Sabirah's hard work. What did you want to know?'

'What did you find on the laptop?'

She looked at Sanchez.

'You can speak in front of Alice. I've told her you've got Rick's laptop with his latest work.'

On a previous unofficial investigation with Chapman, Sanchez had seen Antonia shoot the man who held a gun at Sanchez's head, and she also knew both Antonia and Chapman had killed others earlier. The fact they still enjoyed their freedom told Antonia she could trust her. Antonia got up, put on the lights, and lowered the blinds.

'What you doing?' Chapman looked puzzled.

'Check your phone.'

'Signal's gone.'

'Good.' Antonia still didn't like sharing this. 'Someone's buying shares in companies linked to Trident, through Nieto's company.'

'What for? That ship, or should I say, submarine, has sailed.'

'We don't know, but just looking got him in trouble. What happened to him?'

Chapman spread his hands. 'He died in a road accident. He fell out of a van.'

'Fell, or someone pushed him?'

'Fell or jumped. He was on his own.'

'Why would he jump?'

Chapman looked uncomfortable. 'He had burns—'

'From the crash?'

'Before. They'd bandaged some burns.'

'Torture.' Antonia felt sick.

'Looks like it.'

Sanchez's olive complexion had paled.

'Do you want water?' Antonia fetched three bottles from her fridge without waiting for a reply.

They drank, then Chapman said, 'Did you find anything which could help us discover who did this?'

'I'm still looking. He had a row with Nieto the Tuesday before he disappeared.'

'What about?'

'He'd had a few drinks and thinks he mentioned something about insider dealing and the Trident investigation.'

'Insider dealing?'

Antonia looked from one to another. 'None of this goes further—'

'That's a given, Antonia,' Sanchez said, and Chapman nodded.

'She's used inside information to make millions, even billions, since the crash in '07.'

'When do you intend publishing?' Chapman said.

'I'm hoping next Tuesday, but Geoff's got to make sure there's nothing actionable in it. We also think she's behind the death of her finance director, the one before Rick's wife.'

'She struck me as capable of anything,' Sanchez said. 'She knows about you, Antonia, and mentioned the bullshit about your link to terrorism.'

'Could Harding have mentioned that?' She remembered Chapman's certainty Harding worked for her old enemy, Reed-Mayhew. How much money had Reed-Mayhew now amassed?

'He could have. It's a shame we don't have more from the laptop.' Chapman looked disappointed. 'But you've given me a bit to push his wife and Nieto. I'm sure she'll be there.' He stood. 'I see the patrol's here. I'll check they've got a safe house ready for you. Unless you've arranged your own?'

She held his gaze. 'Not this time.'

Antonia opened the blinds after they left. That they'd tortured Grainger changed things. Who else would they target?

◆ ◆ ◆

Wanting to keep Voight off balance, Chapman and Sanchez arrived at her house early. As he'd expected, Nieto had accompanied Voight and answered the door.

'You're early, Inspector. Don't you realise it's inconsiderate to your hosts to arrive early?'

'They didn't do etiquette at my school. Is Ms Voight home?'

'I realised you haven't shown me your identification.'

'Your receptionist checked them.'

She stood with her hand out and they both showed their ID cards. Once she'd examined them, she stepped aside. Voight came out of a side room and gave an apologetic smile.

'Ms Voight, can we check Mr Grainger's study and your bedroom?'

She glanced at Nieto before replying. 'Of course, I'll show you.'

'Hang on, we'll come with you,' Nieto said.

'You worried we'll plant something or are you scared of what we'll find?' Sanchez said.

Nieto gave her a glare that should have turned her to stone, but disappeared into the room Voight had come out of.

They split up. He checked the study while Sanchez did the bedroom. The study looked too tidy, like someone had searched it and didn't want you to know. After half an hour, Sanchez came in and closed the door behind her.

'Nieto's hanging about on the landing, by the bathroom.' She kept her voice low. 'He's not taken any clothes.'

'What do you mean?'

'There's nothing missing in the wardrobe. It's huge, and it looks like they've let a Stepford wife loose designing it. Every item has its own place. And nothing's missing. They've got two sets of matching luggage, and again, it's all there.'

'Good work. Nothing doing here, haven't even found his laptop.'

'Hasn't Antonia—'

He held a finger to his lip.

'Sorry.' She glanced at the closed door and moved closer. 'What do you think of her demeanour? She's behaving like an abused spouse.'

'Let's finish this room and we'll go back down. I'll separate them and you see if you can find out anything.'

Twenty minutes later, they'd searched everywhere except under the carpet. They'd even moved pictures and ornaments that might conceal a safe. Back downstairs, they found both Nieto and Voight sat at a long kitchen table, nursing large glasses of red wine.

Nieto saluted them with her glass. 'I'd offer you some, Inspector, but suspect you're not allowed.'

'You'd be right. Ms Voight, I couldn't find your husband's laptop.'

'He'll have taken it with him. He took it everywhere.'

'But he doesn't appear to have taken any clothes.'

Voight gave Nieto a look of panic, then said, 'Yes, he did.'

'I can't see any gaps in the wardrobe.'

'He had what he called his assignment clothes. He kept them in a wardrobe in the spare room. They've gone.'

I'm sure they have. 'What about luggage?'

'He . . . He kept a battered old Samsonite backpack in the same place. He didn't like the Louis Vuitton stuff – too showy, he said.'

'Could you show Sergeant Sanchez where he stored it?'

'Yes, of course.' She stood, hesitant.

'I'll show her.' Nieto took charge.

'Ms Nieto, I've got a few questions for you.'

Sanchez left with a reluctant Voight.

'Nicely done, Inspector. A waste of time, but . . . Now, what do you need to ask me?'

'I understand you had a row with Mr Grainger a few days before he disappeared. What caused it?'

'I don't know what you're talking about.'

'Tuesday, he came to your house for a meal.'

'Oh, that. I wouldn't call it a row. Rick likes his whisky and can get argumentative. Likes to provoke people. I just told him to behave.'

'So, no row?'

She stared at Chapman.

'Is that a yes or a no?'

'You really are a pain in the arse, Inspector.'

'How long has Ms Voight worked for you?'

She seemed thrown by the change in tack. 'Four years.'

'And what happened to her predecessor?'

'He had an unfortunate skiing accident.'

'Not unfortunate for everybody.'

'What the hell do you mean?'

He didn't answer.

'You jumped-up busybody, I'll make sure you're reprimanded for your impertinence.' Her cheeks had grown red.

'I meant it turned out okay for Ms Voight, you having a vacancy.'

Sanchez and Voight returned to break the silence. Chapman checked with Sanchez, who gave a small shake of her head.

'Thanks, Ms Voight,' Chapman said. 'If you remember anything, please don't hesitate. You've got my card.' He started for the door.

'One thing,' Sanchez said. 'Do you have a car?'

'Yes, a Tesla.'

'Where is it?'

'Someone stole it.'

'Have you reported it?'

Voight gave Nieto another panicked look.

'You told me Rick borrowed it, Erika.'

'Yes, of course, I'm not thinking. The grief.'

'Can we have the details?' Chapman said. 'We can check for any sightings, find out where he's been since he disappeared.'

'Of course.' She gave Sanchez the details.

'What's happened to your dog?'

'What?'

'There's a lead hanging by the back door, and a chewed-up tennis ball in Mr Grainger's study.'

'Buster was ancient. They had to have him put down,' Nieto said.

'What a shame. Thanks again, Ms Voight. Ms Nieto.' He followed Sanchez out to the car. 'Anything?'

'I asked her if Nieto was coercing her or if anyone had threatened to harm either her or Rick but she played dumb. Said she didn't know what I was talking about.'

'Did you believe her?'

Sanchez shook her head. 'Absolutely not.'

'Nieto is definitely pulling her strings. And the bullshit about the car *and* the dog. A pack of lies.'

'No doubt. But, boss . . .'

'Why do I get the feeling you're going to tell me off?'

'Don't let Antonia get too close to this investigation.'

'You think she's involved?'

'I'm sure she isn't. But I've heard rumours Harding's convinced you're in her pocket.'

'We both know it's bollocks.' He strode to the car. Sanchez was right. He wouldn't be the first officer crucified for something he hadn't done.

CHAPTER 31

After spending a weekend in the strange hotel the police had booked her into, Antonia wasn't in the mood for the email from Geoff Stokes, and rang him straight back.

'How can we have received an injunction from JN Partners?'

'I've no idea, Antonia. Have you discussed the article with anyone?'

Neither Chapman nor Sanchez would have said anything, would they? 'The only thing I can think of is Rick Grainger might have said something to his wife.' *Or his torturers.*

'However it's happened, Nieto's solicitors are demanding the right to see any accusations against her and the right to reply.'

'That's ridiculous.'

'We'll fight it, of course. But you can't publish the article until I give you the go-ahead. Sorry, Antonia, and I'm sorry to hear about Rick. He seemed a decent man.'

'He was. Thanks, Geoff.'

She called Sawyer in and asked her to take a seat. 'I'm sorry, Jean, your article won't appear tomorrow. Nieto's taken out an injunction.'

'How did she find out?'

'I'm assuming Rick mentioned something to his wife or left something she might have seen. He had another laptop, didn't he?'

'Yes, he used a Windows laptop most of the time.'

Antonia would ask Chapman if he'd found it.

'Can you say when my article will appear?'

'I'm sorry, Jean, I can't yet, but we will publish it. Don't worry.'

Sawyer got up to go. 'Are we covering the dispute with Zungharistan?'

'Rick mentioned it a few weeks ago, but we've got a report from one of our sister publications on the site. We don't have the resources or expertise to cover it. Why?' The profile they'd got following their last big story meant they now had a network of partner publications they shared stories with, and this gave them much better international coverage.

'I'd never heard of it, but one of JN's clients comes from there.'

Grainger said he'd gone with his wife. Antonia had assumed on holiday, but was it a work trip for her? She'd park it for now. She didn't want to complicate matters. 'Let's leave that alone for the moment.'

Sawyer left and Antonia got hold of Chapman. 'Did you find Rick's laptop?'

'No, nor anything which could help us track his movements. Did you want anything else?'

'Yes. We've had an injunction about our Nieto story. She's somehow got wind of it.'

'Well, it wasn't from me.'

'I didn't think it was. Just telling you.'

'Okay, thanks, but I've got a busy morning.'

With a distinct impression of being fobbed off, she ended the call. She'd spent the weekend thinking about Grainger and who would have killed him. It had to be whoever he was investigating. She'd tried getting hold of some of his contacts, but they'd either not picked up or given her the cold shoulder.

He'd given her a few local contact numbers, and she rang them now. The first few went to voicemail or rang out, but she finally got hold of someone. 'Hello, Mel?'

'Who's that?'

'Antonia. I'm a friend of Rick Grainger.'

He didn't speak for a long moment, then said, 'I heard about Rick. Unpleasant business.'

'He gave me your number before he disappeared, and I thought you could help me find out who's behind what happened.'

'I thought he died in a road accident.'

Antonia didn't want to scare Mel off but needed him to realise why she needed to speak to him. 'It was, but I don't think Rick was there by choice.'

Another long silence preceded his reply. 'I understand. Rick said you're okay, so that's good enough for me. Do you know the fancy new restaurant opposite HMS Belfast?'

'I can find it.'

'You can buy me lunch. See you on the terrace at one.'

'Great. How will—'

Thinking he'd lost the signal, she rang him back, but it rang out. She'd have to hope he turned up and recognised her.

Would her police escort drop her? It shouldn't take them long and she imagined they'd welcome a change of scenery. Before she left, she had time to check up on Sawyer.

'I've looked at companies with a market capitalisation of over fifty billion, but there aren't many in the UK. I've expanded it to Europe.' Sawyer turned her screen so Antonia could read it.

None of the household names listed would get involved in something so risky. And would they torture and kill anyone? Three names, one of which Antonia knew well, sat on a separate list. 'What are these?'

'They're companies which comprise agglomerations of related companies. None could manage such enormous sums alone, but together, and with the access to leveraged funds they've got, they could just do it.'

A surge of adrenaline increased her pulse. *Don't get blinkered.* 'Can you get a bit more background on each one and see if there're any links to Nieto's company, no matter how tentative?'

'Of course.' Unlike Antonia, who hated sifting data, Sawyer loved these assignments. 'Have you seen the latest on Zungharistan?'

'Go on.'

'They've recalled their ambassador and threatened to arrest ours.'

'It's escalated quickly.'

'They've accused him of spying.' Sawyer didn't hide her obvious glee at this development.

'I'll check it out.' She'd better speak to her police escort and make sure they'd give her a lift.

She found them drinking coffee in Zabo's office and, as she'd suspected, they couldn't wait to get out. On the journey, she checked the story Sawyer was following. A dispute with a small country far away wasn't likely to become critical and the connection to JN Partners could only be a coincidence. Her mind strayed to Sawyer's second list. She hadn't realised GRM had grown so fast. She knew Reed-Mayhew had taken over a large prison provider in both the US and Russia, but he must have expanded into other areas. They needed to monitor his businesses more closely, otherwise he could become too big and powerful to take on.

They arrived at the end of Lower Thames Street and pulled over by the barrier. After persuading them she'd be safe in such a public place, she set off to find Mel. Despite her reassurances, she recognised the risks and remained on high alert. The riverside thronged with tourists and local workers enjoying the sunshine at lunchtime. She scanned the crowds, looking for familiar faces or threats, and arrived at the restaurant to find it almost full. She checked the tables but didn't see any with just one man at them. Had Mel let her down?

Maybe he was delayed. Prospective diners were queuing by an open-sided bar, and she joined them. She assumed he knew what she looked like, but she hated not knowing who she'd meet. She split her attention between the diners and people arriving. A few men paid her attention, and instead of ignoring them as usual, she checked them out.

Despite realising the futility, she'd built up a mental picture of Mel from his voice. Most of the men she looked at preened, and she dismissed them. One got up and came towards her, but a glare stopped him. She'd almost given up when a bulky man wearing jeans and a Grateful Dead T-shirt approached.

'Antonia?'

'Mel?'

'Yep, I've booked a place round the corner.' He set off without waiting.

Antonia looked at the police car, just visible through the crowds. Mel strode away from her, seeming focused on getting away. She'd better hurry before she lost him. Two minutes later, they arrived at a seedy-looking bar with a few tables out on the pavement. One sat on its own, positioned so those at it could observe their surroundings. Mel made his way to it, and she joined him.

'Less crowded and the food's better.'

Seeing diners getting their meals at the last place had made her hungry. 'What do you recommend?'

'The lobster thermidor is excellent, but on a day like today, I'd go for a nice crab salad with fresh granary bread.'

Antonia studied the unpromising exterior of the bar. 'You're joking?'

'I don't joke about food.'

They ordered from an ancient waiter and while they waited, Mel introduced himself.

'I'm a forensic accountant specialising in fraud and money laundering. I did twenty-five years in the Met, eleven in Financial Crimes, and branched out on my own.'

'How do you— did you know Rick?'

'Met him while I was still a plod, but we kept in touch, and he uses me now if he's working in my area.' As he spoke, Mel maintained a check on their surroundings.

'I'm happy to pay you for any help—'

'Wouldn't hear of it. He was a mate, and I'll do what I can to help you.'

'Were you working with him on his last story?'

'He ran a few things by me. Once I saw who might be involved, I warned him to take care. But he obviously wasn't careful enough.'

'You know what happened, then?'

'When I got your call, I made some enquiries. Still got mates in the job. Nasty business, poor lad.'

'Who were you worried—'

Their food arrived, and he waited until the waiter had left. 'Shall we eat?'

Despite her impatience, Antonia nodded. Mel concentrated on his food, except to carry out his regular scan of their surroundings. He finished and patted his ample stomach.

'What do you reckon?'

'Excellent. I'll come here again. Can you tell me who you were worried about?'

'Someone Rick said you knew well—'

'Reed-Mayhew?'

'Yup.'

'How's he involved in Rick's investigation?' Her mind raced.

'He didn't say. Rick gave little away. But he asked me about the woman his missus works for. She's a piece of work. She's a good friend of Reed-Mayhew. They must have met at cold-blooded-bastard school.'

'There's no link between their companies.'

'You've just not found it.' He winked at her. 'He's got a lot of money in this place that's in the news—'

'Zungharistan?'

He nodded. 'Not in his own name, but he's got into lithium, cobalt and nickel mining in a big way. Enormous demand for batteries, so makes sense, but he could come unstuck if things go pear-shaped and they throw all the Brits out.'

Antonia's thoughts swirled. Reed-Mayhew was more than capable of getting Grainger tortured to death. But his links to Nieto brought everything into focus. If Grainger had let slip he was investigating Reed-Mayhew at the dinner, Nieto could have passed the message on.

◆ ◆ ◆

As Gunnerson left his office, Chapman let out breath. He hadn't liked cutting Antonia off, but having Gunnerson walk in had left him with little choice. She wasn't in Harding's pocket, but she'd clashed with Chapman before about his closeness to Antonia and her publication.

Sanchez came in with her tablet. 'They've got the autopsy and forensics from the van.' She sat in his visitor's chair as he opened the email they'd both received.

It had arrived half an hour earlier, so Sanchez would have read and digested it. He sat back. 'Give me an executive summary.'

'I'll start with the two in the front. They're who we first thought they were from the documents on their person. Low-level thugs who'd disappeared off our radar two years ago. Not sure what they've been up to, but it doesn't look like they're reformed characters.'

'Can we find out where they've been, speak to known contacts and relatives?'

'Louisa and Greville are both on it now.'

'You don't need me, do you?'

'Of course we do, boss.' She shook her head.

'Okay, I get the message. Cause of death?'

'Catastrophic injuries consistent with being in the front of a van hit by a lorry at speed.'

'Is that what it says?'

'You asked for the executive summary.'

'What about the back of the van where they'd put Grainger?'

'Don't you want me to tell you about Grainger's autopsy?'

'I didn't know the guy well, but I liked him. Give me the sanitised version.'

'Okay. Severe burns inflicted on at least two separate occasions. Left arm, the bandaged one, happened one or two days before the right—'

'The night he disappeared?' Poor guy.

'Evidence of heat damage to hair all over the front of his body, like he stood too close to a fire. Scorching to his clothing with actual burn damage to his right sleeve. Clothing, cheap mass-produced, available through dozens if not hundreds of outlets. We're trying to narrow it down . . .'

'Cause of death?'

'The bumper of the camper van smashed his skull, but he was unlikely to survive his burns. They also found traces of hydromorphone in his urine.'

'They gave him painkillers?'

'Looks like it.' Sanchez returned to the report. 'In the rear of the van they found a heavy-duty polythene bag, suitable for carrying a body, with traces of his burnt skin on the inside. They found traces of blood between the metal floor and the plywood panels on it.'

'Grainger's?'

'They belonged to two other people. One of them disappeared eight months ago. The other's not on our database.'

'Shit! They've been using the van as a hearse.'

'Looks like it. It belongs to a company based in Bermuda. No record of the actual owners. No surprises there. We're trying to find out where they garaged it. One thing which might help us is they found traces of mineral oil mixed with tiny aluminium chips in the treads.'

'Workshop? There must be hundreds of those.'

'They also found bits of sand subjected to great heat, so they think an aluminium foundry.'

'Dare I ask if we're looking for those?'

'Darren is.'

'Anything else?'

'Not at the moment. I'll help Darren.'

'Can you let me have the details of the victim you identified from the blood found in the van?' If they could find a link between them and Grainger, it could help catch the killers. He doubted the two dead thugs transporting Grainger would be the ones ultimately responsible for the killings, even if they'd done the deed. They were just tools.

The extra leads from the van gave him a boost, which soon evaporated when Harding's sidekick Koval summoned him to the chief superintendent's office.

He guessed he'd been called in because he'd visited Antonia yesterday. The patrol must have reported him. Aware of his precarious position, he determined not to wind Harding up. When he got summoned in, Koval sat behind him, clicking a pen, driving Chapman mad. To block it out, he fantasised about assigning the inspector the most tedious task he could think of. He'd have to make do with giving Harding a headache and hope he took it out on her.

'Inspector Chapman, what did I tell you last time I saw you?'

'You said a few things, boss. Do you want to give me a clue?'

Koval sucked in a breath and Harding reddened. 'In particular, people leaking to the press.'

'Yep, I remember now. What about it?' So much for not winding Harding up.

'You went to see a reporter immediately after interviewing a grieving widow. The publication has since written a detailed story about her husband's death. You leave me no choice but to take disciplinary action.'

'You're joking?' Harding didn't look like he was. 'The deceased worked as a reporter for the publication. Of course they're going to write about him. I imagine every paper has done so—'

'But none of the others quote his wife.'

'They quote *his wife*, not a police officer. She knew the reporter, so why wouldn't she speak to them?'

Harding looked disappointed. 'Why did you go there?'

'I'm investigating the death of an employee. His assignment might be relevant. I'm speaking to everyone who—'

'I want you to keep me appraised every time you interview anyone from there. Did you record your conversation?'

'I did not.'

'In future you will record all your transactions with the paper, in particular the editor, and send me a transcript.'

'Is that all?' He braced himself to rise.

'No, Inspector. I've received a complaint about your behaviour from the widow—'

'Was it from Ms Voight?'

'What? Stop interrupting me. She's too upset to complain, but your behaviour towards her was unacceptable.'

'In what way?'

'You insulted her employer as well.'

'These are just unfounded—'

'The receptionist witnessed your insults—'

'He's lying.'

Harding ignored this interruption. 'In future you will not talk to Ms Voight or Ms Nieto without my express permission. When you do, Inspector Koval will accompany you, and you must record all your conversations. Do you understand?'

Stick it up your arse. 'Yes, sir. Anything else?'

'Yes! You'll share full details of your investigation with Inspector Koval, every day.'

'Okay, we haven't much so far, but you're welcome to look at it. You might be able to help us.' Chapman smiled at Koval.

He had no intention of letting Harding, or his acolyte, keep tabs on his investigation. He didn't trust the chief super as far as he could throw even his expanded carcass.

CHAPTER 32

After lunch, Antonia returned to the office to get an update from Sawyer.

'Hello, Nadimah, what are you doing here?' Antonia did a double take of the leather jacket on the back of her chair, almost identical to one of hers.

'I'm helping Jean.'

Sawyer looked up from her laptop. 'Nadimah was a bit bored, but she's been doing some basic research for me. She's collating share sales and purchases with transactions of the same value made by companies we're investigating to discover who's buying and selling them.'

'How's it going?'

'Okay.' Nadimah didn't look too enthusiastic.

'Jean, can you focus on GRM? And you mentioned JN Partners had a client in Zungharistan—'

'Have you seen they're threatening to arrest all British people there now?'

'Are they?' Now she knew Reed-Mayhew had links there. She needed to keep up with this dispute. 'Can you get me the name of JN's client?'

Antonia returned to her office with the name and logged into the Zorro research database. Like so many companies linked to Nieto, a series of shadowy proxies owned this one. But it enjoyed favoured status in a country the president and his family ran like a feudal kingdom. The possibility they didn't benefit from the company's activities ranged between zero and none.

On an impulse, she checked if any of the president's family had ever lived in the UK. A sister spent three years at Oxford, studying politics and history, but from the reports, appeared to spend her days sleeping and nights partying. She checked which university Nieto attended. Oxford, and they'd both attended the same college for two years.

Sawyer came in with her findings. 'I've found links between Nieto and Reed-Mayhew. They attended a networking event in 2005. Nadimah found it.' She placed her laptop on the desk and showed Antonia the screen.

A magazine article headlined *THE CLASS OF '05*.

Underneath it, a photo taken in the grounds of a posh country hotel. Had Antonia seen it before? Sixteen young people dressed in evening wear stood in two rows. An arrow from each led to a potted history of their business successes. Every one of them fabulously successful. Antonia studied the left side of the photo, where a youthful Reed-Mayhew, looking like a sixth-former, stood next to a tall, elegant woman who looked ten years older. Nieto, much younger than she was now, but unmistakable.

The article listed the net worth of the participants – none less than fifty million and in Reed-Mayhew's case, far more.

Antonia tapped the screen. 'When's this article from?'

'It's two years old.' Sawyer frowned. 'I've not found any business links between them, but I'll keep looking.'

'Oh, okay.' Antonia tried to keep her disappointment out of her voice. 'Tell Nadimah good work.'

Sawyer reached for the laptop.

'Hang on. Can I have a closer look at the photo?' She focused on the opposite end of the image and recognised a name. She'd interviewed the man, although she didn't recognise the hirsute youth staring at the camera with a cynical smile. He'd displayed the same photo in his study, but she'd not paid it much attention. She'd kept his contact details. 'Thanks, Jean.'

His PA put her through. 'Antonia, long time no see. How can I help you?'

'I'm doing a profile on one of your fellow class of '05 participants.'

'I didn't realise you did fluff journalism.'

'It's something we're trying out.' *Over my dead body.*

'Tell me it's not the golden boy, Mayhew – or Reed-Mayhew, as he now styles himself.' He laughed. 'I forgot, it wouldn't be. I doubt he'd talk to you without his solicitor.'

'It's not him.' Antonia hesitated, uncomfortable sharing the name of someone she *was* investigating. 'It's Jacinda Nieto.'

He gave a throaty chuckle. 'She's an . . . interesting woman. Mayhew pursued her for the entire weekend. She wanted nothing to do with him. Called him "Adrian Mole" behind his back, but I've heard they've worked together a few times. Amazing how attractive a few billion, or not so few in his case, makes you.'

'I didn't realise.'

'I haven't got all the details, but they asked me if I wanted to join them on the last one, a mining venture in Zungharistan, but I declined. It looks like I made an excellent decision, the way it's blowing up over there.'

Antonia suppressed her excitement, and with a promise to keep in touch, ended the call. She needed to speak to Grainger's wife. Chapman suspected she knew something. If she could appeal to her loyalty to her husband, maybe she'd speak to her. She must be aware of her company's links to Reed-Mayhew. And Antonia believed he'd caused Grainger's disappearance.

Although sure Voight wouldn't be at work the day after she'd learned of her husband's death, she rang her office to confirm.

Despite Chapman's chilly response last time she'd rung him, she called his mobile. 'Am I allowed to speak to you?'

'Yeah, I'm in my office on my own. How can I help you?'

'I've got a link between Nieto and Reed-Mayhew. I know he was behind Rick's disappearance—'

'We don't *know*, we strongly suspect.'

'Of course it's him. Derenski worked for him when he killed Alan. Hughes worked with Derenski, and his brother was waiting for us at Rick's lockup. What more do you need?'

'Evidence?'

'I'm sure I can persuade Voight to talk to me.'

'Not a good idea. She's in thrall to Nieto—'

'She might want someone to get her out of there.'

'Both you and Sanchez broached the subject, but she blanked you.'

'But last time I saw her, she still thought Rick was alive, and you're police—'

'So?'

'Come on, Russell. What if you were like Harding?'

Chapman huffed. 'I still think it's a bad idea.'

'I'm going round.'

'Don't, Antonia.'

'I'll have two of your guys with me. If you're so worried, meet me there.'

'Harding's warned me off.'

'I'll tell you how I get on.'

She'd be happier if he came, but maybe Voight would talk if she went on her own. At least she'd have the two constables with her. Antonia thanked Nadimah for her help, gave the number of her latest burner to Zabo and told him her destination.

The two constables discussed the situation in Zungharistan in excited tones as they drove her to Clapham. She had a quick look on her phone. The overwrought report she read mentioned the president had got involved and made a speech about his country being 'disrespected'. They then mentioned the nuclear arsenal the country inherited from the Soviet Union. Why did adults behave like kids?

A tingle of unease lodged at the back of her brain, but they arrived at their destination before she could follow it up. Telling the officers she'd be less than an hour, she rang the doorbell.

She'd almost decided she'd had a wasted trip when the door opened. 'Yes?' Voight peered out from behind the metal bar, her voice weak and nasal.

'Erika, it's Antonia. Can I come in?'

'Antonia?' She sounded drugged.

'I worked with Rick.'

'Of course, sorry.' She removed the bar and opened the door. She still wore a dressing gown and hadn't combed her hair or applied make-up.

'Are you okay to talk?'

'Of course, please come in. So kind of you to come.' Her red nose and bloodshot eyes told of how she'd spent her time.

Antonia waved to her escorts and followed Voight into the house, where they sat in a comfortable sitting room facing each other. 'Have you not had visitors?'

'A few this morning. I've been back to bed.' She gestured at her dressing gown, her hands fluttering. 'The doctor gave me some-thing. Can I get you a drink? I'm having tea.'

'A coffee.' While she waited, Antonia studied the room. Silver photo frames covered the upright piano in the corner. Grainger and various people she assumed were family members, but none of Voight. A large dog accompanied Grainger in several of them. From the next room, she heard voices and her senses sharpened.

Just one voice, then it stopped. Voight returned with two mugs on a small tray, one coffee and one tea.

'Did I hear voices?' Antonia said.

'Rick's sister called. She's coming over this evening to discuss the funeral arrangements.'

Antonia mumbled platitudes. 'Where's your dog?'

'He . . . He barks whenever we have visitors. He's Rick's dog. His brother's looking after it.'

Antonia picked up some confusing signals from Voight and struggled to read her. 'I know this will be painful, but have the police told you much about what happened to Rick?'

'What have they told you?'

'There's a rumour someone beat him up before the car hit him.'

'Who would do that?' Her eyes glistened.

'Do you know a man called Gustav Reed-Mayhew?'

Voight looked confused. 'What? He's a well-known businessman.'

'Do you know him?'

She frowned. 'I've met him once at a fundraiser. Why?'

'Do you do business with any of his companies?'

'It's none of your business.'

She needed to change tack. 'I'm going to tell you something in confidence. Reed-Mayhew arranged the murder of my boss because we got too close to one of his schemes. He had me drugged and beaten up twice. We think he's behind your husband's death.'

'No! Do you have evidence for any of this? Why haven't you taken it to the police?'

Antonia sipped more of her bitter coffee. 'I don't trust them. He's got a few in his pocket.'

'Why would he have killed Rick?'

'Because he was working on a story exposing Reed-Mayhew's crimes.'

'What crimes?'

'I don't know.'

Voight looked incredulous. 'You're his boss.'

'But he never told me. Where's his laptop?'

'I don't— He took it with him.'

'Like he took the dog and your car?'

'Why are you behaving like this?'

'How much of the mining company in Zungharistan do JN Partners own?'

Voight's eyes widened. 'Who told you?'

Antonia picked the mug up but decided not to have any more. She missed the edge of the table and the mug fell, smashing on the floor and splashing coffee on her jeans. Voight glanced behind Antonia. She turned to follow the gaze, but her body didn't obey. A figure appeared. Who? But she couldn't focus. Her heavy head pulled her sideways and her eyelids dropped.

The cost of the uniforms she'd bought for Hakim, starting his new school, and Nadimah, who seemed to grow every week, had eaten into Sabirah's savings. She'd spent most of the weekend searching job sites. And four hours knocking on doors and checking job vacancy cards this morning had left her despondent.

She should be enjoying the last two weeks of the long holiday with the children, instead of wandering around looking for work. Her work suit, smart but too heavy for the weather, stifled her. She went into a café, more to have a break than because she wanted to eat or drink anything. She ordered tea and toast and took it to a table in the corner. Her phone buzzed, an unknown number.

'Hello, Sabirah Fadil.'

'Ms Fadil, it's Tim Eve. Sorry it's taken so long to get back to you.'

'Okay, Mr Eve. How can I help you?' What did he want?

'Tim, please. I'd like to offer you the job, if you still want it.'

Is this a joke? 'What are you offering?'

'Erm, the job you applied for, but conditional on you achieving the required ARBs within six months.'

She held in the whoop and swallowed. 'Can we discuss this? I'm near to the office.'

'Of course, shall we say in an hour?'

'Yes, bye.' She let out a yelp and her neighbours stared at her. 'They have offered me a job.'

The three women at the nearest table all applauded and congratulated her. Sabirah thanked them and finished her tea. Should she ring the children? And Mrs Curtis and Antonia. No, she'd wait and then tell them when she'd received the job offer in writing.

She arrived early and introduced herself to the receptionist, remembering to tell her why she'd come. The woman smiled, seeming to have forgotten the misunderstanding of last time.

Eve came straight out.

'Mrs Fadil, please come through.'

Sabirah sat facing him, still not convinced of what he was offering. 'Are you saying you will pay me the full salary offered in the advertisement?'

'Yes, we recognise what you can offer. We realise you can't work unsupervised until you have achieved the standards required in the ARB, but provided you pass the Prescribed Examinations within six months, we'll be happy.' He looked nervous. 'Are you going to take the job?'

Sabirah wanted to yell with joy but made do with a big grin. 'Yes, thank you.'

'I thought you could start in two weeks if that's okay?'

'Yes, thank you.' *Stop saying thank you like an idiot.* She could take the children away, safe in the knowledge she would come back to a good job.

She completed the formalities and, an hour later, left with a written offer of a job in her handbag. The brief journey home took too long. She couldn't wait to see her children's faces when she told them. As she entered Vincent Terrace, the sight of the two houses in harmony gave her a lift. She let herself into the house and rushed upstairs to their apartment.

'Nadimah, Hakim, I'm home.'

A fed-up-looking Hakim came out of the kitchen. 'Nadimah's next door helping Jean.'

'What's wrong?'

'I'm bored.'

'Okay, let's go somewhere nice for our dinner and then tomorrow we can visit the zoo.'

He lit up. 'Can we?'

'I'm celebrating my new job.' She told him and they danced a jig. 'Let's find your sister.'

Nadimah was in Jean's office on a spare laptop. She let out a yell and hugged her mother. Her daughter seemed to have grown, even since yesterday. Jean joined in the congratulations, and thanking her, Sabirah led her children out of the office.

Her phone rang. Mrs Curtis. 'Sabirah, I want you to take the children and stay with my cousin in the west of Scotland—'

'Sorry, I can't. The children have school and I've just started a new—'

'You don't understand. If there's a nuclear strike, London will probably be hit first. At least you'll be safe up there.'

Sabirah's mind went blank. Zungharistan. She hadn't really paid attention to what was happening there. Had chosen not to, probably. Now her thoughts churned with the idea they might have escaped one war, only to be caught up in another unthinkably horrible one. 'Will you be coming?'

'No. My place is here, I've had my life.'

Sabirah didn't know what to say. Her children had stopped and looked at her expectantly. Had they heard Mrs Curtis? 'We're just coming home, can I speak to you then?' She ended the call. The sense of panic that had seized everyone back home when they feared nuclear weapons had arrived on their doorstep returned, fresh and real.

'Everything okay, Mamma?' Hakim studied her with his big brown eyes.

'Of course.' She forced a smile and ruffled his hair. 'Come on, let's go.'

'Can I change if we're going out?' Nadimah said.

'You'll take ages,' Hakim complained.

'Two minutes. Please, Mamma.'

'Go on.'

She ran on ahead. By the time Sabirah left the offices, Nadimah was already on the pavement, halfway to their home. She looked so grown-up. A van pulled out of a parking space opposite, engine roaring. It swerved towards Nadimah.

Sabirah screamed a warning and ran down the steps. The van stopped across the pavement in front of her daughter. The side door flew open and two men wearing black, with matching ski masks, jumped out. They grabbed Nadimah and threw her into the van.

'NO!' Sabirah ran and reached the open door.

A pair of pitiless eyes stared out of two eyeholes. Behind them, Nadimah struggled with the other man. A fist shot out and caught Sabirah flush in the face. She fell and then the door slammed as the van disappeared down the road.

CHAPTER 33

When the news of Nadimah's kidnapping reached Chapman, he demanded he investigate the crime. He argued it had to be linked to Grainger's death and persuaded Gunnerson, who told him she'd take care of Harding.

He arrived at Vincent Terrace with Sanchez. Police cars filled the street, and he had to park round the corner. With a sense of déjà vu, he accompanied Sanchez to the front door. The two of them had first come here looking for Antonia, a murder suspect, eighteen months ago.

A uniformed constable answered the door.

'Chapman.' He showed his ID. 'And DS Sanchez. We're here to interview the witnesses.'

'Someone's here already.'

'I'm taking over.'

A grizzled figure Chapman recognised came to the top of the stairs looking irritated. 'What you doing here, Chapman?'

'I'm taking over. It's linked to my murder investigation.'

'Nobody's told me.'

'Do you want to contact Control?'

'Yeah, I bloody well do.' He made the call, making his displeasure clear when told to hand over to Chapman.

'What have you done so far?' Chapman asked.

'Just arrived, so I'll leave it with you.' He summoned his team and stomped out of the house.

'Friend of yours, boss?'

'We clashed when I was a DCI and he still a DI. Still hasn't forgiven me. Let's make a start.'

He climbed the stairs and found Sabirah and Hakim in their comfortable living room. Sabirah had made it much cosier since she'd inherited it from Antonia, who'd left it as she'd found it. Sabirah sat at one end of the sofa and her son stood beside her, his arm across her shoulders and looking far older than eleven.

'Mr Chapman, what's happening?' She dabbed at her swollen nose with a tissue.

'Hello, Sabirah, Hakim. We're taking over. Can you tell me what you saw?'

'I told the other man.'

'I'm sorry, you're going to have to go through it again.'

He and Sanchez took the two chairs opposite, and Sanchez placed a recording device on the coffee table. 'Okay if we record you, Mrs Fadil?'

'Sabirah, please. Of course.'

Chapman led her through an account of what had happened, asking a few questions to clarify points whenever she faltered. 'Has someone looked at your nose?'

'It's fine. I don't think it's broken.' She dabbed at it with the tissue.

'If you're sure. Had you noticed the van earlier?'

Hakim raised a hand. 'I did.'

'When did you first see it, Hakim?'

'Before Mamma came home, maybe half three.'

'Was the patrol car outside?' He needed to warn Antonia about this.

'No, they left earlier.'

If Antonia hadn't gone to see Voight, there was no way the kidnappers would have gone ahead with two officers outside. 'What can you tell me about the van?'

'It was a sprinter, not one of the big ones. It had the logo of a courier company on the side, but the driver drove round the block twice until he found a parking space, instead of just stopping in the road.'

'Did you see the driver?'

'He stayed in the cab on the phone, but you couldn't see inside properly, just that he was holding the phone to his ear.'

They must be using a screening device. 'But definitely a man?'

'Yeah, big, with a beard.'

'Okay, did you get the number?'

'When they grabbed Nadimah, I memorised it. I told the other policeman.' He recited the registration number.

'Well done. And, Sabirah, you sure you didn't get a good look at the man who hit you?'

'Just his eyes. He wore a' – she groped for a word – 'mask.'

'And you can't think of anyone who might have done this?'

Sabirah's brow furrowed. 'She had trouble at the school. They threw some boys out.'

This didn't sound like a school dispute, but you never knew with some parents. 'Do you have any names?'

'Sorry. The school will know.'

Sanchez made a note of the school.

'Okay, Sabirah,' Chapman said, 'we're going to monitor your phones in case they get in touch, and we'll have some officers stay with you. Okay?'

She nodded. 'Do you think they want ransom? I have little.'

'I think it's a case of mistaken identity and they'll release her when they realise.' He hoped he was right, not wanting to contemplate any other possibility. After instructing Sanchez to make the arrangements, he joined the rest of the team outside. He took them next door, where Eleanor and the staff waited for an update.

'Inspector, I'm glad you're here. The other officer told us nothing, just to wait here.'

'Sorry, Eleanor. Right, everyone, we need to move fast. I want everyone to give a statement to my colleagues here. Even if you think you saw nothing, you may have, and it could help us find Nadimah. Can we use the other offices, Eleanor?'

'Please do.'

'Do you want to see the footage from our camera, Inspector?' Jean asked.

'Can we also have a copy?'

'I'll email it to you. Tomasz has it on his screen.'

Antonia's new assistant reminded him of her old boss, Alan. He rotated his screen so Chapman could see it. It showed the street outside, vehicles on both sides of the road with the trees separating it from the canal providing a green backdrop. It could have been a still until a car drove past. Then a woman with a pram and a dog appeared on the opposite pavement.

'Is this the van?' Chapman pointed at the vehicle with the distinctive logo on the door.

'Yes, Inspector.'

'Can you focus in on the driver?'

The image zoomed in, but sunlight glinted off the window, making it impossible to see into the cab. The image returned to the street scene. Then Nadimah appeared out of the door, almost skipping down the path to the pavement. The van pulled out and crossed the street, and the kidnapping occurred almost exactly as Sabirah and Hakim had described.

Sawyer returned from her office. 'I've emailed the footage to you from when the van arrived.'

'Great. Did anyone recognise the woman with the pram and the dog?'

'I think she lives on the next street.' The young assistant reddened at the attention. 'She sometimes comes out of a house with her dog in the morning. It's on my way here.'

'Do you know the address?'

'Erm, I can show you the house.'

'Okay . . . Tomasz, isn't it? I'll ask one of my constables to take you round once they've finished. Do you know if Antonia took her phone?'

'She took a burner.' He recited a number, which Chapman punched into his phone.

Unavailable. *Shit, what a surprise.* He contacted Control to get the contact details for her escorts.

'There's an issue, Inspector.'

'What issue?'

'They've lost contact with her.'

'Right, I'm on my way.' He hoped it was just a mix-up but had a bad feeling.

Louisa Walker cut through the rush-hour traffic like wire through cheddar, leaving honking and doubtless cursing motorists in her wake. Chapman held on tight and closed his eyes for most of the journey. A second patrol car, blue light flashing, sat behind the one that had been keeping a watch on Antonia.

Walker braked and Chapman released his seatbelt, getting out as the car stopped. A constable and a sergeant watched him from the porch of Grainger and Voight's house.

'Chapman.' He flashed his ID. 'Which one was watching her?'

The constable raised a hand. 'Me, boss.'

'What happened?'

'She went in an hour and a half ago. We—'

'On her own?'

'Yes, boss. She didn't want the woman to know we were here—'

'What woman?'

'The one who lives here.' He described Voight. 'She came to the door and Antonia waved, then went in.'

'Then what?'

'She said give her an hour, so we gave her an extra five minutes, then I tried the doorbell. No answer. I looked in the windows and saw nothing, so we checked the back. There's a gate, but we climbed over and checked the back door. There's a conservatory and a couple of French windows, so you can look into most of the house. Then we rang it in.'

'Right, break in.'

'You sure, boss?' He pointed at the stained-glass panel in the door.

'What's round the back?'

'One of the French windows looks ropey.'

'Tell your mate to break in through there.' Chapman pointed at the constable's radio.

A minute later the alarm wailed and by the time they found the spare key for the front door and let him in, Chapman wanted to rip it off the wall.

'Get the alarm silenced and the rest of you, search.'

He took upstairs, checking the bedroom Sanchez had searched yesterday. He found the walk-in closet. Three suitcases and most of Voight's clothes had gone. 'Shit.'

The alarm quietened, and he returned downstairs and gathered his forces. In the kitchen, three uniformed constables, the sergeant and Walker. 'Anything?'

'I found two mugs in there, boss.' Walker pointed to a room behind her. 'I've bagged them.'

Nobody else offered a contribution.

He addressed the sergeant and her constable. 'I want you to start a house-to-house in the street, find out if anyone saw anything at all today. Her clothes have gone, and I assume she didn't carry them out the back while you two' – he indicated her guards – 'watched the front door. You can go with Louisa and check if anyone round the back saw anything. Make sure to ask them if they saw her loading cases in her car during the last twenty-four hours.'

Once they'd dispersed, he rang Control, reported Antonia missing, presumed snatched, and ordered reinforcements plus a forensics team. He also reported Voight as a potential fugitive. Thinking about Nieto, he added her name, knowing it would raise flags with Harding if nobody else.

He cursed himself. He should have met Antonia here, Harding or not. His phone buzzed. Sanchez.

'Russell, what's happened?'

'Antonia's disappeared. There's nobody here, and half Voight's clothes have gone.'

'Bugger. Okay, here we've got statements from everyone. We've tracked the woman with the dog. She thinks the man in the van had a beard but isn't sure. He had a phone up to his face and turned away from her. A team arrived to monitor Sabirah's phones. I've spoken to the head of Nadimah's school and got the boys' details. I'll go—'

'Leave them. I'm pretty sure we can link this to what happened to Grainger. Did you notice what Nadimah was wearing? She looked like a mini Antonia.'

'Not so mini, she's one sixty-seven.'

Five foot six in old money. 'I suspect they thought they'd got Antonia.'

'They look nothing like each other.'

'Not to us, but if you've got a description, mixed race or Syrian, and they've both got shortish hair.'

'Okay, what do you want me to do?'

'Check the traffic cameras there and the ones round here. They needed a vehicle to get Voight and Antonia out. Can you also have a look at the camera footage from the front door of *The Investigator*? See if we can get anything from the shot of them dragging Nadimah into the van. We also need to follow up the aluminium castings. If they've taken them to the same place they took Grainger . . .'

The memory of seeing Grainger in a body bag, arms a charred mess, sickened Chapman.

◆ ◆ ◆

The headache and nausea told Antonia what had happened. How had she let Voight drug her? She lay on her side on a hard floor. Opening her eyes made no difference. Her right arm moved without restriction, but her left lay under her. She rolled on to her back, freeing the arm. It tingled as the circulation returned. A metallic, chemical stink faded before she identified it.

She checked her legs, also unfettered, but no shoes. They must have decided the drugs would keep her under control. She rolled over, and pushing herself off the floor, got to her knees. Another smell. Rats' droppings? But faint. She shuddered. As her sight grew accustomed to the darkness, she discerned shadows. A thin, pale line at floor level suggested a door. She rose, keen to get up from rat-height.

Her legs wobbled and bile rose in her throat. She reached out until her hand touched a cold, hard surface. Metal? Had they put her in a van? But it felt different. The rough floor under her bare feet felt like concrete. She bent to confirm it, and moved too fast, having to use her hands for support again as she swayed. Her palm vibrated, and a sound reached her through the walls. Like a giant's footsteps. She shuffled to the wall and placed her ear against it.

BOOM!

Then another. Where was she?

Taking care not to kick anything, she kept one hand on the wall and completed a circuit of her prison. Less than four paces each side, and empty. The corrugated walls didn't have any gaps she could find, even where the faint line suggested a door.

The banging continued, and she stretched, her movements getting more vigorous as she worked at expelling the drug from her system. She stopped, breathing elevated, but not straining, her muscles warm and ready for action. The banging had stopped. She'd not noticed it end. Where had they brought her? She pressed an ear against the metal side. A low rumble, like a train in the distance, made the wall vibrate, faint, but detectable. Then voices, coming nearer.

She tensed, listening as they got louder. The strip under the door grew brighter, and now became a rectangular outline around the entire door, like a halo. She waited as the voices approached. She stood to the left of the door, tense, but willing her muscles to relax. Whoever opened it would get a big surprise. A key turned. A chain scraped across metal. Then a squeak as someone drew a rusty bolt.

The door swung outwards, flooding her eyes with light. Two blurred outlines appeared in the opening. Antonia launched herself at the nearest one, catching him with her bony forehead. Warm blood spattered her top, and the man cried out. Another stood to her left. She threw a punch, catching him a glancing blow. He spun away, quick to react, but her other fist smashed into his cheek, and he reeled.

The first one, still clutching his nose, reached inside his jacket. A front kick smashed his elbow into his ribs, and he dropped whatever he'd reached for with a clatter. The other one had moved out of range. He held a knife in front of him, the tip swaying. Antonia, still unused to the bright light, concentrated on his feet.

His left foot slid forward. Antonia moved to her right, away from his blade, but kept her weight on her left leg. Instead of resetting, he overreached, his arm straight as he stretched to stab her. She swayed back, and as the blade slashed the air in front of her face, her left forearm smashed into his elbow. He screamed and dropped the blade.

A kick to the side of his unprotected knee hit with a crunch, and he fell. The other one retrieved his blade and retreated several metres away, glancing at the huge pair of double doors behind him. The large space they stood in had dirty whitewashed walls and a high roof. An oily metallic odour infused the atmosphere. Railway sleepers between metal uprights stuck out from the perimeter walls to subdivide the space.

Most of the compartments contained dregs of metal and swarf, but two contained chunks of crushed aluminium. A small digger, its dirty bucket glistening with oil, sat in a corner. What was this place? She checked the man she'd disabled. He lay watching her, hugging his injured arm, and his eyes full of hatred. Her attention returned to the other one. He'd edged towards the door. She moved away from him, relaxing her stance.

He ran, and she caught him one pace from the door. She rammed her shoulder into his ribs, slamming him into the wall beside it. He fell senseless, leaving a smear of blood on the whitewashed breeze block. Voices came from outside. She looked at the first man. He prepared to shout. She ran at him, launching herself from two metres away and snapping his head back with a flying side-kick. She recovered her balance and ran to the big doors.

At the side of the doorway, she waited, straining to hear. The voices grew faint, then a door closed, and she couldn't hear them. She waited five minutes, senses on high alert, and then pulled the nearest leaf of the door open. It led her into a wide corridor, going left and right. Which way had the voices gone? She guessed and ran left.

After twenty paces, the corridor turned ninety degrees, then ended with a roller-shutter. Next to it a door, and she checked it. It opened into a small sluice room with shelves full of cleaning products on one wall and a sink opposite. She backed out and examined the roller-shutter, but padlocks held the chains in place.

A man's laughter made her freeze, and she looked for an escape. The storeroom. She closed the door and waited in the darkness. The stench of bleach and cleaning fluid caught in the back of her throat and made her eyes smart. Voices rumbled from outside. Her pulse hammered. Chains rattled as the shutter lifted. The voices faded, then stopped. As the adrenaline drained from her system, her foot started hurting. She waited, counting to three hundred before opening the door a crack.

Silence. She opened it and stepped out. Three men stood in a line across the corridor. Two carried shotguns and flanked the third, who held an automatic. He gave a nasty smile and pointed at a trail of bloody footprints leading to her. The other two laughed. A cruel sound.

'I believe you're looking for me, Ms Conti.' His nicotine-hoarsened voice had fuelled many of her nightmares. She'd found Danil Derenski, the man responsible for Alan's murder.

CHAPTER 34

The early morning news accompanied Chapman on his drive into work. As last night, it focused on the news from Zungharistan.

> *Following the explicit nuclear threat to the UK, the Prime Minister is chairing an emergency meeting of NATO at Chequers. The US President cannot attend because of a prior engagement, but the Vice President will fly in to RAF Brize Norton forty miles away.*

Chapman snapped off the volume. The imminent threat of nuclear destruction wasn't conducive to the effective working of his brain. The fact he'd had four hours' sleep already played havoc with it. He was old enough to remember the tail end of the Cold War and seeing leaflets advising people to hide in their cellars. Not much use for people living in a flat like him. He wasn't sure whether he wanted to survive a nuclear winter. He arrived at work in good time – travelling before six had its benefits – and made his way to the deserted office before making himself a coffee.

He spent the next hour reading more of the statements his team had taken from people around both kidnap sites. If they'd mistaken Nadimah for Antonia, they must realise their mistake by now. And what would they do with the poor girl? He didn't know what to make of the fact they'd not released her, not wanting to dwell on any of the options. The call from Abby when she'd seen the news had been hard enough.

He sipped his coffee and studied the statements. The vague and contradictory descriptions of the car seen parked at the back of Grainger's house, given by five different people, meant they needed to check almost every car they filmed. The cameras didn't cover the back gate, so they couldn't see anyone leaving.

Sanchez had spent three hours helping the camera operators track the vehicles and hadn't finished. Add to that the plethora of footage from all the doorbell and household cameras in the vicinity meant they would wade through it for days.

At seven Sanchez came in. 'Do you want another?' She gestured to his mug.

'Yeah, cheers.'

She returned with two coffees three minutes later. 'Are you ready for a debrief? I'm waiting for a couple of updates.'

'Give me half an hour. I've almost finished the statements.'

She returned forty minutes later with another coffee and her tablet. He almost refused the drink but decided today his caffeine levels could go sky high.

'Okay, what do you have?'

'We used the new overnight service to get the cups we recovered analysed.'

'How much did we have to pay?'

'Now someone's snatched a young girl off our streets, they've removed the budget constraints.'

'Can we both put in for a huge pay rise?'

'No chance.' Her smile faded. 'They found traces of sodium thiopental in the coffee cup.'

'That doesn't sound good.'

'No. It induces rapid unconsciousness but soon wears off. But once she's unconscious, they could have given her anything to keep her out for as long as they wanted.'

The thought of Antonia, helpless and unconscious at the mercy of someone like Nieto, set his teeth grinding. 'Any joy finding Nieto or Voight?'

'Neither has surfaced anywhere, but it's easy for someone with Nieto's wealth to disappear.'

'I've put in a request for an unexplained wealth order for both women—'

'But we know how Nieto made her money. They'll just get it thrown out, on appeal if not initially.'

'But it's the easiest way to have her assets temporarily suspended. Gives us time to find something more substantial to sink her.'

'You've not gone through Harding?'

'Of course not. I've sent it to his replacement at Financial Crimes. I've heard she's fuming because of all the crap he left behind when he came here.'

'Crafty.'

'I've been called worse. Any update on the vehicles from yesterday?'

'The van's genuine. But it should have been in a bodywork garage awaiting collection. Nobody missed it until four this morning when the courier went to collect it.'

'Bloody hell, I thought *I* got up early.'

'The traffic camera system lost it yesterday but found it again this morning when a couple of fifteen-year-olds wrapped it round a lamppost. They claim they found it on the local school playing field.'

'Where?'

'Brentwood.'

Chapman's interest sharpened. 'We found Grainger's body near there.'

Sanchez made a note on her pad. 'Okay, we know they screened the van used to snatch Nadimah, but they obviously planned to use it to snatch Antonia, so had prepared. If we assume they'd not planned to seize her from Grainger's place, they might have nothing protecting the cars they used. Seventeen vehicles which could fit what we're looking for left the road at the back of the house in the timeframe we're investigating. None of them were screened, but five are no longer detectable on the system—'

'Five?'

'If they're in a garage overnight we won't detect them. Some people put the car in theirs.'

'Of course, I'm thinking crime.' He drank some coffee. His hands shook even before he swallowed it.

'I'll get them to do a visual check in the area in case they changed plates. Long shot, but we can't afford to ignore anything.'

'Definitely.'

'What about the schoolboys?'

'In the van?'

'The ones Nadimah had trouble with.'

Chapman took a deep breath. 'Just check neither of the lads who crashed the van were involved. But the witness said the driver had a beard.'

'*Possibly* had a beard. But I agree, it's not these lads.'

'And what's happening with the aluminium smelting—'

'Casting. Smelting would make our job easier. Grev got the list. Do you want me to narrow it down to the Brentwood area?'

'Give it a twenty-five-mile radius.'

'Okay. Anything else?'

'Not unless you've got anything. I'm going to take Darren to JN Partners, intimidate a few bankers.'

'Okay, I'll get in touch if anything comes up.'

Chapman collected Darren Baxter and set off. Unlike the last time he'd taken Baxter on a visit, he didn't think he'd need his colleague's muscle, just his unsmiling, intimidating expression. They arrived at JN Partners. The same young man sat behind the reception desk.

'Officers, Jacinda isn't here. How may I help you?'

'When did you last hear from her?'

'She rang this morning. What's this about?'

'Where did she call from?'

'She didn't say.' The receptionist's gaze kept straying to Baxter, who stood to Chapman's left, so the two of them weren't 'in frame' together.

'Can you check?'

'Sure.' He returned his attention to the screen.

Chapman signalled to Baxter to move. Baxter, who stood near the front corner of the desk, rushed to the rear.

The receptionist leapt to his feet. 'What you doing?'

Chapman moved to the other side and took a snap of the screen, which showed a list of all the calls received this morning.

'That's confidential.' He killed the screen and sat, his attention oscillating between the two officers.

'What time did she ring?'

'I don't have to tell you.' He swallowed.

'What's going on here?' a deep, gravelly voice demanded.

Chapman faced the speaker: a short, wide man in an expensive suit, wearing a gaudy painted silk tie. 'We're looking for Ms Nieto. She's wanted in connection with a serious crime.'

'She's not here. What's your name?'

'Chapman, and yours?'

'Why do you need my name?'

'For when I'm giving evidence in the trial.'

'What trial?' Doubt appeared in his confident demeanour for the first time.

Both officers stared back, dead-eyed, and he gave his name.

'Make sure neither of you, or anyone else who works here, leaves the country without telling me.' Chapman threw a card on the table.

In the lift down, he checked the picture he'd taken. Only two of the calls came from mobiles. One had a name alongside the number, and the other 'Unknown'. They must track Nieto before she got rid of her phone. He texted the number to Sanchez. Urgent trace this.

❖ ❖ ❖

After a restless sleep, Antonia got up, and in pitch black, explored her room. She'd seen it fleetingly when they'd bundled her in and noticed a hospital bed with restraints, but nothing else. A circuit of the room confirmed her impression. She swept the wall with her hand, looking for a switch. Unable to find one, she returned to the bed and lay there, trying not to think of what had happened to Grainger.

As she dozed, the door to the room banged open and strip lights flickered on. Antonia sat up on the bed. The restraints she feared they'd use on her hung down the sides. Derenski and his armed companions crowded in the doorway.

'Get up and stand facing the wall.'

'I need the toilet.'

'I believe your friend didn't bother. He just wet himself.'

The others laughed.

Was this where they'd kept Grainger? She noticed the stains on the bedding, and suppressing an uneasy shudder, Antonia waited.

Derenski took a step back. 'All right, put those shoes on first.'

A pair of cheap trainers lay under the bed, and she slipped them on, wincing as her cuts rubbed against the fabric.

'Okay, come out. There's a toilet here.'

The three men retreated and stood in a semi-circle in the corridor, well out of range. Derenski gestured with his automatic to a door three paces away. She went in and closed it behind her. A light came on, illuminating a small wet room with a toilet and sink, but no window. She used the facilities, cleaned her teeth as best she could and rinsed her face in cold water, drying herself with rough paper towels. She felt better but needed a coffee.

Outside, the three men waited, Derenski holding a pair of metal handcuffs. 'Face the wall, hands behind your back.'

Once they put those on her, she'd be helpless. The two gunmen studied her like a cat would a fallen hatchling.

'The guy whose leg you smashed is their brother,' Derenski explained.

She got the message and turned, the skin on her neck prickling. Derenski tightened the cuffs and pushed her down the corridor. One brother led the way, and her other captors followed her. The air grew hot and dry. They paused at a door. Her mind raced as she imagined what lay behind it.

The lead man opened the door and hot air, like a dragon's breath, belched out. She followed him into a large room. On her left, a metal chair of unusual design sat on two rails leading to a steel door at the far end of the room. Heat haze made it shimmer. She'd seen similar chairs before. It resembled one she'd found Chapman tied to. And she knew its purpose.

'Ms Conti, I hope you slept well.' Nieto stood on the other side of the door.

'Why am I here?'

'We need to find out what you know.'

'What, everything?'

'You won't be so smart in a few minutes.'

Were Chapman's team looking for this place? They'd also be searching for her. But Nieto must be confident they wouldn't find her. Antonia needed to keep her talking.

'Why have you done this? You've already prevented me publishing my story.'

'I'm asking the questions.'

'Go on then, ask one.'

'Tell me about the article we blocked. What was it about?'

'Your insider dealing.'

'And?'

'The possibility you had your FD killed four years ago.'

'Nothing else?'

'No.' Sweat trickled down Antonia's back.

'Nobody cares about insider dealing.'

'Or murder?'

'You haven't got evidence. Anyway, that's not what Rick was working on.'

'No, he never told me what he was working on. He should have done last Monday, the day he disappeared. The day you brought him here.'

'It wasn't me, dearie.' Nieto gave a smile.

'Reed-Mayhew.'

'So, you know.'

'Mr Derenski here works for him, and I put two and two together.'

'I don't believe you.'

Antonia shrugged. 'What are you working on with Reed-Mayhew?'

'No questions. I'm not a Bond villain who's going to tell you everything.' She smiled. 'What I will tell you is Reed-Mayhew helped you achieve your greatest triumph.'

'What do you mean?'

'The information which enabled you to bring down the government. Who do you think brought it to you?'

'One of Rick's contacts.'

She chuckled. 'The lady with the pram works for me. She got the papers from one of his companies.'

Antonia tried to digest the information. 'Why would he help me?'

'He wanted Trident two stopped. How do you feel, knowing he used you, and you're helping him greatly increase his wealth and power?'

Antonia wasn't sure she believed her. 'How am I helping him?'

'You're never going to know. Now, no more questions.'

'What put you on to Rick? The dinner party?'

'I told you—' Nieto paused. 'Okay, I'll tell you this much. Rick could be very indiscreet after a drink and told me he knew I was working with Mr Reed-Mayhew.'

'"Mr" now. Is it no longer "Adrian Mole"?'

'My, you have been busy. Let's find out what else you know.'

'I've told you—'

'I don't believe you.' She signalled to Derenski, and he handed the automatic to a brother, grabbed Antonia's arm and pulled her towards the chair.

She resisted, but the nearest brother raised the shotgun and pointed at her midriff.

'A very painful death, Ms Conti.' Nieto looked like she'd enjoy witnessing it.

'How will I answer your questions if I'm dead?'

'I believe being shot in the knee also hurts like hell.'

'And bleeding out from the femoral artery is also quicker.'

Nieto addressed the gunman. 'Use the automatic.'

He retrieved it from his brother and pointed it at her knee. Now she'd studied them, she recognised them as the two who'd accompanied Derenski when one of them shot Alan. She wasn't sure which one but would try to remember.

'Let's see how tough you are when you're bleeding,' he said.

Sweat drenched Antonia's back, and it wasn't just the heat. 'I know what you did to Rick, and you won't let me go.' She spoke to Derenski. 'I'm going to fight you every inch of the way. Shoot me in both legs and break my arms, but you won't get me in there in one piece.'

The standoff lasted long seconds until Nieto said, 'Fetch her.'

Derenski released Antonia and, pushing her away, collected his automatic. He limped to the door, favouring the knee she'd smashed for him. The brothers kept Antonia covered. Who was he fetching? She didn't have to wait long.

'Antonia.' A terrified Nadimah stood in the open doorway, Derenski holding a gun to her head.

◆ ◆ ◆

'Nieto's switched her phone off?' Chapman couldn't hide his disappointment.

'Afraid so, boss. She rang from—' A loud blast from a taxi he'd cut up drowned Sanchez's words.

'Sorry, where?'

'Rainham.'

'Essex?' Chapman brought up the mental map of London he carried in his head. He'd driven past Rainham on his way to finding Grainger's body. 'How far from where we found Grainger?'

'Ten miles?'

'Right, how's the search for aluminium casting works going? Do we have any in the local area?'

'We found seven in the twenty-five-mile radius you gave us. Not sure how far those are from Rainham. Can I get back to you?'

'Yeah, sure.' He ended the call and concentrated on the traffic.

'We should have stayed with the receptionist until they'd tracked Nieto down, boss.' Baxter looked as unhappy as Chapman felt.

'If he warned her. But then what? Wait until she stops, and our guys catch her. She won't have Antonia in the back of the car with her and our priority is finding Antonia.'

'She could be on her way out of the country.'

'Yeah, but she's going the wrong way. If she's going from Stansted or City—'

'There's a small airfield at Thurrock. Nip over to France or Holland and then—'

Chapman pressed redial and got straight through to Sanchez. 'Sorry, boss, I've not finished—'

'Can we get someone to Thurrock airfield and make sure Nieto isn't taking off from there? Close the airfield, if you must.'

'Okay.' Sanchez shouted instructions, then came back on. 'Right, I've got the list now. We've got three near there. The closest is Hangman's Wood Industrial Park, North Stifford.'

'Bloody appropriate name, if they're there. Okay, we need to narrow it down.'

Baxter raised a hand. 'Boss, why don't we ring each one asking if they do castings—'

'Why warn them?'

'I meant posing as a customer, boss. Then ask if you can pop down later. If they're cool with it, let's move them down the list.'

'Great idea, Darren. Did you hear, Alice?'

'Got it. Speak later.'

Chapman contemplated heading towards Essex, but they'd need backup, and they'd reach the station in five minutes. He hoped Antonia and Nadimah were both okay.

Back at the station, he found a small crowd huddled round Greville Sanderson's monitor in the main office. His team had grown, with reinforcements drafted in from other departments.

'What's going on, Louisa?'

'US Vice President's just made a speech saying, because we're not renewing Trident, we're on our own.'

'I meant with finding our two kidnap victims.' He turned to Sanderson. 'Grev, turn that shit off and get back to doing our job.'

'But, boss, this could end in nuclear war—'

'I don't care. We can do nothing about it. But we *can* find these two people.'

Sanchez came out of his office. 'Glad you're here. The Hangman's Wood site is looking most likely. The other two were both fine, eager even, for us to go round. This lot weren't answering their phones. We also traced a car seen behind Grainger's house yesterday to a school five miles away. It would have stayed hidden until September, except the astronomy club came in early to paint the outside of their observatory.'

'Not the local state school, then. Do we know who owns the car?'

'Someone stole it from a long-stay car park near Stansted. The owner's in Lanzarote for two weeks.'

'Good work, Alice. Have we got backup organised?'

'You happy to go?'

'Short of a flashing sign saying "We're here!", I'm happy.'

'Good. I've booked an armed response team from Essex and done the paperwork for our team to go over the border. They'll arrive in an hour.'

'It will take us one hour to get there. Let's go.'

'It depends who's driving,' Sanchez pointed out.

'Right. I'll go with Louisa. Do you want to follow in Darren's car? He's the second-fastest driver in the team.'

They arrived at the rendezvous point ten minutes before the armed response team and waited. Chapman wanted to go now, almost certain they'd got the right place, but every minute, doubts assailed him. What if they'd come to the wrong site, or they arrived too late?

The teams from Essex arrived and, following a quick briefing, they set off in convoy.

The site looked derelict. A recce, using a tiny drone camera, identified fresh tyre tracks leading to one of the big sheds at the back. None of the other buildings looked occupied. They couldn't see any surveillance cameras and planned to go in through a side door near the main roller-shutter. One team covered the rear exit, and the rest gathered at the front.

Chapman's crew held back, bulky in their flak jackets, Baxter's covering half his torso. Chapman swallowed as they waited for the breaking-in team to do their work. A hollow feeling in his stomach accompanied a sense of not being able to fill his lungs. Sanchez gave him a tight smile, her face pale but determined. Sweat trickled down his neck.

A bang, then the prescribed warning shouts. The team swarmed in through the opening. Another bang from the back and more shouting. Chapman's crew waited, each second dragging. He edged towards the opening, his crew following.

The shout of, 'ALL CLEAR!' acted like a starting pistol. He charged into the space. Along the left wall, a row of offices. The rest comprised an undivided space. Chapman walked to the nearest office, where armed figures stood around. A desk, broken chairs and rusting filing cabinets lay abandoned on the stained carpet. A musty smell and mouse droppings confirmed its status.

The uniformed inspector came up to Chapman and pointed through the doorway. 'You can see where they parked, but they've gone.'

CHAPTER 35

'She's thirteen, Derenski. Is this how you get your kicks, Mr Big-Shot, holding guns to a young girl's head?' Antonia ignored the threats from the two gunmen behind her.

A tic fluttered at the corner of Derenski's eye, and he turned crimson. He pointed at the nearest gunman. 'Take over for me.'

'With this?' He tapped the stock of his shotgun.

'Use your knife. She's a kid.'

Nieto pointed at the man's weapon. 'Give it to me.' She took the shotgun and pointed it at Antonia's legs, her expression saying she'd be glad to use it.

Derenski pushed Nadimah to the gunman, who grabbed her, seizing her neck in the crook of his elbow, and holding a knife he'd produced at the angle of her jaw.

'Stop fucking struggling.' The knife nicked her skin, and blood dripped down her neck.

Nadimah froze in shock.

Derenski came up to Antonia, pistol pointed at her head, and grabbed her face with a meaty hand, squeezing her cheeks together. 'I'll show you how much of a big-shot I am—'

'Derenski,' Nieto said. 'I'm not paying you to get your kicks. Get her in the chair. You can have her when I've finished.'

His gaze flicked to his employer, his anger diverted, but then he focused on Antonia. Giving her cheeks a painful squeeze with a hand stinking of garlic and sweat, he pushed her away.

'Bring the girl to where Conti can see her.' Nieto gestured with her shotgun.

Her captor dragged Nadimah to the side, so Antonia would be able to see her from the chair. She glanced down at Nadimah's feet. Unlike Antonia, she still wore her own shoes. Antonia made eye contact with her and gave her a smile. Despite having just arrived, Nadimah's forehead shone with sweat.

Derenski pushed Antonia towards the chair. She stumbled, her feet moving about in the too-big trainers, but he grabbed her upper arm.

He placed his lips near her ear. 'When she's finished with you, if you're still alive, I'm going to smash your knees. Nice and slow. You won't have the pleasure of the months of rehab, but you'll thank me.' He prodded her in the back. 'Get in the chair.'

'Like this?' She wiggled her cuffed hands.

'Stop.' He grabbed her wrists, then pushed the automatic into her ear. 'Don't try anything—'

'Derenski, you shoot her, I'll shoot you.'

'Fucking bitch,' he muttered into Antonia's neck. The pistol disappeared. Then two hands gripped her wrists and pulled them together.

'You're hurting me.'

He laughed, then a key clicked, freeing her hands. He spun her round to face him. The chair was a pace away. Once they secured her to it, she might as well be dead. And so might Nadimah. Derenski pushed her towards it. The back of her knees hit the edge, and she fell backwards. Derenski grabbed her shoulders and held her up before thrusting her into the seat.

He studied the chair with a frown. 'Which arm?'

Nieto pretended to ponder. 'You're right-handed, aren't you? Let's go for the right.'

He disappeared behind Antonia. She looked at Nadimah. Her captor's attention wavered, and he held the knife a few centimetres away from the girl's cheek. Antonia again made eye contact and her gaze travelled down to Nadimah's feet.

Behind Antonia, metal clanged against metal and Derenski huffed before reappearing with a bracket. He tried sliding it into the slot at the front of the right arm, but it wouldn't fit.

'Help him, will you?' Nieto snapped at the gunman.

'But . . .' He tapped his shotgun.

'I've got her covered.' Nieto moved across so she could see Antonia. This brought her nearer to the heat source and she wiped her brow.

'No offence,' Derenski said, 'but I'd rather one of my guys covered her. I've seen what she can do.'

'I'm not a helpless damsel. Just get her in the chair.'

The gunman looked at Derenski, who shrugged. He placed his shotgun on the floor behind him and, grabbing Antonia's left wrist, he leant across and studied the bracket. 'I think it's the wrong one.'

'Give me strength.' The barrel of the shotgun had drifted towards the floor and Nieto raised it. 'I thought you'd done this before.'

Derenski half-turned to her. 'The other guys normally do it.'

His automatic stuck out of the back of his belt. Antonia recognised the model she'd used just before Christmas and visualised taking the safety off. She checked that the confrontation between their bosses had distracted the two brothers. Then, making sure Nadimah paid attention, she grabbed the automatic, and shoved Derenski with all her strength. He stumbled towards Nieto.

The brother holding Nadimah cried out, and the girl screamed.

Antonia released the safety and shot the brother holding her wrist in the face. Blood splashed her, and her ears rang. A shotgun blasted and even through her damaged hearing, she heard Derenski's scream.

Nadimah used her solid shoes to stamp on her captor's shin. He released her, and she threw him. He landed on his back, his knife skittering across the floor.

Derenski fell forward. Nieto, holding the smoking shotgun, watched, horrified, and Antonia shot her. She dropped her weapon and fell.

Nadimah, who'd learned at the gym to run once you've downed your assailant, didn't, and instead stamped on his throat.

'Run, Nadimah!'

She hesitated.

'Get help!'

With a wide-eyed look, Nadimah ran.

Nieto's shotgun had fallen near the man Nadimah had felled and he grabbed at it. Antonia sprang from the metal chair and shot him in his chest. She moved across and snatched the shotgun from his hands, throwing it towards the back wall. With her ears still ringing, she didn't hear Derenski.

He leapt on her back, forcing her to her knees. She dropped the automatic. His forearm swung across her throat, and he pulled her head back. She snapped the back of her skull into his head with a crunch that made her bones shudder. His hot breath sprayed her neck as he grunted.

She swung an elbow into a not-so-solid midriff. Hot liquid seeped through her sleeve. She did it again and he let go, staggering back. She leapt away and spun toward him. Holding his side with a blood-soaked hand, he reached down with the other and scooped up the automatic, bringing it up in a smooth arc.

Antonia charged, aiming her shoulder at the injured spot. Even through her ringing ears, she heard his scream. She pumped her legs, shoving the heavier man, despite being disorientated and unsure which way she was going. The increased heat told her, but she didn't stop. Her loose-fitting trainers slid off and her bare foot slipped in Derenski's blood. She fell to the floor.

Derenski's momentum kept him moving until he slammed into the metal door, screaming. His clothes smoked, then flames flickered. Antonia scrambled back and got to her feet. Nieto, still alive, had curled herself into the foetal position.

Derenski, now a flaming crucifix, stumbled away from the metal door. Antonia couldn't look away. He staggered a few paces, then fell on Nieto, engulfing them both in flames. Nieto's screams punctuated the sound of burning. Black smoke billowed off the two bodies.

Antonia looked away. In the doorway stood the man she'd disabled yesterday when trying to escape. The brother of two men she'd just shot. And the automatic in his hand made up for any injury he might be carrying.

◆ ◆ ◆

The armed response team had gathered near the entrance and huddled round their commanding officer. Chapman's team stood near the back, waiting for him to finish his call to Gunnerson.

'Of course I thought she was here.' He walked towards the back door, keen for his team not to witness his humiliation.

He heard the shot as he stepped through the doorway. Where had it come from? A loud boom, a shotgun, followed. It came from a building fifty metres away and to his left. He ran towards it. A door stood next to the roller-shutter in the centre of the wall. Behind him, footsteps clattered.

He reached for the handle, but the door was locked. He'd landed a kick, shaking the frame, before Baxter reached him.

'Here, boss, let's do it together.' Baxter stood alongside him and draped an arm across his shoulders.

Chapman did the same, stretching to reach across his colleague's shoulders. 'Ready, after three.'

They lifted their inside feet. On two, another shot sounded, and they both slammed their heels into the door. With a splintering crunch, it flew open. As they removed the damaged timber, the first of the armed officers arrived.

'You stay back, sir.'

'Fuck off.' *Don't be stupid, Chapman.* 'Go on, make sure you bring them back.'

Six officers swarmed through the opening. Then the inspector arrived. 'Right, guys, you four go round the back and secure any openings. Let me know if you need help. The rest of you come with me.'

Another two shots, this time higher pitched. 'Those are ours. Let's go.'

Chapman watched as they followed their colleagues. His heart racing, but his brain working even faster. He'd hoped Antonia had fired the earlier shots, but why had a copper? Had one of them seen a black face with a gun and shot first? No, they knew what she looked like.

Sanchez arrived. 'You dropped your phone.'

He took it from her, and it rang straight away. 'Russell, what's going on?'

'Sorry, Yasmin, it's the right place, wrong building. Shots have been—'

'I'll get some ambulances—'

'Alice will have.'

Sanchez nodded.

'Okay, I'll get the heli and get the circus out. You say shots. Any of ours?'

'The last two.' He hoped they were.

Gunnerson sighed. 'Three-ring circus then. Keep me posted.'

A cry of, 'ALL CLEAR!' came through the open doorway. Chapman pushed past Baxter and ran inside. A corridor led away from him, and he sprinted, turning the corner too fast. Ahead, dark-clad figures milled around. Two bodies lay on the floor. His steps faltered.

The smell of smoke came from a cloud seeping out of an open door beside the bodies and gathering at ceiling level. Then the unmistakable stench of burnt human overpowered everything else. He stared at the two mounds on the floor. What had Antonia worn when she disappeared? Denim-clad legs lay tangled before him. She always wore jeans. But *not* black Doc Martens.

He got closer and saw the pale skin. Relief surged through him. He peered through the open door, where more bodies lay. Dare he look?

'We need some extinguishers.' The cry came from inside the doorway.

'Come on, Darren.'

Chapman ran back to the entrance and he and Baxter stripped the police vehicles of their extinguishers before returning. The fear something had happened to Antonia consumed him, but he forced his legs to keep going.

Smoke still poured out of the open doorway and three of the armed response team took the extinguishers to a burning mound halfway across the room. Chapman followed them in as they attacked the fire. Two bodies lay on opposite sides of the room, both dead from gunshot wounds. He inspected them, relieved to see neither could be Antonia. One, his face a ruined mass of blood and bone, unrecognisable. The other he recognised with a start. The man who'd shot Alan Turner.

Chapman studied the smouldering mound. It must be Derenski. As the extinguishers knocked the fire down, he saw the limbs. Two bodies, one a woman. 'Antonia!' He rushed forward.

'Inspector.' A constable stood next to Baxter. 'They're in there.'

'Where?'

'Through those doors.' He pointed down the corridor.

Chapman ran to the doors and barged through them. They swung shut behind him, cutting off the stench of smoke. He stopped. Doors lined the short corridor, one ajar. He poked his head in. An armed officer, helmet on the floor, murmured to someone on a hospital bed.

'Antonia?'

'Mr Chapman?'

'Nadimah, how are you?'

The constable stepped aside. Nadimah, red-eyed and exhausted, lay on a none-too-clean bed.

'Are you hurt?'

She shook her head, ready to burst into tears. He leant over and hugged her. She gripped him, sobbing, and he murmured platitudes. After a while, her sobs receded. Guilt skewered him as he fought the urge to leave her to find Antonia.

At last he straightened. 'Where's Antonia?' Flecks of blood speckled the back of Nadimah's hands.

'The lady's next door removing the blood from her eyes,' the constable said.

He rushed out and ran to the next door. Bloodstained clothes, stinking of smoke, lay in a pile. Had they been there before?

He knocked on the door. 'Antonia?'

He knocked harder. 'Antonia?'

The door opened and Antonia stepped out, wearing baggy institutional pyjamas, sleeves and legs too short.

'What the hell you wearing?'

She scowled, looked down, then grinned. 'All I could find. There's a dressing-up box in that room.' She pointed across the corridor.

'How are you?' He wanted nothing more than to scoop her up and hold her, but stood, awkward and uncertain.

'Been better. You remember last December?'

'Yeah, of course.'

'I feel as bad as I did then, times two.'

He gave in and embraced her, wanting to carry her away. She held him.

'Boss?' Sanchez watched them. 'We need to preserve the evidence.'

'Of course.' He untangled himself.

'I'll go to Nadimah.' Antonia paused. 'Derenski's in there. *Was.*' She ducked into the first room and the constable came out.

Sanchez gave an apologetic smile. 'Sorry, Russell, Harding's here.'

'What?'

'He's with a bigwig from Essex.'

'Fuck! Where is he?'

'Back where all the shit went down. Is Antonia okay? It looks horrible.'

'She said worse than December.'

'Poor her.'

'I'm more concerned with Nadimah. How much did she see?' He straightened his collar. 'Let's see what Harding wants.'

A very pale Harding came out of the main room, looking like he wanted to throw up. Behind him, a uniformed superintendent from Essex. They walked past the two bodies and stopped.

The superintendent wagged a finger at Harding. 'I'm sorry, Ian, this is mine, and I'm not letting you big-city boys ride roughshod over us.'

'My team has dealt with the case. The people in there are known criminals, responsible for kidnappings, multiple murders and various serious financial crimes. It's a very complex case and we've got the resources to deal with it. You haven't. I'll speak to the commissioner, and she'll speak to the Home Secretary, and you won't have a say.'

The superintendent chewed the side of her mouth.

Harding gestured at Chapman. 'Inspector Chapman is on top of the case.'

She glared at Chapman.

Chapman wasn't prepared to let Harding cover this up, which he would if he got it. 'Boss, if Essex are struggling for resources, I'm happy to give them all the help they need. These shootings have happened on their patch, so it's quid-pro.'

Her expression softened. 'It sounds a very sensible offer.'

'We can't spare you and your team, Inspector.'

'Why not, boss? We'll be *helping* Essex, not taking the case. We can do most of it from our office.'

'What a good idea. Thank you, Inspector, I'll be in touch.'

'Walk with me,' Harding hissed at Chapman and strode away.

Chapman followed and caught up with him.

'What the hell are you playing at?'

'It's a sensible—'

'You know I want the case.'

'Why?' Chapman didn't need an answer.

'What do you mean, why?'

'There's a woman in there, the kidnapper you mentioned, who you warned me not to investigate—'

'I didn't.'

Chapman ignored the lie. 'And how did you know Derenski's here?'

Harding hesitated. 'Who?'

'You needed to be quicker than that. Don't interfere in this, like you tried last time. It won't end well for you.'

'Are you threatening me, Inspector?'

Chapman glared back at him until Harding stalked away.

Nadimah stared out of the side window as the car carried her and Antonia through dark streets. In the front sat Chapman with Walker driving.

'Are you okay, Nadimah?' Antonia said.

'I, I don't know. I feel bad I left you—'

'Don't be silly. I told you to go.'

'Yes, but I should have come back to help.'

'And do what? Get shot yourself?'

She shrugged. 'I should have warned you when I saw the other man, not run away to hide.'

'You did the right thing. We're both alive and . . . you were fantastic.' She put her arm round the girl's shoulder.

Nadimah snuggled into Antonia and within a few minutes, her breathing slowed and deepened. Antonia closed her eyes, wishing she could sleep, too. The stench of burning flesh still clung to her nostrils and although she'd showered when the forensics team finished with her, she still felt dirty. A blast of cold air as Chapman opened the door jerked her awake.

The door to Eleanor's house opened and two figures ran towards them. Sabirah and Hakim met Nadimah at the car and held her in a sobbing, laughing, talking scrum. Antonia watched until Sabirah saw her and summoned her to join them.

'Thank you, Antonia, for bringing her back.' She turned to Chapman, standing beside the car. 'And you as well, Inspector. Thank you.'

Antonia untangled herself and watched as the family walked back to the house. 'I'll say hello to Eleanor. You coming in, Russell?'

'We'll give you a lift home, but I'll wait here. I'll just be in the way.'

'Nonsense. Come on.' She put her arm through his and followed the happy family inside.

The evidence that Eleanor had been crying, the first time Antonia could recall it happening, took her breath away, and she knelt beside the chair to hug her. Chapman stood to one side, embarrassed by the effusive thanks and the raw emotion on display.

Antonia stood. 'I'll get going. Busy day tomorrow.'

'You're not coming in,' Eleanor said.

'You try stopping me. I'm publishing Nieto's story—'

'You can't. The injunction—'

'She's dead. I'll deal with it tomorrow. I'm too tired now.' After saying goodbye, she followed Chapman to the car.

He stopped before they reached it. 'I'm going to her company tomorrow. We're taking it apart. I'll let you know about anything which might be useful.'

'What about Harding?'

'Leave him to me.'

'Thanks, Russell.' She stopped herself, aware of his colleague in the car.

A few minutes later, they pulled up outside her house, and thanking them both again, Antonia let herself into her home. Although exhausted, she needed to perform one task before having another shower and going to bed.

She collected a tumbler from the kitchen and knelt before Alan's whisky collection. The memory of the first time she'd ever tasted any returned. She'd arrived on Alan's doorstep, on the run from the police, wet, cold and terrified. After he'd got over the shock of seeing her, he'd stuck her in front of the fire while he poured her a generous measure. The image of him turning bright red when she'd accused him of trying to get her drunk was so real, it made her heart ache.

She shook herself and after pouring a generous measure of Alan's favourite Springbank Scotch into the tumbler, she saluted him.

'I got him for you, my dear friend.' Derenski hadn't pulled the trigger, but he'd been responsible, and she was certain one of the two brothers she'd shot *had* killed Alan.

She sipped it and took the glass up to the bathroom. In the shower, she pondered Nieto's claim that Reed-Mayhew had helped her. Why? He'd only have done it if doing so helped him in one of his schemes. Nieto had hinted it was a big one. Tomorrow she'd find out what it was, and try to stop it.

CHAPTER 36

Voices in the hallway outside her office alerted Antonia to the fact she was no longer alone in the building. Despite only getting three hours' sleep, she'd woken alert and full of energy.

Her door opened and Sawyer and Miles stood in the opening. 'Antonia. You're back.' A big grin split Miles's face.

Sawyer rushed in. 'Is Nadimah . . . ?'

'She's fine. Safe home with her mother.'

'Oh, thank God.' Sawyer's eyes shone behind her lenses.

'We've got a lot to do, Jean, Miles. Come in and sit down.' She waited for them to get comfortable. 'Jean, we're publishing your story.'

'What about the injunction?'

'I've left a message with Geoff. Nieto's dead and once word of her involvement in kidnapping and torture—'

'Torture?' Sawyer examined Antonia anew.

Apart from a few bumps and scrapes, most of Antonia's injuries from yesterday had been on her body and weren't visible. 'Not me, or Nadimah. Anyway, once her powerful friends discover what she'd been involved in, they'll distance themselves from her.'

'Okay, what do you want me to do?'

'It doesn't need much more. I've written an account of her attempt to suppress the story and her death, including the events leading to it. I was there for most of them. Can you concentrate on finding the links between her and Reed-Mayhew? I don't care how you get the information.'

'Okay.' Sawyer gave an unsubtle wink.

'What about me?' Miles said.

'Reed-Mayhew wanted the last government to fall. I want to know why and who in the current administration has links to him. Why he wants them in power.'

'Okey-dokey.'

Antonia continued sifting through Grainger's notes until Eleanor arrived at ten. 'Tell me you arrived in the last hour.'

'Sorry, the last four?'

Eleanor sighed. 'I remember being young.'

'How's Nadimah?'

'Remarkably composed. You wouldn't think she'd been through an ordeal. How bad was it?'

'Bad enough. She missed the worst, but they held a gun at her head, and then a knife at her throat.'

'We saw the nick. Sabirah's furious.'

'The girl did a brilliant job. She took one kidnapper out, using the training she'd just got at the gym. I signalled what I wanted her to do, hoping she'd understand, and she did.'

'Hmm. I remember a time you thought her too soft.'

'We all make mistakes, Eleanor.'

'Yes, we do. Have you seen the Prime Minister's statement?'

Antonia had almost forgotten about the crisis facing the country. She clicked on the link to her news browser. 'What's she said?'

'Let's just say I doubt any anti-Trident protest will get much support.'

'She hasn't?' Antonia clicked on the first report.

The UK is now committed to the renewal of nuclear deterrent.

'Of course.' She opened a new page and clicked on the share price index. She'd bookmarked the relevant shares and brought them up.

'What is it, Antonia?'

She moved the screen so Eleanor could see. The share price change column showed just green figures. Every single share had risen by at least fifty per cent.

'What are we looking at?'

'The shares Rick investigated. All have shot up, and that's before they've announced any deals.'

'Someone's got lucky.'

'Not luck.'

'You think someone has engineered this crisis?'

'I'm sure of it. Nieto attended university with the president's sister. Reed-Mayhew owns shares in one of their biggest companies. I don't have the proof yet, but I bet he was buying the shares.'

'Wow, that's audacious, even for him.'

'But look at the rewards.' Even as they watched, the shares rose.

Antonia's mind raced. How could she prevent Reed-Mayhew from benefitting? Even now, he could sell his shares and take huge profit. His already solid position would become unassailable.

'Sorry, Eleanor. I need to focus.'

'What will you do?'

She told her.

'It's a risky proposition.'

'I know, but I'm not standing by.'

◆ ◆ ◆

The atmosphere at JN Partners following the news of Nieto's death puzzled Chapman. The police hadn't shared the circumstances of her death, and after the initial shock, people reacted in two distinct ways. Many appeared concerned about their future, but amongst a certain group, a sense of excitement seemed to prevail. His team were interviewing all employees, he and Sanchez concentrating on the senior staff. Ensconced in the opulent panelled boardroom full of expensive antiques, they'd just interviewed one of the senior partners.

'Bloody hell, he'll be on the Bolly tonight.' Chapman shook his head. 'How many shares does he own?'

Sanchez checked their data. 'Ninety-two thou.'

Chapman calculated. 'He's eleven million down. I'd be crying.'

'But he thinks he's going to do better in the long term. They'll split Nieto's share, paying today's price, based on the precedent she set when she bought her finance director's shares. And once the shares bounce back, they'll make millions.'

'Cold bastards. How can they? A colleague's just died.'

'It's what they do here, make calculations on the financial implications of every event. Plus, it's a promotion opportunity.'

Chapman understood the latter. 'Right, who's next?'

'Roger Dieng. He's Erika Voight's deputy.'

Chapman's interest sharpened. 'Okay, get him in here.'

Sanchez used the intercom and a minute later, a tall, elegant man in a well-cut suit walked in. He sat and light glinted off his dark forehead. He appeared to fall into the 'concerned' camp and after establishing the preliminaries, Chapman started.

'You're aware Ms Voight is under arrest in Ankara airport, pending extradition on various charges.'

'No, sir, I did not know. Is she okay?'

Chapman exchanged a look with Sanchez. 'As far as we know. It means an opportunity for you because she won't be returning.'

Dieng laughed. 'Not for me.' He became serious. 'I wouldn't want the job, although with Nieto gone, things may change.'

'Did you not like Ms Nieto?'

'I didn't dislike her.'

'Was there something about you *she* didn't like?'

'Nothing like that, Inspector. I just don't like her business methods.' He looked uncomfortable.

'Would you care to elaborate, Roger?' Sanchez said.

'Like you English, us Senegalese don't like to speak ill of the dead.'

'In a police investigation, it's often unavoidable.'

Dieng studied his hands for a long moment. 'She was too lucky. Every call, even those where she went against our analysts, came out right. I did a calculation. If we'd followed our analysis instead of her "hunches", we'd be sixty per cent less successful.'

'That's a lot.'

'It would still leave us in the top ten UK funds. At the moment, we're way ahead of all the others.'

Chapman had discussed this with Antonia. 'You think she indulged in insider dealing?'

Dieng's eyes widened. 'Has this anything to do with her death?'

'What else were you worried about?'

'We're buying shares in engineering companies in a particular field.'

'Nuclear submarines?'

'You're well informed, Inspector.'

'Do you want to elaborate?'

'As you seem to know so much. I wasn't happy about it for various reasons. We're buying some shares on our behalf, which I considered too risky after the recent government decision not to renew Trident, but we're also buying shares for two people I don't think we should represent.'

'You're going to have to tell me who they are.'

'We have a reputation—'

'When the details of Nieto's death come out, your company will *not* have a reputation. Not one you'd want.'

'Oh my.' Dieng ran a hand across his face. 'I discovered this information by accident. Only Nieto and Ms Voight can access details of our confidential clients. They share information on a secure encrypted email only the pair of them use. I discovered Ms Voight's password by accident.'

'By accident?'

'Okay, I took steps to find out her password. She trusted me with it. I'm not proud . . .'

'You did the right thing.'

'Thank you, Inspector. The two companies are GRM and the Zunghari Development Corporation.'

'Does the latter possess any link to Zungharistan, the country?'

'It's supposed to be the country's sovereign wealth fund, but it's a piggy bank for the ruling family.'

Chapman wanted to end the interview now and let Antonia know what he'd discovered. Reed-Mayhew was clearly involved in manipulating the markets, with the help of the Zunghari president.

'Are you prepared to speak to the press about it?'

'I . . . I hadn't thought about it.'

'I believe *The Electric Investigator* is working on it.' Chapman ignored Sanchez's look of incredulity.

'Oh, right. Good to know who I need to speak to.'

They finished the interview and Sanchez waited until Dieng left. 'You know we recorded the interviews?'

'But you turned it off for the last guy, didn't you? I didn't hear you warn Dieng he was being recorded.'

She burst out laughing. 'Your face. I could have milked it for weeks. I forgot to turn it back on.'

◆ ◆ ◆

After the call from Dieng, Antonia rewrote parts of Grainger's article. The email he sent, and the supporting documents, went to Geoff Stokes, although Antonia would 'publish and be damned' if necessary. Alongside Sawyer and Miles, she worked on the two articles throughout the day. By early evening, she'd almost finished and waited for the okay from Stokes.

At six, Eleanor came into her office. 'Have you seen the news?'

Antonia put the main news channel on, turned the screen and read the transcription.

> *The president of Zungharistan has accepted that the dispute with the United Kingdom resulted from a mis-understanding. The dispute arose because a senior diplo-mat from Zungharistan was refused entry to the UK. It turned out that the diplomat in question didn't have a valid passport at the time. The president has apologised and offered to compensate in full any British citizens who lost out because of the dispute.*
>
> *British businessman Gustav Reed-Mayhew, in Zungharistan on unrelated business, is believed to have helped broker the rapprochement.*

That's why he'd got Nieto to organise her torture. He was in Zungharistan, making sure he could take the credit for something she believed he and the president had already arranged. Antonia couldn't imagine Reed-Mayhew gladly missing an opportunity to watch her suffer. She opened the share price screen. The green had now become red.

Eleanor frowned. 'Why did the president make the announcement now? The shares are dropping and both he and Reed-Mayhew will lose out.'

'No, they won't.' Antonia pointed to the share price. 'It's higher than when the previous administration signed the last deal. He bought his shares after that deal was cancelled and the shares crashed.' She clicked on another tab. 'Look at the number of transactions. Someone has sold huge numbers of those shares. It will be all the proxy companies Reed-Mayhew and his co-conspirator set up. They're taking the money and running.'

'Can't we stop them?' Eleanor looked distressed.

'I'll do my best.'

'Geoff's coming over later.'

'Oh, okay. In which case, I'll need to concentrate on this now.'

She started typing before Eleanor left the room. She'd not made much of Nieto's links to the Zunghari president's sister, or Reed-Mayhew's shares in the Zunghari mining company, but intended to. Not only did it hurt to see someone like Reed-Mayhew profit from corruption and crime, if he kept the billions in profits he'd made, he'd become untouchable, and she couldn't allow that.

Two hours later, she let Eleanor know she'd finished. She arrived with Geoff Stokes, who looked around Antonia's office.

'Much more suitable for a woman of your status, Antonia.'

Unsure if he was being funny, she thanked him and gave him a memory stick with her work on it. She found Chapman chatting to Sawyer and Miles and invited him into her office.

Stokes cleared his throat. 'The article on Nieto, I have no problem with. She instigated the injunction and, as she's now deceased, we should be fine to publish. There are also the circumstances of her death, which further strengthens our legal position.' He sipped water from a flask he'd produced from his briefcase. 'Regarding the second article, and the addendum, which I will come to later, I have issues—'

'I'm publishing it all, Geoff.'

He looked pained. 'I feared that would be your reaction. However, I'd be failing in my duty if I don't give my advice. The connection you make between Reed-Mayhew and Rick Grainger's death is unsustainable.'

'He killed him – or paid those thugs who died with him to do it. They took me to the room where they tortured him.'

'Inspector.' Stokes addressed Chapman. 'Have you found evidence of either Mr Grainger or Mr Reed-Mayhew at the premises Antonia refers to?'

'We've got evidence of Rick. Traces in a bed we found there. But there's a huge amount of evidence to sift from the rest of the premises, plus CCTV of the surrounding roads.'

Although she suspected the bed she'd lain in was the one they'd put Grainger in after torturing him, having it confirmed made her queasy. 'Okay, I'll remove reference to Reed-Mayhew being there until we have evidence. Anything else?'

'The suggestion of collusion in the addendum, between Reed-Mayhew and the Zunghari president—'

'We've got evidence of them meeting and buying shares through Nieto's company.'

'All circumstantial. You can mention them and let people draw their own conclusions. You're uncharacteristically emphatic in the piece. I suspect the emotion of Mr Grainger's treatment affected your usual impeccable judgement.'

She looked at Stokes, who seemed sincere. 'Okay, I'll change it.'

An hour later, she'd finished. They gathered in her office and watched on her screen as Sawyer uploaded it. All her energy drained away, and she wanted to sob.

'I'll lock up,' Eleanor said.

'Thanks, I'm shattered. Thank you, everyone.'

Chapman stood. 'Do you want a lift?'

'Yeah, thank you.'

◆　◆　◆

The taxi from the railway station drew up outside Sabirah's home and she paid the driver. He helped unload their luggage and get it to the front door. She gave him another five-pound tip.

'Come on, you two, let's get this upstairs and then—'

'Then I'm going to bed,' Nadimah announced.

'It's only five and you've just spent ten days lazing about in St Ives.'

'But we got up before six this morning.'

'Only because you wanted to go to the beach on the last day. Hakim and I were quite happy to stay in bed. Anyway, we're going next door. Antonia invited us. Something's going on.'

'Oh, okay.'

Mentioning Antonia soon perked you up, young lady. The darker skin from days lying in the sun hid her daughter's small scar from the knife. She seemed to have recovered from her ordeal, but Sabirah wanted her to get counselling, to see the professor who'd helped Antonia. She'd ask her to speak to Nadimah.

Half an hour later, they'd changed and made their way next door. At the door to Antonia's office, Nadimah pushed past her and charged in, giving Antonia a tight hug as soon as she stood. She'd grown almost as tall now, although she still needed heels to match her. Several others were already there, and Sabirah greeted familiar faces.

They'd set a large television up on a stand and it played silent images. Food and drink covered most surfaces, apart from Antonia's

444

desk. As Sabirah confirmed they'd 'been lucky with the weather' and had 'caught the sun' to various people, the room filled up. Nadimah stayed close to Antonia, seeming afraid to be separated from her.

Eleanor arrived and Sabirah rushed to her side. As they exchanged greetings, a tension settled on the room. Someone increased the volume on the television.

> *The government announced today that they will seize the profits made by both GRM and the Zunghari Development Corporation after the High Court in London decided they are the proceeds of crime.*

A loud cheer drowned the reporter's next few words. People danced and hugged each other. Antonia had separated herself from Nadimah and Chapman held her. Someone had frozen the action on the screen and started it again when people fell quiet.

> *The government has already seized the profits made by JN Partners pending a police investigation. We understand that following days of unrest in the capital, the president of Zungharistan and his family are under house arrest.*

More restrained cheers greeted this. Antonia released Chapman and made her way to a sideboard, where she picked up a tray with a bottle and some glasses. She came towards Sabirah and Eleanor.

'What's this?' Sabirah studied the amber liquid. 'I only drink champagne.'

'Springbank whisky. It's in honour of Alan.' Antonia's eyes shone.

'I will try it, for Alan.'

Antonia poured a measure in four glasses, gave one each to Sabirah, Chapman and Eleanor, then took one.

'To Alan.'

Acknowledgements

This is the bit where I can, in a small way, acknowledge those who've helped me on my journey to get this novel published.

The support of my family and friends continues undimmed, and I want them to know I never take it for granted.

Members of my writing group, South Manchester Writers' Workshop, give me constructive advice on my writing, and continue to contribute to my improvement as an author.

Thank you to C. J. Harter. Chris, your comprehensive report improved the manuscript significantly.

My agent, Clare Coombes, from The Liverpool Literary Agency, who gave me valuable feedback on the finished manuscript. Her professionalism and continued support is much appreciated.

Finally, the people at Thomas & Mercer, starting with Victoria Haslam, who continues to be a hugely supportive champion of my work.

David Downing, of Maxwellian Editorial Services, Inc., who made editing this novel as pleasurable as the last two. His continued wisdom and insightful feedback gives me great confidence that my novel will be in the best possible shape.

Jill Sawyer, who copyedited the manuscript, picking up my verbal tics and innumerable errors, while suggesting further improvements.

Gill Harvey, who did the proofread and eliminated those errors that always slip through and threaten to undermine all the work that has gone before.

Dominic Forbes, whose excellent cover compliments the brilliant two he designed for *A Long Shadow* and *A Stolen Memory*.

Thank you also to Nicole Wagner, Dan Griffin, and their respective teams.

Last, but not least, a huge thank you to Sophie Goodfellow, Emma Mitchell and the rest of the team at FMcM who have made sure my books remain in the public eye.

About the Author

Photo © 2021 Steve Pattyson Photography

David Beckler writes fast-paced action thrillers populated with well-rounded characters. Born in Addis Ababa in 1960, David spent his first eight years living on an agricultural college in rural Ethiopia where his love of reading developed. After dropping out of university he became a firefighter and served nineteen years before leaving to start his own business.

David began writing in 2010 and uses his work experiences to add realism to his fiction. David lives in Manchester, his adopted home since 1984. In his spare time, he tries to keep fit – an increasingly difficult undertaking – listens to music, socialises and feeds his voracious book habit.

Follow the Author on Amazon

If you enjoyed this book, follow David Beckler on Amazon to be notified when the author releases a new book!
To do this, please follow these instructions:

Desktop:

1) Search for the author's name on Amazon or in the Amazon App.
2) Click on the author's name to arrive on their Amazon page.
3) Click the 'Follow' button.

Mobile and Tablet:

1) Search for the author's name on Amazon or in the Amazon App.
2) Click on one of the author's books.
3) Click on the author's name to arrive on their Amazon page.
4) Click the 'Follow' button.

Kindle eReader and Kindle App:

If you enjoyed this book on a Kindle eReader or in the Kindle App, you will find the author 'Follow' button after the last page.